Praise for *Lone 1*

"*Lone Dog Road*, Kent Nerburn's long .... return, is a revelation. It takes us on a journey through a barely known world where cultures rub against each other and the old knowledge of the first Americans struggles to find voice in a world that has forgotten it exists. Nerburn has lived in this world between cultures. He has traveled its roads and knows its people, and his characters breathe with the life of these travels. Join him on this journey to a world between worlds. It is a journey that asks big questions for which there are no easy answers, and a glimpse into the very heart of the American experience."

— **ROBERT PLANT**

"Great stories are born in the heart and from there make their way into the world. *Lone Dog Road* is a great story deeply rooted in the human heart. Using the vast canvas of the Great Plains, Kent Nerburn paints with his words the hardscrabble lives of the people who by choice or by chance call that place home. The result is breathtaking in its beauty and heartwarming in its humanity. Nerburn is a storyteller to be celebrated, and *Lone Dog Road* is a story to be treasured."

— **WILLIAM KENT KRUEGER**, *New York Times* bestselling author of *Ordinary Grace* and *This Tender Land*

"*Lone Dog Road* is swift, compassionate, and instantly credible. Everyone in its pages is searching for home — the young brothers fleeing federal pursuit, their wise and weathered great-grandfather, the traveling gospel singer, and so many others. Kent Nerburn writes like a trusted friend in this sturdy outstretched hand of a novel — grab it and hang on."

— **LEIF ENGER**, author of *Peace Like a River*

"*Lone Dog Road* is one of those special novels that opens a door into another reality. Though Kent Nerburn is not Native, he has the magic needed to portray reservation life in the shadows of South Dakota's

Black Hills. *Lone Dog Road* is poignant, heartfelt, and educational. Read it and learn."

— **DAN O'BRIEN**, author of *Buffalo for the Broken Heart* and *In the Center of the Nation*

"Kent Nerburn is one of those rare individuals who has been invited to see over the fence into another culture. A lifetime of listening quietly to Native Americans of many nations has invested his work with a wisdom that has won him the admiration of Native American readers and cultural leaders and allowed him to create a nuanced and poetic account of being 'Indian' in a white man's world. He writes with grace, and he manages to tell sad stories with a deep affirmation. The integrity of Nerburn's heart and the careful insights of his prose are abundant on every page of this remarkable novel of trial and redemption."

— **CLAY JENKINSON**, director of the Dakota Institute

LONE
DOG
ROAD

Also by Kent Nerburn

Neither Wolf nor Dog: On Forgotten Roads with an Indian Elder

*The Wolf at Twilight: An Indian Elder's Journey
Through a Land of Ghosts and Shadows*

*The Girl Who Sang to the Buffalo: A Child, an Elder,
and the Light from an Ancient Sky*

*Chief Joseph and the Flight of the Nez Perce:
The Untold Story of an American Tragedy*

Voices in the Stones: Life Lessons from the Native Way

Native Echoes: Listening to the Spirit of the Land

Simple Truths: Clear and Gentle Guidance on the Big Issues in Life

Small Graces: The Quiet Gifts of Everyday Life

Ordinary Sacred

Forgiveness: Reflections on Life's Hardest Journey

*Make Me an Instrument of Your Peace:
Living in the Spirit of the Prayer of Saint Francis*

Letters to My Son: A Father's Wisdom on Manhood, Life, and Love

Dancing with the Gods: Reflections on Life and Art

LONE DOG ROAD

a novel

KENT NERBURN

New World Library
Novato, California

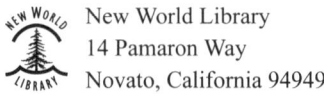

New World Library
14 Pamaron Way
Novato, California 94949

Text design by Tona Pearce Myers

Library of Congress Cataloging-in-Publication Data

Names: Nerburn, Kent, date, author
Title: Lone dog road : a novel / Kent Nerburn.
Description: Novato : New World Library, 2025. | Summary: "Set in the Dakota High Plains during the drought-stricken summer of 1950, *Lone Dog Road* tells the story of two Lakota boys who embark upon a quest to replace their great-grandfather's channunpa (sacred pipe) after it was broken by a government agent"-- Provided by publisher.
Identifiers: LCCN 2025007436 (print) | LCCN 2025007437 (ebook) | ISBN 9781608689941 paperback | ISBN 9781608689958 epub
Subjects: LCSH: Lakota Indians--Fiction | Brothers--Fiction | North Dakota--History--20th century--Fiction | South Dakota--History--20th century--Fiction | GSAFD: Domestic fiction | Novels | LCGFT: Fiction
Classification: LCC PS3614.E456 L66 2025 (print) | LCC PS3614.E456 (ebook) | DDC 813/.6--dc23/eng/20250228
LC record available at https://lccn.loc.gov/2025007436
LC ebook record available at https://lccn.loc.gov/2025007437

First printing, May 2025
ISBN 978-1-60868-994-1
Ebook ISBN 978-1-60868-995-8
Printed in Canada

10   9   8   7   6   5   4   3   2   1

New World Library is committed to protecting our natural environment. This book is made of material from well-managed FSC®-certified forests and other controlled sources.

In memory of Bud Thompson, Leonard Little Finger,
and Ruthie Fevig, mentors and friends

◊ ◊ ◊

LAKOTA LANGUAGE RESOURCES, GLOSSARY, AND PRONUNCIATION

In Lakota, as with all oral languages that are translated into written text, there are differing opinions on spellings, diacritical markings, and even definitions and meanings themselves. I have attempted to honor the sources from which I have obtained the words and spellings used in *Lone Dog Road*. The usages and spellings, and even the meanings, herein reflect the opinions of my sources. I have left them as I received them, in order to respect the understandings of the people who were kind enough to share their knowledge with me.

My primary sources are the elders of the Lakota Language Consortium (Lakhota.org); my Lakota and Dakota friends, especially Dar Walks Out and her uncle, Henry Brings Them Back; Eugene Buechel's *Lakota Dictionary*; and numerous Lakota and Dakota texts in which Native speakers used words in the way they had learned them.

At Lakhota.org, the Lakota Language Consortium provides a wealth of digital resources, including a dictionary app that allows you to listen to the pronunciation of each word in both male and female voices.

LAKOTA WORDS AND PHRASES

akíčhita: warrior
Aŋpétu-Wí: the sun
Áŋpó-Wičháȟpi: the morning star
čhaŋnúŋpa: a sacred or ceremonial pipe
čhaŋnúŋpa-íŋyaŋ: pipestone

Čhaŋpȟásapa-Wí: July

čhaŋšáša: red osier dogwood bark that the Lakota mix with their tobacco for smoking

Čhaŋšáyapi: "the place where trees are painted red," Redwood Falls, Minnesota

ciye: older brother

hahó: an expression of affirmation or gratitude

Haŋhépi-Wí: the moon

hásapa: a person with black skin

háu: an expression of greeting or approval

Háu, mitákuyepi. Hello, my relatives.

hiŋháŋ: owl

hiyú po: a calling for all to come closer

hokšíla: boy

huŋká: a relationship created by ceremony that binds two people together in a bond stronger than friendship, brother- or sisterhood, or family

huŋkáyapi: those who have been made *huŋká*

ȟuŋwíŋ: putrid, rotting, decomposed

ič'íč'upi: to give of yourself, to sacrifice

Iktómi: the trickster, the spider, the weaver of webs

iná: mother

inipi: ceremonial sweat lodge

íŋyaŋ: stone, rock

Inyan Sa K'api: the quarry at Pipestone, Minnesota, where the sacred red stone is dug

íŋyaŋša: red pipestone

ištáničatȟaŋka: horned lark

iyéska: mixed-blood

khéya: turtle

kȟolá: friend

Lé-aŋpétu kiŋ čhaŋtéwašteya napéčhiyuzape ló. Today, I'm happy to shake your hands.

lekší: uncle

maškétu: friend (woman speaking to a woman)

mitákuye oyás'iŋ: we are all related / all my relatives

Mníšoše: Missouri River
načá: chief, leader, wise adjudicator
nisúŋkala: younger brother
owáŋka: altar, sacred area
Pahá Sápa: the Black Hills, the sacred home of the Lakota people
pȟahíŋ: porcupine
pȟeží zizí: matchbrush, a yellow wildflower
philámayaye: thank you
šišóka: robin
šúŋka: dog
Taŋyáŋ yahípi. Welcome to all.
tȟakóža: grandchild
tȟáŋka: big
tȟatȟáŋka: buffalo
thezí tȟáŋka: big belly
thíŋpsiŋla: prairie turnip
thiyóšpaye: an extended family group
Tȟuŋkášila: 1. grandfather; 2. Creator, God
uŋčí: grandmother
uŋkáŋna: grandfather
wablúška: bug, insect
wačháŋtognake: to be generous, to have compassion
Wačhíwiŋ: Dancing Woman (a name)
wagmíza-wasná: pemmican-like cookies made with corn
wakȟáŋ: sacred, holy, possessing spiritual power
Wakȟáŋ Tȟáŋka: Creator, God
wakíŋyaŋ: thunder being
wamákȟaškaŋ: an animal; things that move upon the earth
waŋblí: eagle
wašíču: white person
wasná: pemmican
wičháȟčala: old man
Wičháȟpi-Oyáte: star people; the stars as beings
wičháša wakȟáŋ: a man endowed with spiritual power
winúȟčala: old woman
wóhaŋpi: cooking for a feast

wóksape: wisdom
wóohitike: bravery, courage
wóphila: thanks, gratitude
wówačhiŋtȟaŋka: patience, perseverance
wówaȟwala: gentleness, humility, self-effacement
wóžapi: chokecherry pudding
ziŋtkátȟo: bluebird

Lakota Pronunciation Guide

An accent mark over a vowel indicates the word's stressed syllable.

a	almost like *a* in *father* but shorter
e	like *e* in *bed*
i	like *i* in *khaki*
o	somewhat like *o* in *pork*
u	like *oo* in *took*
aŋ	like *o* in *money*, nasalized
iŋ	like *i* in *pink*, nasalized
uŋ	somewhat like *u* in *tuned*, nasalized (no English equivalent)
b	like *b* in *boy*
č	similar to *ch* in *discharge* (unaspirated), not like *g* in *gin*
čh	like *ch* in *chin* (aspirated)
č'	like *č* but followed by a glottal stop
g	like *g* in *got*
ǧ	like the standard French *r* (as in *Paris*) (no English equivalent)
h	like *h* in *hat*
ȟ	close to the Spanish *x* in *Mexico*, but more guttural
k	like *k* in *skip* (unaspirated), not like *k* in *kip*
kh	like *kh* in *khaki*
kȟ	connect *k* and *ȟ* (no English equivalent)
k'	like *k* but followed by a glottal stop
l	like *l* in *lamp*
m	like *m* in *map*
n	like *n* in *nap*
p	like *p* in *spin* or in *happy* (unaspirated), not like *p* in *pin*

ph   like *p h* in *steep hill* when pronounced fast
pȟ   connect *p* and *ȟ* (no English equivalent)
p'   like *p* but followed by a glottal stop
s   like *s* in *so*
š   like *sh* in *shop*
t   like *t* in *still* (unaspirated), not like *t* in *till* or *d* in *dill*
th   like *t h* in *sit here* when pronounced fast
tȟ   connect *t* and *ȟ* (no English equivalent)
t'   like *t* but followed by a glottal stop
w   like *w* in *was*
y   like *y* in *yes*
z   like *z* in *zero*
ž   like *s* in *pleasure*
'   catch in the throat, like the pause in *uh-oh*

LONE
DOG
ROAD

Runners

A BIG LONESOME SOUND

Levi

"Sit down, Reuben."

"I'm scared."

"Sit down. Grandpa said you had to listen to me."

"Grandpa's dead."

"You don't know that."

"Yes, I do."

"No, you don't. Just sit down."

I grabbed him by the arm and pulled him down. I hated to do it. He didn't understand. He never understood. He couldn't. But he was stubborn, all the time. I think sometimes people with something wrong with their brains are born stubborn, because that way they don't do things that get them in trouble. They don't do anything. Like sit down when the train is going around a curve.

"You could fall out."

"I won't fall out."

"How do you know?"

"I won't. I know."

He had that pinch-face look with his hair all sticking up like a porcupine. I reached over and tried to brush it flat. "Look, Grandpa said you had to listen to me. Momma, too. And I want you to stay sitting down."

"Grandpa's dead and I don't have to listen to nobody."

"Grandpa's not dead. You always say that when you can't see

5

someone. Momma told us we had to run. She said I have to look out for you."

He turned his back to me and stared into the darkness.

◊ ◊ ◊

We were lucky to get on the train. I had thought for a minute we were going to die. I had seen the older boys do it, running alongside like dogs on a hunt, just real relaxed until they were going the same speed as the train, then grabbing the ladder on the side of the boxcar and swinging themselves up, like getting on a horse. But they were older, and they could lift a saddle above their heads and throw rocks so far you couldn't see them land. We were just little, Reuben and me, with me only having eleven years and Reuben only having six, and Reuben was different in the head and would never do what anyone said. But we had to go. We had to get away. Momma had said so.

"Just get on the train," she said. "They're coming and they'll take Reuben away, like they did your grandpa. Now run down to the tracks and get on the train. Make Reuben do what you say. Don't let him run away and don't let anything happen to him. I'm telling you that. You listen to your mother."

"I'm listening, Momma, but Reuben doesn't listen."

"You make him. You tell him I told you. You tell him Grandpa said so, too."

The train was really loud. I had to shout to make Reuben hear me.

"Momma told me, Reuben. She said I have to make you listen and do what I say."

He was all bunched up with his arms around his knees.

"You shouldn't have pushed me."

"I had to. The door was really high."

"Yeah, but it hurt."

The train was screeching and crashing and shaking all around.

"I almost couldn't get on. You saw it. I was hanging there, the train going faster. I could have fallen under. My legs would have been cut off. What would you have done then?"

"It hurt when you pushed me. You didn't have to push me."

He covered his ears and pulled his jacket over his head.

It was dark in the car. It smelled like old grain, kind of sweet and sickening. The wheels kept making that clacking sound, and there were all the screeches when we went around turns, and we couldn't see even to the other end of the boxcar.

I put my mouth next to Reuben's ear. "Do you think there's anyone down on the other end?"

"There's no one there," Reuben said.

"Are you sure? I thought I heard a sound."

"There's no one there. I can tell."

That made me feel better. Reuben could tell those things. He could go into a room and feel what was in there. He could look at piles of things and tell you how many there were. Sometimes he wouldn't talk at all, even when people talked to him, then the next day he'd say exactly what someone had said. It was like hearing an echo.

"How'd you remember that?" I'd ask.

"What?"

"What the people were saying last night."

"I don't remember anything."

"But you just said everything they said."

"No, I didn't."

"Yes, you did."

Sometimes he made me so mad I wanted to hit him. But I never did. I just wanted to.

◊ ◊ ◊

I didn't know where the train was going. I should have been all sad, running away and not knowing where we were going. But I was too scared. And besides, when Reuben was along he took up all the place in your mind, just thinking about him and what he was going to do next and keeping him from doing it, or making sure he did something he was supposed to. It was like having a baby, or maybe a mule.

I was getting so mad at him for not sitting down and not caring if I fell under the wheels that I forgot to be scared. That's why I sometimes liked having him around. There were lots of things to be scared of, and Reuben filled up all the scared places in my mind. Besides, I figured that Creator wouldn't let someone like him be hurt, so if I stayed close,

I was probably all right, too. He was like a good luck thing. But he made me really mad.

We'd been going for lots of hours when the train slowed down. I could see the lights of a town up ahead, like a bunch of fireflies out on the prairie, all gathered together in the dark. It made me feel good but it made me feel sad — there were families there inside those lights, just laughing together and eating supper. It made me think of Momma and Grandpa.

The train whistle blew, big and lonesome. Four times. *Wooooo. Wooooo. Woo. Wooooooooo.* Sometimes the engineer would let that last *wooooo* go on for a long time, like it was crying out into the night.

I thought of what it must be like to be inside one of those warm houses, hearing that sound, all cozy in a bed. Maybe it made them want to get away, to get on one of those trains and ride away to some place they'd never seen. But maybe it just made them happy to be warm inside their bed. It made me feel sad. It went way off in the distance.

The train slowed down.

"Come on, Reuben," I said.

He was all curled up in a ball.

"Let's get off. There's probably some nice people there. People are nice to kids. Even white people."

"Leave me alone," he said. "I'm sleeping."

"You always say that. I know it's a lie."

"No, it isn't. Not this time. I'm sleeping."

"How can you be sleeping when the train's rocking so hard?"

"It reminds me of when Momma rocks me. Leave me alone."

He pulled his knees in close and pulled his jacket up tighter over his head. I think he was crying.

"Come on," I said. "We can get some food."

I was going to try to lift him up and move him, but the train jerked and I fell over. Then it started speeding up. The town just kept going by. I could hear the whistle. *Woooooo. Woooooo. Woo. Wooooooooooooo.* Then the town was just a pool of lights disappearing in the distance.

I sat down with my back against the wall. I thought of those houses. I was wishing I was home.

AT NIGHT YOU'RE AFRAID
OF EVERYTHING

Levi

Morning is good when you're traveling. At night you're afraid of everything. In the day you know what you're afraid of.

I like to watch the sun come up. There's all sorts of sounds and everything is changing. Grandpa calls it the dawn chorus. Everything is happy and just starting to come alive.

I used to sit with Grandpa and watch the sun come up. He'd come into our room, real quiet, and touch me on the shoulder. Sometimes I was already awake, but I'd pretend I was still asleep. It made me feel good to hear his footsteps and feel his touch. He was always real gentle. Then we'd go out in the front of the house, not saying anything. He'd put his finger on his mouth, then point to the sky. We'd just sit and watch and listen, seeing how the sky went from dark to purple to pink to bright, and hearing all the birds and animals rustling and singing.

I was thinking these things when I opened my eyes. The sun was coming in through the boxcar doors.

The train was stopped. I don't know why it was stopped. I could hear the engine making sounds way up front. I looked outside. It was the purple time, just turning to pink. There was nothing around anywhere, just hills.

"Come on, Reuben," I said. "The train's stopped. Let's get out of here."

Reuben made a growling sound. He sleeps really hard. You can't just touch him on the shoulder. He gets mad when someone tries to wake him.

"Come on," I said.

I could hear men walking along. They were hitting things on the wheels or the sides of the cars. I could tell by their voices they weren't looking for anything. They were laughing a lot and weren't talking fast or low or anything.

I dragged Reuben way back into the shadows at the back of the boxcar. He made some sounds, but they weren't very loud.

"Be quiet," I said. "There's some men out there."

He made another growling noise and went back to sleep. I knew he'd stay quiet.

The men went by, talking and laughing. They must have been checking something. I snuck up to the door to see where they were. Outside the sky over the hills was turning bright. It was going to be a hot day.

The men were way down the tracks. I could hear their voices getting real small.

"Come on, Reuben," I said. "Let's get out of here."

Reuben growled again. He was like a baby bear sometimes. I grabbed him by the arm, like Momma did. I figured if she did it, it was okay for me to do it. You're going to have to be his momma and poppa now, she'd said.

I pulled him up.

"We're getting off here," I said. "We're going to run real fast. There's some train men out there, but they're old and won't chase us very far. We'll run straight toward the hills."

"Let me sleep," he said.

I pulled his arm really hard. "We're going to run now. You can sleep later. We need some food."

"I'm hungry," he said.

Sometimes it was really easy to move his mind around.

◊◊◊

We jumped out and fell down and rolled down the hill that the tracks were on. The train men never saw us. Reuben scratched his knee a little and I cut up the bottom of my hand. It wasn't too bad.

There was a river running under a bridge way down at the bottom of a gully. It was an old wooden bridge made out of big pieces of lumber all covered with tar. You could smell it really strong. I think the bridge is why we were stopped. Part of the train was on it.

We ran down to the river. It wasn't very big, just kind of puddling. I think the bridge was more to go over the gully than the river.

We drank a lot of the water. It tasted pretty good. I found an old bottle and filled it and stuck a piece of my shirt in it. I did not know what else I could do.

The train started up again. It moved really slow. The bridge creaked. I thought that maybe we should get back on. But the train picked up speed until it was going too fast. Then it was gone. There was nothing around, not even a road.

Reuben was chasing after some butterflies on the bank by the river. There were lots of them. They moved like white ribbons, all flying together.

Grandpa had told us that it was good to chase butterflies because it made you quick. He said he'd seen them fly into the mouth of a man once and that man could make music after that. Reuben liked to chase them with his mouth open. He wanted to make music, too, he said. He always did what Grandpa said. Grandpa was the only one he really listened to.

I missed Grandpa, even more than I missed Momma. With Momma I got to say goodbye, and she had made me go. With Grandpa, they just took him. It was like he was still out there somewhere.

I thought about when those men came to get him. He lifted his head real straight and stood up. He wouldn't let them touch him. He walked to their car, not looking at anyone, even Reuben and me. He just walked to their car and got in.

Reuben came back and sat down. He was breathing hard. The train whistle was far away. The only sound was the wind and a little bit of a trickle from the water.

"Do you ever think about Grandpa?" I asked.

Reuben pointed to the butterflies. "I see Grandpa," he said. Sometimes the things he said didn't make any sense but made a lot of sense at the same time.

"I miss Grandpa," I said.

Reuben put his head on my shoulder. "I wish a butterfly would fly in my mouth," he said.

"Do you want to eat?" I asked.

He made a snapping sound with his mouth and made his funny grin, with all his teeth showing. It made me happy. It was the same way he smiled at Momma.

I reached in my bag. I didn't want him to see that it was almost empty. He always kept things like that in his mind, things about empty and full and how many there were of something.

"I've got some bread," I said.

"How much?"

"Lots. Here's some *wasná*, too."

Reuben liked *wasná*.

"I like red food," he said. This *wasná* was full of berries. It was the last food I had that Momma had given me.

We ate until the sun got hot, then we took off our clothes and lay in the water. The butterflies were still flying around.

"Where do they go at night?" Reuben asked.

"I don't know. Where do we go at night? Just wherever we can."

"I wish I could go where the butterflies go."

"Why?"

"Then I wouldn't be scared."

I reached over and touched his hand.

"We'd better get going," I said. I didn't want him to be scared. I was already scared for both of us.

We got dressed and started toward the hills. The sun was behind us. You couldn't see it, because it was everywhere, just light. It felt angry, like fire. I started sweating really hard.

"I don't like this," Reuben said.

"What?"

"Being out here. There's too much sun."

"Tonight we'll sleep in a house," I said.

"How do you know?"

"I just do."

He called me a liar under his breath, but I pretended I didn't hear. I knew where we were going now.

We were going to find a house.

A DIFFERENT KIND OF HOUSE

Levi

It was hard walking in the hills. Reuben doesn't walk fast, and when he gets mad he just stops. So I had to keep him from getting mad. I started singing songs he liked — powwow songs, school songs, the songs the nuns taught me in church.

Reuben liked it when I sang. He has a beautiful voice. He can sing like an Indian way up in his throat or like a white man way down in his chest. People stopped and listened when he sang. Sometimes we would be somewhere and I would start singing and he would listen to me. Then he would start singing and I would stop. He would know all the words just from hearing me sing it once even if he had never heard the song before. People couldn't believe he could sing the way he did.

We kept walking and I tried to sing along with our steps. Pretty soon Reuben started singing. I kept making my singing softer until it was only him. He had his eyes closed even though he was walking. Reuben never noticed anything else when he was singing.

We walked all day this way, with Reuben singing and me worrying about what we were going to eat and where we were going to stop. The sun was like a fire. I thought I was going to get sick. Once I did a little, but Reuben didn't see me. He was still singing. I don't know how he walked like that with his eyes closed.

We ate our lunch in a gully. I was scared for snakes, but we didn't see any. We had *wasná* again, and bread. There was a little stream, but the water was almost gone and it wasn't very good. We drank some

from my bottle. We had *wasná* and bread for supper, too. I didn't like
eating the same thing, but that was all we had.

I was right about a house. We walked until the long shadow time.
Then I saw one in the distance, all broken down and gray and leaning
like it was half blown over. There was no glass in the windows. It
looked like no one had lived there for a long time.

I pointed at it and made Reuben look. He was still singing.

"See? I told you we'd sleep in a house," I said.

He made a snarl face.

"I don't want that house," he said.

"This is the only one we've found."

"I want a different kind of house," he said. "A house with people,
not a ghost house."

"There aren't any ghosts there," I said.

I didn't like it when Reuben talked about ghosts. That was white
people talk and it scared me. Grandpa talked about spirits all the time,
but they were like the memories of people who had died and stayed
around to watch us and help us. But ghosts were something else, like
something that scared you and did bad things to you. They were like
a white people idea because white people thought dying was the end
of everything and there was a god waiting who would do bad things
to you if he didn't like you. That's what they taught me in the school.
Grandpa told me not to listen to them. He said dying was just crossing
over to another place. He said the spirits you meet there are friends,
not ghosts.

I finally got Reuben to go in. It was all dusty and smelled bad.

I cleaned off a place on the floor and laid out our jackets to make
a bed.

"Here, lay here next to me," I said. The wind was starting to blow
hard outside. It was a dust wind.

"I don't like it here," Reuben said.

"I don't like it here, either," I said.

I could hear the wind making scream sounds outside the house. It
was blowing dirt in through the cracks.

Reuben curled up on the jackets and pushed his head up onto my
chest.

I put my arms around him and held him like Momma did. I liked it when he let me hold him. I wished there was someone to hold me, but I didn't tell Reuben. I was trying to be a momma and poppa for him.

We slept all curled up together. I kept waking up. The wind kept blowing and there were noises outside. But Reuben just kept breathing hard. I wished I could sleep like him.

I had lots of funny thoughts that night, almost like dreams. Sometimes when it's really late you can't tell thoughts from dreams, especially when you're not sure if you're asleep or awake. I kept seeing Grandpa. It was like he was there with me.

I lay all night. I kept my eyes closed. It was a really long time.

When the sun started coming up I thought I felt Grandpa touch me on the shoulder. But when I opened my eyes he wasn't there. I closed them again and started to cry just a little.

Maybe Reuben had been wrong about ghosts. Maybe it was the spirit of Grandpa he had been feeling.

◊◊◊

Morning didn't feel very good. I started to get sick from not eating. I wanted food really bad. But mostly I wanted food for Reuben. Now I knew what it was like to be a full-grown. You had to worry for everyone, not just yourself, and not let them know.

Light was coming in through the cracks in the boards. I looked around the room. There were books and paper lying everywhere, and spoons and some broken dishes. They were all rotted and ruined, and dust had blown all over them. I wondered why they were there. Why didn't the people take them with them when they went away? It was like maybe something bad had happened and they had just got up one day and left.

I didn't like that thought. I didn't like any of my thoughts. They were all about being hungry or scared or what we were going to do. I started to talk to Grandpa, real quiet, under my breath, so Reuben wouldn't wake up.

I thought maybe if that feeling on my shoulder was really Grandpa's spirit he would answer me.

"Grandpa, I'm really scared," I said. "I don't know what to do. Momma just said to run away. She told me to stay away from the aunties because the government men would be looking for us there. She thinks they would take Reuben like they took you."

I looked out through the broken windows at the long, empty hills. The sky was full of flying dust.

More than anything I wanted to see Grandpa.

"Where are you, Grandpa?" I asked. "Why did they take you away? You never hurt anybody. You always talked soft, even when you were mad. Everyone listened to you. They came to you when they had a problem. You knew all the old ways. You knew how to heal people. I want to be like you, Grandpa. I want to know about all the birds and the animals. I want to help people. I want to make people happy."

I was getting all sad inside. I didn't want Grandpa to see me cry, even if he was only a spirit.

I felt something standing behind me.

I turned around. It was Reuben.

"I want to see Grandpa," he said.

MISSING GRANDPA

Levi

I should tell you about Grandpa so you know why I am missing him. Grandpa is really old. He isn't really our grandpa. He's Momma's grandpa. But we call him Grandpa. Everyone does. He likes that.

Grandpa said he'd been really good at baseball, but he'd got hurt bad falling off a horse, so he had to stop playing. Now he walks with a limp, all crooked, with his one side dipping down every time he takes a step.

He'd been on a team once and liked to talk about it a lot. He even tried to play catch with Reuben and me, but he couldn't see very well and the ball always went past him and one of us had to go get it. He is always smiling and he likes to laugh, real quiet, kind of sneaky sounding, so no one hardly even hears him.

Grandpa isn't very tall, not much taller than me. But you can feel him in the whole room when he comes in.

His fingers are all bent. When he reaches for things it's like a bird claw.

Momma has to help him do his hair. He doesn't like it hanging down but he won't cut it. He says Creator gave it to him and he doesn't want to insult Creator by cutting it.

Once I asked him why my hair was cut. He said, "I'm old. Creator wants different things from you."

That made me feel better because they made me cut my hair in boarding school. They had cut it off real short when I first got there and washed my head with kerosene and some tar that really burned.

17

Now I keep it short. Not real short, but just kind of short so I can shake it dry when I wash it.

Reuben's hair is short-like, too, but his is all spiky and stuck up. The kids call him "*p̌hahíŋ* head," the porcupine boy. I don't want him to have it cut off shaved-like in boarding school.

Momma likes to tie Grandpa's hair so it hangs down his back, like a horse's tail. She does it real gentle. She runs her hand along it before tying it up. The two of them laugh a lot when she does it.

One time I had asked Momma about Grandpa's hair, if it had always been long like this even when she was a little girl. Her eyes got far-like and she said that he had cut it all off when Grandma died. He kept it short for a year, she said, then he let it grow back.

"When did Grandma die?" I asked. She didn't say anything. I never asked about it again.

Grandpa is the greatest man I ever knew. His words always sound like they have a smile in them. He drinks lots of coffee. He is always up before the sun, going to his prayer place up on the hill to say his morning prayers. Then he comes down and makes coffee, a whole pot, and drinks it while sitting at the table. Sometimes he looks at books or magazines. He can't read words but he looks at pictures a lot.

He spends lots of time talking to the old ones who have walked on. Sometimes I see him out back on the hill, smoking his *čhaŋnúŋpa* and facing in all the directions, cupping the smoke and bringing it around his head, and talking to them. He does it in Indian. He doesn't speak English unless there are white men around. Then he only says what he has to. He can speak good English when he wants to.

Sometimes he lets me be with him when he smokes. He does not let me smoke with him. He says it is not time. He says I have to learn many things first.

He's showed me how to fill the *čhaŋnúŋpa*. "Someday you will do this," he said. "You must only use your right hand." He wants me to learn everything right, the old way, the way he was taught. He doesn't want me to forget the old ways just because I'm going to the school with the nuns and priests.

Grandpa really likes Reuben. When Reuben makes the rest of us mad by not doing something or not listening, Grandpa just laughs and runs his hand through Reuben's spike hair.

He treats Reuben different. All the aunties and grandmas in town are always hugging and squeezing us kids. But the grandpas and the other men don't do that. They just show us. They say it's important for a man to be strong inside his own body. But Grandpa is always touching Reuben, moving his arm in a certain way or facing him toward the sunset or some other place, or running his hand through Reuben's hair.

Once I asked him why he did all these things to Reuben. He said Creator gave Reuben different understanding. "He doesn't learn like you do," he said. "I need to put understanding into him in other ways."

Momma told me that when Reuben was really little she had put him on a cradleboard when she was out gathering berries. She had set the cradleboard under a tree so Reuben could listen to the wind in the branches. His arms were tucked really tight in the blanket so he had to learn about the big things around him and not just grab at little things.

She left him there while she went to pick berries. When she got done and was coming back she heard Reuben making funny sounds like chattering.

She saw a prairie dog sitting on the top of his cradleboard, making sounds the same as Reuben's. It was like they were talking. Reuben was just a baby and couldn't say anything in people talk.

That night when she told Grandpa he just nodded and smiled. That's when he started doing all the things with Reuben that were different from me.

Grandpa told me that I should always watch everything because Creator has made everything in a certain way. The seasons keep coming in the same way, the animals all do things the same way. That's how we learn, he says, by seeing the patterns that Creator has put in life. When something is different and not part of the patterns, that thing is *wakȟáŋ*. It has Creator's special touch.

Reuben is *wakȟáŋ*, he says. He does things different. He knows different things. It is important that we learn what Creator wants from Reuben, he says.

He takes Reuben to special places; he tells Reuben stories he doesn't tell anyone else. He keeps Reuben by him all the time.

It makes me sad that he does all these special things for Reuben. I asked him why Reuben gets to learn these things and I don't.

"Reuben has a special task in life," he said. "It is important that we learn what it is."

"I want a special task in life, too," I said.

"You have a special task," he said. "Your task is to protect others. That is why Creator gave you Reuben for a little brother."

Grandpa never gets mad with people. He smiles even when other people are angry. He has to smile in our house a lot, because Momma gets angry a lot. It's never hitting angry, and it's never at Grandpa or at Reuben or me. It's mostly at the *wašíču* and the things they've done.

Grandpa tells her to stop thinking about the *wašíču* and that things will all work out in the Creator's time. She said she doesn't have all of the Creator's time.

Then they argue and Grandpa just smiles. "Your mother is a grizzly bear," he says. Then he smokes his *čhaŋnúŋpa* and laughs.

SWEET GIRL

Danton

I think it all began on the day I had to put Sweet Girl down.
That was her name — Sweet Girl — and if ever there was a dog
that lived up to her name, it was my dear sad-eyed Sweet Girl.

I had seen it coming for weeks. She'd just been lying around, panting, not eating, no interest in squirrels or balls or even being petted. I'd
get her up, help her walk a little, have a talk with her, ruffle her ears in
the way she liked. She'd wag her tail once or twice, then settle back
down in the dirt and close her eyes. I knew what I was looking at, but
I just couldn't bring myself to call it what it was.

Then one day we tried to walk, she made it about ten steps and col-
lapsed. She tried desperately to get up, pulling herself with her front
legs, but her back legs wouldn't move. She looked up at me with the
saddest eyes I'd ever seen and gave me that "I'm sorry. I just can't do
it anymore" look. Just about broke my heart.

I put her in my arms and carried her home, whispering to her about
what a good dog she was. I held her all night, listening to her labored
breathing, telling her stories of all the good times we'd had. The next
morning I lifted her into the pickup and drove her into town to Doctor
Jameson and did what had to be done.

I buried her in her old favorite blanket down by the river, cried
until I was all cried out, then threw everything I had in the back of my
truck and headed west.

Why I chose west, I don't know. I think it was just that I wanted
to get away from everything, and south was too bright and north was

too cold and east was the direction of people. West was the direction of space. And I needed space. Space can do a man good when he's all tied in knots.

I didn't much care where I ended up. I was just moving, with a head full of doubts and private griefs, putting miles behind me and chasing the top of the next hill.

I kept the seat next to me empty. That was Sweet Girl's spot, and in my heart she was still sitting there like she had done for fourteen years, all alert, looking out the window, panting and smiling that dog smile that says, "I'm the happiest dog in the whole world." No one else was going to sit there, at least not for a long while.

The road is a good place to think, especially in the great empty spaces of the West. There's nothing to grab the attention, just earth and sky. Thoughts pass through the mind like clouds, taking shape, then fading and disappearing, only to be replaced by another.

I did a lot of reflecting on that drive. I'd reached the age when there was as much of my life behind me as in front of me, and the patterns were becoming clear. I was a loner, and probably always would be. One girl — a beautiful Romanian woman I'd been involved with back at the university — had said I was just a typical American male, afraid of commitment, making a virtue out of riding off into the sunset in search of some higher purpose when I was really just a coward trying to find a way out of town.

Maybe she was right, but I didn't see it that way. Ever since I was a kid I've always kept to myself. My mother used to chase me out the door and say, "Adey, you need to play with the other boys," and I'd just go sit under a tree or lie on my back and stare at the shapes in the clouds or set up races between twigs in the water rushing down the stream.

I didn't even talk until I was five. My grandparents had come down to northern Michigan from Quebec and my whole family still had a French accent. The Anglos didn't like us because they thought we stole their jobs, and the French didn't like us because they thought we'd betrayed our heritage when my grandpa had changed our name from D'Antoine to Danton. It sounds silly now, but I was afraid I might have a French accent when I talked, so I learned to just keep my mouth shut. After a while, it just became second nature for me to be a watcher rather than a talker.

It wasn't that I wasn't thinking. I was thinking all the time. I'd spend hours walking in the woods and talking to my dog, Skipper. But otherwise I just kept my own counsel and tried to blend into the woodwork.

The fact is, I've never felt like I belonged. I've wanted to be part of things, to help other people and be part of their lives, but it just never happened. I'd try something, hope to connect, and when it didn't work out, I'd just move on.

Even during the war, when the whole country was united, I felt like an outsider. I was turned down for conscientious objector status because the draft board said my religious convictions were "not authentic enough." What's more authentic than not wanting to kill another human being? But that wasn't good enough for them.

So I ended up doing alternative service working in the shipyards in Duluth, where I kept to myself, did my job, and went home to my little cold-water room in the Seaway Hotel and spent my nights listening to the dark, brooding sounds of Lake Superior outside my window.

College didn't work either. I was the best student in the department and had fellowship offers and promises of a bright future in academia. But what was going on outside the window was always of more interest to me than what was going on in the front of the classroom. So I left the one place where I might actually have fit in and took odd jobs where no one knew anything about me and no one asked. A stint helping out an old Norwegian carpenter, some short-term trucking gigs, a summer on the ore docks farther up Lake Superior at Beaver Bay. Good experiences, but nothing that stuck.

The only constant was Sweet Girl, that raggedly little pup who became my constant companion and confidante from the moment I found her shivering by a dumpster in Copper Harbor until the day I buried her in that lonely ground on the banks of the Iron River.

Now she's gone, and the gray is starting to show, and the weight of the past is feeling greater than the lure of the future.

I guess that's how I ended up in this little shack on the edge of this Indian reservation in western South Dakota. Run out of gas, run out of time, run out of energy, run out of hope. It doesn't much matter. One day you just stop, say, "This'll do," and try to make peace with the shape of your own life. No more running. No more seeking. Time to take a stand.

But this place, this place.

People can talk about it, but until you experience it you can never really understand. Just hills, endless hills, rolling and rolling like treeless waves, and nothing but the moon and a coyote howl and the occasional whine of a distant semi to give it shape.

Sometimes I would go up on the rise behind my cabin and look out over the land and try to figure out how far away a particular hill was. Was it five miles or fifty? Was that storm spitting the lightning in the distance an hour or minutes away?

I'd hear the scream of a nighthawk and think it was talking to me, or the cry of a distant owl and feel it was sending me a message. I swear to God sometimes it made me think I was losing my mind.

THE JOB

Danton

I really didn't need a job. I had a few dollars in my pocket, enough to last a half a year or so. But I could feel myself getting out of balance. There are lots of ways to go crazy, and I could feel things sneaking up on me in a way I didn't like. Besides, if you're going to stop moving, you've got to find out what it means to stay still.

Most of the folks around here had been born within a day's journey and they knew this land and its moods better than I ever would. I figured I'd just settle in, listen more than I talked, and learn what they had to teach. Maybe it would even be a good fit.

But it turned out that most of the locals were as private as I was. They were quick to help if you got stuck in the snow or a fence blew down, but otherwise, all you got was just a nod and a wave and a quick "How you doing?" or a comment about the weather — friendly enough for the day-to-day, but nothing to scratch the surface of your life.

I'd become friends with some of the Indians — well, at least as close to friends as a white man could become. They'd show up at my door asking for food or help with some car trouble, or sometimes they'd just come and sit in front of my house.

I could never figure out what they were all about. They'd come inside when I was gone and eat my food — this was not the kind of country where people locked their doors — but they'd never take anything.

Sometimes they'd leave something — a feather or a stone or a bundle of sweetgrass. Sometimes they'd come over and sit around until I fed them. Then they'd eat and go and never say a word. But I never felt afraid. They were almost a comfort. They fit in this place in a way that I never would.

That's part of why I'd taken the job, too. I liked the Indians. There was something peaceful about them. They weren't always moving and twitching inside their own skins. They said the Creator had placed them here and that's where they were supposed to stay. They didn't have that itch they couldn't scratch, or at least didn't seem to. I figured maybe some of it would rub off. You become where you are just like you become who you're with or you become what you do, and this job checked at least some of those boxes.

The job title was "agent assistant for boarding school recruitment." The description didn't say you had to be white, but you could tell. It had so many qualifications that no Indian would have them. I don't know if they really even wanted to hire someone. Maybe it was some government mandate. But I showed up, fit the requirements, and got hired on.

The guy I worked for was half Indian — a mixed-blood, they called him, except when they called him a "breed," for half-breed, which made his eyes get small and his jaw get tight.

He was a big threatening guy who walked like a bear. His name was Darwin Bazile but everyone called him Two Finger, and he was just about the meanest man I had ever met. One day we were driving through the town and we came upon a dog in the middle of the road — dead, half dead, I couldn't tell — and he just drove right over it, never slowing or stopping.

"Jesus, Two Finger," I said. "You could have swerved or something."

He turned and looked at me with eyes as dead as a corpse.

"Why?" he said.

◊◊◊

When I'd taken the job I'd thought it was going to be about helping get kids to school, but it turned out there was no helping involved. The job was to catch runaways or grab kids for the boarding schools, pure and simple. Though the job description had called it "recruiting," it was just plain kidnapping. You'd get a name from the Bureau of Indian Affairs for the tribe and directions to some house, then you'd just go out and grab the kids and ship them off to the boarding school.

When I first started, I thought the Indian boarding schools were some distant relative to the Swiss finishing schools or the rich ivy-covered campuses in New England where politicians send their kids — some place where the kids could learn proper behavior and get a leg up on getting a good job. I figured it was probably a good thing for kids from the reservation.

But, boy, was I wrong. The Indian kids came home in the summer with stories of beatings and starvation and a whole lot worse. I probably should have quit, but I guess I didn't quite believe them. I'd hated school as a kid and I'd told stories just about as wild. So I just kept doing what I was told and not looking much beyond the end of my own nose.

The town itself was a dusty little outpost on the western South Dakota plains. This was reservation land, and the Indians outnumbered the whites about ten to one. At first I worried that the Indians were all going to rise up one day and take back the town. What with the way their kids were treated and the way the store owners wouldn't give them any credit and followed them around while they were shopping, I figured the day would come when they'd just say, "We don't have to take this anymore," and we white folks would find ourselves on the small end of a mob or getting run out of town with only the clothes on our backs.

But after a few weeks I realized that nothing like that was going to happen. Sure, there were troubles — mostly man-on-man stuff, or man-on-woman, usually fueled by alcohol. But something big — whites against Indians, that sort of thing — wasn't going to happen. Folks, both Indian and white, had made their peace with the poverty and the dust and the way the world worked. They mostly kept to themselves, came to town to do what they had to do, then went back to their homes out in the hills. Any bad things that happened took place inside the four walls of their houses or out along the fence lines, and most of it stayed there unless blood or guns were involved. The law was seldom called. Folks tended to like to solve their own problems.

The big excitement in town was to go to the little café down the street at lunchtime and sit with the old-timers and eat whatever Lucie, the owner, had made. Lucie was a big German woman with a heavy accent who called everyone "honey" and usually cooked up a pot of some kind of stew or soup and sold it to you for whatever you were able to pay. There was no menu, no choices. Just take what she made and pay what you could.

Most of the old-timers who came to Lucie's were Lakota who didn't speak much English, at least not when they were in the café. They talked together, laughed a lot, smoked up a storm, and drank more coffee than I had ever seen anyone drink in my entire life. I'd show up about noon, nod to the regulars, take my seat, and keep to myself. Though we never talked, I fit in pretty well. I'd grown up in jeans and T-shirts and work boots, so at least visually I looked like I belonged. Pretty soon they just accepted me as part of the furniture.

Two Finger never came to the café. "I don't eat with Skins," he said. And that was that. My guess is that the Skins didn't want to eat with him, either. But that was a theory that never got tested. They wanted nothing to do with him. He wanted nothing to do with them. It fit the pattern of life out here just fine.

THE GRAB

Danton

Working with Two Finger really weighed on me. There was something affectless about him, something empty and indifferent. At first you didn't notice it, because he was so volatile in his anger and rage. But it was all surface anger, almost more of a sadistic glee, like the pleasure children take in squashing a bug or throwing gasoline on prairie dogs and lighting them on fire, which Two Finger once bragged about having done as a child. But beneath the surface was something dark and empty, like the inside of a tomb. It made me afraid to be around him.

I don't know where he got the name Two Finger. He was like lots of folks on the rez — he just had a name that people called him and no one questioned it. You just accepted it for what it was. I suppose this was because the Indians had all just been given Anglo names sometime in the past, and no one gave a damn whether it was the right name or not, so they all used nicknames that had something to do with some personal history or some defining characteristic. All I know is that Two Finger had all his fingers, so his name probably came from something I didn't want to know about.

Two Finger looked just white enough so that the Skins didn't like him, and just Indian enough so that he couldn't go into a white town without getting in trouble. He was a big heavy-jowled guy, about six feet four, with a pockmarked face and small, snakelike eyes. His skin was an ugly yellow color that I had never seen on a person before. He was probably in his mid-forties, but it was hard to tell. He wheezed when he walked and he had a slow, lumbering manner that made him seem like a threat to everything small and delicate in any room he entered. Even if he had liked me, I wouldn't have liked him much. But he didn't like me. He didn't like anybody.

I suppose he was the perfect guy for the job of rounding up kids for the boarding schools. He didn't care if the kids cried or their parents begged or if someone grabbed a gun and threatened him. He was stronger than they were, meaner than they were. He had the government behind him, and he didn't care if he died. That made him someone no one wanted to mess with.

The high point of the job for Two Finger was doing a "grab." A "grab" was when the parents resisted and you had to take the kid by force. "Grab 'em like a fish and watch 'em wriggle," he said, baring his teeth like a ferret.

I hated the grabs. Pulling kids away from their families seemed like a cruel and unnecessary way to do something that could have been done more gracefully. The one time I told Two Finger that I thought there must be a better way to do it, he grabbed me by the shirt, almost lifting me off the ground. "You're not getting paid to think," he said. His voice was so filled with menace that I never brought it up again.

What bothered me the most about the grabs was Two Finger's utter lack of emotion about ripping kids away from their families. He'd get sent a name, make a grunt, say, "Come on, Danton," and we'd get in the car and drive to the home. He'd push his way into the house and stand like some dark hulking force while the parents begged and pleaded, then he'd grab the little boy or girl and throw them into the back seat of the car, where they'd sit sobbing and shaking until we got back to town and handed them off to the school officials. Sometimes he wouldn't say a word the entire time.

That's why I was so taken aback when I walked into the office one day to find him walking back and forth and chortling, "We've got ourselves a Lone Dog. We got a fucking Lone Dog." He was licking his lips like someone anticipating a long-awaited meal. "Come on, Danton," he said. "This one is going to be fun."

I followed him out to the car, uncertain of what was happening. I didn't know who the Lone Dogs were. I didn't know where we were going. I didn't know what had gotten Two Finger so animated. The only thing I was certain of was that it wasn't going to be fun.

BROKEN

Danton

The Lone Dogs lived deep in the hills about ten miles out of town at the end of a road that had been named by them or for them — Lone Dog Road. There were four of them — an old man, his granddaughter, and two kids. I was told that the old man was well regarded in the community, though I had never heard his name mentioned before.

Apparently the Lone Dogs were refusing to send their younger boy to the boarding school, and some faceless government official had determined that it would set a bad precedent to let a man of influence in the community keep his family members out of the school. Two Finger had been tasked with making sure that didn't happen.

Lone Dog Road was a washboard affair pocked with craterous holes and strewn with rocks the size of human skulls. It was hard on cars and even harder on the people in them.

By the time we got to the Lone Dog house, Two Finger's glee had changed to anger.

He finished the Lucky Strike he was smoking and flipped it out the window into the bone-dry grasses that grew up to the side of the road.

"I'll take care of this one," he said. "You just back me up."

The Lone Dog house was little more than a tar-paper shack cobbled together out of spare timber and salvaged windows. I couldn't imagine how it survived against the brutal summer winds and merciless winter blizzards.

"I hate this goddamn heat," Two Finger said as he pushed himself out of the driver's seat and lumbered toward the door. He was sweating and wheezing and cursing under his breath. The temperature was approaching a hundred degrees, and it wasn't even noon.

He stopped long enough to light another cigarette and take a deep drag, and flipped it into a tiny flower garden on the side of the house. Then he pushed open the front door and walked in without even bothering to knock.

The family was sitting together around the breakfast table — the grandfather, the mother, the older boy who was maybe ten or eleven, and the younger boy who appeared to be about six or seven.

The grandfather nodded like he had been expecting us. He was a little man with long white hair pulled back into a ponytail. He was polishing a red stone pipe and seemed almost indifferent to our presence.

The mother was a different story. She stood up when we came in and blocked our path. She was tall and masculine, close to six feet, with dark hair, hard cheekbones, and piercing blue eyes the likes of which I had never seen on an Indian. She pulled the younger boy close and placed herself protectively in front of him. The older boy stayed seated with his eyes down.

I had never felt frightened on a grab before. Most Indian folks tended to be subservient in the face of government authority, and Two Finger's presence took away any remaining thoughts they might have had about putting up resistance. But there was a latent violence here, especially on the part of the mother. Her eyes had a cold rage that sent a chill through me.

The younger boy peered around from behind her. He had big luminous eyes and a shock of black hair that stuck up in all directions like a dandelion. He was as cute as a button, but there was something slightly off about him. He never blinked; he just stared. He reminded me of a wary animal, taking in everything, but understanding nothing. Even at first glance, it was clear that he was no one who belonged in a boarding school.

Two Finger gestured toward the mother, as if he expected her to just hand the boy over to us.

She took a step toward him and stared right in his face. She was absolutely devoid of fear.

Two Finger curled his lip and gestured toward the boy again. The mother did not move. There was something lethal in her stillness.

I was about to speak up when the old man hoisted himself from his chair and stepped between them.

"Come, come, there is no need for anger," he said. He held out his pipe. "Come, let us smoke together."

Two Finger brushed him aside.

The old man persisted. "No," he said, holding the pipe out like an offering. "We should smoke about this."

Two Finger looked down on him as if he were a bothersome insect and swatted the pipe out of his hands. It fell on the floor and broke into pieces.

Suddenly, it was as if all the air had gone out of the room. The old man stared down at the pipe, then up at Two Finger, then back at the pipe. He bent over and carefully picked up the pieces and walked out into the yard without even looking at us.

The mother stared at Two Finger with a coiled fury. I think if she had been holding a knife she would have tried to kill him.

Two Finger seemed almost pleased. He leaned against the wall, casually lit a Lucky Strike, and puffed on it triumphantly.

Both boys had moved in behind their mother. The older boy's eyes had gone completely blank.

Two Finger looked at the three of them and curled his lip into that ugly ferret sneer.

Through the door I could see the old man lifting the pipe pieces to the sky and chanting something in Lakota.

"Come on, Danton," Two Finger said. "Leave the old man to his witch-doctoring. We can come back tomorrow and take the kid."

He flicked the cigarette at the feet of the mother and boys and walked out to the car.

◊ ◊ ◊

To this day I don't understand why Two Finger didn't grab the boy right then. Perhaps he wanted to draw out the family's discomfort and suffering, like his professed desire to have them wriggle like a fish on the end of a line. Perhaps he was actually a little afraid, like I was. But whatever the reason, we headed back to town empty-handed, with Two Finger chortling and chuckling and chain-smoking his beloved Luckies.

He drove in his usual fashion — too fast and with no concern for the realities of the situation. At some point we hit a pothole, a tire blew, and we ended up in the ditch. Neither of us was hurt, but the event threw Two Finger into a rage.

"Fucking Lone Dogs!" he shouted as he climbed out of the car, as if they were somehow responsible. "Fucking Lone Dogs!" He kicked the side of the car until it dented.

An Indian man in an old pickup appeared out of nowhere and helped us change the tire. Two Finger cursed the whole time, shouting about hexes and spells. I tried to give the man a couple of dollars, but he just smiled and shook his head, got back in his truck, and disappeared as quietly as he had arrived. The incident further enraged Two Finger, causing him to drive even faster on the remaining journey back to town.

"I knew it," he said, pounding the steering wheel. "I knew we should have taken him. Tomorrow. Tomorrow we grab that fucking little Lone Dog kid."

CASTING SPELLS

Levi

Grandpa is the reason Reuben and I are running. One day two government men came to our house. They said they were there to take Reuben to boarding school, the same one where I go. There was a white man and a mixed-blood.

Momma was angry when she saw the men coming. She had on her "grizzly bear" face. That's what Grandpa calls it.

"It's all right, my girl," he said. He had a full smile. "Let me take care of it."

The school men came in without knocking. It was a big insult. The mixed-blood's eyes were hard and small, like black stones. They were cold-like, like a snake. The white school man stayed back. His eyes had some kindness. Some sadness, too.

The mixed-blood tried to take Reuben. Momma pulled Reuben up close to her. He held on to her leg and looked up at her.

"Get out of my house," Momma said.

The mixed-blood was showing a dark spirit.

Grandpa tried to get the mixed-blood to calm down. He held up his pipe. "Let's smoke together," he said. Grandpa liked to smoke when there was anger in the room.

"We're not smoking about anything," the mixed-blood said. "We're taking that kid."

He hit Grandpa's pipe out of his hand. It fell on the floor and broke.

Grandpa's grandfather had given him that pipe. He had made it with his own hands.

Grandpa just looked at the pipe pieces on the floor. He was more still than I had ever seen him.

He picked up the pieces and walked out the door past the school men. He never even looked at them.

That night Leonard Eagle Feather came to our house. He saw a car go into the ditch when he had been driving home. He said it looked like a government car.

The driver was a mixed-blood, he said. He kept swearing in *wašíču* words and talking about how Grandpa had put a spell on him.

Leonard helped them change a tire and get the car back on the road. Then he came to our house to tell us what had happened.

He and Grandpa talked for a long time, and Momma, too. They were still talking when I fell asleep.

◊ ◊ ◊

The next morning Momma got Reuben up early and sent him up the hill to hide. She told him to stay there and not come down.

Pretty soon the school men came back. They slammed the car door hard. We could hear angry voices.

The mixed-blood pushed in again without even knocking.

"We've come for that boy," he said. He was talking to Grandpa. We were sitting at the table.

"You can have this boy," Grandpa said. He was pointing at me.

"We already have him. We want the other boy."

"He will not go with you."

The mixed-blood got mad at Grandpa and told him to get Reuben. Grandpa said he didn't know where Reuben was.

The mixed-blood said Grandpa was lying and that he knew Grandpa had put a spell on them and made their car go in a ditch.

Grandpa just laughed.

"If there's a spell on you, I didn't do it," he said. "Maybe you did it to yourself when you broke my *čhaŋnúŋpa*."

Then he got up and turned his back on the man. It was a big insult.

He waved his hand in the air, like to say goodbye. "Maybe other bad things will happen to you, too," he said. "I don't know."

That got the mixed-blood really angry. He started shouting really loud.

"Take your anger outside of my house," Momma said.

The *wašíču* school man tried to make the mixed-blood calm down. The mixed-blood kept shouting.

Grandpa closed his eyes and said something real low in Lakota.

That made the mixed-blood even more mad.

"See?" he said. "Now you're putting curses on us. I know what you're doing."

"I'm not putting curses on you," Grandpa said. "I was praying. You have a *wašíču* brain."

That made the mixed-blood act crazy. I thought he was going to hit Grandpa. He took Grandpa by the arm, really hard-like.

"Now you're coming with us," he said.

Grandpa pulled away from him. "I will go with you," he said. "But you will not place your hands on me."

I ran over and held on to Grandpa.

Grandpa put his hand on my shoulder. There was strong calm in his hand.

He made himself straight and walked out of the house. He did not let the school man touch him.

That's when Momma made us run.

She gave me the bread and the *wasná* and told me to get Reuben.

"Don't go anywhere you know," she said. "If you do, the government men will find you. Get on the train and don't get off until you see morning. Creator will protect you."

I took the bread and the *wasná* and went up to get Reuben.

That's when we ran down to the tracks and hitched on the train.

I don't know what happened to Grandpa.

WHAT YOU WERE HIRED FOR

Danton

The ride back to town was one of the most uncomfortable I've ever experienced. Two Finger made me sit in the back seat with old Lone Dog. I don't know if he thought the old man might try to escape, or if he just liked the idea of putting us next to each other out of spite. I kept looking at Lone Dog out of the corner of my eye, thinking I should say something. But he was silent and taciturn, sitting motionless with his hands folded in his lap and a placid expression on his face.

Two Finger drove in his usual fashion, chain-smoking and wheezing and letting out a violent curse when he hit an unusually bone-jarring bump or pothole. He seemed to have completely forgotten about the little Lone Dog boy.

We drove the entire trip without speaking, with the old man's unearthly air of calm permeating the entire car. I felt dirty and ashamed. I could not wait to get away from the whole situation.

I left the two of them standing outside the office and hurried to my truck. I was almost sick to my stomach for what we had just done.

I spent the whole night tossing and turning, filled with self-recrimination and doubts.

The next morning did not bring me any more peace. I was seriously contemplating just packing up my truck and heading further west, but I had to see this through. The little boy's face, peering out from behind his mother's dress, haunted me. He was like God's own innocent.

I drove into the office, uncertain of what I was going to do.

Two Finger was already there, an almost unprecedented occurrence for a man who seldom arrived before noon, if he arrived at all.

"I don't feel good about this," I said, steeling myself for the response.

"About what?" he answered, spooning the dregs from a cold can of chili.

"About us taking that boy."

"There ain't no 'us,'" he said, licking at the spoon. "'You.' You're going to go get him."

The comment shocked me. I had imagined many responses, but this had not been among them.

"Why me?" I asked.

Two Finger squinted and leaned toward me.

"I'm busy," he said.

He tossed the chili can across the room toward the wastebasket. It hit the rim and bounced onto the floor.

"Besides, what the hell do you think you were hired for?"

I stood there motionless, dumbfounded and confused.

"Go on. Go get him. Use your college-boy charm. Find the little bastard and bring him back here."

I didn't know what to say. Two Finger was right: This was what I had been hired for.

I left him sitting at his desk paging through a *Stag* magazine and headed out Lone Dog Road, contemplating the very real possibility that this whole South Dakota venture had just been one more bad choice in my life of questionable choices.

But I couldn't forget the image of that little boy with his wide uncomprehending eyes and that sprig of dandelion hair. I couldn't leave him to Two Finger.

NO WELCOME IN HER GREETING

Danton

Mrs. Lone Dog met me at the door, but there was no welcome in her greeting. She stood on the threshold with her hands on her hips, blocking the doorway. She made no offer to invite me in.

I had not paid much attention to her on the previous visits. I had been too concerned with the boys and Two Finger and the old man. Now it was just the two of us, face-to-face, and I could feel the full force of her intimidating presence.

She was hard-edged and angular, somewhere in her early thirties with thick black hair tied back in a kerchief. She must have had a case of smallpox or some other disease as a child; her cheeks were textured with scarring.

She might have been pretty in a different circumstance. She had broad cheekbones, an aquiline nose, and a strong, square jaw. But there was a darkness in her, not unlike the darkness in Two Finger, that took the beauty away and made her seem cold and frightening.

But what struck me most were her eyes — they were a translucent blue, almost like ice. I had never seen anything like them before, especially in a Native person. They burned with some distant fury, but they generated no light.

"Good morning, Mrs. Lone Dog," I said, making sure that she heard me use her name. I wanted to show that I honored and respected her as a human being, not like Two Finger who just called people, "Hey, you," or didn't even address them at all. "I'm here about your boys."

She stared at me with those terrifying eyes and gave no response.

I was used to Indian silences, but hers had a threat within it that set me on edge.

"We need to talk about your boys," I said finally, unable to take the silence any longer.

"Where's my grandpa?" she asked. Her voice was flat and without emotion.

The wind had picked up and was blowing a fine silt across everything. I shielded the side of my face with my hand in an attempt to keep the grit from getting in my eyes.

"Can I come in?" I asked.

"Where's my grandpa?" she repeated.

I didn't know how to respond. I had no idea what Two Finger had done and no idea what he was planning.

"I left him in town with Two Finger," I said.

"He's eighty-seven. He's an elder. You had no right to take him."

"I know. But it wasn't my call."

"I'm sure nothing is your call. Save me your apologies. You will not enter my house."

She turned and shut the door in my face.

I retreated to my truck and sat for a long time trying to figure out what to do.

The wind rattled the windows and blew skeins of dust across the hood. A tumbleweed skittered around the fender and bounced off across the prairie. The whole situation felt wrong, even dangerous. I just wanted to get out of there. But I knew I couldn't return to Two Finger empty-handed. If I didn't have the boys, I at least needed to have some sort of an explanation. So I went back to the house and knocked again.

Mrs. Lone Dog opened the door wide and stood before me with her arms crossed across her chest.

"What?" she said. I noticed she was holding a kitchen knife.

"I'm really sorry. This is not my idea."

"That's not stopping you."

"It wasn't right what Two Finger did," I said, trying to establish some kind of rapport. "He treated your family with disrespect."

I knew I was going far beyond what I had a right to say. This sort of personal admission, especially when I was there in an official capacity, was completely inappropriate. But the image of her younger boy staring out from behind her with those innocent eyes would not leave me.

She stood silently, regarding me with contempt.

Suddenly, without thinking, I blurted, "I don't think your boy should go to that school."

I couldn't believe it when I heard the words come out of my mouth. It was like an out-of-body experience. All the loneliness, all the misgivings I had about the job, my hunger to be liked by somebody or at least understood, all met in that moment as I stood staring at that ice-eyed woman who was blocking the doorway in front of me.

She looked at me with disdain. The dust was burning my eyes and cutting my face.

"Bring me my grandfather," she said, and slammed the door.

A FRIGHTENED MAN

Danton

"**G**oddamn it," Two Finger thundered, slamming his fist on the desk. "Letting a fucking squaw push you around." He leaned across and fixed me with a dark, menacing stare.

I had prepared myself for his anger, but I had not expected this level of threat. I had even crafted the rudiments of a speech that would explain why I had come back empty-handed. But face-to-face with his violence, my words failed me.

"I think she needs to see her grandfather before she will tell us anything," I stammered.

Two Finger slashed his hand across his desk, knocking a coffee cup to the floor.

"Who's in charge here? You? Some fucking squaw? Some crazy old man with a pipe?"

"It's family," I said. "I think we need to respect that."

"You think. You think."

He walked to the other side of the room, flexing his hands into fists.

"You're not paid to think."

He punched the wall violently, hard enough to break an ordinary man's hand. For the first time I truly saw what the families feared when he came to take their children.

"I'm just telling you what I saw," I said. "I think we need to find the old man and bring him back to her if we want to find out anything."

He spit into the wastebasket and turned toward me.

"You want to find the old man? You think that's going to do it? Then go do it. It ain't that hard. He's in the back room."

The information shocked me. It had never occurred to me that Two Finger had been intending to hold the old man like a prisoner.

I knew there were some old cells in the rear of our building that had been part of the old jail before the new one had been built across the street. I had been back there once, and they were dank, musty, urine-smelling cubicles filled with desks and old tires and file cabinets turned on their sides. I didn't even think there would have been room to put the old man back there, much less any legitimate reason to do so.

I found the old man curled up on a wooden bench in one of the cells. He probably hadn't slept much. Two Finger hadn't even bothered to give him a blanket.

He pushed himself upright when I came in. As I opened the cell door he stood up, almost at attention. You could feel the ghost of generations of warrior training in his manner.

"Going home, Mr. Lone Dog," I said.

He nodded and stepped toward the door.

Again, I was struck by the quiet dignity of his manner. It was clear that movement was hard for him. But he carried himself with such self-containment that he seemed to control all the space around him.

I had seen this before in Indian men and had come to look upon it with awe. They could own a room without ever saying a word. I could only imagine what it must have been like for government treaty negotiators to confront a group of men like this and try to convince them that they must now be subservient to the wishes of the Great Father in Washington.

Luckily, I didn't have to negotiate anything. I just had to get old Lone Dog back to his home in the hills and try to convince him and his granddaughter to at least talk to Two Finger about the issue of the younger boy and the boarding school.

I had wanted to take the government car, but Two Finger hadn't offered it and I didn't dare ask him. So I had to take my pickup. This was going to be hard for me. It was the first time anyone had sat in the passenger seat since Sweet Girl had died.

The old man followed me out to the truck, again refusing any offers of assistance. He pulled open the door and paused for a second. He looked at me, then down at the seat, and smiled slightly, as if he knew something. He touched the seat and nodded, then slid in with a single move that defied his bad leg and his age, and placed his hands in his lap. He sat motionless with his eyes closed and an almost beatific smile on his face.

It was strange having him in Sweet Girl's seat, but somehow it didn't bother me as much as I had expected. He seemed at peace and that put me at peace. We rode in silence down the main street and out into the hills.

Despite Lone Dog's calm demeanor, I soon found myself feeling the need to explain and apologize. I considered several approaches, but none of them seemed right. Finally, I just said what was on my mind.

"I'm sorry about Two Finger. What he did to your pipe."

The old man opened his eyes and touched me on the arm. "He is a frightened man," he said. "He has a frightened spirit."

This was not the response I had expected.

"Still, I feel bad about it."

The old man held his hand up, as if to stop me from the direction I was going. "You had nothing to do with it," he said.

"I was there. I should have done something."

He pursed his lips into that tiny smile and stared into the distance. It was an interior-facing smile, full of private thoughts and knowledge.

"His spirit is on a long journey," he said, tapping me on the knee. "So is yours."

Then he sat back, placed his hands on his lap, and closed himself off like an animal that does not want to be seen.

YOU ARE THAT MAN

Danton

We drove up the path to the old man's home just as the sun was dropping behind the distant hills.

The wind had calmed, but the sky was still gritty with dust, diffusing the waning sunlight and casting everything in a blood-red glow. The light reflecting off the windows of the house made it seem as if its interior was on fire.

The heat had settled over the land in a breathless haze. I could only imagine what it was like for old Lone Dog in this weather. I'm sure the temperature was still over 100 degrees, and he was dressed in jeans and a long-sleeved shirt buttoned at the collar and the wrists.

I didn't know whether to offer him assistance in getting out of the car or just let him do it on his own. He had always refused assistance in the past, but the ride had been long and I was sure he had not had anything to eat since we had brought him in the day before.

I was still trying to decide what to do when he spoke up from the passenger seat.

"You will come in," he said. It was less an offer than a command.

I had not expected this. I knew I had to find out about the boys, but I had hoped to resolve the issue in the relative neutrality of their front yard. His daughter had made it clear how she felt about me entering her house, and I did not want to confront her anger again.

"I'm not sure..." I started to say, but he had already opened the car door and was stepping into the dust.

"Come," he said, with an air of even greater authority. "You will come in."

I didn't want to say "yes," but I couldn't say "no," so I just deferred to his status as an elder and followed him meekly up to the house.

His granddaughter had heard the car drive up and was waiting in the doorway. The old man was preoccupied with keeping his footing and did not notice the cold look she was giving me. I shrugged as if to say that I was just following his instructions, but her manner did not change.

"The *wašíču* comes in," the old man said. Obviously he was aware of the dynamic between his granddaughter and me, even though he appeared to be paying no attention.

"Grandpa!" she said.

"No, Ree girl," he answered. "The *wašíču* comes in."

It was the first time I had heard anyone use her name.

He bent down and touched the small clump of yellow flowers in the garden patch next to the door. "Ah," he said, with an air of satisfaction. He smiled up at her as if there was nothing else under discussion. "*Pȟeží zizí*. This is doing well," he said, stroking the plants as if they were small animals.

"Do you know this flower?" he asked me.

"No," I said. "I don't know very much about plants."

He gave me his little smile. "Good for colds."

His granddaughter had taken him by the elbow and was helping him toward the house. She cast a hard stare over her shoulder at me as if trying to shoo away a stray dog.

"Ree girl, this *wašíču* stays here," he said. "I have some things to say to him."

Her eyes widened, but she said nothing.

None of it made any sense. Anything he had to say he could easily have said during the drive.

His granddaughter helped him in the door and guided him to his rocking chair.

She made no effort to offer me any hospitality. I stood in the doorway, trying to figure out what to do.

I didn't dare ask about the boys, though I knew I would have to address the issue soon enough. But this was not the moment.

It was almost as if the old man was reading my mind. "You are here about Reuben," he said. "That is why Two Finger had you bring me home."

"Yes," I said. "That's what I'm supposed to do, but…"

The old man gestured me to silence.

"We will talk about it soon. Granddaughter, give him water. This is a hot day."

Ree was clearly not happy with my presence. Nonetheless, she did as her grandfather instructed, ladling me a glass of water from a pail before withdrawing to a corner and standing with her arms folded across her chest.

"Good," he said, as if all the preliminaries were now over. "Now I have some things to say. Sit. Sit."

I moved tentatively to the bench by the table and sat down across from him.

He pulled a crumpled cigarette from a pack in his shirt pocket and lit it with a wooden match. "Smoke?" he said, offering the pack in my direction. I shook my head and tried to look relaxed.

"This job you have taken with that Two Finger," he began. "It has a bad heart. When I heard about the new *wašíču* with that job, I asked about you. My friends, they see you at lunch. They watch you. They say your eyes are sad. They say you are confused. They say you are not good for that job and that job is not good for you.

"I know those boarding schools where you are sending the children. I know what they do to their little spirits. I let Levi go because he is strong and needs to know *wašíču* ways. But Reuben is not like Levi. That school is not a place for him.

"I knew you would be coming for him soon. I have waited to see you. Now I have seen you. Now I know what my friends know. Now I am going to tell you some things."

I shifted uncomfortably in my chair. I felt like a schoolchild who had been called to the principal's office.

"You do not belong in that job. You do not know what you are doing. You are like a little child. You do not know the good things. You do not know the bad things. You have come to our country like an animal with a wound. You do not see the things around you. You think only about your pain. You are lost in yourself."

The psychology behind his assessment was uncomfortable, but it had a kernel of truth.

"That Two Finger man," he continued, "he has a much greater wound. But it has healed wrong. You have not healed wrong. Your healing can still be good. My friends say you are a good watcher. Good watchers are good listeners. So I am going to teach you now. I am going to teach you about Reuben. I want you to listen. This is important."

I nodded uncertainly. I had no idea where this was going.

The old man pressed forward. "I was not raised in *wašíču* language," he said. "I do not think in *wašíču* thought. You *wašíču* have more words than we do, but they come from a foreign land. I am going to tell you in words from the ground where my grandfathers walked."

His speaking had assumed a formal tone.

He turned to his granddaughter. "I want you to witness this, my girl. That is why I invited him into our home. If I call you to witness, then I am bound by Creator to speak the truth." His granddaughter said nothing, just stared at me with those cold blue eyes.

He turned his attention back to me. "There is *wašíču* remembering and there is Indian remembering," he said. "*Wašíču* remembering is about things that have happened. It is easily forgotten. That is why you write in books. You do not want to forget things that have happened.

"Indian remembering is different. It is not in books. Some of it is in stories. But some of it is in a place you don't know about.

"You have seen an animal when it searches for food? How does it know where to look? Have you seen a bird return to its home in the spring? How does it know where to go? This is the kind of remembering we Indian people know.

"You are trying to stop us from our way of remembering. That is why you steal our children for your schools. You fill them with *wašíču* words and beat them when they use their own words, because you think that words carry the way of remembering. Taking our words might stop our *wašíču* remembering but it will not stop our Indian remembering.

"All of us knew this Indian remembering at one time. It was passed to us by our elders. It was in our language. Our language is different from yours. It does not name things, it calls things. When we call them, they listen and they speak back to us. Your words give things names, but they are your names, not their names. Nothing listens when you talk to it in your words.

"But your words are strong. They cover the earth like a blanket. Nothing can escape them. Your people knew that if you covered our words with your words, your words would smother our words and our words would die. You thought we would lose our Indian remembering. Many of us did. But some who remained strong in Indian remembering could not have it taken away by the smothering of our words."

I was having difficulty following him. His way of expressing himself was strange and elliptical.

I started to ask him a question. He held up his hand to stop me.

"You listen. You do not try to speak. When you try to speak, it tells me that your ears have stopped listening. It tells me you have gone to your mind to find something to say. I do not want you to go to your mind. Your mind must stay open to the things I am saying.

"There are not too many of us left who have the Indian remembering. The young ones, they want to have it but they have learned to think through your words, so they hear it only in the most distant way. They try, but your words have stopped their ears to our Indian remembering. Some of us, the old ones, the ones born with our own tongue, we have Indian remembering. But we are dying off. Soon there will be none of us.

"But there are also the ancient ones. They are not the same as the old ones. The ancient ones come into the world with this remembering. They do not need the language because the Creator has placed this remembering in their spirits.

"Reuben is one of them. He has Indian remembering. It is in his spirit."

The old man's voice had turned very soft. He was keeping to his formal way of speaking, but his words were flowing slowly and calmly, almost hypnotically, almost like a song. I imagined this was how the children were taught in the old days. Though I was confused, I felt honored to have him speak to me like this. I felt like I had been taken inside a place where few white people ever got to go.

Out of the corner of my eye I could see his granddaughter stiffening. Every time the old man paused she would lean forward as if to interject something or to stop him from going further. But each time he would glance at her and she would pull back and cross her arms more tightly across her chest, as if trying to hold in her words. She knew she was there to be a witness, not a participant.

"Now I will tell you why Reuben cannot be allowed to go to that school," he said. He leaned in close. "I want you to hear me.

"Reuben does not understand the world like we do. All things he sees and hears go right to his spirit. He cannot hold the world away from him with words and thoughts.

"Your *wašíču* world now covers our Indian world. It surrounds us and controls our lives. It is loud and it is demanding. It makes the memories that fill up our days and drowns out our Indian way of remembering.

"Memories have great power. They must be treated with care. They are like spirits. They fill the heart and shape the mind. Memories that are near and loud are like noisy spirits. They keep the heart from the deep remembering.

"Most of our memories that come from the *wašíču* ways are bad memories. The memories from those schools are the worst of all. They have broken the spirits of many of our people. I am watching Levi close so he does not have his spirit broken.

"When you are old, like I am, you can push these bad memories away with good memories, because you have traveled down so many pathways and seen so much of life. But when you are young, the bad memories can hold you, because your memories are so few. There is nothing to push the bad ones away.

"Reuben holds his memories strong. He cannot understand the world around him, so when he gets a memory, he holds it close. Those are the places he can go in his mind. If we let him go to that school, his mind will be filled with bad memories that he cannot escape. They will turn his spirit dark and close his ears to the deep memories.

"He must not go to that place. His spirit will die in that place. I will not let that happen. I will not let his spirit die in that place."

He stubbed his cigarette out on the arm of his chair and put his hand on my arm.

"Now you must listen to me carefully. Now I will tell you why you are here.

"I cannot protect Reuben. I am old and the *wašíču* will not listen to me. My granddaughter cannot protect him because she is a woman and *wašíču* do not respect the mind of women. Only a *wašíču* man can protect him."

He paused, as if to let the gravity of what he was about to say set in. "You are that man."

I am not sure if the shock was greater to his granddaughter or to me.

"Grandpa!" she said, breaking her silence.

She began speaking rapidly in Lakota. She continued until her grandfather held up his hand. "You are here to witness, Granddaughter. You are not here to contend with me. I have said what I have said."

He turned to face me. All the mirth was gone from his eyes.

"You," he said. "Have you understood me?"

I was unsure what to say. For weeks I had been getting more and more bothered by the job. Two Finger's treatment of the Lone Dogs had brought me to the brink. But I was not sure that I wanted to give myself over to the vision of an elderly Lakota man.

Old Lone Dog saw me hesitate. He tapped his temple with his forefinger. "This is not about the workings of your mind," he said. "This is about your spirit finding its way. Listen to me. I am an old man and I have walked far on the road of life. I have walked where you are walking. I may not know your mind, but I see the trouble in your spirit.

"You are a man without a purpose. You do not farm. You do not ranch. You work for that Two Finger who has a stone in his chest.

"You have no wife. You sit each day in the café, saying nothing. You act as if watching, as if to learn. But you did not come here to learn. You would not be with Two Finger if you had come here to learn.

"You are a lonely man. You are out here to escape. I do not know what you are escaping from. That is of no concern to me. All I know is that Creator gives us each a task. When we are called into this life from the other side, it is for a reason. 'Come out, come out,' Creator says. 'I have need of you in this world.' That is why we are born.

"Our task in life is to find out why Creator has called us. Sometimes Creator shows it to us easily. Sometimes we must search very hard.

"I am giving you a gift. I am showing you why Creator called you into life. You do not have to search anymore. You have been given your purpose. You have been called to be a protector of a little one who has an ancient spirit."

I felt the hairs stand up on the back of my neck.

His granddaughter was looking on in horror as her grandfather spoke.

"Grandpa!" she said, and began speaking again in Lakota.

"Speak English," he said. "If he would trust us then he must hear us. It is not good to hide behind our words. Speak in his language."

She switched to English in deference to her grandfather's wishes. "I don't care if he trusts us. I don't trust him. I don't trust any white man and neither should you. Have you forgotten what has been done to us?"

Her grandfather reached over and touched her gently.

"You are young, Granddaughter. Your eyes have not seen what my eyes have seen. I have forgotten nothing. I have seen the worst of who they are. I have seen it for longer than you have been alive. There are good ones among them, as with all people. They just see the world through small eyes. Their minds are small places."

He touched his chest. "But that does not mean their hearts cannot be opened. This man is a good man. He is just confused."

His granddaughter was clearly upset.

"Grandfather, do you remember when I was a little girl and they sent me away for the summer to work in those white people's houses?"

The old man nodded.

"Do you remember that Anishinabe girl who was my friend? Do you remember what happened to her?"

"You are holding to a thin reed. You should let it go."

"No, Grandpa. There was truth in that story. I have seen it. So have you."

"Granddaughter, the *wašíču* are here. They are not leaving. Will you fight against them your whole life?"

"I will not fight against them, but I will not trust them."

He patted her on the hand.

"Go ahead. Tell that story, Granddaughter. It will be good for you to say it out loud. You carry too much poison inside."

"It's not about poison. It's about survival. It's about survival for my boy. Sometimes holding to the old ways makes you blind."

"As you will, Granddaughter," he said. "Tell the story if you must. Perhaps it will be good for the *wašíču* to hear it. But I want you to use his name. A person only becomes real when you say their name. Tell her your name, Mr. School Man."

I was almost afraid to say it. I felt like I was giving something important away. "Adrien Danton," I said.

"Ah, a good name. Now you can place the story before him, Granddaughter. Tell Mr. Adrien Danton your story. Clear your heart."

Ree walked over and stood across the table from me. There was no thought of her sitting down; there was nothing conversational about this exchange.

"All right, Mr. Adrien Danton," she said, saying my name in a way that made it sound almost dirty. "Here's your story.

"When I was a girl they sent us off to live with white people in the summer. The boarding school people did that. The people you work for. Like your Mr. Two Finger. Like the *wašíču* government.

"They said they wanted us to learn how to be civilized, but they really just wanted us to be slaves.

"Some of the girls were lucky. They got to go home to their families in the summer. The rest of us, they just picked us like choosing cattle. 'You go here. You go there. You go with this family. You go with that family.'

"I went with a family that was really mean. I won't bring them alive again in my heart by saying their name. They practiced the Christian way and they made me work every day except Sunday when they made me pray all day.

"They didn't have any children and they treated me like a slave. I had to wash clothes. I had to iron. I had to get up in the morning before the man got up and stay up until after he went to bed at night. I had to cook and clean and do anything they said. I didn't even have a bed, just a quilt and an old mattress under the stairs.

"The man hit me sometimes if he didn't like the way I did something. It wasn't hard, but it scared me. I was never hit at home. They treated me worse than their dogs.

"There was another girl. An Anishinabe girl from up north. She was my best friend. She got sent to a very kind family. This girl had her own bedroom and everything. They let her play with their own children. They even called her their Indian daughter.

"They lived in town. They were rich even for *wašíču*. All she had to do was help them make meals and wash clothes. She was like part of their family, not like one of their dogs. We were all so jealous.

"One fall when I came back to school she was already there. Her eyes were sad and she didn't want to talk. I asked her what had happened. She said her *wašíču* family had turned mean to her and now she was afraid.

"I couldn't believe it. We had all wanted to be her.

"I kept asking her what had happened. She didn't want to tell me. But then she started crying and came over and we hugged and she told me.

"She said there was one day when she was supposed to make a dinner. The people had some friends coming over. She made the table beautiful in the white man way with china and special glasses. She even went out and found flowers and ironed all the napkins. She was so excited.

"She was supposed to make them fish. She thought, 'I can do that.' Her grandmas had taught her how to cut the fish and cook it in the Anishinabe way. She thought she would make her family so happy.

"She waited outside for the man with the ice truck to bring the fish. When she saw it, she knew that fish. It was a kind of fish that only came from a lake her father used to take her to. It was a lake where there is no water coming in and no water going out. These fish were long like snakes. She was raised not to eat these fish. Her people said they were half snakes. She was afraid of them. She did not want to touch them or cook them.

"The woman came into the kitchen and asked her why she wasn't cooking the fish. She told her she was afraid. She told her that her people had said these fish were part snake and should not be eaten.

"The woman got mad and told her she had to cook them.

"She wouldn't.

"The woman hit her across the face and made her go outside. She told her she was ruining the dinner and from now on she had to sleep in the back room with the dogs.

"She brought the minister out to their house and had him pray over her. He made her read the Bible and told her those were old superstitions and she had to forget all those things, and that her parents and grandparents were wrong.

"For the rest of the summer they kept their other kids away from her. The minister came all the time and made her pray and read the Bible. They even were going to try to make her eat some of that fish, but she kicked and cried and wouldn't do it.

"So they sent her back to the school early and she was there all by herself until the rest of us came back.

"There, that's your story, Mr. Adrien Danton."

The story seemed too fantastic to be true. But this woman may have been many things, but she wasn't a liar.

"That's a sad story," I said. "People shouldn't treat each other so badly. But, I'm sorry, I don't see what it has to do with me."

"*Wašíču* can be kind and friendly as long as you agree with them. But if you disagree with them, their way always wins. Their words count for nothing. You learn to trust only what you see."

"I assume you mean like me working to get kids to the boarding schools."

"Well, you do, don't you?"

"I said I didn't think Reuben should go to that school."

"Those are words. You are still here in my house. You are still working for Two Finger. You are still coming to get Reuben. You are like that family, talking kindness. But you don't even know your own mind. You are like a dog barking on the front end and wagging on the back. I don't know which end to believe. I'm not sure you do, either."

She moved in close to me. She was speaking almost directly into my face.

"I thought I was born to fight for my people, not for a child. But now that Reuben is here I love him more than anything in the world, more than you love anything. You live alone. You have no family. You do not know what it is to have a child, especially a child like Reuben.

"Grandpa's right. You live inside the small room of your own mind. That is an easy place. Reuben's life is a hard place.

"If you want to help me keep Reuben from that school, that's good. It might be good for your spirit like Grandpa says. I don't care. I don't believe like Grandpa. I don't believe you were chosen for anything, not to do with Reuben. I don't want you to think you have any part to play in his life. I will fight anyone who hurts him until I kill them. Do you understand?"

Her voice sent chills through me. Her blue eyes burned with an icy fury.

While she was speaking, her grandfather had gone to a shelf in the back corner of the house. He returned with an old dusty baseball glove that looked like something from the 1930s.

"Do you like baseball, Mr. Danton?" he asked. "I was a hell of a shortstop."

A GOOD SEAT FOR REUBEN

Danton

I don't know when I'd ever been so happy to get out of a house.
I'd driven up to the Lone Dog's intending only to bring an old man
home and pick up a young boy for the boarding school, but somehow had found myself pinned down by a furious ice-eyed woman who
compared me to someone who beat a young girl for refusing to cook
fish that looked like snakes and lectured by the old man about my spiritual destiny and his time playing shortstop.

It was like I had crossed into an alternate universe. And, in some
way, I had.

But the old man was right: I really was a confused man. It's just
that the term had suddenly taken on a whole new meaning.

The only thing that was certain was that I could no longer work for
Two Finger and do the work that I was doing. Listening to old Lone
Dog and his granddaughter had convinced me of that. The deeper issue
of my responsibility to Reuben was more difficult.

What had the old man meant and how should I take it? Maybe he
was just playing upon my hunger for family and human connection
to enlist my aid in finding his great-grandsons. Or maybe he truly believed that I was meant to be Reuben's protector as part of some grand
cosmic plan. Or maybe he was just an old man with a touch of senility
and some well-worn phrases that evoked a different spiritual time and
way of looking at the world. And what was I to make of Ree's comments that had come very close to being a threat?

When Lone Dog had walked with me out to the car after the

confrontation, he had not said another word about the protector issue, but had instead gone on about his baseball days and watching Satchel Paige pitch in Bismarck in 1935.

"If you ever didn't think that the Creator gave some people special gifts," he said, "you never saw Satchel Paige pitch." He mimicked a pitching motion and flashed me a wide grin. "Could have thrown a fastball right through the door of this here truck. Would have come out the other side."

When we reached the Ford, he leaned over and stared in through the passenger window at the front seat. "I want to ask you something," he said. "When you brought me out to this car from that jail place, you hesitated before you had me sit down. Why did you do that?"

"You don't miss anything, do you?" I said.

He flashed me that impish grin again. "I was a shortstop. Couldn't let the ball get past me. And we Indians never miss anything. That's why we're still here."

His formal manner had almost completely disappeared and he was treating me more like a son or a friend than a representative of the government. I decided to be open with him. In a sad way, this was the most human connection I had experienced since arriving on the rez.

"It has to do with my old dog, Sweet Girl," I said. "That was her seat. No one had ever sat in it since she'd died."

"Ah," he said. "So you do understand."

"What?"

"I was worried you were a practical man. I couldn't understand why the Creator chose you. Now I see that you are a spiritual man. You just don't know where to look."

He pointed at the seat.

"That seat. Where your dog was. Your old dog made it sacred. You didn't want anyone on it.

"That's how we feel about the land where our parents and grand-parents are buried. They made it sacred with their blood and their bones. We've been mourning for that land ever since you started cutting and plowing and building on it.

"Yes, I think the Creator chose well when he chose you. That will be a good seat for Reuben to sit on when you find him."

DARKER THAN NIGHT

Danton

I probably would have just driven away if the wind had not come up. Old Lone Dog noticed it first. The sky was darkening in a strange and ominous way. There was a sound to it, a kind of rumble, like something moving toward us.

I looked to the west. The sky was completely black. It was something darker than night, something alive. And it was moving.

"You better come back in," Lone Dog said. "You can't drive in this. It will choke your truck."

I had heard about the dust storms of the '30s. The old-timers never tired of telling stories about how the wind had blown at 50, 60 miles an hour for days without cease and how the cutting dust had stripped the paint from their houses.

Our current dust storms were not as bad, and certainly not as continuous or frequent, but they had become a fact of life, with folks covering their car radiators with canvas panels and the landscape dotted with abandoned windmills that were able to pull up nothing but sand. People had just come to accept this situation as normal.

But there was something about this wind that was different. The air had been heavy all day — portentous, looming, like before a storm but with an overwhelming dryness. It puckered your skin as if pulling the moisture from it.

I had thought little of it as I had brought old Lone Dog home — just another hot day with a particularly harsh wind. But now it had taken on a strange edge.

Lone Dog looked at the sky. "Yes, you should come back in," he said.

I shut the truck door and followed him back to the house. The sky in the west was a rolling darkness.

Ree was already stuffing the cracks with rags.

She threw me some towels and pieces of cloth. "Get to work, Mr. Adrien Danton," she said. The tension between us had been replaced by a common concern about the storm.

Lone Dog was staring out the window. "Don't get many like this," he said, "but when we do…" He let out a long whistle.

The house had been built poorly. It was really nothing much more than a converted shed. The walls were made from horizontal planking that had been salvaged from various sources — rough sawn, not finely milled, so where the pieces fit together there were cracks and seams. The tar paper on the outside had covered them over, but on the inside the gaps were evident. As long as the tar paper held, the dust could be kept to a minimum. But if some of it tore, there would be nothing to stop the dust and silt from blowing through the house in streams.

For whatever reason, the Lone Dogs had never addressed the issue properly. Putting pieces of batten over the cracks would have been better than the flimsy tar paper. And prudence would have dictated at least holding the tar paper down with furring strips. But none of this had been done. Instead, they had addressed the issue from the inside, stuffing the cracks with rags and putting towels across the bottom of the doors when the weather demanded it.

During my construction days with the Norwegian carpenter, I had gotten pretty good at doing mortise and tenons. Given a decent chisel and an afternoon, I could have shored up that house and made it a hundred times more livable. But that was neither an option nor a possibility at the present time. What had to be done now was to seal up the house against whatever was looming on the western horizon.

Ree nodded me toward a corner of the room where papers were being rustled by some indeterminate wind intrusion. Old Lone Dog was going around turning the cups and dishes upside down to keep them from filling with dust.

"These big ones," he said. "You can feel them on your skin."

We worked until we had used up all the rags and towels. The sky outside had turned darker than anything I had ever seen.

I was scared and uncomfortable and just wanted to be home in my own house. The wind had gotten as loud as a freight train and kept our minds from thinking about anything else.

The house was small and claustrophobic. Aside from a lean-to bedroom and a tiny kitchen, there was only this one large room with a rocking chair in the center and the wooden table and bench by the wall. A potbelly wood stove and a broken-down purple couch took up the other wall. One makeshift shelf held Lone Dog's baseball glove, a baseball, and various pots and dishes. There was no sink, only a chipped enamel dishpan and the bucket where Ree had ladled water for me earlier in the day. It was the kind of house where everyone had their place and collective survival was based on not violating each other's privacy.

I did not know where to sit or what to do. The old man had settled into the rocking chair that was obviously his personal place. Ree had taken a seat on the bench facing the old man. Since the couch was covered with clothes and old newspapers, my only choice was to keep standing or to sit on the bench with her — an act that felt uncomfortably intimate in light of our interactions up to this point. I backed up and leaned against the wall as casually as I could, trying to give the impression that this was the most comfortable and logical place for me to be.

The wind was now buffeting the house with ferocious intensity. The silt made a hissing sound as it hit against the tar paper on the outside walls. Dust was somehow making its way in through the cracks and under the door, despite the efforts we had made to seal up all the openings with rags and towels.

I could see that Ree was getting upset. She was leaning forward with her elbows on the table and her hands folded in front of her. Her jaw was tight and her knuckles were tensing and relaxing almost involuntarily. She was staring directly at her grandfather with a look somewhere between anger and pleading.

I stayed back as far as I could. I was actually worried about the safety of my truck in the brutal winds, but what was going on in the house was even more concerning. At one point Ree said something to her grandfather in Lakota. He responded in kind and she shook her head violently.

I could tell that the conversation had something to do with me and the boys. They kept glancing in my direction and several times I heard the words "*wašiču*" and "Levi" and "Reuben," though they made no effort to include me or explain what the conversation was about.

They continued in this fashion for almost five minutes while the old man rocked back and forth in his chair, staring intently at his daughter and never taking his eyes off her.

I heard a sound from outside, like a piece of tar paper being ripped from the house. It fluttered and flapped, like a sail that had broken loose from a mast. For a quick moment, all our attention was drawn to the wind raging outside.

Ree looked at her grandfather, then at me. The old man had his hands steepled over his mouth and nose. It was clear that he was waiting for his granddaughter to speak.

"Mr. Adrien Danton," she said. "Would you go find my sons?"

Encounter

WE'RE NOT RUNAWAYS

Levi

Thinking about Grandpa had made me really sad. I didn't want to have to act like a full-grown. I was scared and feeling really alone.

I could feel myself starting to cry. I dug my fingernails into my arm to give myself a different pain. Reuben came over and sat down by me.

"Why you crying, Levi?" he said.

"I'm hungry, Reuben," I said. It was only half a lie.

I was telling lots of half lies now. Grandpa said when you start telling half lies they will take over the truth and pretty soon you will be telling whole lies. I didn't want to be telling whole lies.

I did not like the sky outside. It was only noon-like, but the air was all dark and angry. It made my skin feel hot and itchy.

Reuben pointed to a bird. It was sitting on an old fence post, making a strange sound, like screaming. Other birds were flying funny, like they didn't know where to go or were trying to get away from something. They were all making lots of noise.

"This is a bad day," Reuben said.

There was lots of dust in the air. It got in my hair and my eyes. It burned really bad. The wind was really strong.

I took some shirts from our bag and tied them around our faces.

"Keep your face covered," I told Reuben. "We'll walk low to the ground."

I looked up for the sun to know which way we were going. It was like it was behind a fog, except that the sky was brown. The birds were having a hard time flying.

Reuben and I bent over and tried to walk close to the ground, but the wind was too strong. The dust was blowing everywhere.

"We should go back to that house," I said.

"No," Reuben said. "That was a bad place."

We bent into the wind and tried to walk. I had to keep Reuben close. If he got even a few feet from me I wouldn't see him.

"This hurts my eyes," Reuben shouted.

The dust was in my teeth. It made my lips crack.

"We've got to go back," I said.

Reuben started coughing. "I want to go back, too," he said.

The sky was like it was alive. The sun was disappearing.

It was night-like, and it was only the middle of the day.

◊◊◊

We got back in the house. The whole floor was covered with dust, snow-like. It was blowing in through all the cracks and in the holes for the windows. It burned really hard like stinging when it hit you.

We got in a corner and huddled up together. Reuben kept the shirt over his head. "What's happening?" he said.

"I don't know. I think it's like what Grandpa talked about," I said. "The *wašíču* are turning over the earth too much. He said it was not good for the earth to be upside down, and that Creator was going to come and take it all away."

"Grandpa knew about everything," Reuben said.

"I know."

The wind blew hard against the boards of the house. Outside the window, dirt was flying through the sky.

Reuben put his arms around me. "I wish we could be with Grandpa," he said.

"We're going to be with him," I said. "I promise."

I shouldn't have said it. I didn't even know where Grandpa was. But I was worried about Reuben. Grandpa taught me that when I made a promise I had to keep it.

We sat against the wall. We had the jackets over our heads.

We had no food. Reuben knew it, too.

"I don't think we should stay here," I said. "We need to get to a town."

The sky was still full dark, but the dust wasn't as strong. I thought maybe we could run through it.

"Okay," he said. "Let's go."

We wrapped the jackets around our faces and ran out holding hands. I really wanted to help Reuben. He felt little and scared.

We stumbled for a long way. It was hard breathing with the jackets over our faces. Reuben fell down some. Our skin was covered with the dust and dirt. Our hair was full of dust.

We found a road. It was just dirt, not very wide. There were no cars on it. The dust was everywhere.

"Someone will come," I said.

"Someone will come," Reuben said back. It was like he was saying whatever I was saying now, because he couldn't have any ideas.

"Stay close," I said.

"Stay close," he said. I could hardly hear him. The wind was too loud.

We sat on the side of the road, holding hands, waiting. The dust moved along the ground in long lines really fast, then it curled up into the sky.

I saw a light in the distance. It was all hazy and small. It was coming toward us. Then it was two lights. It was a truck. It had its lights on in the dust.

We waved at the driver. He stopped and opened the door. It was hard to open. The wind almost blew it shut.

"Get in," he said.

We climbed in and sat in the seat. There was a sandwich wrapped up in some paper. I tried not to look at it.

The man looked down on us and smiled. He was *wašíču*. He looked really tall.

"Indian kids, huh?" he said.

"Yes, sir."

"I haven't seen you before. You're not from around here, are you?"

"We're going to see our grandfather," I said. It was a small lie, but I could not tell a *wašíču* man we were running from a boarding school man.

I looked at Reuben. I wanted him to stay quiet. He closed his eyes and put his head against me. I knew he wouldn't say anything now.

"So, where's your grandpa?" the man asked.

I didn't know what to say. I had started down the path of lying and I did not know how to stop.

I had heard the government men say the word "Hiawatha," so I said, "Hiawatha." I didn't know where Hiawatha was.

The man looked at me real funny.

"Why don't you come home with me," he said. "You don't want to be out in this dust. We can get you cleaned up and fed."

"We're not runaways," I said.

The man just smiled. He had a really kind face.

The man lived in a house with a porch on the front. It had been white once but now it was mostly gray. It had a barn and some other buildings. There were some trees around it, but the leaves were mostly blown off. The wind was blowing really strong. The dust made the sky all brown. The sun was almost not even there.

"You go in and meet the missus," he said. "I'll unload the truck."

"I can help, sir," I said. Grandpa had taught me always to help people. He said that was what a man was supposed to do.

The dust was feeling sharp like knives. It made me think what it would be like to have my skin pierced for the Sun Dance.

"I'll tell you what," the man said. "You carry this bag into the house."

He gave me a burlap bag from the truck. It was full of flour and other food. I could smell coffee in the bag. It made me think of Grandpa.

Reuben had run to the house. He didn't like all the dust. It was hurting his eyes.

"Is that your brother?" the man asked.

"Yes, sir," I said.

"He doesn't talk much."

"He's other-minded," I said. I wanted him to know before Reuben did something wrong.

The man smiled again. He smiled a lot.

"As long as you're some-minded," he said. "I know a lot of folks who got no mind at all."

That made me smile. "No, sir," I said. "Reuben has a mind. He can add up numbers and remember things and sometimes even talk to animals. My grandpa says he is *wakȟáŋ*."

Once I said it I wished I hadn't. It's not good to talk to white people about the old ways, even good white people. Grandpa told me it was always good to stay quiet around white people. They think different, he said, and they hear words different. He told me their language is a trick.

"I've got some animals he can talk to," the man said. "Once this weather settles down. Couple of stubborn ones. Maybe he can talk some sense into them."

"Yes, sir," I said. I didn't know if he was saying a trick.

I looked around. There were fields around the farm, but you could hardly see them through the dust.

"So your grandpa's in Hiawatha?" the man asked.

"Yes, sir," I said. I was walking more on the path of lying, because I didn't know where Grandpa was or where Hiawatha was. But I wanted the man to think about where we were going and not where we had come from.

We started walking to the house. The man put his arm on my back. It was real soft and gentle, kind of like the way Grandpa touched Reuben. It made me feel good and not think about the dust.

"You boys could use some food."

"Yes, sir," I said.

The man smiled again. "Better than that old sandwich on the seat of the truck."

GOOD LIKE MOMMA TAUGHT YOU

Levi

The rancher man's house was beautiful inside. It had rugs on the floor and electric lights with shades. I had never seen electric lights until the boarding school. Now I was seeing them in a house.

I wanted to see the man's wife. I wanted to know what she was like.

Reuben had found a dog and was petting it. We had a dog once, but it got killed. His name was Mato. Someone shot him. He was my dog. I was sad for that. I'm still sad for that.

Our people don't let dogs in the house, except really little ones. Reuben liked seeing a dog in the house. This dog was old.

The man came in and took off his shoes. They were all brown with dust. He had a bandanna over his face. He pulled it down and took a big breath. "Did you find the missus?" He was talking to Reuben.

Reuben didn't say anything. He was lying on his side and looking into the dog's face. Their noses were almost touching. The dog's nose was pink like a school eraser.

I tried to sit in a chair and be good for both of us. I was worried that Reuben might say something wrong.

"Thank you for giving us a ride, sir," I said. I was trying to talk like the priests at the school taught us.

"You looked pretty lonely out there by the side of the road in all that dust."

"Yes, sir. We were."

"What's your name?"

"Levi," I said.

"And your brother's Reuben. Levi and Reuben. Bible names. Levi and Reuben on the side of the road, a long way from home."

"Yes, sir."

He had a funny way of talking, like he was finding things out without asking.

"I'll go and find the missus," he said. "She'll get you boys something to eat."

He went into the kitchen and through into another room. I could hear the door close.

I leaned over and grabbed Reuben by the shirt collar. "Don't say anything," I said. "Just be good, like Momma taught you."

"I like this dog," he said.

"You've got to promise me you'll be good."

"His fur is soft. He's like Mato."

"Reuben, we've got to be nice to these people. They could send us back. Don't say anything about running away."

The dog was thumping its tail just a little. It was old and yellow with the fur rubbed off its elbows. Reuben touched its ears and made noises. The dog licked Reuben on the nose. I think it was understanding him.

Reuben wouldn't answer me. I was getting really mad. I got down on the floor right next to him. I didn't want to talk loud so the man would hear us.

"You've got to promise me you won't say anything," I said. "You've got to listen to me."

Reuben was making dog sounds.

The man came back in through the door. He looked down at us. His wife was behind him.

The man was smiling. His wife was smiling, too. She had a plate with some bread and meat and some glasses and a pitcher full of milk.

She was Indian, like us.

When Reuben saw her, he got up. He ran over to her and put his arms around her, like she was our mother. She rubbed his hair. He started crying.

"You smell good," he said.

She laughed real soft, just like Momma.

"You eat," she said. She was speaking English.

I hoped it wasn't a trick.

CLEANING UP

Levi

The food was good. I didn't know whether to eat like at home or like they taught me in the boarding school. Grandpa would have thrown a piece of the meat in the stove for the spirits. The school would have made me fold my hands and pray to the Jesus man. Reuben was eating all the bread and was eating with both hands. He was really hungry.

"You eat as much as you want," the woman said. Her voice was so soft, like singing. The man just smiled.

He went into another room. I could hear him getting water.

When we were done he took us into that other room. There was a metal tub. It was filled with water. Steam was coming off it.

"You boys clean up," he said. "You're pretty dusty. I'll bring you some clothes."

He left us in the room and went away. I was glad. I didn't want to take off my clothes in front of him.

I washed Reuben first. He didn't like the hot water at first, then he liked it a lot. He didn't want to get out. I poured water on his head to get the dust out of his hair. It made the water all dirty. I didn't even want to get into it, but I did. Reuben got a lot more clean than I did.

When we were done the man came in with some clothes. I think he had been waiting outside the door until he didn't hear splashing.

"Here," he said. He handed us some shirts and pants that were for boys. They fit me pretty good, but they were too big for Reuben.

"Just roll them up," he said.

I wanted to ask if there was a boy here, but I didn't. Grandpa said it was a white man thing to ask questions. People will tell you what they want you to know, he said. People's lives are like their house, he told me. They will invite you in if they want you in.

Reuben was trying to make the clothes fit. He was pulling up the pants really high. The man helped him with a rope for a belt and rolled his pants and shirtsleeves up.

We walked out into the other room. The woman was sitting there in a chair. When she saw us she started crying.

I didn't know whether to like these people or to be afraid. I didn't know what to think about an Indian woman with a *wašíču* man. The only Indian women I had seen around *wašíču* men were the ones who worked at the school. They had mostly become like the *wašíču* men and were really mean.

This woman didn't seem mean. I stood quiet with my eyes down like Grandpa had taught me, out of respect. But Reuben ran over to the wife woman and put his arms around her again. She put her arms around him, too. They held each other for a long time. It was good to see him happy. It was good to see her happy, too. She had sad eyes.

I wanted to look at the rancher man's eyes. I wanted to see if they were mean like the *wašíču* men at the school. I had to know what to do to protect Reuben.

I looked up, just for a minute. The rancher man didn't see me. He was looking at Reuben and his wife. His eyes were good eyes. They were full of smiles.

WHAT HELL IS LIKE

Levi

The house had a picture of Jesus, just like in the school. Our house didn't have pictures. Grandpa said the world was full of the Creator's work. Why should you make pictures of it when you can see it in the real way?

But I had never seen the real Jesus. So I thought it was a good thing to have pictures of him. That way I could think about him more.

I never would have told that to Grandpa. He didn't care about Jesus. That was for white men, he said. We Indians have our own ways, he said.

The picture of Jesus in this house was of him kneeling by a rock with his hands folded. The sky was glowing and he was looking into the sky.

Reuben saw me looking. "Who's that *wašíču?*" he asked.

"That's Jesus," I told him.

"Why is he wearing a dress?"

"I don't know. He lived a long time ago."

"Women wear the dresses," he said. "Why is there light around his head?"

I didn't want to talk to Reuben about Jesus. He was too little to understand.

I had learned about Jesus in school. He was really good. He helped people and gave them food. He was strong, too, like an Indian. When they stuck him in the side with that spear and put him on that cross, he was just like an Indian at Sun Dance with the piercings and the tree. He just took it and did it for the people.

I was sad that he had cried out one time. People at the Sun Dance never cry out. It must have really hurt him. Some of the other kids said he wasn't brave because he cried. I thought he was really brave. It would hurt to have nails through your hands and feet.

What scared me most was the place he could send me. The priests and nuns told me about it. They said that Jesus had been born in a desert place and walked around talking to people and telling them how to live, and if you didn't do what he said, you would go to a place where there was fire all the time and you would burn and burn and never burn up. It was under the ground, they said. It was called the hell place.

One of the priests even took the hand of a boy who was talking in class and burned it with a cigarette. He just stuck it in his hand and turned it around until you could smell the boy's hand burning. The boy was shaking, but he didn't cry.

"That's what hell is like," the priest said. "If you don't do what Jesus says, you will go to this place and it will burn like that all over you forever," he told us.

I didn't want to go to this hell place. I was really scared, but I didn't want anyone to know. I didn't want Reuben to go there.

Sometimes I cried at night thinking that Grandpa and Momma would go there unless I told them about Jesus, but I never told them. I thought maybe if they didn't know, Jesus would just forget about them and let them go to the Indian place where we go when we die. But then I thought that if I didn't tell them, maybe Jesus would be mad at me and I would go to that hell place. It made me cry even harder, but I never let anyone see. I didn't understand why Jesus would send me there, or Grandpa or Momma or Reuben. His face was kind as he kneeled at that rock. He had good eyes.

The rancher man saw me looking at the picture. "Do you know who that is?" he said.

"Yes, sir," I answered. "It's Jesus."

He smiled at me. "So you must go to school, then?" he said.

I did not want to answer. This man scared me. He could learn things just by asking questions.

I didn't want him to know anything about me. He might put me in his truck and take me to that school. Reuben, too, and Reuben didn't know anything about Jesus. And the priest might burn his hand and beat him with belts, or do other bad things to him. I kept my eyes down and didn't say anything.

The rancher man put his hand on my hair like Grandpa did to Reuben and ruffled it a little. "That's okay," he said. "You just rest easy. You don't have to talk." At first I didn't like him touching my hair. Then I liked it. It reminded me of Grandpa. I wanted to ask if he thought Jesus was going to send Grandpa and Momma to that hell place. And Reuben, too. But I didn't.

Reuben was back on the floor talking to the dog. The dog's eyes were runny and sad. Reuben's nose was touching his. His tail was wagging. It made me think of Mato. I tried to stop my thinking.

Reuben was saying words in dog talk. He has a special talking he does with animals. Grandpa had said it was okay and that we shouldn't try to understand it. I think it was the same one he had used for talking to the prairie dogs when he was little. Grandpa said it was *wakȟáŋ* and we should never interrupt Reuben when he was talking it.

The rancher man didn't know this. He just went up to Reuben and said, "You like Mister Bones?"

That was the dog's name. I had never heard of a dog named Mister Bones.

Reuben looked up. He was really confused. I think he was in his animal mind.

He made that face where he pushes his lips out.

"Don't talk to me," he said.

The man smiled and started to say something. His wife came over and put her hand on his shoulder. She shook her head and said something real soft. The man nodded and walked away.

The wife bent down close to me. "You take care of your little brother," she said to me, real soft like whispering. She was talking Indian. "You need to be very careful for him."

"Yes, ma'am," I said. "I will."

NIGHT SPIRITS

Levi

That night we slept in a white man bed. I had never slept in a bed like that. It was soft and Reuben and I could get down real tight against each other in the middle and pull the cover over us. It was like a sack made of feathers. It was the best bed I had ever slept in.

"See?" I told Reuben. "I said we would find a good house."

He put his head in my chest and rubbed me with his hair. He was all clean and smelled good. We were having fun.

The Mister Bones dog was right by the side of the bed. He was following us everywhere. I wanted to pet him and hug him. I wanted him to be my friend like Mato. But I let him be mostly Reuben's friend. I wanted Reuben to be happy and not scared.

"I wish we could live in this house forever," Reuben said. "I like this Mister Bones."

I could hear the man and woman talking in the next room. They were talking soft and laughing. He called her "Lillie." She called him "Karl-Martin." There was happy in their voices. It made me feel good to hear them. You can sleep better when you hear people laughing.

I had decided to like this Lillie woman. She had talked nice about Reuben. It made me trust her.

I wanted to give trust to the Karl-Martin man, too, but Momma had told me never to trust a *wašíču*. He had kind eyes, but the Jesus in the picture had kind eyes, too, and he sent people to the hell place if they didn't do what he said. I wanted to know if this Karl-Martin man's kindness was a trick. I wanted to know if he was going to give Reuben to the school men.

Reuben was singing a dog song. He was doing it in his dog talk so I couldn't understand. But I heard him say "Mister Bones" in it, so I knew it was a dog song.

It made me happy to hear Reuben sing. I liked it when Reuben was happy. I knew he couldn't be happy in that boarding school.

Things happened at that school that I did not want in my mind. I didn't even tell Momma and Grandpa some of them, but I think Grandpa knew. He could tell things like that.

Like the time I saw a matron running down the hall with something all wrapped in a blanket. She was holding the blanket tight, but there was crying from inside of it.

She shouted at us to get back in the room. There was a little girl sobbing really loud somewhere way down the hall. There was like a clank from the furnace door and then a real bad smell, a *ȟuŋwiŋ* smell. I knew that smell from roasting meat when we were hunting, but I didn't want to believe it.

That girl who was sobbing was gone the next day. The other girls said she had a baby. None of us ever saw any baby.

I saw lots of these things and they made me scared for Reuben. I did not want him in a place like that. I did not want things like that in his mind.

Reuben had stopped singing. He was making snore sounds. He was full asleep.

I put my arm around him. I could not go to sleep. The night spirits would not leave me alone. I kept thinking about Reuben and the boarding school and if I should give trust to this rancher man.

I could hear them talking in the next room. I did not know how to think of this man. He was always asking questions. Grandpa told me that you should only ask questions to learn about the world, never to try to look inside people.

This Karl-Martin man's questions were always trying to look inside me. I did not want him to see inside me. But I had to answer. I had to show respect. We were guests in his house.

It made me feel good that he had an Indian wife. I thought if she could like him I could like him. But I still had some fear. Momma said that *wašíču* always think they know what is right for Indian people. This man might think it is right to take Reuben back and bring him to the boarding school. The boarding school would kill his spirit. I do not want Reuben's spirit to die.

Reuben was curled up against me. He was making sleep sounds. Mister Bones was making sounds, too. The wind outside was not so loud. The man and the woman were still talking, but it was soft and I couldn't hear. It was only me and the night spirits.

I told them they should let me sleep. I don't remember anything after that.

DOORS TO THE HEART

Lillie

Life has been so lonely here since we lost Joseph. I have not been
able to throw his clothes away. I have not been able to enter his
room. I see him everywhere in this house.

Now two little boys are sleeping in his room. In his bed. Indian
boys. Indian like me. I can't tell you the joy I feel at hearing those two
little voices in the next room.

How did Karl-Martin find two little Indian boys on the road in this
wašíču country? It must have been Creator speaking. Why else would
they be here, at our house so far from Indian country, our house so
lonely for the presence of a boy?

For three years now I have listened to that room and heard only
silence. When Joseph was alive there was life in that room. Sometimes
at night he would make a sound like a snuffle or a small cry. I knew
it was only him having a dream, and it filled my heart with love. I
would go to his room and watch him sleep. I would say a prayer for
his dream, that it was a dream brought by good spirits. My eyes would
fill with tears at the gift Creator had given me.

How lucky I was. I did not think I would ever be a mother. I was an
Indian girl in a white town, and the boys did not treat me with respect.
There were good boys in town and I liked them. But their mothers
did not let them like me. I had to stay alone. I dreamed of meeting an
Indian boy, but none ever came.

For my whole life I was mad at my father for moving to that town.
He went there to work on the railroad. He said it would be good for

me to be around white people. He said it would be good to learn the *wašíču* ways.

He never understood how it hurt my heart. He grew up on the reservation. He had friends. If only he and Mother had given me some brothers and sisters. But there were no brothers and sisters. I was always alone. If it wasn't for Ida, I think I might have killed myself.

Ida was lots older. She was Indian, like me. She was my best friend. She lived in town, too. But she went to the Indian boarding school, so I didn't get to see her much during the school year.

Ida had grandparents who lived out in the country. They were rich Indians. They had a big house. In the summer we would ride our bikes out there and play. They had Indian things like drums and cradleboards and lots of carvings made of pipestone. Ida's grandfather had brought them from their home country in Minnesota. He said he wanted to keep the old ways alive.

We would go upstairs and put the cradleboard on our backs and pretend we had babies. We would put a doll in the cradleboard and walk around and sing to it and tell it stories. I would be the mother. Ida would be the grandma. It was fun to play like we were Indians in the old way, not Indian girls living in a white town.

I loved Ida's grandmother. She would sit us down and teach us about the old ways. She would tell us the stories and ask us to tell them back to her.

I didn't go to the Indian school like Ida did. Father said the Indian school was a bad place and the Indian ways were dying. He made me go to the white school. He said I had to learn to live like a white person.

I tried to learn the white man ways to make him happy. I got all A's. I was the best speller. I won a geography contest about the world. The teacher could point to any place on a map and I could say its name. But I didn't have any friends.

When Father died, I told Momma I wasn't going to go to that school anymore. I wanted to go to the Indian school. I wanted to go to school with Ida. Momma didn't like it, but she let me go.

The Indian school was not a bad school like some I heard of. They did not like our Indian ways, and there were some mean teachers, but there were some good teachers, too. They made us go to Mass and pray, but they didn't hurt us, at least they never hurt me or the other girls I knew.

Our Indian school had a library. The librarian was Miss Robideaux. She said I was her favorite student. She would choose a book for me and say, "Here, Lillie. You should read this book." Then we would talk about it. I read *Little House in the Big Woods*. I read *My Antonia*. I read *Jane Eyre*.

Oh, how I wished I could have been a white girl like the girls in those books. But I had an Indian skin.

When I finished that school, I thought I would never go back. But then Miss Robideaux died. They wrote me a letter. They said she always talked about me. They said they wanted me to be the librarian. It was a great honor that they would ask an Indian girl like me. It was a great honor that Miss Robideaux had remembered me. I said I would take the job.

It was there that I met Karl-Martin. He was older than me. He was a teacher in the school. He had come from the east and was studying to be a priest. He was a white man, but his heart was like an Indian. He helped the boys and girls. He let them talk Indian when he was around. He never hit them. He had a kind smile.

I liked that he talked to God. He would sometimes call him *Thuŋkášila*, like we Lakota did. He could have gotten in trouble for that. But he said that God answers to every name. The children loved him. He had a good heart.

Sometimes he would come into the library. We would talk until it closed, then we would talk longer. Sometimes we would go down by the river and talk about our lives. I felt myself falling in love. He did, too. But he was going to be a priest, and a priest cannot have a wife. So I went back to my aloneness and my books.

Then one summer he went away. He went to help an old farmer. When he came back in the fall he said he did not think he could be a priest. He asked if he left the school would I go with him and be his wife. He said we could get a farm.

I could not believe Creator had sent a man to me. I had been waiting for an Indian man. Now Creator had sent me a priest white man. I was afraid, but I said "yes."

We bought this farm. It was just a few miles down the road from where Ida's grandparents had lived. Ida lives there now. Karl-Martin said it would be good for me to be close to my friend. But it was a bad farm. The land had not been cleared well. The last family had left. Now the bank owned it. They said we could pay them from the crops. They liked that Karl-Martin had been a priest. He said he would work harder and longer than any farmer they had ever known.

But Karl-Martin was not a farmer. His eyes are on the sky, not on the earth. He does not have love of the soil in his hands. He cannot make things grow.

I said we should leave. I said we should try a different way. But when Joseph was born Karl-Martin said we had to stay. He said he would work harder. He said he would make the farm grow. He would have something to pass on to Joseph.

But now Joseph is gone and we are still here. It is a hard time. The sky is bad. There is no rain. There are days when dust rises up and turns the sky dark. The crops are small. The earth is more about death than life. There is death inside our house and death outside in the fields. All I think of is Joseph. I think about him every day.

When Joseph died, Ida came to help. She told me that in our Indian way we must grieve for a year. Cut our hair short, set a place at the table, give the first taste of every meal to the one who is gone. Then after a year we must let them go. Their spirit has stayed around to help us.

She said it is not good to try to hold them after that, that they worry for us if we do not let them go. She said it is not good for them always to be looking back to us, thinking about us. Their journey is hard, too. We must set them free, just as parents must set their children free.

I have tried to do that. But it has been three years and still I call for Joseph and I think I hear him calling for me. I have found my smile again, but it hides sadness. It has made me ashamed to see Ida.

Why can I not let him go? Is it wrong to hold so strong to a mother's love?

Ida says that my heart was made sick by that boarding school, that I listened too much to the priests. She says I see like a *wašíču*, where life is only between birth and death and you fear what is on either side of them. She says I would not be so full of sadness if I thought in our Indian way, where our earth life is just a small part of our path, and Joseph has just walked on, that he has just left his earth body behind him.

I asked her, "Why then do we mourn, if this is just a small part of the path?" She tells me it is because grief is just our spirit's cry of surprise when someone we love chooses to cross over to a different world. She says that mourning is good and that we must hold it tight, then lay it down. She says it is right to want to hold hands with the spirit of those who have walked on, and that they want to hold hands with us, too, and watch over us and care for us because they know we feel sadness, but then they need to turn their eyes away from us and look toward their own journey, and we must let them go.

That is why those two boys made my spirit cry and sing when I saw them getting out of the truck with Karl-Martin. It made me think of Joseph, but I saw two new spirits walking strong toward me. Karl-Martin was smiling, and Karl-Martin's smile had been gone since we lost Joseph.

Tonight we talked late, like we used to, like when we first met. Joseph's spirit was making us talk. Karl-Martin has not wanted to talk since Joseph died. His way is to bury the dead, to place them in the ground and let them be. He has closed the doors to his heart and lives with the pain inside. It has been left to me to mourn with an open heart.

I have tried to talk to him, but he will not hear.

"We can have more children," I said.

"We are too old," he said. He turned away from me then and I never saw him again.

Until tonight, when the young boys came. There were tears in his eyes. The boys had taken the stone from his heart.

Now those boys are in the next room. I can feel them. They are like a warm fire, giving me peace. In my heart I can see them in Joseph's bed, under his cover, clean, snuggled together, wearing Joseph's clothes. I had cried when I saw the older boy in Joseph's shirt and pants after they had bathed. Now my spirit is singing for what I have seen. It is good that they are here. Creator has given us a gift.

"What shall we do with them, Karl-Martin?" I asked. "We should get them home. Their family will be sick with worry."

I could see Karl-Martin was thinking hard. "Yes," he said. "But there is something here we do not see. The older boy said they were going to Hiawatha to visit their grandfather."

I knew that place. It was a hospital-type prison where they locked up Indians. It had been closed for years.

"We need to find out more," he said. "You talk to them. You have their trust."

"Should I do it now? I think they are still awake."

He touched my cheek with his hand.

"No," he said. "Morning will be soon enough."

That night Karl-Martin loved me. It was good to feel him again.

WHITE MAN SHOES

Levi

When I woke up, the room was bright. Reuben was gone. Mister Bones was gone, too. There was no dust. The wind was gone, too. It was a blue-sky day.

I went downstairs. I had never been in a house with an upstairs before, only the boarding school.

The wife woman was sitting at the table. She was cutting bread.

"Good morning, Levi," she said. She was speaking *wašíču*.

"Where's my brother?" I asked. Grandpa says I am his protector. I must always think of him first.

The woman pointed out the door. She did it our way, with her lips. It made me feel good.

Reuben was on the back step with Mister Bones. He was sitting with his arm around him, like friends. He was talking soft. I could not hear his words. I think they were dog words.

The man was not here, only the woman. It made the room an Indian room.

"Come here, Levi," she said. "Sit with me." There was bacon cooking on the stove.

I sat in a chair. She looked long at me, holding me with her look.

"Tell me, Levi," she said. "Why are you here?"

I wanted to put my eyes away and say nothing. But she just sat.

I tried to stay quiet, but her words would not go away. She had put them between us.

"You can tell me," she said.

"We were just walking," I said. "We were going to the Hiawatha place."

She reached across and touched my face, real soft, with her fingers.

"You are Lakota. You should not lie. That is for white men. The Hiawatha place has been closed for twenty years. Tell me now. Why are you here?"

I felt strong spirit power in her. My words got heavy in my mouth.

She pulled on me with her eyes. "Why?"

I thought to stay quiet, like I did around white men, and then she would leave. But she was Lakota. Her silence was longer than my silence.

"Some school men came to take my brother," I said. The words came out like stones. I was afraid. "My momma told us to run."

"Where are you running?"

I did not want to say. I had not told anybody. Not even Reuben. I was holding it close in my heart.

The woman saw my hiding.

"Who is your family?"

"We are Lone Dogs."

"I know that name," she said. "The Lone Dogs are good people. They do not make liars."

"No."

"Just because you are running, you must not forget who you are."

"No," I said. It was like she was drawing the words out of me.

"It is good that you are doing what your mother says, that you are protecting your brother. He is other-minded. He should not go to a *wašíču* school. But you cannot run forever. Tell me now. Tell me why you are here. Tell me where you are going."

I started to cry. She was pulling sadness from me.

"They broke my grandpa's *čhaŋnúŋpa*. The school men." I couldn't stop the words. Her spirit power was calling them out. "They came to our house. They wanted to take Reuben. Grandpa said they couldn't have him. They broke his *čhaŋnúŋpa*. Momma said to run."

"And how are you here? This is far from your home."

"We got on the train. Momma said to get on the train. She said to stay on it until we saw morning. Then we got off."

"So you do not know where you are?"

"No." I could feel crying in my eyes.

She put her arm around me. She was warm, like that cover on the bed.

"And you do not know where you are going?"

My eyes were filling strong with tears.

"Momma said not to go to the aunties or the uncles. We are just running."

She wiped my cheek with her apron.

"They broke his pipe," I said again. My mouth wanted to say it. I couldn't stop saying it. "They broke Grandpa's *čhaŋnúŋpa*."

She looked at me with a smile way of knowing. "A man does not say something twice unless he wants to be heard," she said. "Four times you have told me about the *čhaŋnúŋpa*. Wait here."

She went out the door past Reuben to her husband. He was chopping wood in the back. I could hear them talking. They talked for a long time. He came in with her. He wore a white shirt. He sat down next to me.

"Tell me about your grandpa," he said. "His *čhaŋnúŋpa*."

I did not want to talk to him. I did not have strong trust in him. Grandpa said I should turn my tongue around when *wašíču* talked to me.

The woman saw my fear. She touched her lips. She smiled at me with her eyes.

"You talk," she said. "This man is good. He is my husband. I would not have taken him for a husband if his heart was not good. You can trust him. He has a good heart."

She touched my arm. "Talk."

My words started coming. "Grandpa was teaching me the *čhaŋnúŋpa*. He showed me how to get the *čhaŋšáša*. He showed me how to put it in the pipe. Sometimes he would let me light it. His grandpa had given it to him. He told me when I touched it I was touching my ancestors' spirits. He said when we smoked it the ancestors were listening. The school men broke it." I was talking fast. I could feel more tears in my eyes.

The Karl-Martin man sat silent. The *wašíču* teachers in the school only became silent when they were angry. This man's silence came from respect. My heart was sad but I was feeling more to trust him.

"What did your grandpa do when the school men broke the čhaŋnúŋpa?" he said.

I thought to answer him.

"He pulled his spirit close. He could do that. He got all the pieces. He gave one to me. He took the rest outside and buried them. He stayed there for a long time."

The Karl-Martin man smiled at me. "You are a smart boy," he said. "You say only what you have seen."

"Grandpa says I should only say what I know with my own eyes."

"Your grandpa is a wise man. Now, I will ask you about the boarding school."

This man was talking like an Indian. He was laying one thing on the ground at a time. "Tell me what you are learning in the wašíču school."

"I am learning to fix shoes," I said.

"You are learning to be a shoemaker."

"Yes, sir," I said.

"Do you like fixing shoes?"

I was getting scared again. This man was making me walk where he wanted. I thought he might be tricking me.

"I like fixing shoes," I said. A boy in school told me that if you do not know where a white man is going, just say his words back to him.

He sat for a long time. "How old are you, Levi?" he said.

"I have eleven winters."

"Do you wish to be a man?"

"Yes, sir."

"What must a Lakota man have?"

I looked at his wife. She smiled again and nodded.

"I don't know the words in English," I said.

"I will help you," she said. Her voice was quiet, like Grandpa's. "Wówahwala."

I knew that word. "He must walk quiet. Not place himself first."

"Wačháŋtognake."

"He must give to others. Give what he has."

She smiled at me. "You can do this," she said. Her words were soft like music. "Say them in Lakota if you don't know them in English."

I put my eyes down. I tried to remember what Grandpa had taught me. I tried to put it in *wašíču* words.

"He must be strong," I said. "He must have strong caring for others. He must have no fear to serve. He must leave wrongs behind."

The woman was nodding.

The words were coming easy now. "He must have *wóohitike* — be brave in all things. He must give no thought for thanks."

They were words Grandpa had taught me.

"He must have respect for all things. He must bring food to the old. He must show right to the young. He must hold his mind close and have a heart for all people."

The Karl-Martin man looked at me. He thought long. He held me strong with his eyes.

"Does he need to know how to fix white man shoes?"

I felt strong shame. I started to cry.

A GRAVEYARD FOR PORK CHOPS

Levi

I was feeling kindness from this Karl-Martin man. He did not show anger. He spoke soft, like an Indian.

"Come along with me, Levi," he said. "Reuben will stay with the missus."

I did not want to leave Reuben alone. Momma said I had to take care of him. I wanted to stay near to him.

The Karl-Martin man saw my fear.

"Reuben will be fine," he said. "You have my word."

It made me scared to hear a white man give his word. Momma told me not to listen when a white man gave his word. She said white men had been giving us their word for years. When we trust their word, we die, she said.

I thought to turn and run and hold on to Reuben. I could see him on the porch. He was talking to the Mister Bones dog. He was happy.

"Reuben will be fine," the man said. Twice he had said it. "We need to feed the animals. I can use your help."

This made my mind divided. I was scared for his word, but when someone asks for help you must give it, especially when you are a guest.

He put his hand on my shoulder. We were walking then. He did it in a good way.

"I used to have a boy," he said. "He was like you."

I decided to give him my help.

We went toward the barn. It was a blue-sky day, not a dust day. There were birds.

The old Mister Bones dog came to walk with us. He walked next to me, licking my hand. I walked slow so he could keep up. He had a bad limp.

"That Mister Bones dog walks like my grandpa," I said. I thought to make a joke with this man. He had a good spirit. "My grandpa fell off a horse. He used to play baseball."

"Well, old Bones never fell off a horse and he can fetch a ball when he has to. But he just kind of wore out. A limp doesn't stop anybody. Just slows them down. Right, Bones?"

The man had a smile in his voice. I liked talking to him. I liked that he talked to his dog.

"Why is his name Mister Bones?" I asked.

The Karl-Martin man laughed. "The old fella lives for bones," he said. "Doesn't chew them. Just buries them. This whole yard is like a graveyard for pork chops." That made him laugh even more.

I hugged Mister Bones. He licked my face. His tail was full wagging. He was a good dog. He felt like Mato in my heart.

We walked together to the barn. I felt friendship in this place.

The man had one horse. It was not strong looking. He had a cow, too. And there were chickens. It was a white man kind of farm.

He gave me some gloves. They were old, not too big. Boy size. It made me proud to wear them. He had me lift hay and bring it to him. It was on the other side of the barn. I helped him feed the horse. There are lots of them on our reservation. I like to ride them. The older boys race with them. Someday I want to have a horse. This man's horse was friendly.

I worked hard, not resting. Grandpa said to always work hard and to help if you want to be a good man. I want to be a good man. I want to be like Grandpa.

I had not done white man work before. The hay was heavy. It made my arms sore. Once I dropped a bale. We had been working for a long time. The sun had gotten hot. The string dug into my hand. I felt shame. I should not have dropped it.

The Karl-Martin man did not get mad. He laughed and told me I had done well. He was like the uncles. I felt good to like him then.

He told me to sit on one of the hay bales. He took out a metal bottle. He called it a thermos. He said it had belonged to his father. His father used it when he worked in a factory place in somewhere called Cleveland. I had never seen one before.

It was full of water that was cold. I could not believe it was cold. We had been out in the sun all day. He said to drink as much as I wanted. He had not had any. I didn't want to drink much so he could have some.

"You drink it all if you need to," he said. "You worked like a man."

That filled me with good feeling. No white man had ever said a good thing to me before about being a man. I knew how to be a man in the Lakota way. I did not know how to be a *wašíču* man. I thought it meant to follow orders. That's what they told me in boarding school. I did not think it meant to work hard like with the hay.

I drank some water. I gave some to Mister Bones. He drank it out of my hand. His tail was wagging. He was really thirsty.

I thought to give the thermos jar back to the man.

He would not take it. "For you and Bones," he said. "I'm doing fine."

I wanted to like this man. I wanted to give him my trust.

"Levi," he said. He sat close to me, right next to me. He was using my name. "I want to ask you some hard questions."

He had been asking me questions all the time. I did not know why he would ask me about asking me questions.

"Yes, sir," I said.

"The missus and I have been talking. She is from your people. She knows your ways better than I do." I could see sadness in his face. I did not know why his eyes should show sadness.

"We know you are running. We know you're afraid for your brother. You are right to be afraid. I know the boarding schools. I worked in one. Your brother should not go to one of those schools."

He was not walking a straight path. I felt fear again.

"Where are you going? We want to help you. We're not going to give you to the school people."

I thought to be quiet, to tell him nothing. Then I thought of what the missus had said, that I was Lakota, that my family did not make liars.

I reached in my pocket. I had the piece of Grandpa's pipe he had given to me when it broke. I showed it in my hand. I did not know if I should let a *wašíču* touch it.

The Karl-Martin man did not take the piece. He closed my hand around it with his hand. "You keep that," he said. "That's yours."

I gave the thermos jar back to him. This time he took a drink.

"*Philámayaye*," he said. "Isn't that the word?"

I felt respect in him. I thought to tell him my heart.

"Here, have some more," he said. He handed me that thermos jar again. It was like the *inipi*, where all the men drank water together.

I was feeling more trust. I thought to talk to him in the Indian way.

"My grandpa has strong power," I said. "He is teaching me. He says it's too soon to know who I am. He does not think I have medicine power. He thinks maybe I have a strong heart to lead. He wants me in the boarding school to see if I am brave, to see if I am reed or oak."

I held out the pipe piece.

"This pipe was from his grandfather. My grandpa was teaching me that pipe. He told me that pipe would be in my hand someday. A school man came to get Reuben. He broke the pipe. Now I have this piece. The rest Grandpa put in the earth."

The pipe was talking through me now. It was giving me courage. Now I was going to tell him what was in my heart. I had not said this to anyone. Not even Reuben.

"My grandpa said this pipe came from the *Inyan Sa K'api* place. He said that is where the stone is from — that our people have a special place where we get that stone. He said it is in the sunrise direction. I am going to that place to get him some new stone. His legs are old. Mine are young. I can go to that place. I am taking Reuben. I will get Grandpa stone for a new pipe."

My spirit was scared for saying this. I had given full trust to a *wašíču*.

The man had kind eyes for these words. He put his hand on my shoulder. His touch was soft. He had a full smile. My spirit stopped being afraid. I had said what was in my heart.

WALKING WITH A GHOST

Lillie

When I saw Karl-Martin and Levi coming back from the barn, I was afraid for what I was seeing. They were both smiling. Karl-Martin had put away his smile after Joseph died. Now he was smiling again. Levi was smiling, too. They were walking close to each other. They were both heavy with sweat. Levi was wearing Joseph's gloves.

I stopped what I was doing and went out on the porch to meet them.

Karl-Martin had his arm around Levi's shoulder. "This young fellow is a hard worker," he said. "We got half the hay put up."

I told Levi to take Reuben and Mister Bones to get some water from the pump. I was afraid for what Karl-Martin was thinking.

"Karl-Martin," I said. "You're not thinking to have those boys stay?"

He took my hands and held them in his. "No," he said. "It did my heart good to have a boy next to me, and God knows I would have him if I could. But I know better. There's a ghost in this house. Even if we could keep him here, he would be walking with a ghost."

"I feel good to hear you say that," I said.

He squeezed my hands gently. "We use our words differently, you and I, Lillie. But we see with the same eyes. Even if I could keep young Levi with us, I wouldn't do so. Our Joseph couldn't live between two worlds. I would not make another boy live with a divided heart just to fill my own emptiness."

It made me happy to hear these words. But it hurt me to hear him speak of Joseph's struggle. It made me go back to his death in my mind.

Karl-Martin saw my sadness. "I'm sorry," he said. "I know I shouldn't talk about Joseph's dying around you. I know you don't even want to say his name. You think that by not saying his name he will disappear from your life. But I think you're wrong. Your silence just makes a shrine in your heart, an altar no one else can approach."

"I am a mother," I said. "I will do what I do."

"And a Lakota. You will not let go of the past."

We had walked this road many times before. The past will always be alive for a Lakota, more alive than for any *wašíču*. If we do not speak of it, it is because we do not wish to make it more alive than it already is. We cannot run to the future like the *wašíču* do, looking always for something new, something better. We honor the past and carry it with us. I will make no apology for this. It is my Lakota way of praying. I make my prayer in the silence of my heart.

I would have said more to Karl-Martin, but he is my husband. When we are walking separate paths I will always let his words walk the farthest.

"If you would not keep them, what would you have us do with them?" I asked. "The boarding school men will be looking for them. And their mother will be filled with worry."

Karl-Martin had a strange look in his eye. "I've watched Levi now all day. He's a quick learner. And strong."

"What are you saying?"

"Do you remember the old Lakota man at the boarding school who said that a young Lakota man should not hope to live to an old age? That he should die on the battlefield, fighting for his people?"

"That old man was crazy. And those days are gone. You're making no sense, Karl-Martin."

"No, I am making sense. I've been doing a lot of thinking. Those days are gone, but the Lakota heart is not gone, or at least it should not be. That old man wasn't crazy, he was just talking in the Lakota way, pointing to one thing to teach about something else. He was saying that to be a Lakota man, you need to be willing to risk your life for your people."

"You are still talking in circles, Karl-Martin."

"There are many battlefields, Lillie. Levi worked hard today. He wants to be a man. I could keep him here, show him how to be a man in our way, to become a farmer with hard work and farm skills. He could be the man we wanted our Joseph to be. If I could change the world to have it be that way, I would. But I can't. Levi needs to be a man in the Lakota way. He needs to find his Lakota heart."

"These are good words, Karl-Martin. But they are going nowhere."

Karl-Martin paused in the way he does when he is about to say something important.

"He wants to go to the *Inyan Sa K'api*, Lillie. The pipestone place in Minnesota. To get new pipestone for his grandfather. He wants to go alone, with just his brother."

I could not hear these words, not through my mother ears. "Karl-Martin, that place is days away. Little Reuben is just small. He needs protection, he does not need challenge. And Levi is only eleven. He is too young, as well."

Karl-Martin made his face hard. "The Creator places our path before us," he said. "We must walk it when it is shown to us."

I don't like it when Karl-Martin speaks in this way. It is as if he is trying to be an Indian, trying to twist things for my ears. "I do not hear strength in that, Karl-Martin," I said. "I hear cruelty."

Karl-Martin's voice was firm. "I am not saying this is easy. And I do not say it easily. But I am saying it."

I could hear the boys returning. The water was splashing in the bucket. Reuben and Levi were laughing. Mister Bones was barking. I could see him limping in circles around the boys. They were all playing. Our house was filling with life.

Reuben pushed open the screen door. The bucket was filled to the top. Levi was carrying it with both hands. He was struggling.

"I brought it full," he said. He was tall with pride. "Reuben helped me."

Reuben made a face like a grin and clenched his fists. "I helped get water," he said.

Karl-Martin let them struggle with the water. Then he got down on his knee so his eyes would be looking at their eyes. "You've done good work," he said. "Thank you for helping." He reached to shake their hands. Levi took his hand. He looked to be surprised to hear a white man thanking him. Reuben ran and grabbed me around the knees.

Karl-Martin held Levi's hand in his. "Go wash up," he said. "Take some of that water you just brought in. Now we've got plenty." Levi grinned and took Reuben by the hand. Levi was still wearing Joseph's clothes.

Karl-Martin turned to me. "We'll talk more tonight," he said. "After the boys go to bed. For now we should let this rest."

◊ ◊ ◊

My spirit was troubled all through supper. These were small boys. Eleven years is not yet a man; not even a man in the making. I knew the school agents would be looking for them. It was not good to send them off, but it would not be good to keep them here. I did not know what to do. When the boys had gone to bed, Karl-Martin sat with me. I could tell his heart was soft.

"Lillie," he said. "I have prayed in my own way about this. These boys have been sent to us, just like Joseph was taken from us. I believe it is God giving us another chance."

"No, Karl-Martin," I said. "I think that is your guilt talking. This is not about us. It's about these boys. These boys have not been sent to heal your wound."

He walked to the window and stared out into the night. His back was to me. I could see his face reflected in the glass. The moon was rising over his shoulder. It was round and distant.

"Since we lost Joseph, every day I've lived with pain," he said. "I can't live my life with this pain."

"What will you do, then? Will you end your life, like Joseph did?"

It was a hard thing to say. I was afraid to hear his answer. But he was talking from his heart to me. He never talked from his heart to me. I had to know.

"No," he said. "I will not end my life. But I'll do what I must to end the pain."

We spoke late into the night until the moon became small in the top of the sky.

It was never good to argue with Karl-Martin. He would say what he believed. Then he would stand firm with it. Words would not change his heart.

He thought to send those boys off, like Levi wanted. I thought to keep them, to find their home. He saw like a man. I saw like a mother.

"They are too young," I told him. "These are dangerous times. This is a year of bad dust. It is the season of fires. The days are hot and the nighttime winds are strong. Something bad is in the air. When these things come, these boys will be alone and crying. They will be looking for their mother, not seeking to become men. I believe you are wrong to do this."

"There is good and bad in all decisions," Karl-Martin said. "Only the Creator knows if the steps we take are on the right path. You are a mother. A mother seeks protection. I am a father. A father seeks courage."

"You are talking like an Indian now," I said.

"It's not just the Indian way," he said. "The boy Jesus left his family when he was twelve. They found him teaching in the temple. He said he must be about his father's business, and he did not mean his earth father. It's time for these boys to be about their father's business. And that is to be a Lakota."

"You're spinning a web in the sky with your words, Karl-Martin. Let me put your words on the ground. Levi is only eleven years old. It could kill him."

"And they would make him a shoemaker, Lillie. There are many ways to die."

A MAN CAN GET THIRSTY

Levi

When I woke up the Karl-Martin man was smiling down at me. He stood tall, like the tallest man I had ever seen.

It was another blue day, not dusty. Some clouds.

The sun was behind his head like the picture of Jesus.

"Good morning, boys," he said. His voice was soft. Music-like. Reuben made a bear sound.

There were clean clothes for us, all folded, on a chair. They were like clothes for a *wašíču* boy, but not like stiff boarding school clothes. There were white shirts from soft cloth and blue jeans and a leather belt with a silver buckle.

"Pull these pants on," he said. "It will just take a minute."

We pulled on the pants.

He put the belt around me and made marks on it with a pencil. He rolled up the legs and folded them so they wouldn't be too long. Mine were almost right. Reuben's were way long and he had to fold them almost to the knees.

"Now take them off and give them to Mrs. Steinbach. Then go get your breakfast. The missus has it on the table ready for you."

The wife woman was standing in the doorway. Reuben and I went behind the door to take off the pants. We did not want to do it in front of a woman.

Reuben leaned in close. "Who's Missus Steinbach?" he said. He had a scared face.

"That's the wife woman. It must be their name."

"Why does he call her the missus? Is that a *wašíču* name?"

"It's not a name. It's what *wašíču* call each other. Mister and Missus. It's the respect way. We have to do it in boarding school."

"But she's not *wašíču*. She's Indian, like us."

He was making me mad. The Missus Steinbach woman was waiting.

"I don't know, Reuben. Just take off the pants."

He wouldn't stop talking. He was hard pulling on my sleeve.

"Why does Mister Bones have a respect name? Is he a *wašíču*?"

I was full angry. He had gone inside his mind.

"Dogs can't be *wašíču*. Dogs are just dogs."

"But he's a Mister."

"Take off the pants," I said. I grabbed him hard on his shoulders. I felt sad to do this. Grandpa would not want me to do this. But he was being other-minded. We had to show respect.

I took off the pants and gave them to the Missus Steinbach woman. I thought to see if she was angry. But there was more sadness in her face.

We went downstairs. I did not like being in my underwear, but we had long shirts on, so it was not so bad. There were eggs and bacon. They were on plates for us. There was milk, too, in glasses.

The Mister Steinbach went out to the barn with the belt. The Missus Steinbach took the jeans into another room.

Reuben ate really fast. He liked bacon. Mister Bones was right there. He was pawing my leg. His tongue was out. He had a dog smile.

"Give him bacon," Reuben said.

"No. You give him bacon."

"I ate all mine."

"Then take him over on the floor," I said. I do not like to eat with a dog looking at me. He was pawing my leg. He had a trickster face.

Reuben went to the floor with Mister Bones. They did that dog talking where they touched their noses together.

The Mister Steinbach came back. He had the belt. He went to the other room and got the jeans.

"Give them a try," he said.

We tried them on. The pants were not long now. He gave Reuben a rope to hold his up. He gave me the belt. It had a buckle with a horse and rider on it. It was a cowboy waving his hat while the horse tried to throw him off.

"Do you like it?" Mister Steinbach asked.

I had never seen a belt like that.

"You treat it right," he said. He was giving me the belt.

He handed me a bag. It was like a parfleche, but with straps that you could put over your shoulders. He put it on my back.

"Is that too heavy?" he asked.

"No," I said. It was a small lie. The straps cut into my shoulders.

The Missus Steinbach came into the room. She looked at Mister Steinbach. I could feel sadness between them.

Reuben had on his new pants. They fit right now. The shirt had long sleeves. He was flapping them like a bird and making bird sounds. He had a big smile.

Mister Steinbach got down on his knee. He looked me in the eye in the *wašíču* way.

"Levi," he said. He was holding me with my name. "Mrs. Steinbach and I have talked. I have watched you. You have worked with me. You did not complain. I believe you have a strong heart and a strong body. You have said a Lakota man must have *wóohitike*. To be brave in all things. Do you have *wóohitike*?"

"I want to," I said.

"I believe you do," he said. "Mrs. Steinbach told me another word. *Wówačhiŋthaŋka*. Do you know that?"

"Yes," I said. "It is to keep going and not stop and not be afraid. Grandpa taught me."

"Do you have *wówačhiŋthaŋka*?"

I put my eyes down. I did not want to say. *Wówačhiŋthaŋka* is a full man thing.

"Mrs. Steinbach believes you have *wówačhiŋthaŋka*. She says you could not have come this far without it."

The Missus Steinbach was nodding. She was standing far back. She had a sad smile.

Mister Steinbach stood up. Missus Steinbach came to me. She took both my hands. She stayed standing.

"Levi Lone Dog," she said. She had claimed my full name. "I'm speaking to you as a mother. I'm speaking for your mother. She has sent you running. She did this because she loves you. She wants you to keep Reuben from the boarding school. She has told you to care for him. You are brave. You have come a long way. I know you wish to honor your grandfather. That is a good thing. It is a man thing. But your Lakota heart must first take care of your brother. Do you understand that?"

Her words were strong.

"Do you understand that?" she asked again. She was holding me with her eyes.

"Yes," I said, soft-like.

"I want your word." She would not let go of my hands.

I was scared. No one had ever asked for my word.

I looked at Reuben. He was talking to Mister Bones. Mister Bones was rolling on his back.

I thought of Grandpa. I stood up strong. I made my back straight, like Grandpa did when the school men took him. "I give you my word," I said, man-like. It felt good to say it.

"I want to hear you say it again."

"I give you my word," I said again, more loud this time.

It felt good to put strong words in front of me. All my life I have stayed behind my words. Now I was putting my words in front of me. I was making a promise with my words.

The Missus Steinbach hugged me. It was a warm hug. It made me feel happy. She gave me a piece of paper. It was folded. She put it in the pocket of the shirt.

"Today is a good day," she said. "Care for your brother. Make your journey in safety."

I had not known we were leaving. Now I knew it.

Mister Steinbach came to me. He put the parfleche bag on my back. It was heavy.

"You are a good man, Levi," he said. "You can do this."

I looked down.

"You will get the stone for your grandfather's *čhaŋnúŋpa*."

We walked out to the road. "I am going to tell you what to do," he said. "We have a friend. She is Mrs. Steinbach's oldest friend. She is Indian like you, only Dakota. Her name is Miss Ida. She knows the place of the red stone. She can help you."

Missus Steinbach pointed to my shirt pocket. "You give her that note," she said.

"Yes, ma'am."

"Be sure."

"Yes, ma'am."

She tied bandannas around our necks. Not too tight, just loose. "You use these if the dust gets strong," she said.

It made me scared to think of the dust.

Mister Steinbach came in front of me. He pointed up the road. It was into the sun.

"It's about six miles. I would drive you, but this is your journey. You'll cross a little creek. There's a big oak tree. All by itself. You'll see it. Miss Ida's house is on the right. It has green shutters. You should be there by noon."

I didn't know what shutters were but I didn't say anything.

Missus Steinbach had put food in the bag. "You've got bread, *wasná*, some cheese. Jerky," she said. Her arms were crossed. She was smiling her sad smile.

"Oh, I have something else for you," Mister Steinbach said. He reached into his work bag. He took out his thermos jar. "A man can get thirsty when he's traveling," he said. "Here."

He gave it to me. I took it with both hands like Grandpa taught me to do when getting a gift.

"You make sure he keeps it full, Reuben," he said. Reuben clenched his fists and shook his head up and down like he does when he is too happy to talk.

I saw strong sadness in their faces. Reuben ran over and put his arms around the Missus Steinbach. Mister Bones went with him.

"Off with you now," Mister Steinbach said. "God speed. Six miles. Across a creek. Big oak tree. A white house with green shutters."

"You give her that note," Missus Steinbach said.

The road looked long. There was heat spirits rising from the fields. It was going to be hot.

"We're going, Reuben," I said.

I took his hand and we started walking. I turned around to see Mister and Missus Steinbach.

They were holding hands, too.

Pursuit

ČHAŊNÚŊPA HAS BROUGHT YOU

Ida

When I saw them two little Indian boys coming up the road, I knew it had something to do with Lillie. There's not too many of us Indian folk around here. They was walking like they were coming from somewhere. Like they knew where they were going.

Oh, they was cute, the two of them, with those red bandannas on their necks. The one acting all big and standing straight with his hair all combed, and the little one kind of wandering like a puppy, pulling this way and that, heading up the drive to my house.

I rolled my wheelchair out onto the porch when I saw them. "You boys, you come on in," I said.

The older one, he walked right up to me and handed me a note. He put his arm out straight, like handing a note to a teacher. "Are you Miss Ida? Missus Steinbach told us to give this to you." He was all serious, like a little man full of business to do.

"You come in. It's hot out," I said. "I have food, some good things to drink."

The little one, he run right past me, right into the house. The older one, I could see he was upset, like the littler boy should be acting more polite.

"It's all right," I said. "You come a long way. That little one, he's your brother?"

"Yes, ma'am," he said. "His name is Reuben. He's other-minded."

111

He was using boarding school manners. I could see he felt shame for his brother.

"Come," I said. "I have fresh bread."

I could tell they were good boys. I put them at the table. The young one ate with his head all down over the food. The big brother kept those boarding school manners with "yes, ma'ams" and "no, ma'ams." He was all full of fear, like he might do something wrong. The little boy, Reuben, he ate all full of joy. It made me feel good to watch him eat.

The note from Lillie was written in Indian. That told me it was important.

It said the boys had run because the boarding school men were after them. She thought to get them away from her house because the school men might come there. She said they were on a journey, that I should hear it from their own mouths. She thought that I could help them.

I wondered what journey they were on. They were just young. My house would not be safe from the school agents. They would come first to all Indian houses. I live just up the road. We are the only Indians around. They would look everywhere. They would find those boys.

I watched the young one, watched his eyes. I could see he had different sight. He looked in, not out. I could tell he needed protecting. If Lillie thinks I can help these boys, I thought, I must do it.

Lillie is my oldest friend. I have known her since she was just little. We are like sisters. She lives the *wašíču* way, but the old ways are strong within her. Sometimes Indian people can live like *wašíču* but keep a strong Indian heart.

I wanted to know more about this journey.

"Why are you here?" I said to the boy, Levi. "Why did you come to me?"

He reached in his pocket. "Missus Steinbach said to show you this." It was a piece of red stone, pipestone.

Then I knew.

"Why do you have this?" I asked.

"My grandpa gave it to me. Some school men were at our house to take my brother. They broke Grandpa's *čhaŋnúŋpa*. This is from that *čhaŋnúŋpa*. He gave it to me. He said to carry it with me."

I took the piece of the pipe. I held it in my hand. It was warm, almost hot. It had strong power.

"Come," I said. "Leave your brother to eat. We are going to talk."

We went to the living room. I wanted this boy to be comfortable. I put him in the soft chair. My grandfather's chair. He sat straight. Kept his eyes down, showing respect. He had been raised well.

I wheeled close to him. I touched him on his arm, just soft. I could feel him shaking.

"It's okay," I said. "*Čhaŋnúŋpa* has brought you to me. Tell me how *čhaŋnúŋpa* broke."

He told me about his grandfather and the bad school agent who had broken the pipe.

"*Čhaŋnúŋpa* does not break unless it wants to," I said. "*Čhaŋnúŋpa* must have wanted to break." That made him feel better.

We talked for a while. I wanted to make him feel less fear.

"You wait," I said. I wheeled to the kitchen, to my special bowl. It was full of *wagmíza-wasná*, the corn kind of cookies. I make them the old way, with chokecherries.

I gave him some.

"It tastes like Momma's," he said. He was smiling. I knew then he was feeling more calm. I thought to talk to him more about the pipe.

"Give me the *čhaŋnúŋpa* piece," I said.

He took it from his pocket.

"Lay it on the table."

I started singing, real soft. "*E ha ya e ho yo-I, e ha ya e ha. Ya e ha-a-you-I ye-yo, e ye ye ho-yoi.*" It was the pipe prayer song.

"Do you know that?" I asked.

He nodded in his eyes-down way.

"You look around you. What do you see?"

The room had many things made from the red stone, the *čhaŋnúŋpa-íŋyaŋ*. My grandfather had carved them.

"My people are Yanktonai. Santee. Mother is Yanktonai. She is from the *Inyan Sa K'api*, the place of this red stone. Creator made my people protectors of this stone. That's why Mrs. Steinbach sent you to me."

While we were talking, little Reuben came in from the kitchen. He had a joy smile on his face. He had *wóžapi* all around his mouth. He licked his lips to show happiness.

"Come here, Reuben," I said and reached my arms to him.

"*Uŋčí,*" he said. "Grandma." And ran to me.

"You wear the *wóžapi* more than eat it," I said.

I wiped the corner of his mouth with my sleeve. He smiled his joy smile at me and put his arms around my legs. I have no feeling there, but I could feel him in my heart.

WHAT *KHÉYA* SAID

Ida

Oh, it was good to have that little boy holding on to me. We old never get held. There was joy everywhere in me. My heart was full of thanks to the Creator.

I thought to know more their journey, to see if they were just running or if Creator was guiding them. I knew that Lillie had sent them to me to find this out.

"I want you to do something," I said to Levi. "I want you to go to the shed behind the house. There is a tub there, like for washing, with holes on four sides, like doors. I want you to bring it here."

He went to get it. He did not ask why. He was a good boy.

"Reuben," I said. "Do you know *khéya*, the turtle?"

Reuben looked up from holding me and shook his head up and down.

"There is a gully down by the road. *Khéya* lives there. I want you to go get a *khéya*. You sit and watch. You will know which one."

Reuben was happy. He ran off to get *khéya*. There was no fear in him.

Levi came back with the tub.

"Set it on the floor in the middle of the room," I said. "Make the four holes facing the four directions." My grandfather had given me that tub. It had power for teaching. You never throw away something with power for teaching.

Reuben came in with *khéya*. He was breathing hard. He had run fast.

"Show me," I said. The *khéya* was just small, like a baby's hand.

"Let me see him," I said. The *khéya* turned his head up to me. He had small wise eyes.

"Why did you pick him?"

"I sat. He came to me."

"Good," I said. "Now put *khéya* under the tub. Then I want you to watch."

Reuben put *khéya* under the tub.

"Reuben, which door will *khéya* come out?"

Reuben smiled wide. He pointed to the east-facing hole. "There."

"Beat on the tub, Levi," I said.

Levi beat on the top of the tub. *Khéya* came out the east-facing hole, like Reuben said.

"Do it again," I said. "Which door, Reuben?"

He pointed to the east-facing hole, the same one. *Khéya* came out that hole.

We did it over and over. Every time Reuben was right. Every time *khéya* came out of the east-facing door. He was never wrong.

"Why that one, Reuben?"

"It's the sun-coming-up direction," Reuben said. "Where we're walking." That's all he would say.

Then I understood.

He took *khéya* and held him close. He ran his hand down *khéya*'s shell, like petting. He looked up at me. He was smiling big. "*Khéya*'s house is on his back," he said.

"I want you boys to leave me alone with *khéya* for a while. You go outside. I'll call you to come in."

The boys went out.

I held *khéya* close to my chest, close to my heart. *Khéya* stayed still, the same stillness as me. We breathed together. He did not move.

I closed my eyes. He was very old.

I breathed with *khéya*. *Khéya* breathed with me. We could feel each other's spirit. I did not feel time.

I held *khéya* close to my face. I blew my breath on *khéya*. *Khéya* took my breath. I gave *khéya* my spirit.

I called to the boys.

"Reuben, come in here," I said.

Reuben came in the door.

"I want you to take *khéya*. I want you to close your eyes. I want you to be more still than you have ever been in your life. I want you to hold *khéya* against your chest. I want you to do it until I tell you to stop."

Reuben nodded. He did not ask why. He took *khéya*. He made a pinch face and closed his eyes. He put *khéya* against his chest.

"Now do not move," I said. "I want you to feel *khéya*."

Reuben kept his pinch face. He did not move. He did not even breathe.

"Stop now," I said. "What did you feel?"

Reuben grinned big at me. "I feel *khéya*'s heart."

"You are a good boy," I said. "Now you go out with *khéya* and tell your brother to come in."

Reuben ran out. He had Levi come in.

Levi sat in the chair. He was serious-faced. He kept his eyes down.

"Levi, I want to ask you something. I want you to tell me the truth. Can you do that?"

He nodded, all serious.

"Where are you going with your brother?"

I could see his spirit struggling. I touched his cheek, just soft.

"It's okay," I said. "You speak when the words come to you."

We sat quiet. I let his spirit come to rest. We could hear Reuben talking to *khéya* outside the door.

I took his hand in mine. It was like touching a lily pad.

"Levi," I said. "Mrs. Steinbach sent you to me. You must tell me the truth. You must have *wóohitike*. Tell me where you are going."

I knew the answer. I knew it when he had shown me the piece of *čhaŋnúŋpa*. But I needed to hear it from his voice.

He started talking. The words came soft, like whispering.

"You must speak strong," I said.

"The *Inyan Sa K'api* place," he said, like he was trying to hide the words.

"Strong."

"We are going to the *Inyan Sa K'api* place," he said. "The place where the stone for *čhaŋnúŋpa* comes from."

I was glad to hear him say it.

"And why are you going there?"

"We are going to get stone to make Grandpa a new *čhaŋnúŋpa*." His words were strong now.

It made my heart smile to hear him speak the truth.

"Does Reuben know?"

"He is just little. He only knows each day. I can take care of him. Grandpa says I am his protector."

"One should always listen to a grandpa," I said.

Hearing me say good words about his grandpa made him feel more peace.

"You are a brave boy," I said. "And a good brother."

He still would not look up, but his face showed pride.

I kept his hand held in mine.

"Levi," I said. "I am double-minded about letting you and your brother go. The *Inyan Sa K'api* place is a long way and you are just young. But I believe that Creator has sent you here. I believe that Creator is guiding you on this journey. So I will help you."

Then I said the words that had been buried deep in my heart.

"Now I have something to ask of you, Levi. All my life I have thought to go back to that place, the place of *Inyan Sa K'api*. The place of my people. But Creator took my legs from me. I believe now he has sent you to me with your strong legs. I believe he has sent you so I can make my journey. Now I am going back. I am going back with you. I send my spirit with you. Because of you boys, I am going home."

Reuben came in through the door. He was holding *khéya*.

"*Khéya* had friends," he said. "We talked."

He made funny sounds like talking then pulled with his hands like a turtle swimming.

He put his arms around my neck and hugged me. "You are *Uŋči*," he said. His face had a full smile.

"What did *khéya* tell you?" I asked.

"We are going to a place of red stone," he said. "That's what *khéya* told me."

WÓOHITIKE

Levi

I was feeling fear to go again. It had been five nights we had been gone. I didn't tell Reuben. I didn't tell anyone.

The Ida woman was hard to leave. She was Indian, like us. She had a smile in her everywhere. She had soft hands. She made me feel safe.

I thought to stay and help her. Grandpa would have liked that. But she said we should go. She said we should do the *čhaŋnúŋpa* journey.

Reuben did not like to go. He said it made him afraid.

"There's a bad thing in this day," he said.

"What?" I asked him.

"Just a bad thing," he said.

I was feeling fear, too. I didn't know if it was coming from inside or outside. But we had to go. Now we were going for Miss Ida, too. We were carrying her spirit home.

This country was strange to me. It was different from where we live. The air was heavy. The *wablúška* were different. The birds were different. So were the plants. Everything was different.

Grandpa had told me about a big river called the *Mníšoše* that the *wašíču* call the Missouri. He said it is like the blood running through our land. He said it keeps us alive. Our people live on the sunset side, he said, where there are hills and the singing grasses. More *wašíču* live on the sunrise side, he said, where it is good for their way of farming. I think we must be on the sunrise side now. We must have crossed over on the train at night. When we walked to Miss Ida's house there was corn right up to the side of the road. It all felt like *wašíču* land.

It did not feel good for a Lakota to be here, I thought. But I would get Grandpa new stone for his pipe. I would have *wóohitike*. I would have courage. We would keep going to the sunrise way.

I tried to think like Grandpa would think. Grandpa taught me that when you don't know something, you must listen closely. You are following a new trail. You must look with new eyes.

I would do that. I would listen closely. I would look with new eyes. I would find the place of the red stone and get the stone and bring it to Grandpa. I would be his legs to get the stone for a new pipe just like we would be the legs for Miss Ida to bring her spirit back to *Inyan Sa K'api*.

Reuben didn't know any of this. He knew only we were running to a red stone place and that he wanted to see Grandpa.

I thought to make him feel good and not feel fear. I thought to tell him this would be an easy trail.

"It will be three days, Reuben," I said. "Miss Ida said that."

"I know," Reuben answered. "*Khéya* told me."

Reuben's whole mind was inside of *khéya* now. Everything he was doing was *khéya*-thinking.

Miss Ida had said to stay on the road. It was small, not wide, only dirt with fields on both sides, and sometimes a house. There were no cars. She said if we saw a car we should wave. She said we should not be like lost dogs, looking lost and scared. We should look like we knew where we were going. She said that *wašíču* people wave and smile at each other, not like our people who just go to where they are going and don't look at anyone when they walk. She said to say we were going to our grandfather's place if someone stopped. It is not a lie, she said. It is not good to lie, even to *wašíču*.

I was happy wearing the clothes Missus Steinbach had given me. Reuben, too. They were clean, like white shirts, not store kind, but made by hand. They made me feel safe. They made me feel like I could be in this *wašíču* country and not be scared. They made me think of the Steinbachs. I wish we would have stayed with them.

Reuben's shirt was too big. It made him look funny, like with the sleeves too long. We kept the bandannas on our necks. He was running in circles, flapping his arms, with the sleeves flying like wings, making bird sounds.

"What are you doing?" I asked.

He touched his bandanna. "We look like *šišóka*," he said. "The robin bird. I am flying." He made more bird sounds. They sounded just like *šišóka*. They made me laugh.

I was watching Reuben's eyes. I could see they held fear. He was being a bird to make me happy.

"Come here," I said. I thought to hold him. Being held makes you feel less fear. I thought of Momma holding me. And Missus Steinbach. And Miss Ida. I put my arms around him. I could feel shaking in him. He was close to crying.

"Don't be afraid, Reuben," I said. "We are going to get the red stone for a new pipe for Grandpa." It was the first time I had said it to him with words. I wanted him to feel less fear. You have less fear when you know where you are going.

"That Miss Ida made me think of Grandpa," he said. He was full crying now.

His crying made me want to cry. My crying was close to my eyes. It wanted to come out.

"Can we go back?" he asked. It was the first time he was backward-facing.

"Be like *khéya*," I said. "Be sunrise-facing."

He sniffed twice and wiped his nose with his sleeve.

He put his head against me. "I will be like *khéya*," he said. "I will stop being like *šišóka*. *Šišóka* wants to be in her nest. *Khéya* keeps his house on his back."

SPEAKING THEIR NAMES

Danton

It was hard to believe the boys could have gotten this far. I was a hundred miles from their home, out of the high plains and into farming country. The whole land had lost its Indian feel. This was the land of the settlers now. Germans, Czechs, Swedes — all manner of folk who had come from places across the ocean, staked a claim, built some solid little Main Street town, and made the land bear fruit as commanded by their Biblical God.

The air was heavy and turbid, with an oppressive weight that burned the lungs. Corn and wheat and a dozen low crops I didn't recognize stretched out on either side of me as I drove down the razor-straight gravel roads that bisected the fields.

It was a sobering drive. This land was fecund and fertile, but dying of thirst. You could almost feel the crops withering and struggling under the weight of the drought. And behind it in every town, in the stores and the cafés and the people you met on the street, you could sense the desperation of the men and women who had given everything they had to these fields.

I felt for these people. They were hardworking, God-fearing folks who were being blindsided by forces they couldn't control. I'd see them sitting in the cafés, sharing stories of the '30s when the dust and the drought had left this landscape dotted with abandoned farms and devastated fields that they had picked up for pennies on the dollar, and were now in danger of losing to the same indifferent forces that had destroyed the dreams of people a generation before.

In some ways these were my people — the western edge of the tillers and harvesters who had made their way across the continent from the Atlantic, believing in the bounty of the soil and hard labor, until they had hit the great waterless places of the Great Plains and been forced to choose between stopping and settling on the last arable land for a thousand miles or continuing westward and trading their plows for branding irons and barbed wire and going from raising crops to raising cattle and sheep.

Some couldn't face the change; some relished it. Soon enough they separated into the men of tractors and overalls and the men of the cowboy hats and horses, and, for the most part, the Missouri was the line that separated the two.

Now, however, they were all — farmers and ranchers alike — threatened with the same peril. When the sky turns against you, whether with dust or drought, it doesn't matter if the death it brings is to cattle or crops, in the end it is the same. It is the death of dreams. And dreams were dying here.

◊ ◊ ◊

I had not intended to range this far from home when I had set out to find the boys. Five, six miles at most is what I had expected.

But here I was, driving down a gravel road on the far eastern edge of South Dakota, following out a string of leads and clues that had me looking for a weather-beaten farmhouse and a mailbox with the name "Steinbach" painted on it.

Ree had said that she'd sent the boys to the railroad tracks and told them to hop a freight. Kids had been doing it for years, she said — she herself had done it as a teenager — and they all knew the curves and grades where the train slowed down.

She had instructed them not to get off until the sun came up. If they got off too soon, she had told them, the school men could find them and bring them back.

I'd talked to a couple of maintenance workers I'd seen inspecting the tracks. They'd said the line was the next thing to be abandoned; there was one train a day and the engineers drove it the same way all the time, so it was easy to guess where the boys might have gotten off. The first stop in the morning would have been near the town I had just visited, so that was where I had started. It wasn't much to go on, but it was something.

The old men drinking coffee in the café on Main Street had told me I should try the Steinbach place. Their house was nearest the tracks, they said.

They were curious about what I was up to, but no more than they would have been about the doings of any stranger passing through town. This was farm country and runaway Indian boys didn't interest them much. None of them had seen any boys, but they promised to alert the local sheriff if they did. I chatted with them about the weather and the crops for long enough to be neighborly, then went by the sheriff's office to leave my contact information, and set out to find the Steinbachs' home.

I didn't know if the Steinbachs knew anything about the boys, but it made sense at least to have a talk with them. According to the directions I had been given, their house was just a few miles up the road.

I'd been told that they were private folk who pretty much kept to themselves. The woman was Indian and the man had worked at a boarding school for a few years. Some of the folks in town thought maybe he had been a priest. There were lots of rumors about them.

The sky was blue and cloudless as I drove out to the Steinbach house. This was one of the calm days. Abandoned farmsteads were everywhere. Silt was piled like waves against the sides of buildings. The gravel road kicked up clouds of dust that covered my windshield. I ran my wipers, but they just smudged and smeared my view.

The Steinbach home was set back from the road in a stand of oak and tangled undergrowth. The house itself had once been a tidy white country farmhouse with a small sitting porch in front and a half story upstairs. But the weather and years of neglect had caused the paint to fade and the porch to sag, and it now felt like a sad memory of someone's happier time.

A man I assumed to be Steinbach was standing on the front porch as I drove up. He was tall — maybe six feet four — gaunt, with huge hardworking hands that hung like anvils from the sleeves of his white muslin shirt. He was square-jawed and hawk-beaked, with a vigilant gaze and an erect stance. His hair, which was turning from blond to white, was thinning and swept back. Even at a distance, it was obvious that this was a man who gave and took nothing easily.

I drove up casually, as if this were just a leisurely visit. These were times when I was glad I owned a pickup. People's first impressions in these parts were formed by your shoes, your vehicle, and your hands. Though it was obvious by my hands that I was not a laborer, my worn-down work boots and my dusty Ford half ton at least marked me as someone who belonged in this country. I could only imagine how I would have been received if I had driven up in the government-issue black Plymouth sedan that gave Two Finger so much pleasure when he pulled up to someone's house to execute a grab.

Even so, Steinbach's greeting was anything but neighborly. He stood with his legs apart and his arms folded across his chest. There was no aggression in his manner, but it was clear that he was holding his ground.

"Mr. Steinbach?" I said, stepping out of the truck with as much confidence as I could muster.

He nodded silently. He had placed himself directly in the center of the two steps leading up to the porch. In every way possible he was a human wall, dividing his world from mine.

"Hate to bother you," I said, offering the standard opening apology all Midwesterners have bred into them. "My name's Adrien Danton."

I reached out to shake his hand, which he met with a perfunctory formality. His hand was huge, almost twice the size of mine.

"Can I sit for a second? Too much road time."

He nodded and stepped aside, opening the porch to me but keeping the door blocked. I could tell that he saw me as a representative of some kind of officialdom — someone with a paper or a message or an edict to deliver — and he wanted to waste no time getting to the heart of the matter.

He pointed to a weathered wooden straight-backed chair set against the front window. An old yellow dog lay wheezing in the corner. I reached out to pet it, but it showed no interest in me beyond a single wag of the tail. So I settled in with an almost excessively theatrical sigh of appreciation.

Steinbach himself remained standing. He offered me neither food nor drink.

"What can I do for you?" he asked.

I wanted to defuse any underlying tension as quickly as possible, so I decided to forgo any pleasantries or formalities and meet his no-nonsense manner with one of my own.

"I'm looking for a couple of Indian boys who ran from their home back on the reservation. Their mother is worried about them."

He remained silent. He had not heard enough to warrant any response on his part.

"They're about six and ten. Eleven maybe. The younger one is slow, maybe a little retarded. That dust storm the other day really got their family worried. I said I'd help them out. They figured as a white man I'd probably have a better chance of getting folks to talk to me."

My explanation did not soften or move him.

"Why are you asking here?" he said. "At my house." He was still holding his ground, offering nothing.

"They hopped a freight. Track workers said the first place they could have gotten off would have been close to here."

Through the window I could see the shadow of his wife moving in the background, trying to get close enough to hear without being seen. More than ever I was convinced that these people knew something. Otherwise, curiosity would have brought her out to the porch to at least listen to the conversation.

Too much was on the line for coyness, so I decided to lay everything out.

"I used to work for the government, helping round up kids for the boarding schools. But I couldn't take pulling kids away from their families, so I quit. I'm partly responsible for those boys running away. I'm just trying to help get the little guys back home."

Steinbach nodded. All six feet four of him loomed above me, staring down at me with an expression of practiced indifference. He ran his hand through his thinning blond hair.

"I'm sorry to hear about the boys," he said. "But they haven't been through here."

He offered no further guidance, no speculation about where they could have gone or people I should talk to.

He let his silence hang in the air for long enough to inform me that he had nothing more to say, then offered me his huge, calloused hand in a final handshake.

There was nothing more to be gained by extending the conversation, so I accepted his handshake and told him to contact the local sheriff if the kids came by. I said I would check in there before I left the area.

"I wish you well in your search," he said as an act of closure to the conversation.

The old dog flubbered once in the corner, as if to add a note of finality to the proceedings.

I backed awkwardly toward the steps, trying to find a graceful way to take my leave from the situation without making it look like a full retreat.

"Their names are Reuben and Levi," I said. "If you see them. Their mother is really worried."

As I turned to walk down the steps, Steinbach's wife emerged in the doorway.

"Please sit down, Mr. Danton," she said. "It was good that you have spoken their names."

HUNGRY FOR COMPANY

Danton

My initial impression of the Steinbachs could not have been more wrong. My calling the boys by name had changed their attitude completely. Mr. Steinbach had merely been serving as the gatekeeper, leaving all the decisions on matters of the boys to his wife's discretion.

"You know them by name," she said. "Not just as some Indian boys. That tells me you care about them." She beckoned me through the doorway. "You are welcome in our house."

Mrs. Steinbach was a singularly striking woman. She, like Ree, was close to six feet tall. Her features were every inch Lakota, with wide cheeks, a dark, dusky complexion, and slightly narrow eyes. Her hair was thick and rich and peppered with gray. She was broad and powerful and moved silently but with absolute authority.

Though they could have been sisters, she and Ree were like polar opposites. Ree was all angles and edges and exuded a barely suppressed anger. Mrs. Steinbach had an ethereal air, almost a distant sadness, as if she wasn't fully present.

It was fascinating to see her wearing a typical farmwife housedress, and quite a contrast with Ree in her tight jeans and blue workman's shirt. It was ranch versus farm played out in the dress of two forceful, prepossessing Native women.

I was immediately taken by the graciousness of the Steinbach home. It was far different from what the outside would have led me to expect. There were several overstuffed easy chairs and an upright piano, all centered around a braided oval rug and a coffee table with a scattering of *National Geographic* and *Life* magazines.

The walls were covered in rose-patterned wallpaper, and one corner of the living room was taken up by a cupboard-style bookshelf filled with old hardbound books and what looked to be a complete set of the *Encyclopaedia Britannica*.

A Maxfield Parrish print of two young girls lying between two pillars hung on the wall next to a picture of Jesus praying on a rock that I must have seen in every home in Michigan when I was growing up. It was a room built for comfort, and it immediately put me at ease, though I was curious at the absence of any Indian objects or decoration.

I tried to sneak a glance at the book titles — books and photos always offer an insight into people's lives — but Steinbach had taken a seat across from me and was commanding my attention. His wife had retreated to the kitchen, leaving just us two men to face each other.

"We don't get many visitors," he said, leaning back in his chair and clasping his hands behind his head. His open, relaxed manner was the exact opposite of the stern formality he had exhibited on the porch. "Wife's Native. Not a mix folks take to around here. We mostly stick to ourselves."

"Can keep you out of trouble," I said. "I'm pretty much the same way."

"Still and all, every once in a while a man just feels the need of company."

He nodded toward the kitchen where I could hear his wife chopping vegetables. "You know how the Indians are. Why say two words when one will do?" It was an expression I myself had used more than once in describing the Indian folk I dealt with back on the reservation.

He took an amber half-pint bottle of whiskey from a cabinet in the bottom of the bookshelf. It was dusty and had not been opened.

"Drink?" he asked. "These are dry times."

"Not a bad idea," I said. Alcohol was expensive and precious in these parts. If he was offering to open a new bottle for me, it was a true gesture of hospitality. It would be wrong to turn it down, and a drink might just make him more amenable to a conversation about the boys. "Just a little, though. I'm not much of a drinker."

He set a glass in front of each of us, poured a solid shot into mine, and filled his about halfway.

"Now tell me about those little runaways," he said.

I told him the story of Two Finger and the pipe and old Lone Dog and the jail cell.

"Sounds like quite a bastard, that Two Finger fellow," he said.

"Tip of the iceberg."

"An old man shouldn't be in a jail cell. And the pipe. You don't disrespect someone's *čhaŋnúŋpa*."

His use of the word was a great relief and set me at ease. It told me he understood. It made sense that he would have some sensitivity to Indian practices, given his Native wife. And I was warming to his increasingly affable and welcoming manner. I found myself opening to him more than I had expected.

"I got myself in way too deep," I said. "Getting involved with Two Finger and the boarding school stuff. I'm a Midwestern kid. Michigan. The Upper Peninsula. I came out here just looking for something new. I didn't know anything. I just took the job to pick up a few dollars and fill some time. I figured the boarding schools were probably good for the kids. You know, three squares and the three R's."

Steinbach had a knowing look on his face. "That's what most people think, until they see one in action."

"You have any dealings with them?" I asked.

"Some," he said, lifting his glass to his lips. It was a shut-down answer that told me that this was not a subject he wanted to pursue.

We sipped at our whiskey and shared stories of our upbringing in the east. He had come from Ohio, a little town named Gnadenhutten. He didn't say how he had ended up out here and I didn't ask. I figure people share what they want when they want. Beyond that, their lives are their own business.

The comforting aroma of frying chicken was filtering in from the kitchen.

Steinbach noticed me turning my attention in that direction. "You'll stay for dinner?" he asked.

"I really shouldn't," I said, though the prospect was appealing. The afternoon was getting long and I needed to find a place to stay for the night. "I'm trying to get a lead on those boys."

Mrs. Steinbach walked in from the kitchen. "I think we can help you with those boys," she said. "If you'll share our table we can talk about it. Please stay."

The aroma from the kitchen and the possibility that I might get some leads on the boys was too much to turn down.

"If it's not too much trouble."

"Guests are never trouble," she said, smiling.

I was quickly taking a real liking to her. She was a strange combination of kindness and reserve, and she had an easy domesticity that reminded me of my grandmother, as if making meals and welcoming guests into her home was the most fulfilling thing in the world to her.

"It's not much fun cooking just for the two of us," she said. There was a wistful edge to her voice.

Though the Steinbachs were gracious and welcoming, I could tell they were still gauging me, trying to decide where to draw the line on their friendliness and hospitality. But they were clearly hungry for company. I think that my obvious pleasure at being in a home where a meal was being prepared softened them to me. It had been so long since I had been involved in anything domestic. The aroma of frying chicken and baking bread took me back to my childhood and the summer cookouts under the oaks and the elms with the breeze blowing warm off the shores of Lake Michigan. It was enough to make me weep.

The meal was a delightful amalgam of Lakota and traditional farm-style cooking, with pan-fried chicken, a whole-grain bread, a root vegetable Mrs. Steinbach called *thiŋpsiŋla*, and a berry dish that she said had been her mother's specialty.

We ate slowly, savoring our time together. We talked about the boys, but only in generalities. Though it was hard, I kept my questions to a minimum. It was important that the Steinbachs not think I was interrogating them. There was a fine line between having them know I was concerned about the boys and having them think I was just using them to get information. They had already indicated that they might be able to help me. An unwarranted sense of urgency on my part might have given the wrong impression.

After the meal Steinbach said I should come out to his shop and we could talk more without disturbing his wife. She believed in being in bed when the sun went down, he said, and already the sky over the fields was turning from deep orange and crimson to a darkening purple.

We walked casually out to the barn behind his house, watching the evening descend. The fields beyond the copse of trees looked shriveled and anemic in the waning twilight. The stars came out — one, then another, until the entire sky was filled with pinpoints of light. All around us the sound of cicadas filled the air.

He lifted the heavy black hasp on the door of the shed. "The house is my wife's domain," he said. "This place is mine. It isn't much, but a man needs a spot of his own."

"My dad used to say that every man ends up in the garage," I said.

"When you've got no garage, a shed will do," he answered.

I was enjoying his company. Once past the initial formality, he had proven to be a kind, caring man, almost poignantly hungry for human contact. "I love my wife to the end of the world," he'd said. "But, damn, those Indian folk, they pretty much say only what they have to, and that's it."

I could relate to his loneliness. I lived with my own loneliness every day. I did my best to turn it into solitude, and mostly that worked. But I was unfettered and could pick up and leave anytime I wanted to. He was tied to a home and a marriage and a piece of land that looked to be dying before his eyes. Mine was the loneliness of freedom; his was the loneliness of entrapment.

It was a convoluted bond, but I think we both felt it acutely.

YOU COULD SMELL THEM
BURNING

Danton

Steinbach's shop was a little eight-by-ten add-on shed attached to the barn, with a potbellied woodstove in the corner and a single salvaged window facing out to the fields. He gestured me to an old wooden chair and dragged a hay bale in from the barn for himself. He took a metal pie plate from the shelf, set it on the bench, and ladled about a quarter inch of water in it from a bucket that was sitting on the floor, then placed an old glass kerosene lantern in the pan and lit it with a wooden match. The light flickered up, making shadows dance across the walls.

"Can't be too careful," he smiled. "Dry country."

It was a typical man's shop, smelling of axle grease and motor oil, with a workbench and tools and piles of scrap of the sort a man would need to keep a farm running. Rolls of barbed wire and a bolt cutter were stacked in the corner.

He had a few tools I didn't recognize — tools brought over from the old country by some ancestor, I was guessing — and a selection of wood files laid out on a chamois cloth. The usual collection of pliers and wrenches and screwdrivers and hammers were scattered haphazardly across the surface of the bench.

In the far rear corner of the bench stood a stack of hardbound books by authors like Étienne Gilson, Rudolf Otto, and Rudolf Bultmann, none of whom I had ever heard of. On the wall where most men would have had a pinup or a calendar of Marilyn Monroe, he had a piece of paper with a handwritten verse on it. I stood up so I could read it. It was written in a formal hand.

A PSALM BEFORE SUNRISE

And what will be more blessed than this day?
Will tomorrow's sunrise be more beautiful than this dawn?
Will a child's touch be more precious?
The earth more filled with love?

In a yesterday long forgotten we sought this day
And called it blessed.
Now that it has arrived,
Will we throw it aside for dreams of an unknown tomorrow?

Send light into my heart, oh Lord,
That I might not turn away from this sunrise.

Send joy into my heart, *Thuŋkášila,*
That I might sing a song only for this day.

He had settled in on the hay bale and was sipping at his glass of whiskey. "Wrote that a few years ago," he said. "I used to be in the seminary. Thought I was going to be a priest."

He poured another strong shot into my glass. "I read it every morning before I start my day."

I didn't know quite how to respond, either to the personal revelation or the devotional intimacy of the verse.

Steinbach sensed my discomfort. "That's all right," he said. "Religious talk makes lots of people nervous. They think someone is going to try to sell them something or convert them or make them read passages from the Bible. I'm not that kind of guy. I just — well, I think about things like that. I thought maybe I'd let you read it. You seem to be an open-minded fellow."

I didn't know if this was Steinbach or the whiskey talking. We had made it through almost half the bottle, and only a few of the sips had been mine.

"No, it's fine," I said. "It's good for a man to speak from the heart."

"Only worthwhile place," he said.

I took a sip of the whiskey. The conversation was becoming uncomfortably intimate. I wanted to steer it in a different direction.

"It was nice of your wife to have me stay for dinner," I said. "That was the best meal I've had in years."

"I get it every day," he smiled. He tapped his stomach, as if to show how much weight he'd put on, though he looked to me like he didn't have an ounce of fat anywhere on his body. "We're poor, but we live rich."

"Lucky man."

"I tell myself that every day."

He reached under the workbench and pulled out a small box.

"Here," he said. "I want to show you something."

The box contained several small wooden carvings of birds. They were rudimentary and crude, almost little more than long bullet shapes, each with real bird feathers attached to its sides for wings. They were not much bigger than hummingbirds, which they actually resembled. One had a long piece of curved wire for a beak and another had a tiny cone of tin fastened to its front. They all had tiny blue beads for eyes. He cradled one in his hand. It was crude, but heartfelt.

"I can't decide if I should paint them or stain them. What do you think?"

"There's enough brown around here these days with all the dust," I said. "I think you should paint them. We can use a little color in our lives."

A broad grin crossed his face. "You think like I do, Mr. Danton. I like your style."

He pointed to the eyes. "These are beads left over from a cradle-board my wife made. Blue. Indians call it the color of forever. Seemed like a good choice for something that spends its life in the sky."

"Why do you keep them out here?" I asked. "You should put them in the house on your bookshelf."

"I just make them to make them," he said. "I don't make them to

show them. They're not that good. I do a lot of it with files." He nodded toward the chamois on the bench. "Every time I make a stroke I
say a little prayer. It's kind of a meditation for me."

Again, he was veering toward religion.

The sky was descending toward purple; the night was getting dark
and the air was starting to get heavy. I needed to find a place to stay.

Though we had not yet talked about the boys, it felt like a good
time to leave. I could come back in the morning and continue the conversation.

"I should get going," I said.

A glow flashed far over the horizon. A few distant rumbles of
thunder rolled in the distance.

"Amounts to nothing," he said. "Just heat lightning. Wish it was
more. This whole land is dying of thirst."

He put his hand on my wrist, a gesture of friendship more than
restraint. "Stay a little longer. We can make a place for you to bed
down."

The option was appealing. The streets of these small South Dakota
towns roll up after dark, and I didn't even know if the nearby town had
a hotel.

"You sure it's okay?" I asked.

"More than okay. It would be our pleasure."

I looked through the shed door at the growling sky. Another
faraway flash of lighting illuminated the distance.

"God, it's big out here," I said. "I never get used to it."

"Don't think we're meant to get used to it," he answered. "Keeps
us humble."

The thunder rumbled again. "Voice of God," he said. Then he let
out a short laugh. "Oh, I forgot."

"No, that's okay. I can use a little religion."

"Stay out here very long and you'll get a lot of it."

He finished the last of his whiskey. He looked fondly at the half-
empty bottle.

"Thanks for sharing this with me. I never drink like this," he said.
"It's probably been a year. I was saving that bottle for a special occa-
sion." He shook his head and smiled. "I guess you're it."

I was feeling a little woozy. I could not imagine how Steinbach was feeling. He had drunk far more than I had. I was thankful I wouldn't have to drive anywhere.

The light from the kerosene lamp flickered in the slight evening breeze, casting shadows across his creased, angular face. He walked to the doorway, put his massive hands on either side of the doorframe, and stared out at the star-drenched sky. "You know, Mr. Danton, I didn't come out here expecting to marry some Indian woman. I didn't expect to marry anyone. I was going to be a priest. They sent me out here to work in the boarding school." He shook his head and smiled. "I didn't know what I was getting into. Kind of like you with that Two Finger fellow."

That explained the knowing look he'd given me when I had mentioned my job.

"Funny thing, life," I said.

He gave a short laugh. "You live it forward, understand it backward."

"Nice phrase."

"Søren Kierkegaard. You probably never heard of him." Then, after a long pause, "Why'd you do it?"

"What?"

"Come out here."

"Oh, nothing too deep. My old dog had just died. I had nothing. I could never make it work with any woman. So I just said, 'The hell with it' and headed west."

"Military?"

"Nope. Alternative service."

"But why here? Why South Dakota? Why the rez? Why work with that Two Finger?"

"I guess the air just came out of my tires. Seemed as far away from everything as I could get. I just took that job for something to do. Like you said, I didn't know what I was getting into. One day I'm looking for a place to spend a summer. The next day I'm chasing Indian kids across the plains. Now I'm sitting in a shed in some farmer's yard, drinking whiskey and watching for rain."

Steinbach laughed. It was all shorthand — just thoughts bubbling to the surface through the alcohol — but he seemed to be enjoying it.

"How about you?" I said. "It looks like the priest thing didn't work out."

He smiled a long, weary smile. "No. Things took a left turn."

"What? Pretty Indian woman catch your eye?" I knew I was getting personal, but the whiskey was having its way.

"Well, a little bit. But that wasn't it. It was a lot deeper. Religious kind of stuff. You probably wouldn't be interested."

"No, I really am," I said. The drink had loosened our tongues and I was enjoying this man's company. His piety wasn't oppressive, and his openness was refreshing. I realized I hadn't had more than a passing conversation with anyone for several months.

Steinbach pulled the hay bale up closer and sat down across from me. He put his huge hands on his thighs and leaned forward until we were face-to-face. "Okay. This is going to sound strange. But it was the fires."

"What?"

"Prairie fires. You ever seen one?"

"Not up close."

"Well, until you're up close to one you don't know what they are."

He pointed out across the fields. "Look out there. See that lightning?"

Vague sheets flashed over the horizon.

"Does that do anything to you?"

"What do you mean?"

"Does it feel personal? Like it's talking to you?"

He wasn't making much sense, but I was willing to follow him wherever he wanted to lead. "Makes me a little apprehensive," I said. "Makes me think about distances, about what might be coming. But no, nothing personal."

"That's the way I was. Maybe a little more religious than you. That's why I ended up out here — religion. I wanted to go to where the big forces spoke. But it was all abstract. Philosophical. Reminders of God everywhere. But nothing personal."

He nursed the last few drops of the whiskey in the bottom of his glass. The sweet scent of the nighttime breeze blended with the chirping of the cicadas, filling the night with a heavy peace.

"In some ways I'd never felt so at home. These were God-fearing folks. This was God-fearing land. Everybody bent a knee to the big forces. Not like city folks who figure a nice suit and a fat bank account put you in control. I'd listen to the old farmers. They're tough as hell, never crack a smile. But they had an honest humility. Windstorms, sandstorms, droughts, tornadoes remind you you're not in control. A couple of five-mile-high thunderheads and a tornado or two and I was right there with them. But I was always different, always an outsider."

He looked at me with an earnest innocence. "You sure you don't mind me talking about this, do you? I never get to talk like this with anybody. Heck, I never get to talk with anybody about much of anything. Take an Indian wife and the town shuts its doors, not that they were ever open too much anyway."

"No. No. Please."

He pointed again to his pile of books on the bench. "So I'm reading those, the folks out here, they're reading seed catalogs. Try talking about *Mysterium Tremendum* with them instead of Atlee Burpee."

I was way out of my league and we were veering far from the notion of prairie fires, but I didn't want to interrupt him. He was speaking from the heart even if his heart was getting a little help from the bottle.

"So I'm working at the boarding school. Each year they march these little kids in. Scrub them up, stand them in rows. Sweet little Indian kids. Most of them scared. Put the girls in dresses, guys in little suits, feed them good meals, put a little meat on their bones. I'm supposed to be teaching them history and religion.

"They're sitting in rows in these little wooden desks, hands folded, eyes wide, too scared to act up. Heck, most of them couldn't even understand English. And you know the two things that got to them the most?"

"No."

"The crucifix and the globe. They couldn't stop looking at that guy nailed up on a cross and they couldn't stop looking at that globe, thinking that was what the world was like. They called it 'Mister Steinbach's earth ball.'

"One little fella came up to me and said, real serious, 'Mister

Steinbach, I'm afraid for winter.' His name was Ezekiel. At least, that's what we called him.

"'Why, Ezekiel?' I asked. He had big round eyes and the sweetest face. He was real shy, having a hard time talking.

"'It's okay, Ezekiel,' I said. 'You can tell me.'

"He kind of pawed the floor with his feet. 'You said that the earth turns with the seasons. I'm wondering if when it turns toward winter, I might fall off.'"

He let out a short laugh. "God, I loved those kids."

Another flash illuminated the horizon for a moment, bringing him back from his reverie. He shook his head as if collecting his thoughts. "Yeah. Sorry. I was talking about how I ended up here."

He placed his hand on my hand.

"Let me tell you a story.

"It was summer. My second year out here. School was closed. I went to work for a local farmer. An old fellow. Needed some help.

"I stayed in a little outbuilding he had. About the size of this shed. I helped with the milking, the farmwork. Just good, solid labor. A chance to meet some of the locals. Good folks.

"It was a bad summer. Bad as this one. Maybe worse. Hot? My God, it was like the devil's breath. And dry. No rain, nothing.

"Everyone spent their days looking at the sky. Churches full. People on their knees, praying for rain, praying for help, praying for anything.

"Folks were just hanging on. A lot like now. Nobody had much. A few cows, chickens, kind of like my place. Everything had to do with the crops. A good crop, you live. A bad crop, you shrivel up and die.

"The old fellow I was working for was growing hay. Not a lot. Just enough to feed his own stock, sell a little to other farmers. It was a living, but just barely.

"There'd been prairie fires around. Lightning, probably. Maybe controlled burns that got out of hand. You'd hear about them. See the glow. But always miles away. Just like that lightning."

He pointed out the door again to the flashes illuminating the distant horizon.

"Then one day something sparked one nearby, maybe a half a mile away. I was out in the field with the cattle, the horses. Suddenly, just across the road, there are these flames, forty or fifty feet high. Smoke swirling, twisting, all black, going up to the sky. You've heard people talk about tongues of fire? That's what it was — tongues of fire. And loud. You can't believe how loud it was."

He grabbed my arm and held it, as if by holding me he could make me understand the power of the experience.

"It started moving toward us. It was like it looked around and saw us, then decided to come for us. In a flash, jumped the road and came after us. Roaring. I didn't know that fires roared. It got to the pasture first, the horses and cattle.

"We were all running. Everything. The horses. The cattle, their little calves. But the fire caught them, just ate them up."

He put his hands on either side of his head and closed his eyes.

"You could smell them burning. They're screaming and dying and everything's got fear in its eyes. It was like hellfire, Mr. Danton, and you're running and the smoke is choking and chasing you and you keep hearing the screaming, and the heat is getting bigger and you're praying and cursing and doing anything you can and you can't turn to look at it because it'll burn your face off. This wasn't like some punishment from God. It wasn't something distant, some idea from a book."

He paused, as if deciding whether or not to go further.

"I don't know how to say this. This thing was alive. It was like it had a spirit. And it was laughing. It had picked us out. You can say I'm crazy, but I'm not crazy. It was chasing us, making sport of us. One of the neighbors told me he killed one of his cattle, cut it open and dragged it through his field with his tractor, trying to make a fire-break. Fire just came right up to the break. Just stopped there. Burned real low, like it was crouching, then jumped right on that cow carcass, burned it up right in front of him, then jumped off and moved on. It did what it wanted. I'm telling you, it had a mind. It was alive. I swear to God I never experienced anything like it.

"Then, just like that, it turned and went away. Silence. Everything black. Carcasses everywhere. The smell of burning flesh, burning hair, the hay.

"And the thing just went away. Like it had finished its work.

"I was crying, praying. And here's what I'm trying to tell you. I wasn't praying to some God out there somewhere. Some *Mysterium Tremendum*. I was talking to that fire, begging it to stay away, praying that it would keep going the other direction and never come back.

"That's when I knew. I'd been all in my books, arguing about the divinity of Jesus, and God running the show like a ringmaster, then here comes this thing, laughing, cruel, turning and seeing us and chasing us. Then, like when it had had enough of us, it just turned and left. It was alive, I'm telling you. It had a spirit. It was alive."

He grabbed my arm again. "Do you think I'm crazy?"

"No," I said. I didn't know what else to say.

"And those mother cows, trying to save their babies, crying, bawling, screaming like people, no different from us. I swear to God they were praying, too, in their own dumb animal way. I could feel their spirits, see them leaving their bodies.

"That's when something changed in me. All the stuff in those books." He pointed to the pile of books on the bench. "Dry as the crops in that field. All the blood sucked out of them. And I'm trying to teach these little Indian kids about some guy named Jesus living in some place they'd never heard of. Telling them their grandparents were wrong. Their parents. When they've got these spirits all around them. Thunderstorms. Dust storms. Tornadoes. Fires like the tongue of the devil."

His thoughts were starting to fall apart. This was no longer being said for my benefit. This was some private confession, an anguished voicing of his personal crisis of faith.

"Don't you see? We got these little kids sitting at a table, hands folded, saying words they don't even understand. 'Bless us, oh Lord, and these Thy gifts.' Tell them they're 'saying grace.' What does that even mean, 'Saying grace'?

"These people didn't say grace like we did, thanking God for food on the table. They talked to the spirits of the animals who'd given their lives to feed them. And I was trying to teach them how to pray."

Outside, the distant thunder rumbled. The light in the lantern flickered.

Steinbach ran his huge hands through his thinning blond hair. His forehead was glistening. "Heaven and hell? You want hell? Watch a prairie fire kill a baby calf and see its mother bawling trying to save it. More hell in those cries and that mother's eyes than all the theology books in the world. If there's a devil, the devil was in that fire, Mr. Danton. Laughing and killing, then turning away like nothing happened."

He pushed the knuckles of his hands into his eyes, as if trying to drive out the vision of something he could not forget.

"I had to leave. I couldn't stay. Do you see? I couldn't teach these Indian kids something that I only half believed. Something that was wounding their hearts."

Then, as if to correct himself, "It's not that I didn't believe in Jesus anymore. It's just that it wasn't big enough. Do you understand?"

His eyes were pleading. It was as if he was asking me for absolution, wanting another white man to tell him that the world he'd discovered was not a figment of his imagination, and that he wasn't betraying his own people and his faith.

"You're a good man, Mr. Steinbach," I said, not knowing quite what else to say.

"Am I? Am I really? Trying to make those kids hate the world their grandparents had given them? Make them hate themselves?"

He was near tears. He walked to the door and stared out into the rumbling distance. He stood for a long time, saying nothing.

Then he turned back. His eyes were filled with more anguish than I had ever seen in the face of a man before.

"I think maybe that's why God took my son," he said.

WE SENT THEM OFF

Danton

It was a hard night. I couldn't shake the image of this giant of a man, locked in his personal anguish, almost begging for absolution while lightning flashed on the distant horizon and vague rumbles of thunder rolled like echoes in the lonely prairie night.

Even harder was sleeping in a bed that I now knew had belonged to a son he had lost. I understood now what the emptiness was that I had felt in the house — that air of sadness that permeated everything, masquerading as peace and order.

I glanced around the room at the little metal airplanes on the dresser, the pictures of birds and animals cut from magazines and thumbtacked to the wall. It was like a shrine, where the door had been shut at the time of death and all had been left, untouched, as a memory too painful to be confronted.

What had happened? What cruel event had taken place, leaving them trapped in unspeakable memories in this great empty space?

I fell asleep slowly, ashamed for my presence in this house. Theirs was a haunted life, and I should have been no part of it.

The next morning Steinbach was up when I climbed out of bed. I don't know how he did it. My head was heavy. His had to be throbbing. But he showed no ill effects from the night of drinking.

He was freshly shaved, wearing a clean collarless long-sleeved muslin shirt buttoned to the neck. He reminded me of the Amish and Mennonite men I had seen riding the country roads in their buggies back home.

Mrs. Steinbach was outside the back door, humming softly and shucking corn. It was shaping up to be another sweltering rainless day.

I wasn't sure how much of the intimacy of the previous night would carry over into the morning, or if its drunken confessionality would shroud our morning in mutual embarrassment.

I approached cautiously.

"Good morning, Mr. Steinbach," I said.

He had a warm smile on his face. "That bottle of whiskey should have scraped the formality off. Call me Karl-Martin." He reached out his hand, as if to seal our newfound intimacy. I took it in mine.

"Adrien," I said. "With an *e*. Or just Danton."

I had noticed his hands yesterday. They were huge, even for a man his size. They were working man's hands, with calluses from hard labor, but far more graceful than I was accustomed to. The working man's hands I had seen growing up in Michigan were usually monuments to hardship, with broken or missing fingers and huge knuckles and scars and ground-in dirt under the fingernails. Steinbach's weren't like that. Though they were massive and strong, they did not exude power so much as precision, like a surgeon's or a pianist's. It was just one more incongruous aspect of this incongruous man.

"Coffee, I presume?" he said.

"You presume right."

He took two mugs from a sideboard next to the stove. I noticed there was a smaller mug set by itself off to the side. I tried not to read too much into it, but it was hard to ignore. Karl-Martin filled my mug from an old white enamel coffeepot that was sitting on the stove, and pushed it across the table to me.

"That was a good night," he said, showing no sign of embarrassment about how much he had revealed about himself.

"For me, too. Thank you."

"So, you want to know about those two Indian boys," he said. "Let me finish fixing breakfast and get Lillie in here."

I was not accustomed to seeing farm men prepare a meal. Usually it was the women who took charge of all domestic activities.

He cracked six eggs expertly on the edge of the frying pan, using only one hand. He fried them quickly, and slid two onto each of the three plates laid out around the table along with forks and knives and the remainder of the loaf of bread his wife had baked the previous evening.

Hearing the clatter of plates and silverware, she came in from the yard and took a place at the table, right across from me.

Karl-Martin poured her a mug of coffee.

"Thank you, Karl-Martin," she said. He nodded and smiled.

There was a strange formality to both their language and their interaction that bordered on ritual. They simultaneously lifted their mugs of coffee slightly, as if in benediction. Somewhat sheepishly, I did the same.

"*Mitákuye oyás'iŋ*," Lillie said. Then, turning to me, "Thank you for spending the night in our home, Mr. Danton."

"It was an honor," I answered, adopting a formal tone that surprised me as it came from my mouth. "Please. Call me Adrien if you like. Or just Danton. It was kind of you to let me stay."

"And you may call me Lillie."

She held her mug in both hands, like a child holding a cup of milk. Each sip was slow and mindful, surrounded by a quiet awareness. She kept her full attention on me, never looking directly at me, but watching my every action over the rim of her mug as I buttered my bread, ate my eggs, and drank my coffee. There was no sense of judgment in her gaze, just a constant vigilance, like one might find in a servant or an animal trying to decide whether to approach or withdraw.

"Tell me more about yourself, Mr. Danton," she said, choosing to keep a formal distance in her address. "And why you are interested in the boys."

I recounted in more detail my dealings with Two Finger, Ree, and the old man, and told her how the boys had touched something deep in me with their concern and affection for their mother and old Lone Dog. I explained how the breaking of the pipe had shocked me, and how Two Finger's response to it had seemed unnecessarily gleeful and cruel.

"Did you see the *čhaŋnúŋpa* break?" she asked.

"Yes."

"Did you see the boys? How they reacted?"

"Yes. The young one seemed frightened. The older one turned almost cold, like something had changed in his heart. It was strange. It was like he wasn't a boy anymore. I had never seen anything quite like it."

She smiled and nodded.

Karl-Martin was observing silently. He had his huge hands steepled over his nose and mouth.

Lillie stood up and walked into the other room. She returned with an abalone shell and an eagle feather, and took a pinch of sage from a small leather pouch she kept on a shelf.

Karl-Martin remained motionless while she placed the sage in the shell and lit it, fanning the smoldering pinch of herb with the eagle feather until the smoke rose up in a small stream and the scent filled the kitchen.

"I want all bad things gone from this place," she said, speaking in an almost formal manner. "If we would talk about those boys, all the bad things you did with that man Two Finger must be placed behind you."

She cupped the smoke and pulled it around her head. Karl-Martin did the same. She fanned the sage some more and gestured toward me. I pulled the smoke around my head as they had done.

She spoke a few words in her native tongue and left the table. When she returned, she took a pinch of a different herb and placed it in the middle of the shell and lit it, fanning it as she had done with the sage. A sweeter smell filled the air. Again, she and Karl-Martin pulled the smoke around their heads and instructed me to do the same.

"You must promise that your heart will be good and you will do only things to help the boys," she said. There was a quiet authority in her voice.

"I will," I said. It felt like a marriage vow.

She lay down the feather and placed the shell between us. The smoke continued to rise sinuously and fill the room with its sweet, soporific aroma.

"I will tell you about the boys now," she said. "Levi and Reuben. Karl-Martin found them walking on the side of the road. They stayed with us. We fed them, washed them, and clothed them. I made sure they were healthy and good. You can tell their mother that they were well cared for and safe. That should put her mind at ease."

She spoke dispassionately, but I could only imagine the feelings she had experienced as she had tucked those little Indian boys into the bed of her dead son and turned to see those planes and paper cutouts on the dresser as she walked out the door.

The information she gave me was comforting, but not sufficient. My job was to find the boys, not merely relay comforting information about them. And this told me nothing about what had happened to them.

"So, where are they now?" I asked.

She looked at her husband.

"You tell him, Karl-Martin."

Karl-Martin had remained silent since Lillie had begun talking.

"We sent them off," he said.

I'm sure the shock on my face was palpable. Those boys were eleven and six. Such an act of callousness seemed completely out of character for this caring, if somewhat enigmatic, couple.

"Why?" I asked, not even trying to hide my surprise. "Where? They're just young boys."

"It was my decision," Karl-Martin said.

Lillie poured me another cup of coffee. The sweet pungency of the smoldering herb was still floating in the air.

"You said you watched his heart change," Lillie said. "Like he wasn't a boy anymore."

"Yes."

"That was čhaŋnúŋpa calling," Karl-Martin said, picking up his wife's thought.

"You know what čhaŋnúŋpa is, don't you, Mr. Danton?" Lillie added.

I nodded. "The pipe. Like the one Two Finger broke."

It was the first time the two of them had spoken together in a conversation rather than deferring completely to the other.

"Čhaŋnúŋpa is not just a pipe, Mr. Danton," Lillie said. "Čhaŋnúŋpa is alive. Creator gave our people čhaŋnúŋpa to heal the people. If the grandfather's čhaŋnúŋpa broke, it was to call someone to awareness. Karl-Martin and I talked. We believe that čhaŋnúŋpa was calling to Levi. We believe it was calling him to manhood. We chose to help him on that journey."

WAGMÍZA - WASNÁ

Danton

I left the Steinbach house in a state of profound disquiet. There was so much going on behind those walls — so much strength and so much love, yet so much sadness and yearning.

The ghosts of abandoned pasts were everywhere. A Native woman who had walked away from her Native tradition, a seminarian who had walked away from being a priest, and a child whose unmentioned death cried out in silent testimony from behind a closed bedroom door.

What had most affected me about their lives was the morality that pervaded their every action, from what it took for them to let me in the door, to the way they prayed before meals, to the seemingly brutal choice they had made to send those boys off on their own.

But what was disquieting was their seemingly cavalier attitude toward sending two boys on a 150-mile journey across scorching, inhospitable landscape in the name of a spiritual quest for manhood and a piece of stone to which they attributed sacred significance.

It was equal parts cruelty and faith, and the Steinbachs seemed at peace with both dimensions. I did not doubt their belief in the spiritual significance of the journey, but it was inconceivable to me that good, caring people could risk the health, and maybe even the lives, of two young boys on a journey so fraught with dangers and uncertainties.

Yet I had to remind myself that Ree had also sent them off, and she was their mother. But she had done it to help them survive. The Steinbachs had done it to serve what they perceived to be a higher purpose. In my mind, it all came down to nothing more than two little fellows, far too young to be out on their own, being sent off in debilitating dust and heat with nothing more than a backpack and a naive but noble dream. And that didn't seem like enough.

The Steinbachs had told me that they'd sent the boys to the home of someone named Ida — an Indian woman Lillie had grown up with, who lived a few miles up the road and mostly kept to herself. "She knows the old ways," Lillie said. "We knew she'd know what to do." How someone who had never even met the boys would know what to do with them was a mystery to me.

"You need to visit her," Karl-Martin had said. "But look out, she'll talk your ear off." I had been tempted to bring up his comment about Indians never saying two words when one will do, but I had long ago learned that you are best served by never asking anyone to explain themselves. Just hear what they say, take it for what it is worth, and do with it what you will. It's the best way to keep the peace.

◊ ◊ ◊

Ida's home was a straight-line drive up the gravel road that passed in front of the Steinbachs' house. I drove it slowly, hoping against hope that I might see the boys playing in a drainage ditch or drawing designs in the dirt with a stick. But I had no such luck.

Ida's house sat alone on the top of a low rise about a quarter mile back from the road. From a distance it looked like a cross between an Andrew Wyeth and a Grant Wood painting — lonely, forlorn, and solitary, yet somehow bucolic and serene. Despite being isolated, it had a feeling of command about it, like it could have once belonged to a banker or a prosperous landowner, though it obviously had seen its better days. Its front porch overlooked the surrounding countryside and felt like a place where a gentleman farmer could sit to survey the fruits of his labors or the labors of those who were in his employ.

Ida was sitting on the porch as I drove up. I was surprised to see that she was in a wheelchair. Neither Karl-Martin nor Lillie had mentioned any disability when they had talked of her.

She was a short, stout woman. My mother would have called her "plump." Like Lillie, she wore a plain print housedress — apparently it was the clothing of choice for the women in this area — and she had on pink bedroom slippers that could charitably have been described as "well loved." She wore thick wool socks beneath her slippers and her feet barely reached the footrests on her wheelchair. The chair itself had the unadorned utility of something that had been made for an institution.

Even in her farmwife housedress, her Native heritage was obvious. Her skin was the color of a chestnut and her straight white hair was pulled back and held in place by a thin elastic headband. Though she and Lillie had grown up together, she seemed to be of a completely different generation. The years had been hard on her; she looked like an old woman.

She waved as I drove up, showing no hesitation or even curiosity about my arrival. It was as if I were just an old friend come by for a weekly visit. She flapped her hand at me like someone waving a hankie, and let out a warm "Helloooo," stretching out the "oooo" as if shouting into a canyon.

I have always been amazed by people who have every reason to be lonely or depressed, but instead have some inner resource that makes them self-contained and almost preternaturally cheerful. Ida was a perfect example. Her smile was full of mirth and enjoyment. She made me feel welcome before I even stepped out of the car.

"Good morning, Ida," I said. "My name is Adrien Danton. Lillie and Karl-Martin sent me."

She rocked back in her chair. "Ah," she said with a chuckle. "Lillie and Karl-Martin. I'll bet it's about them boys. They were cute ones, them two."

Her use of the past tense made me curious.

"You come in and sit a bit," she said. "We will have a good talk."

She spun her chair expertly and wheeled back into the house. There was no concern about my purposes or questioning of my motives.

I followed cautiously and stood in the doorway. "Sit down, sit down," she said. "You go to the living room. I'll make coffee. I make good coffee."

I went into the living room and settled into the one huge soft easy chair that occupied the corner of the room. As I sat down, a large cloud of powdery dust rose up from its cushion. It hung in the air and filtered through the light that cascaded in from the two tall windows that dominated the east wall of the house.

Unlike Lillie's home, Ida's was filled with Native artifacts and keepsakes. There were beaded moccasins displayed on shelves next to carved pipestone buffalo, bear, and eagle heads. A star quilt covered one wall and an assortment of dream catchers hung from the ceiling. Perhaps most interesting, and completely unexplainable, was a galvanized metal washtub sitting upside down in the middle of the room. It had four holes in it, like cartoon mouseholes. I thought perhaps it was some kind of drum or something that assisted her in dealing with her physical limitations.

"Oh, that," she laughed as she wheeled in carrying two white mugs of coffee on a tray. "I'll tell you about it after we have our treats."

She handed me a cookie that she had brought in with the coffee. "Here. You eat." It was sweet and chewy, almost like pemmican, and tasted like corn bread mixed with berries.

"Have you ever tasted cookies that good?" she asked.

"Not since I left home." I smiled. "Makes me think of my mother."

"*Wagmíza-wasná*. My grandma's recipe. I changed it a little."

She took one for herself and nibbled on the edge of it.

"So, how do you know my Lillie?" she asked.

"I really don't," I said. "I just…"

"Oh, that Lillie," she interrupted with a laugh. She obviously wanted to talk more than she wanted to listen. "That Lillie, she was always the stubborn one."

She wheeled herself a few inches closer to me.

"You know, you could never tell her nothing. Her mother and I told her not to marry that Steinbach fellow. We thought he had too much of the Christian in him. But she wouldn't listen. She just married him anyway.

"Now, he's a good man, that Steinbach. A really good man. But we knew she would have to live in the Christian way, like a white man's farmer wife. We didn't think that would be good for her."

"So you know her pretty well?" I asked.

"Oh, she's my oldest friend. I don't see her much anymore, though.

She and Karl-Martin stay mostly to themselves, especially since their Joseph died. Karl-Martin comes by once a week to help out a little. But Lillie stays home. I wish she would come, but I think her heart is still too heavy."

She tried to bite off a larger piece of the cookie but could do little more than pull on it with her lips. It was obvious that she didn't have many teeth.

"I went there to help after their Joseph died," she said. "They buried him mostly in the Christian way, but Lillie wanted something of the old ways. People want to hold hands with their own kind when someone passes. Lillie wanted the old prayers in the old language. I know those prayers."

By now it was obvious that Steinbach had been right: Ida was going to talk my ear off. But the cookies were good and she was a delight. With her crinkled face and her roly-poly presence, she reminded me of the apple dolls the grandmas used to make back in Michigan. I decided to just sit back and let her make her way through her thoughts in her own time. We would get around to the boys eventually, and in the process I might learn more about the Steinbachs and their private ways.

Ida was already running far ahead of me.

"Lillie and me, we met when she was just little. Maybe seven, eight. I was lots older. Already thinking about boys.

"We were living in town. I saw her one day. She was riding her bike down the street. She had streamers on it. They reminded me of the prayer ties my *uŋčí* used to make. She was pedaling so hard with her face all scowly and not getting anywhere. She made me laugh. She still makes that face.

"She was new in town. Our town was small, maybe two or three hundred — mostly Germans and Swedes and people from places I'd never heard of. We kids all knew each other. You knew when there was a new one. Especially one with brown skin, like me. There weren't too many of us there. We mostly had to keep to ourselves.

"I had this one friend, Marina, she was white. She lived way out of town. No one liked her. They were afraid of her. She dressed strange. I think it was some religion. They heard her dad was mean. I was Indian, so nobody liked me either. That made us be friends.

"When Lillie moved to town, I told Marina, 'There's a new girl in town. She's just little. Maybe we could get to be friends with her first. She's Indian, like me. I don't think the other kids will want to be friends with her.'

"Marina thought that was a good idea. I said I would meet this new girl and see if we could be friends. Then we would see Marina and we would all be friends. It was a good plan.

"I didn't know if Lillie would want to be my friend. Just being Indian girls doesn't make you like each other — it just makes you notice each other. And she was Lakota, I was Dakota. The Lakota, they're lots wilder, at least it seems to me.

"But we got to be friends. Lillie and me and Marina. But then Marina died. She got that flu. The doctor couldn't get there in time. So then it was only Lillie and me. Two Indian girls.

"It was good having another Indian friend, even if we were different."

"So, how'd your family end up here?" I asked. "If it was mostly a white town."

"My family, they'd been here a long time. We are Yanktonai and Santee, from *Čhaŋšáyapi* in Minnesota. We came here after the killings by that General Sibley, about a hundred years ago. You know *Čhaŋšáyapi?*"

"No. Never heard of it."

"It's where the trees are painted red. The white people call it Redwood Falls. We didn't want to come here. We came when they hanged all those Indians. President Lincoln, he did that. He saved a lot of them. He should have saved more. But he had that Civil War. He didn't have much time to think about Indians."

She was talking a mile a minute, pausing occasionally to gum her cookie or check to see if my coffee needed refreshing. There was no way I could stop her, nor did I want to. I just kept nodding and hoping she would eventually come around to the subject of the boys.

"It was a sad time, those years. That's what my *uŋčí* said. We liked the *Čhaŋšáyapi*. It was our home. The government had promised us that we could stay there if we sold our land to them. We didn't want to do it, but we wanted to live. They promised us money so we could eat. But they gave our money to the agents who wouldn't give it to us. You don't know this?"

"No," I said, though I had some rudimentary knowledge of the events.

"*Uŋčí* said those were bad times. Nothing would grow. People were starving. The women were crawling on the ground looking for grain to feed the babies.

"Some young boys, they got angry. They didn't like seeing their little brothers and sisters dying. They didn't like to see the elders all curled up, sick from hunger. They said we were begging like dogs. They killed some white farmers.

"Most of our people were upset. We had lived with the white people. They were our friends. It was the government that was treating us bad, not the people."

"That's the way it usually is," I said.

She continued without even acknowledging my comment.

"Lots of those young boys, they wanted to fight. Oh, they wanted to be warriors. They said we could chase the white farmers off because all the young white men were off at that Civil War. They said it would be easy. They said that our leaders had become cowards."

She shook her head and stared at the floor, as if contemplating a hard and painful memory.

"Young boys don't think about war. They think about being heroes. The women, they think about war. They think about the killing. They think about their babies. They think about their grandpas and grandmas. I sometimes wish the women would be in charge."

"It might be better," I said.

"The government sent soldiers. I guess they weren't all at that Civil War. They had lots of guns. There was killing. Both our people and the white people."

"Our men sent us away. They said we should go to the open country, west from the woods country where we lived. They said we could just keep moving toward the sunset if the white soldiers followed us. They said the soldiers would not follow us into winter. They said white soldiers did not like to fight in the winter."

She peered into my cup. "You want more coffee?"

"No," I said. "Just more of your story."

She smiled and patted my hand.

"I like to tell stories," she said. "You are a good boy."

"Some families stayed," she continued. "They were made prisoners. They were taken to that Snelling fort where the rivers meet. Lots of my relatives died there. I still say prayers for them.

"That's when those hangings happened. The men got captured. The government built a big stage and marched all the men up on it. They put ropes on their necks. White people came to watch. Lots of them.

"The men were brave. *Uŋčí* said they were singing their death songs when the ropes snapped. They went to the spirit world with courage. *Uŋčí* said the white people cheered.

"When I heard about that, I didn't want to know anything more about the white people. I said I would stay away from them even though we were now living with them. People who would cheer when other people die have bad spirits.

"That's why I stayed mostly by myself as a little girl, except for Marina, and then when I met Lillie. I liked my dolls. I liked being alone. But Lillie was different from me. She wanted to know everything. She didn't care — white people ways, Indian ways. She just wanted to know.

"And, oh, she wanted a boyfriend. When she found out I went to Indian school, she wanted to go. She said she might get a boyfriend there.

"I told her she wouldn't like the Indian school. You had to live at that school. They treated kids bad. You got hit a lot and they made you learn Christian."

"So why did you go?"

"My dad died and we didn't have any food. My *uŋčí* and *uŋkáŋna*, they lived outside of town. I wanted to live with them but they were too far away. There was no way to get to school in the winter and my mother said I had to go to school.

"I said I would only go to school with Indian kids. I was a stubborn girl." She laughed and clapped her hands together as she said it.

"So my mother let me go to the Indian school. She said I should close my ears to the Christian talk and should tell her if I got hit.

She said I could learn the old ways in the summer from *Uŋčí* and *Uŋkáŋna*."

By now I had realized that *Uŋčí* and *Uŋkáŋna* were her grandmother and grandfather. I wanted to bring her back to the subject of the boys, but she was enjoying herself so much that I didn't want to interrupt.

"*Uŋčí* and *Uŋkáŋna*, they lived in this house. *Uŋkáŋna* bought it with money he got from raising cattle. He said he had the gift to raise cattle. He said it was his gift from the Creator to help take care of his family. He got rich for an Indian. He said the best way to be an Indian in the white man world was to be rich like a white man. Then they would leave you alone. That's why he bought this house.

"I used to come out here all the time. Sometimes I ran away from the boarding school and hid here. They had a dirt cellar for storing. I hid there when the school people came looking for me. They never found me.

"That's why I was happy when that little Levi and Reuben came to my house. They were running from the boarding school, just like I used to. I thought to do what *Uŋčí* and *Uŋkáŋna* did. I would hide them from the boarding school men."

This was my chance.

"Tell me about those boys," I said. "Are they still here?"

"Oh, no," she said. "Creator sent them on. Come. I show you."

She wheeled over next to me and grabbed me by the wrist. "Now, first you go down to the ditch by the road and bring me back a little turtle. Not too big. I'm going to show you something."

If I'd thought that the ways of the Steinbachs were strange, Ida's were absolutely inscrutable. But she was finally talking about the boys, so I did what she said.

When I got back, she was sitting in front of the washtub.

"Did you get one?" she asked.

I held up a little mud turtle about the size of a silver dollar. Its head and feet were pulled inside its shell.

"Let me see," she said.

She took the little turtle in both hands, put it next to her face, and spoke to it softly.

"Now, before we do this," she said, "you tell me why you care about these boys."

I was happy to have a chance to explain myself. I told her about my job and Two Finger and my change of heart. I explained that the boys' mother had asked me to find them and how Lillie had said I should talk to her.

Ida nodded and pursed her lips. "If Lillie sends you to me, I will help. She is like my little sister." She pointed at the tub with her gnarled finger. "Now take that *khéya* and put him under that tub."

"*Khéya?*" I said.

She leaned back in her chair and laughed. "Turtle. I guess you don't know our Indian language."

"Nope, still working on English."

She smiled and patted my hand.

I lifted the edge of the tub and slid the little turtle underneath.

"Now, which hole will little *khéya* come out of?" she asked.

It seemed like a strange time for parlor games.

"I don't know," I said.

"Go ahead, guess. Just guess." She slapped me on the arm and laughed. "Oh, come on. It's just a game."

I pointed to the hole facing the kitchen.

"Now, pound on the tub."

I beat on the tub several times with my fist. After a few seconds the turtle came crawling out of the hole on the opposite side from the one I had chosen.

Ida laughed and clapped her hands together. "Try another time."

I placed the turtle under the tub again and beat on the top.

"Which door?" she said.

This time I chose the one the turtle had come out before. After a few seconds the turtle came out a different hole.

"I guess I'm not much good at this game," I said.

I had no idea why she was having me do this. Perhaps it was some Indian game of chance or perhaps she was a little batty from living too long by herself.

"That little Reuben?" she said. "He did that seven times. Every

time he got it right. Every time *khéya* came out the hole on that side."
She pointed to the hole facing east.

"He's a good guesser," I said.

"No," she said. "He wasn't guessing. He was listening. *Khéya* was telling him where he would come out. *Khéya* was giving him a message."

She wheeled over right next to me. Her manner suddenly got very serious.

"Mr. Danton. Our people are not like yours. You look to the sky for everything. For your gods and angels. We look to the earth. She is the mother. All the animals. All the people. Everything. We all have that same mother. Some of our people feel that connection all the way back to where everything is the same. They can talk to everything else because they know the place where everything came from. Little Reuben is one of these. He can talk to *khéya*. *Khéya* can talk to him. *Khéya* was telling him where he was going."

BLOOD-COLORED STONE

Danton

Once Ida had decided to trust me, it was like the floodgates were loosed. I think my connection to Lillie had opened her heart to me.

She began telling me about her *uŋčí* and *uŋkáŋna* and how they had tried to protect the old ways by living in the new way. "That way no one noticed," she said. "You know, it was against the law to practice our religion. People were put in prison.

"*Uŋkáŋna* would travel over to the place of the red stone and dig it out and bring it back. *Wašíču* never knew he was making pipes for ceremonies. That's why he made these little *khéya*s and *tȟatȟáŋka*s. The *wašíču* thought they were just trinkets. They never knew about the *čhaŋnúŋpa*. Oh, *Uŋkáŋna* was a smart one." She giggled like a schoolgirl and rocked back into her chair with delight.

"Reach up and get one of those carvings, Mr. Danton," she said. "Any one."

I reached up and grabbed a little pipestone turtle off the shelf. It seemed an appropriate choice.

"*Khéya*," I said.

She grinned broadly and nodded her approval. "You speak good Dakota," she laughed. "Do you know about this red stone. This *čhaŋnúŋpa-íŋyaŋ*?"

"Not really. I know you make pipes out of it. I know it's sacred to you. Lillie told me a little bit about it."

"*Čhaŋnúŋpa-íŋyaŋ*. The blood-colored stone. The stone the Creator gave us. It comes from Minnesota where my people come from.

"The Creator made my people guardians of that place. It was given to us to look after for all the people. That place is sacred in our Indian way. The Creator made it. Men did not build it. It's not like your churches.

"After our war with that General Sibley we had to run from that place. But our heart was still there. My heart has always been there. Always I thought to go back there to live in the way of our ancestors. I thought to learn all the old ways and be a protector of the red stone. *Uŋčí* and *Uŋkáŋna* would teach me.

"But my life did not go that way. When I was still a young woman, just at the age to take a man, one of the windstorms came, one of the tornadoes. I was running to the house to get to the root cellar right under here. A fence post got lifted by the wind and hit me in the back. I was asleep for ten days. When I woke up I had no feeling in my legs. They put me in this chair. I never got back to that place of the red stone."

Her eyes were smiling. But you could see the sadness behind the smile.

"That must make you very sad," I said.

"Oh, for years I was sad. I wanted to be in that place. I wanted to serve Creator. But I grew old in this chair. I became an old woman. I had to lay that down. I had to find another peace. So I care for this house and the things that *Uŋčí* and *Uŋkáŋna* have left me. I think that is the task the Creator gave to me.

"When that little Levi showed me that piece of *čhaŋnúŋpa-íŋyaŋ* and told me of his grandfather's *čhaŋnúŋpa* breaking, my heart was like a bird in my chest. I thought, 'Maybe I still have a gift to give. I think that Lillie has sent these boys to me so I can help them with *čhaŋnúŋpa*. I think that Creator has called to me now to serve.'"

She reached her wrinkled hands toward me.

"Give me your hands, Mr. Danton."

She took my hands in a trembling grip.

"I do not know you. I do not know your heart. I only know Lillie, and Lillie has sent you to me. I can go nowhere. I must wait for what the Creator sends me. Creator has sent those boys to me and now he has sent you to me. He has sent you through Lillie.

"Lillie would never harm a child. All children live in her heart through the memory of her Joseph. If she sent you to me, it is because she trusts you. She wants me to help you help those boys."

She squeezed my hands tighter, as if claiming a promise from me.

"I will tell you now some things you won't understand. I will tell you because of Lillie.

"There are places where the spirit world touches the earth world. The earth is very thin there. Creator speaks there. The place of the red stone is one of these.

"The spirit is alive in that place. It is in the stone. The blood of all our people is in that stone. That is why it is the color that it is.

"You people think it is sacred just to us. But Creator does not work that way. It is sacred from the Creator, not from our minds.

"Those young boys — little Levi and Reuben — they think to go there. They think to get new stone for their grandfather. They think to help him get a new *čhaŋnúŋpa*.

"I feared to send them to that place. It is a long way and they are just little. This is *wašíču* country now and we Indian people are not wanted here. There is cruelty in the hearts of some *wašíču* toward us. We make them think of what they would like to forget.

"They know this is our land. They do not know it in their minds but they know it in their hearts. They do not like knowledge of the heart. They want things they can see, things they can touch, things they can change. They do not like things of the spirit that cannot be changed.

"They think if we are gone they will not have to listen to the voice that tells them this is our land. That is why they have made schools to change us. They think they can take the Indian out of us. They think if we forget who we are they will not have to remember who we are. They want to kill our spirit. They do not want to hear its voice.

"I do not think the *wašíču* will harm those boys. But they will not help them. And there may be cruel ones among them.

"I did not think it was good to send those boys to *Inyan Sa K'api*. I thought to hide them. But *khéya* kept pointing east. He kept pointing the sunrise way toward *Inyan Sa K'api* for little Reuben. He kept telling Reuben he must go that way.

"*Khéya* did not point that way for you. He tried to get away from you. He saw you are confused. He wanted to lead you away.

"But I talk to *khéya*. I tell him that Lillie has sent you. I tell him that the boys' mother has sent you. *Khéya* is one of the ancient ones. *Khéya* has the oldest knowledge.

"These are not easy things, Mr. Danton. They are not for *wašíču* ears. But I am telling you."

She let go of my hands and pointed to the tub.

"I want you to take *khéya*, now," she said. "Put him under the tub again. Go. Do it."

I had placed the turtle in the sink until I could take him back down to the gully. I retrieved him and put him under the tub.

"Now, sit back," she said. "You watch."

She whispered something toward the tub. She spoke softly and in a language I did not understand.

"Now, hit the top of the tub. Not hard. Just soft, so *khéya* knows you are there."

I did what she said. We sat for about a minute. Then slowly the turtle emerged from the tub. He came out the hole nearest the window. The hole facing east.

Twice more she made me do it. Twice more the turtle came out the hole to the east.

"Do you see, Mr. Danton? Do you?"

I looked at the little turtle perched on the edge of the table. I swear he was looking back at me.

MAGNETIC NORTH

Danton

I left Ida sitting in her wheelchair on the porch. She was waving at me with a hankie. She was smiling, but her eyes welled with tears. It's hard to leave someone when you know your presence has filled up their loneliness.

I backed out cautiously, making sure that I waved back and held up the little bag of *wagmíza-wasná* she had sent with me.

My heart was hurting for her, and I know she believed fervently in what she was saying, but I couldn't base my actions on a turtle crawling out from under a washtub.

Still, I had promised Ree that I would find her boys. And what Ida had said made sense, even if her logic came from a different world than mine. From what I knew of little Levi, trying to replace his grandfather's *čhaŋnúŋpa* was just the sort of thing he would attempt to do.

The sky was heavy and portentous as I turned back onto the gravel road. The light was getting sickly and green in that way I remembered just before storms back in the Midwest, when the whole sky seemed to be holding its breath.

I drove cautiously, keeping my eyes warily on the roiling mass of turbulent clouds and heavy, oppressive air. How different this was from the weather in the western part of the state, where even a hint of moisture had people coming out to their porches and staring expectantly, even prayerfully, toward the sky. Here, this sky spoke of an impending deluge that made me wonder if I should pull off the road and take cover.

But then, as quickly as they had arrived, the clouds dissipated, leaving barely a drop of moisture, and moved off, rumbling into the distance. It made me think of Karl-Martin's comment about these forces having a life of their own. It was hard not to feel that this storm was toying with us.

Would it toy with the boys, too, if it found them? I wondered. Or would it release its fury on them? How would they endure a blinding torrent of rain that came slashing sideways with a wind that would knock a grown man off his feet? Would they be able to find a place to hide? Would they find people who would help them? Or would they end up huddled somewhere in a cornfield, alone, afraid, and soaked to the bone?

These were boys used to the high plains where the air was clear and the land was arid and everything was governed by light and distance. On these prairies everything was close, heavy, and moist. It was not land that they understood.

I kept imagining the two of them running through ditches, holding hands in their big oversize clothes, earnestly trying to get to the place of the red stone under these alien skies, taking their guidance from a turtle, just as I was being asked to do. It seemed somewhere between cruel and insane.

But Ida had made me doubt my own thinking, just as old Lone Dog had done when he had told me the Creator had called me to be Reuben's protector. One moment she had seemed like a comforting, grandmotherly presence; the next, like someone from a different world with a different understanding that might, just might, reflect a deeper awareness than my own.

I needed to get my bearings, both psychologically and physically. And the Steinbachs were the only people I could think of who could give them to me. Karl-Martin knew this country and he had somehow managed to make an uneasy peace between his white way of understanding and this Native world of portents, presages, and messages from unseen places. And Lillie knew the Indian hearts of these young boys. It was worth the lost time to have them help me navigate these unfamiliar physical and spiritual landscapes I had entered.

I ran my thumb over the smooth back of the little stone turtle Ida had given me. After all, why did I find it so strange that the actions of a turtle could offer me guidance in how to find the boys? Didn't we place our faith in little round dials that gave us directions by pointing arrows at some supposed magnetic stone somewhere by the north pole?

All of this was washing around in my mind as I made the six-mile drive back to the Steinbachs' place.

Coming down the long gravel road from the east, I had a clearer view of their farmstead in all its stark loneliness. If Ida's house sitting on that rise had somehow seemed commanding, the Steinbach home, slightly down in a hollow, seemed barely to be surviving. It sat forlornly on a patch of scrubby ground amid the great dying fields, surrounded by a tangle of brambles and bushes that grew untended and unkempt right up to the porch and the walls of the house.

Like all the rural farmhouses, it was set back in a copse of trees. But the Steinbach copse had none of that fine geometry of the more prosperous farms — no consciously planted shelter band of trees around the perimeter, no gracious manicured backyard that spoke of picnics and family gatherings. The house just stood there, faded and buckled, on its dusty piece of ground, with its falling-down barn and random pieces of rusted machinery poking up through the weeds. If houses had characters, this was a house that had given up. I could not help but think that the death of their son had been the death of their hope, and that they now just survived, carrying on their lives inside a fragile shrine of abandonments and memories.

I tried to banish those thoughts from my mind. But soon enough they were banished on their own when I saw a black sedan parked in front of the Steinbach home. As I got closer, a chill ran through me. It was Two Finger's old government-issue Plymouth. What he was doing there, and how he had found the Steinbachs, I had no idea.

With my heart beating hard, I reversed course and drove back up the road to a cutoff and parked out of sight and waited.

After about a half hour, I saw the Plymouth drive off.

I drove quickly out of my hiding spot and pulled up in the Steinbachs' yard.

Steinbach was standing on the front porch with his hands in his pockets, staring at the sky. Mister Bones was lying at his side, feet splayed out in four directions and head on the floor.

"Well, well, Mr. Danton," he said. "Welcome back. I figured you'd be leaving directly from Ida's."

I was in no mood for small talk.

"That car that was just here. Was that Two Finger?"

"Yes, indeed. Mr. Darwin Bazile. Your boss."

"He's not my boss anymore."

"He seems to think he is. But I can see why you wouldn't want him to be. He's an unpleasant man."

Steinbach stroked Mister Bones's flank with the toe of his boot. "Mister Bones didn't think much of him either," he said with a laugh. "Wouldn't let him past the porch." At the mention of his name, the old dog thumped his tail and rolled on his back, exposing his belly.

I didn't share Steinbach's casual indifference to Two Finger's visit. "What was he doing here?" I asked.

Steinbach kept his attention on the sky. He was obviously more concerned with the weather than with Two Finger. "I thought that one was going to open up this morning," he said, and shook his head in resignation.

"Yes, but Two Finger."

He turned his attention back to me. "Yes. Your Mr. Two Finger. Well, he was looking for the boys, just like you. And for you, too."

"But how'd he find you?"

"You'd left your name with the sheriff. Not always a good idea around here. They must have sent word back to the reservation. Government is government."

I had forgotten about my brief stop at the local sheriff's office. It had never occurred to me that by leaving my name I was leaving a trail. But I had never expected that there was anyone who would try to follow me.

"You didn't tell him anything, did you?"

He smiled almost patronizingly. "If I don't want something to be known, it doesn't get known."

He stepped past me and walked toward the barn. Mister Bones limped after him. I followed closely behind.

"Did he threaten you? Try to intimidate you?"

"Do I look like someone who's easily intimidated?"

Steinbach pulled open the barn door and walked into the dark, musty interior. Far in the back was an old DeSoto half covered by a tarp. The hood was up and an array of tools were lined out on a rag draped over the fender. He walked over and began tinkering with something in the engine.

"I'm sorry to keep pushing on this, Karl-Martin," I said. "I need to figure out what this is all about. You don't know that man. You don't want him getting his hands on those boys."

"Here, hold this flashlight," he said. "Shine it on the carburetor." He adjusted something with a screwdriver.

His relative unconcern was infuriating. "Did he tell you anything?" I asked. "Why he was here? This makes no sense."

He tapped on the fuel pump with the end of a wrench and pulled on some wires and hoses. "He said he'd never lost a grab, and he wasn't going to lose one now."

I was feeling almost frantic. I was not worried about Two Finger causing me any trouble personally. I was never going to work for him again. But whatever had compelled him to drive halfway across a state in search of the boys made me nervous and frightened. Hatred is a tenacious thing, and Two Finger was full of hate.

"I wouldn't worry too much about him finding the boys," Steinbach said, tightening up a radiator clamp. "Folks around here don't open up much to someone they don't know. He's not going to get anything from anybody. And I bought you some time, anyway."

"How's that?"

He pulled his head out from under the hood and wiped his hands on an oily rag.

"I told him that you had a lead on the boys, that they had hopped a freight and were heading for Nebraska to the Poncas. My guess is he's heading that way. He's already out of his jurisdiction. I don't think he wants the trouble of crossing state lines. But if he gets to the Poncas, they'll see that government car and figure him out right away. He'll be blood sport for them. By the time they're done with him he'll either be heading home with his tail between his legs or chasing off to Texas convinced that the boys are heading for the southern border."

He gave a hearty laugh and threw the rag on top of the air filter.

This didn't explain the reason behind Two Finger's presence, but it did give me some reassurance. I knew Two Finger's ways, and he was dogged but not creative. If he thought the boys were headed to Nebraska, he was headed to Nebraska, too. And it sounded like the Poncas knew how to play cat and mouse with the best of them.

This just increased my resolve to find the boys. I appreciated Karl-Martin's confidence, but he didn't realize what we were dealing with. I could easily imagine Two Finger physically assaulting the boys or beating them bloody with a belt if he managed to find them. His behavior knew very few limits when he was angry, and driving a hundred miles in this heat would have put him into an angry state of mind.

"Listen, Karl-Martin, I know I seem pushy about this. But I'm really scared for those boys. You don't know Two Finger. He's mean. Dark mean."

"Probably true. But he's also lazy," Karl-Martin said. "I could tell that just from those few minutes with him. I told him if you got those boys, you were heading right back to the reservation. He was sweating and wheezing and mumbling and cursing. Said the humidity around here was driving him crazy. Couldn't wait to get home. A couple of dead ends and he'll head back west as sure as you're born. And I set him up to get nothing but dead ends."

He picked up the mug of coffee he had brought with him. "You've got to calm down."

He waved his hand upward toward the unsettled sky. "Your Two Finger is the least of the boys' worries. Did you see that storm that passed over?"

"Yes. It scared me for the boys."

"Scared me for them, too. One of these days this sky is going to crack and all hell is going to break loose. Those boys are smart, but if that sky opens up, doesn't take much for those creeks and gullies to be rushing. Pick the wrong place to hide and it can take you with it. I think you should stop worrying about Two Finger and start worrying more about those little fellows out there on their own."

He shone the flashlight deep into the engine. Every surface was completely covered in dust. "Now, help me get this thing running and tell me what brought you back here from Ida's. I figured you'd be off down the road after the guys and we wouldn't see you again."

He tapped on the starter with the end of a wrench. "Come on. We can talk and work. Feels good to have four hands in an engine again. You know anything about cars?"

I could feel the time slipping through my fingers, but Karl-Martin was not about to be pushed.

I quickly checked the condition of a couple of radiator hoses and tested the tension on the fan belt. "I took an old Hudson Terraplane down to the frame when I was a kid," I said. "And we Michiganders — we grow up with cars like kids around here grow up with tractors. Yeah, I know them pretty well."

Steinbach patted the fender of the car. "This was going to be my project with Joseph. It was going to be his car. I'm not much for mechanics. Figured we'd learn together." It was the first time he'd spoken his son's name or even brought him seriously into the conversation.

"When those boys came through, it got me to thinking. Thought I'd give it another try. Hasn't been run for a while. Not having much luck, though."

"Let me give it a shot," I said.

I removed the distributor cap, cleaned and adjusted the points, pulled out and re-gapped the plugs, and primed the carburetor. Frustrated as I was by Steinbach's cavalier attitude toward the boys and Two Finger, it felt good to be getting my hands dirty in a car engine again. And it was a chance to give something back to Karl-Martin for his hospitality.

"Get in and turn the key and pump the gas," I said. He gave me a thumbs-up and slipped into the driver's seat.

With Karl-Martin working the accelerator and me holding the choke open with a pencil, we got the dusty old car to spit and pop to life, filling the barn with clouds of noxious blue smoke.

"Been a while, eh?" I said.

"Thought she was a goner."

Mister Bones obviously had some old dog memories of better days. He had climbed arthritically into the passenger seat and assumed the regal dog position that I remembered so well from my many drives with Sweet Girl.

"Dogs and cars," I said.

"Like bread and butter. We should take old Bessie out for a spin. Give Mister Bones a chance to relive some memories." He started to say something else, but then changed his mind. "Shut the hood and let's see what we've got. We'll get you on the road soon enough."

We opened the barn door wide. The old horse snorted and bucked in its stall, unaccustomed to the rumbling and the cloud of blue smoke that was filling her stable area.

Karl-Martin backed the DeSoto out into the yard and we went sputtering and popping down the road until the engine smoothed out and the car began to purr with a pleasing rumble. Karl-Martin rolled down his window and I reached over from the back seat and rolled down the front passenger window so Mister Bones could stick his head out. Karl-Martin was laughing a big, hearty laugh, quite unlike anything I had heard from him before. It was good to see something approaching joy coming out of him.

"The fields may be dying, but the open road is still there," he said. "You're a lucky man, Mr. Danton."

"Depends on the day and where you're standing," I said.

He tapped some private rhythm on the dashboard and hummed quietly under his breath.

"Feels damn good. Now, tell me about your visit with Ida. What brought you back here rather than setting off direct to find the boys?"

I wasn't quite sure where to begin. I was embarrassed to tell him about the turtle and the washtub.

"Well, like you warned me, she's a talker," I said. "I learned a lot about her and her people. And a few things about your wife."

Steinbach laughed. "Yeah, she and Lillie go way back. She's a strange one, that Ida. Not a bad one. Just a strange one. Got a lot of the old ways in her."

"And she makes good cookies," I said.

"Ah, yes. Her *wagmíza-wasná*. Get them every time I go over there. I try to help her out as best I can. I wish she'd leave that house. Move into town. That's no place for a woman in a wheelchair. Especially in the winter. But she's doing it for her grandma and grandpa. No arguing with that."

He fiddled with the heater knobs, trying to see what still worked. "So, what did she tell you that brought you back here?"

I decided there was no sense in being evasive. I had to tell him about the tub and the turtles and how she believed that one had counseled her to send the boys off in search of the pipestone and that another had counseled her to send me after them.

"Welcome to my world," he laughed. "What do you think about that, Bones? Would you follow a turtle?" Mister Bones licked Steinbach's hand.

Seeing that old gray muzzle was like a knife in my heart. I might not be able to communicate with turtles, but there wasn't a day gone by when I didn't talk to the spirit of Sweet Girl and feel her presence sitting next to me in the seat of my truck.

I reached over the seat and tousled the old dog's head. "Turtles I don't understand. Dogs, yes." Bones turned back and looked at me with his sad brown eyes. He licked my hand and laid his head against it.

Though I was wary of taking instructions from a turtle, I was more than happy to get my consolation from a dog.

MISTER BONES

Danton

L illie suggested I spend the night, then start out in search of the boys in the morning. I was hesitant because I had no certainty that Two Finger was actually headed off toward Nebraska. Steinbach, though insightful, was at heart a trusting soul, more inclined to the spiritual than the practical. Two Finger might be lazy, but he was cunning. He could easily have been playing Steinbach. I didn't want him to have too much of a head start if he truly did manage to get on the trail of the boys. And with every passing minute the boys were getting farther away.

Nonetheless, I agreed to stay. There was little I could accomplish by starting out just as the day was waning. I would be more likely to miss the boys in the shadows of twilight than in the bright light of morning. Besides, a cup of coffee, a bit of breakfast, and a good night's sleep would do wonders for me.

"You need to trust what Ida told you," Lillie said.

"I'm willing to listen to a turtle," I answered, "but I'm not willing to move like one."

She gave me a hard look, but then cracked into a smile.

Before dinner she had gently berated me when I had suggested that it was cruel to send two little boys off across this country on their own, even if it was for noble purposes.

"This isn't all in our hands, Mr. Danton," she said. "Maybe if you paid more attention to the things of the spirit and treated them with more respect, you would have more faith that things were going to

173

work out." Like Ree, she was a strong woman who had no difficulty holding her ground.

We shared a pleasant evening meal of sweet corn, pork chops, and fresh milk. As Steinbach had said, though they were poor, they lived rich.

We ate with that measured formality that characterized all their interactions. They began with their brief Lakota invocation and treated the meal almost sacramentally, keeping their voices low and passing the food with mindful attentiveness.

After we ate, we all retired to the living room. I was pleased that Lillie had decided to join us. It felt like a compliment to me, and I was happy to look upon it in that way. Mister Bones followed after us, excited to be part of a social event.

"You've taken kind of a shine to old Bones, haven't you?" Karl-Martin said.

"If it's a dog, I take a shine to it," I said. "And Mister Bones is pretty special."

"He's still got some moves," Karl-Martin said. "Want to see?"

"Of course."

He took a small piece of pork chop he had carried from the table and held it over the old dog's head.

"Testify," he said. This was Mister Bones's cue to sit up on his hind legs like a prairie dog and bark.

Mister Bones was game, and obviously had once been able to perform this little parlor trick. But now he could only make a feeble effort to lift his front paws off the ground before giving up and emitting a few earnest yips.

"Oh, Karl-Martin," Lillie said. "Leave old Mister Bones alone."

"I gave up studying to be a preacher," Karl-Martin laughed. "Someone's got to carry on the tradition."

She shook her head in disgust. "You *wašíču* and your dogs."

"Better than turning them into soup."

She cocked her head and give him that same hard stare she had given me. This was obviously familiar territory for them.

"Okay, Mister Bones," Karl-Martin said, tousling the fur on the old dog's head. "You gave it a try."

He threw the piece of pork chop in Mister Bones's direction and the old dog limped after it, wagging his tail frantically.

"Does my heart good to see that old hound," I said. "I think about my old Sweet Girl every day. She's mostly the reason I lit out for the territories. Everywhere I looked I kept seeing her ghost."

The minute I said it I regretted my words.

Lillie and Karl-Martin shared a quick glance, but they let it pass.

"What was she like, old Sweet Girl?" Karl-Martin asked, probably more to cover my faux pas than out of any real interest. I should have changed the subject, but this was the first chance I'd had to talk about her since her passing.

"She wasn't much of a looker," I said, conjuring up an image of the old girl in my mind. "She started out mostly black as a pup, but just got grayer and grayer as she got older. In the end her whole muzzle and all the fur around her eyes was white. Made her look like a raccoon. I don't know what breed she was. I thought she might be part shepherd with a bunch of other stuff mixed in for good measure. In the end she was just a dog."

"The best kind."

"Oh, but her eyes. She had big beautiful eyes. Brown ones. A lot like Bones's. Full of soul. She was one of those dogs that was always right where you were emotionally. Not much of a problem solver, but, boy, could she find you when you were feeling down."

"Hard losing her, I'll bet."

"The hardest." The lump was rising in my throat. I kept seeing the image of us on that last walk, when she had fallen down and looked at me with those eyes that said, "Help me," and I had suddenly realized that I hadn't been taking her for walks, she had been going for walks with me because she thought she was supposed to.

I got down on the floor next to Mister Bones and put my face right next to his, as much to hide the tears welling in my eyes as anything else. Bones looked at me with a wise, doleful look and thumped his tail before nuzzling up against me. I could not believe how good it felt to feel a dog next to me again.

"Old Bones was a rez dog," Karl-Martin said. "We think he's mostly Lab. Some kind of shepherd in there, too. Had a snout full of quills when we found him. I'm surprised he stayed with us after we pliered them out. But it never happened again. He's a smart one. Learns fast. Want to see?"

"Sure," I said. If there was anything that could keep my mind off Sweet Girl and the boys, it was focusing my attention on a dog.

Lillie was shaking her head. She had seen this before.

"Come on, Bones," Karl-Martin said. "Time to go out." He led the old dog to the front screen door and let him out, then latched it with a little eye hook.

He grabbed another scrap of pork chop and set it on the floor just inside the screen door. Mister Bones's eyes got wide and he nudged the edge of the screen door with his nose. Once he realized it wasn't going to open, he limped off the porch and disappeared around the house. Soon I heard him at the back door, pawing and scratching and trying to get in. But Karl-Martin had latched that, too.

In a few seconds he reappeared at the front door and began nudging it again. The door rattled but remained latched.

Mister Bones nosed it another time. Again it moved but remained latched.

He pushed it over and over with his nose until it set up a rhythm and the hook began bouncing in its eye latch, finally jumping up and down enough to disengage.

When Mister Bones heard the hook fall free from the latch he pushed the door again so it moved enough for him to snout it open. He pulled at it with his paw, put his nose in the crack, made his way in, and grabbed the piece of meat.

I had to laugh. "Sweet Girl would have just sat outside the screen door staring at me like, 'Why are you doing this to me?'"

Steinbach smiled and patted the old dog's back.

"Like I said, Bones was a rez dog. Resourceful. Scrappy. Can't put anything over on him, can I, Bones?" Mister Bones thumped his tail several times and returned to chewing contentedly on the chunk of meat he had retrieved.

Steinbach and Lillie exchanged glances. Steinbach nodded slightly.

"I've got a suggestion for you, Mr. Danton," Lillie said. "Maybe you should take him with you."

I was stunned. "You mean, take Mister Bones along when I look for the boys?"

"He could come in handy. He's smarter than you in a lot of ways," she smiled. "And you could use some looking after yourself."

"She's right," Karl-Martin said. "The boys and Bones are really connected. No reason for a couple of Indian kids to trust you. You're just another white man who is trying to catch them, especially since you were at their house with Two Finger. But if they see Mister Bones, well, that could make a big difference. Besides, it will give you some company. Seems like you could use it."

Mister Bones looked up at me as if he concurred.

"Probably a good idea," I said. "You sure?"

"Take him up to bed with you. See how it goes."

"Come on, Bones," I said, getting up off the floor. "We've got a long day ahead of us. Time to get some sleep." The old dog groaned and stood up and followed me up the stairs to the boys' room. He spent the night wheezing and flubbering at the foot of my bed. They were just ordinary dog sounds, but they were music to my ears.

Journey

HÁSAPA MAN

Levi

I did not want to be scared. I never saw Grandpa scared. I wanted to have bravery. I wanted to have *wóohitike*. I wanted it in my heart, not just in my body.

Reuben was looking at me. He knew we were lost.

"Let's go into this field," I said.

The bag was heavy. I wanted to sit down.

We went to the field. There was corn all around us. No one could see us. Reuben sat down. He drew circles in the dirt with a stick.

I thought to make him not worried. I took some cookies from the bag. They were the ones from Miss Ida.

"Here. She gave us cookies."

"She was turtle woman," Reuben said. "I like the turtle woman."

He reached in his pocket.

He had the *khéya* from the tub.

"Did you take that?" I asked. Grandpa does not like thieves.

"She told me to. She said she gave him her spirit. She said I should listen to him."

I felt good then. Reuben does not know how to lie.

He held *khéya* up. *Khéya* was kicking with his legs.

"You be careful with *khéya*," I said. "*Khéya* always needs water."

He made his pinch face. "I know that," he said.

He put his face next to *khéya* and said words in his own talk. *Khéya* pulled his head in and his feet, too.

We drank water from the thermos jar Mister Steinbach had given me. It made me feel big again to give Reuben water from Mister Steinbach's jar. When something comes from someone's hand, it has their power in it.

Reuben drank a lot. He poured some on the ground near *khéya*, making mud from the dirt. *Khéya* dug in it.

"I like to make *khéya* happy," he said. He pushed his head into my chest and rubbed it against me. "Like you make me happy." He smiled at me really big.

I felt strong love for Reuben. But I felt strong fear, too.

"Reuben, I need to talk to you, serious-like."

He was talking to *khéya*.

"Reuben, you need to listen. There is something I don't like about this sky. It has anger in it."

Reuben wasn't listening. He was making his talk to *khéya*. I felt to shake him, to make him listen. Someone always took care of him. He never had to listen if he didn't want to. I needed him to listen.

"Reuben, this is not like home where Grandpa and Momma do everything. I know you can hear me. We need to get to the *čhaŋnúŋpa* place. I don't know where we are."

I was close to crying. I did not want Reuben to see me cry. I am his *ciye*, his big brother. I have to teach him the right way. To show fear-crying is not the right way.

He would not listen. He was talking his *khéya* talk.

I lay down on the ground and put my head other-facing so he didn't see. The corn was tall. I could hear him talking.

I fell asleep. I could hear dream words. They sounded like a man voice. It did not sound like an Indian. I opened my eyes. Reuben was not there. Neither was *khéya*. I heard the words. They were from outside the corn. They were not in a dream.

I crawled through the corn toward the words.

Reuben was standing by the side of the road. He was talking to a man all dressed in a jacket kind of coat that rich white people wear when they get dressed up. Except that this man wasn't a white man. His skin was dark-like, like almost black.

Reuben was showing him *khéya*.

Reuben heard me. He waved his hand to have me come to him. He was serious, excited-like.

"Levi, come here!" he said. "Come down where I am!"

I stayed back in the corn. I did not want to talk to this man. I did not know if black skin men were like white skin men. I had seen pictures of these men in magazines, like at Mister Steinbach's house. One time one came to the boarding school to talk to the priests. I did not know if this man had to do with those priests.

The man was dressed like you see in pictures. He had on clothes not for working, with the pants and coat the same, both the same color and shiny.

He saw me, too.

"It's okay," he said. His voice was deep. It had a smile in it. "I won't hurt you."

He had a car, shiny like his clothes. I did not know how a car could have shine with all the dust.

Reuben ran up to me. He pulled on my sleeve. "I waved, like Miss Ida said," he said. He was proud to have done what Miss Ida had told him. He was thinking to be like a grown-up.

I wanted to be angry with him. He should have stayed in the corn.

I thought to pull him back in the corn, to make us run away from this man. Reuben did not want to move. "I waved like Miss Ida said." He kept saying it.

The man had a big smile. It was a kind type of smile. He did not come toward us. "Nice looking turtle," he said.

Reuben ran back to him and held up *khéya*. He made his turtle sound.

The man made to have me come down to where he was. He did not show anger. I went down to him.

"Just stopped to see if you needed any help," he said.

"No, sir," I said. "We're fine." I stood tall like Mister Steinbach said. I did not want to show fear.

"We're not running away," I said.

"That's good," he said. "It's not good to run away."

His smile got big, like he was seeing inside of me.

He was not tall like Mister Steinbach. Mister Steinbach was like sticks. This man was more square-like.

"We're getting stone for Grandpa's *čhaŋnúŋpa*," Reuben said. "Miss Ida said we should go to the red stone place. She was from there. Levi says we're lost." He was trying to be big, to be like me, to show he could talk in the big person way. I wanted him to be quiet. It is not good to say things to people you don't know.

"Who's Miss Ida?" the man asked. His eyes were smiling, they were not hiding. I could see Reuben being proud for talking. "And you're Levi?"

"Yes, sir," I said.

I wanted to stop Reuben from talking. He was saying too much. When you don't know someone, you only go as far as their questions.

"Miss Ida, she has a big house," Reuben said. "It's down there." He pointed backways down the road. "Down that way."

I looked hard at Reuben to make him stop. He didn't care.

"Miss Ida sounds nice," the man said. "I know that red stone place where that stone comes from. I go by it pretty regular."

The sky was burning. I thought to get out of the heat.

"We have to go, Mister," I said.

"As do I. I could take you a ways down the road, if you like."

I did not know this man. I did not feel trust for him. Momma had said only to give trust to someone who has earned it.

"No. We can walk. Come on, Reuben."

Reuben was still waving at the man.

"Wait," the man said. "You're scared of me, I know. You probably don't never see a colored man much. But I want to help you. Really. That's all I want. Let me get out of my singing clothes. Then I'll help you if you like. You think about it."

I heard kindness in his words, not tricks. I tried to tell his eyes like Grandpa taught me. Mostly in white man's eyes at the bottom you can see anger or sadness. I couldn't see the bottom of this man's eyes. I thought to listen more.

The man took clothes from his car. They were like soft clothes, not shiny. He went to the corn. Reuben took *khéya* from his pocket. He put *khéya* on the ground. *Khéya* crawled toward the car.

He pulled on my sleeve. "Levi! Levi!" he said. "*Khéya!*"

He got on the ground behind *khéya*. He crawled behind him. *Khéya* crawled fast toward the car.

"*Khéya* likes this *hásapa* man," he said.

The sky was getting angry-like. It was in my eyes with dust, and my mouth.

"There is a bad thing in this day," Reuben said. He got in the car. He would not get out.

I thought to Momma's words that I had to protect him. I got in the car with him. The man came back. I thought to Grandpa's words that a Lakota man always gave gifts. I took the last cookie and Mister Steinbach's thermos. I held them over the seat to the man.

He took them. He ate the cookie and drank the water. I felt proud. I was doing it the Lakota way. I was being a man.

HALFWAY TO A FRIEND

Brother James

I had just been daydreaming and driving, tapping out a tune on the steering wheel, when that little fella jumped out in front of me and started waving. Gave me a heck of a start.

Truth is, I was pretty well lost. These straight-line gravel roads all look the same, and if you ain't paying attention you can find yourself in the middle of nowhere with no idea where the next somewhere might be.

Not much to worry about, though. All these roads go somewhere. You just got to keep driving till you come to one with a number or a name. Bound to happen soon enough.

It was another day of hell heat, hot enough to make the devil sweat. Skies with no mercy. Sun beating down so hot I burned my hand on the door handle getting into the car.

Still and all, I was feeling good. The show had been a hit. I'd had those people singing and clapping. Doesn't always happen that way. Farm folk can be a tough audience. Especially the men. They think their hands are for working, not for clapping. But the morning shows are mostly women anyway. Men are already out in the field. No time for fluffery when there's crops to be tended. But the women — singing spirituals is near on to praying for them, and in a summer like this, praying is what everybody needs.

This morning I'd hit it just right. All them farm ladies coming up after the show grabbing my hands. "Oh, Brother James, thank you, thank you." Did my heart good. Not many smiles around here these days, and if I can do my part, well, that's what I figure the good Lord put me on earth to do.

Still and all, I didn't want to stick around any more than I had to. I got me a show tomorrow a hundred miles up the road and lots of folks don't like renting a room to a colored man, even if he's in town to put some joy in their hearts. Best to say my goodbyes, pick up my pay, and head off to the next stop and try to get settled in before the sun goes down. Most white folks got good hearts but some of them got small minds. If trouble's out there looking for you, there's a better chance it's going to find you after dark.

So I was just kicking up gravel, looking for asphalt, belting out a verse of "Ol' Man River" and feeling the coins jingling in my pocket when that little Indian fellow come running out of that cornfield jumping and waving.

I thought he might be in trouble. "What's a little tyke like that doing out here in this hell heat?" I thought. But he's smiling and waving and looking happy as anything. If he'd have been in town I'd have thought he was trying to get me to stop to buy some lemonade or some such. But this was a cornfield halfway to nowhere, not some card table on someone's front lawn.

So I stopped and stepped out. Whatever he was doing, if he needed some help I was likely the only person who was going to give it to him. I hadn't seen another car on the road for close to half an hour.

I swear the little fellow's eyes just about popped out of his head when he first saw me. I don't think he'd ever seen a colored man before, but that wasn't his fault. Indian folk kept with their own around here just like we colored folk did. Not much cause to do otherwise if you wanted to stay out of trouble.

That look on his face near got me to laughing. I think if I'd have jumped at him and said "Boo," he'd have died on the spot. But I wanted to help him, not scare him. He was just a little tyke, couldn't have been more than six or seven. I knew there had to be a story there somewhere. Unless something really bad is going on, you don't find a boy that young out alone on the side of the road.

"Hey, little fellow," I said. "What you doing out here? You need some help?"

He looked back to the cornfield, like he was thinking about bolting back into it. If he had, that would have been the end of it. A farmer finding a colored man rooting around in his cornfield isn't going to take kindly to it, no matter what kind of story comes along with it.

But the boy didn't bolt. He was a curious sort more than a frightened sort. He was as much wondering as to what I was about as I was about him. I waved at him like he had waved at me, figuring it was maybe some kind of Indian signal.

He thought about it for a second, then waved back.

"I'm Brother James," I said. "How you doing?"

He didn't say nothing.

"Come on, I'm not going to hurt you," I said.

Folks talk about us coloreds' eyes getting wide, they ain't never seen any eyes wider than that little fella's.

"You never seen anyone like me before, have you?"

He shook his head.

"Come on, I ain't no ghost. I just want to help you out if you need helping. No good reason for a boy to be jumping out of a cornfield in the middle of this heat. You must have been waving for something."

He wrinkled his nose and took a little turtle out of his pocket and held it toward me straightaway. Made no sense, but kids got their own reasons.

"Nice looking turtle," I said.

He put it on the ground on its back. Thing squirmed and twisted until he flipped himself over. Made the little guy grin like he'd just showed something to me. Still didn't say a word.

That's when I saw the other boy. He was just peeping out of the corn, right on the edge, ready to run back in if he didn't like what he saw. He looked a little older, but not by much. Still just a boy.

"Hey, fella," I said, "Come on down."

He didn't have that "I ain't never seen no Black man" look on his face, like the littler guy. He was more thinking he was looking at trouble and trying to figure out how much of it there was.

"I don't mean you no harm, fella," I said. "Just stopped to see if I could be of any help. Your little brother here — he's your brother, right? — he's been showing me your turtle. No more turtles around here than Indians and colored folks. Looks like all of us are a long way from home."

The boy stepped forward. He was doing a lot of measuring. The wind was picking up. Starting to carry the dust. Hard weather to figure, but nothing good in it.

"We're not running away," the older boy said.

I near broke out laughing. If ever I seen kids with runaway written all over them, these boys was it.

"That's good," I said. "Ain't good to run away."

The little one said something about his grandpa and a pipe. He was mostly just chattering. Something about a Miss Ida and going to the pipestone place.

"I've got to change," I said. "These are my singing clothes. But when I'm done you got a ride wherever you're going."

I went in the car and got my driving clothes. "Going into the corn to change. You can sit in the car if you want." I left the door open as an invite.

I didn't know what I'd see when I came back. As likely they'd be gone as in the car. Folks have to take their own measure of a situation.

The sky was starting to act up, blowing with a hot wind, strong enough to make the corn rattle. The dust was rising again, too. Birds were moving, nervous in the face of things. Change was coming too fast.

When I got back, the boys was in the car. Both in the back seat. The little one was holding his turtle. The older one was holding a cookie and a thermos. He handed them over the seat to me, without saying a word.

I took the thermos and took a big swig. When someone is willing to share a drink with a colored man, you're halfway to having a friend.

EMPTY SKY

Danton

These dirt roads can wear you down if you drive them too fast. Dust clouds rising, stones pinging against the undercarriage, bugs splattering against the windshield — just mile after mile of lonely gravel with wilted crops stretching off to forever. Thirsty country with pain written in every field.

If I was going to find these boys, luck was going to have to be on my side, and luck has never been my close companion. But what was I to do? I had to hope that all these various messages and powers that Ida and old Lone Dog had talked about would magically tell the nose of my pickup which road to choose every time I came to a crossroads. And all the time, knowing that Two Finger might be out there, a couple of section lines over, making choices of his own, and perhaps with more success.

I might have been feeling hopeless and depressed if it hadn't been for old Mister Bones sitting by my side, sniffing the air through the open window. If he wasn't such a great dog, it would have felt like a betrayal of Sweet Girl's memory to have him in her seat. But he was as comfortable as an old shoe, and almost as worn out, with tufts of hair missing and a chunk out of his left ear. Seeing him with that "happy dog in a truck" smile somehow seemed just right. It made me think Sweet Girl would have approved.

"You going to help me find those boys, Bones?" I asked.

Bones thumped his tail twice and stuck his snout further out the window, making his jowls flubber and his ears flap in the wind. The old fellow was fully in his element.

The sun was moving toward noon, and the air was thick with a breathless haze. From the moisture in the air, it was hard to imagine that drought had clasped its hands around the throat of this whole country. But all that moisture was in the atmosphere. None was congealing into the great prairie thunderstorms that Steinbach and all the other farmers were so desperately awaiting. It truly was, as Steinbach had said, as if the sky was toying with them.

The road passed over a few drainage ditches and culverts. All were brown and empty, devoid of water. The corn on either side of the road was brittle and stunted, and the rows of soybeans and wheat were colorless and pale. Where cattle and horses were out in the fields, they stood listlessly in place, as if waiting for release from the oppressive heat that was weighing down on every human and animal and blade of grass for miles around. I watched for clouds, for portents of rain. But the sky was empty.

The sun sat like a hazy orb in the back of the lifeless, colorless sky.

I would have closed the windows and endured the heat if Mister Bones hadn't been having such a good time. I had come to hate the high summer heat back in West River. It scorched you and burned you, but you could escape it by retreating to a patch of shade. This heat boiled you and admitted of no escape. How, I wondered, were those two little fellows surviving?

Before I had left Ida's, she had made it very clear that she expected me to somehow protect the boys on their journey, but not to interfere.

"This is for them to do," she said. "But *khéya* also pointed you to the east. You are meant to protect them like a shield." This was much the same thing old Lone Dog had said to me, and it unnerved me.

"How am I supposed to do that if I can't help them?" I asked.

"You will know when it's time," she said.

This heat had me praying that the time was coming soon, and that I was not going to be too late.

NO LIE INSIDE OF HIM

Brother James

It was hard to figure what I had in the back seat.

I checked them out in the mirror, all sitting up straight, kicking the seat with their heels, feet not even touching the floor. I knew what I was seeing, I just didn't know why I was seeing it. I had run away at twelve, and if you think being an Indian kid on the run in South Dakota in 1950 is hard, try being a little Black boy in Sioux Falls in 1935, begging and shining shoes and stealing now and then, and calling home anywhere you could bed down for the night without being seen.

These boys wasn't afraid of me, not in the least. But they weren't doing no talking, either. The older one had manners. He'd been civilized in some fashion. He kept watching real close. "Taking my measure," my daddy called it. The little one, well he was a different sort. He didn't have no distance between his thoughts and what he did. He kept reaching up and touching my hair and saying something that sounded like "Tatanka. Tatanka."

"You do what you have to do, boy," I said. "Take your time and figure it out in your own way." He was fairly climbing over the seat to get to my face and my hair.

I could see his brother was upset. "Don't pay it no mind," I said. "Your brother just lives right up in the front of his feelings. Ain't nothing wrong with that. Kind of refreshing, actually. Folks around here see a colored man, they put on their smiles and pull way back. You got to read them to know what they're thinking. No such issue with your brother. He ain't got no lie inside of him."

The little guy rubbed his hand on my face, like trying to rub off the color like it was paint. "Nope," I said. "This is the way the man upstairs made me."

He put his arm next to my arm, trying to figure out the color. His mind was jumping around like a prairie dog.

Still, I couldn't pull a word out of the older one. He was the one I wanted to get talking. The little one, he was saying words, but the pieces didn't fit together. There was grandpas and pipes and butterflies and freight trains, but they never added up to nothing. And, to be frank, there was something a little off about him. The older one, he was the one with the story.

Sometimes the best way to get someone talking is to put your own stuff out there first. I'd been where this older fellow was, and if he was as smart as I was thinking he was, you weren't going to trick him into talking just by hoping to hook onto something that interested him. You were going to need to get his trust.

Only one thing that I ever knew that took the suspicion out of someone, and that was music. So right off I started singing "Ol' Man River" without saying a word to explain. I had just sung it that morning and my voice was feeling good. Oh, I blasted it out there, filling that old Studebaker loud enough to shake the roof.

The older boy, he didn't say nothing. He just watched, but he was watching hard. He'd been looking out the window, watching the road shimmer in the heat. Now he was looking straight at me.

The younger boy, he stopped all his touching and rubbing and stared at me like I just come down from outer space. His jaw dropped open and he stood up on the floor in back and put his head up close to me, maybe six inches, like he was trying to figure out where my voice come from. I started in with "Swing Low, Sweet Chariot," loud as I could do it, my voice coming from way down inside. His eyes were like to pop out of his head.

"Yep, started singing when I was about your age," I said, like I was talking to myself, more like musing. I didn't want them to think they had to answer. "Had to run away from home. My daddy, well, he loved the bottle more than he loved me. Used to chase after me with a belt buckle. My momma, she told me to go. I tried to make her come with me. But she figured she had a better chance with a man with a job than she did on the street, even if she had to take a whuppin' every once in a while."

I looked in the mirror. Both boys were looking right at me. I figured I had them.

"Yeah, it was tough being on the run. Food wasn't so hard. Folks leave a lot of good eating behind, if you know where to look. But sleeping, that was another thing. On nice days, well, except for the bugs, it can be just fine. Just got to be out of sight. But when the weather gets bad, like today, with the wind all blowing or the rain, well that's when you start to wondering how you're going to make it."

They was paying attention now, that's for sure. The dust was clouding up the sky, hitting at the car and pushing it sideways. Blowing so strong we had to close all the windows.

"You got to start thinking about it before the sun goes down or you can end up jammed in some corner, shivering and crying. And you always got to keep moving. Little Black boy like me, white folks don't like to see him around. Probably the same for Indian kids, too, should they take to running."

"We slept at Missus Steinbach's," the little fellow blurted out. His brother hit him on the knee.

I pretended I didn't hear. "Course, winter doesn't work at all. You ain't gonna make it staying outside, no matter how tough you are. End up like them frozen dogs on the side of the road. But I always found good folks. When you find good folks, you got to trust them. Sometimes you got to take some chances."

The older boy's face was moving. He was good at hiding things, but not that good. I decided it was time to go silent. Let things sink in a bit.

The church ladies had given me some sandwiches at the end of my singing that morning. It made them feel good to do it and it was always much appreciated. Making a dollar was one thing, but saving a dollar was just as good. They'd wrapped them up in wax paper, put them in a paper bag. I hadn't even looked. I always try to keep my goodbyes as close to my thanks as I can. In them small towns, the folks that like you will do anything for you. But the ones that don't, well, you need to get away before they get time to do any planning.

"You boys wouldn't much like a sandwich, I suppose, would you?" I said.

The little guy's eyes got wide.

I could see a little dip in the road up ahead. Little break in the field. Maybe a drainage ditch. Maybe a tiny creek or some such.

"Looks like maybe there's a little creek up here," I said. "Good place to sit. Down low, out of the wind."

I handed the bag over the seat to the older boy. "Church ladies give them to me. Why don't you check them out? Let me know what we got." The little one was just about jumping out of his seat he was so excited.

The older boy did some unwrapping. He didn't say nothing, but I could see he was interested. I was guessing they hadn't had any sort of meal for a while.

Turns out I was right about the creek. It wasn't much, just a trickle. But there was a pull-off place where we could park and sit and eat.

The sky was starting to break open. The wind was slowing, the dust was settling. Little patches of blue were popping through here and there. Damndest weather I had ever seen. Wanting to storm one minute, blowing dust the next. Couldn't never guess what it was going to do. The only thing for sure was that it wasn't going to rain.

Once down by the creek, it felt cozy as a church. The creek wasn't much wider than what a man could step across, but it was still moving enough to be burbling, and the birds was singing and the trees and bushes were hanging over the water letting the sunlight come through in streams and shafts. There was bugs moving on the water and buzzing in the air. The little Reuben fellow saw some butterflies and about went crazy chasing them, snapping at them with his mouth open like maybe one was going to fly in.

I had hardly gotten a word from the boy, Levi. But I could feel him softening. He wasn't keeping his face down so much, but he was keeping his lips sealed. I had to remember what my momma used to tell me, that the best meals take the longest to cook. I wasn't gonna try to take the lid off that pot until it decided to come off on its own.

I kept working on the edges. "Yeah, I do sixty, eighty shows a summer. Singing the old gospel songs in churches and dancing halls and old folks' homes. Got into it when I was just a kid on the run. 'Sister Latrice and the Gospel Choir.' Ever heard of it?"

Levi shook his head. At least he was listening.

"Yeah, Miss Latrice. She took me in, spit-shined me up, and put me out front. White folks loved seeing a little Black boy singing his heart out. When she passed on, I just sort of kept on doing it. Went out on my own. 'Brother James and His Gospel Review.' Been doing it ever since."

"Here." I handed him my business card. "I keep one in the pocket of everything I own. You never know when it might come in handy for selling or preaching or just walking free from a bad situation. Not that there's too many of those. You meet a bad apple every once in a while. People sometimes don't like the idea of some other kinds of folks, but when you get them one-on-one, they mostly got hearts as big as you or me."

The boy took the card, holding it real formal. I'd guessed he'd never seen a business card before.

"Why don't you get out them sandwiches?" I said. "No telling what other fine eatings those good women put in that bag."

Little Reuben had been swatting at butterflies and jumping in the air, trying to catch them in his mouth. When he heard the bag rustling he come running fast as anything, dropped himself down on the ground next to us, and sat there like a puppy waiting for a bone. He took out that little turtle of his and scooped out a hole next to the stream and let it fill with water. When the turtle commenced to swimming, he started beating the air with his fists and grinning like his face was going to explode. I don't think I ever seen anyone who come so close to bursting with happiness at the littlest things.

Levi was just sorting out the sandwiches when I heard a sound coming. It was a grinding kind of sound, like an engine geared real low, working hard. I wasn't much concerned. This wasn't nobody's property, just a creek on a county road.

Soon enough an old green John Deere tractor come churning over the bridge with a farmer on it. He was a grizzly sort with a face as hard as the land. He didn't look much like trouble, but there wasn't much friendly in his eyes, neither. This may not have been his property, but he knew for sure that it wasn't ours.

I was a little concerned. Indians weren't much welcome in these parts, and a Black man, well, you couldn't be sure there weren't some folks still thinking about fitting you for a tree branch, though you had to keep telling yourself that those days was long in the past.

"Howdy," I said and waved up at him. He didn't say nothing, just turned that tractor down the bank by the side of the bridge and come to rest next to us, engine idling and eyes staring.

I was doing some hard figuring when that little Levi popped up, standing straight as anything, like almost at attention.

"Hello, sir," he said in his little boy voice. I about fell over. That was more words than he'd said to me since he'd come out of the corn. He walked up to the tractor and stuck out his hand for the man to shake. "My name is Levi. This here is my little brother, Reuben. This here is Brother James. We're part of his Gospel Review." The man looked at him sideways, but not half so sideways as I did.

The little fella handed the farmer the old crumpled business card and nudged his brother with the side of his knee. What happened next, well, if there's such a thing as impossible I swear to God I was seeing it with my own eyes.

Little Levi bent down and whispered something in Reuben's ear, then the little fella stood up, took his turtle in his hands, and started belting out "Swing Low, Sweet Chariot" in the sweetest voice I ever heard since my own time as a young one with Sister Latrice and the Gospel Choir.

I was about to join in, but I figured I'd let him take this all the way to the end, or at least as far as he could. But he didn't need no help. He got it right, every word, putting it together just like me, except in a boy voice.

When he got done, the farmer just sat there. He reached down and turned off the tractor and sat there shaking his head and grinning.

"Well, I'll be," he said. "You don't see something like that very often when you're out turning up your field."

He just kept laughing and shaking his head, then turned on his key and gave us a wave and ground his way back up to the road.

"You fellas take care," he said.

Levi just stood there, stiff as a statue. Reuben was jumping up and down and waving like he was trying to signal a ship from a desert island.

"Miss Ida said to wave to white people," he said. "I like Miss Ida."

LEAVING THE PATH OF TRUTH

Levi

I was liking this Brother James. He didn't ask questions to get inside me. He let Reuben touch his hair.

Grandpa had taught me to give friendship to everybody, but to keep your trust close. You can take friendship back and give it again, he said. But you can only give trust once. He said to be very careful and to watch before giving your trust.

I was thinking to give this Brother James my trust. I had watched him. He was like the elders — he'd lay something before you and let you decide to pick it up. He had a giving way, not a taking way. I could feel it. Reuben could feel it, too.

I was proud to help him when the tractor man came. All the time in the car I had turned my tongue around, like Grandpa said, not speaking, but only listening.

When that tractor man came, I saw that he had hard eyes. I thought to reach out my hand in friendship, like Grandpa said. Full-growns will believe a boy quicker than a man, he said. Especially a boy with clear eyes. I know how to have clear eyes.

I thought to use my boarding school manners. I shook his hand and gave him Brother James's card. *Wašíču* like things that are written down. I was proud to have that card. I was glad Brother James had given it to me.

I had fear for what I was doing. I was leaving the path of truth. I did not know what Creator would think. I thought of what Brother

James said, that *wašíču* did not like men with black skin sometimes. It made me afraid for him with this tractor man.

I thought of how it was to be a man in the Lakota way — to have strong caring for others, to give what you have, to have no fear to serve. This Brother James had shown these things. He showed strong caring for Reuben and me when he told us he would take us to the red stone place without asking questions. He had shown a strong heart for giving when he gave us his food and let us eat first. He had shown no fear to serve when he did not ask for anything in return like the *wašíču* do. He was being a man in the Lakota way. I would be a man for him in that way, too.

That's why I thought to leave the path of truth when I saw the tractor man. I knew what Reuben was doing when he put his face near to Brother James's face. He was listening close. He can hear any-thing and put it inside him when he listens close. He doesn't know the meaning inside of words, but he knows the sound of words. He hears things whole. I could see him moving his lips while Brother James was singing. I knew he was learning the word shapes of what Brother James was singing. I knew he had Brother James's songs inside him.

I was hoping he would sing when I nudged him. That's when I had the strongest fear. I whispered the first words to him, the words about chariot. I didn't know what "chariot" was. Neither did Reuben. But I knew he knew the word sounds.

At first Reuben would not sing. Then I whispered he should sing for *khéya*, that *khéya* liked this Brother James, that *khéya* had tried to climb in his car. I said Brother James wanted to hear it, that *khéya* wanted him to hear it.

Then Reuben sang.

I do not know if Creator was angry when I left the truth path to help Brother James. I thought of what Grandpa had said about how a man who would lead must make hard choices. I had made a hard choice to speak against the truth to protect Brother James. It felt good in my heart to do it. I felt like a man in the becoming.

Brother James was laughing. We were driving again, going toward the red stone place. Brother James said his father had worked to dig the red stone in a *wašíču* town called Sioux Falls. It was near where he lived now. He knew the *Inyan Sa K'api*, the red stone place of the sacred stone. He had gone there once with his father. He had seen the Indians digging it. He said he would take us there.

He was happy. His laugh was big. It filled the whole car. He made Reuben laugh, too.

"I've seen some things in my day," he said. "But I ain't never seen nothing like that."

He sang the chariot song. Reuben sang it, too. I thought to sing it with them, but I didn't know the words. Reuben knew the words. He knew them all.

We ate the sandwiches. We ate Miss Ida's cookies.

We drank the water from Mister Steinbach's thermos jar.

This was my most happy time since we had got on the train.

Reuben liked Brother James. He did not have fear of him like of a *wašíču*. "He looks like *ťhatháŋka*," he said.

Brother James asked who *ťhatháŋka* was. I told him it was buffalo. That made Brother James laugh even more loud.

"Brother Buffalo," he said. "'Brother Buffalo and the Indian Boys.' I could make a dollar off that." He laughed like to make the whole car shake.

Reuben was wrong. This was a good feeling day.

DIFFERENT ROADS

Brother James

So now I had two Indian boys in the car with me. One was smart as a whip and the other one could sing a whole song after hearing it once. Two boys wanting to go to the pipestone quarry, and me having to decide what to do.

I knew I had to make miles if I was to get them to that place and still have time to find a spot to stay. Got that show tomorrow night. Nice little town. Good folk. They really put on the dog — put posters up and everything. Mayor usually comes. Brother James is a big event for them. Got to be ready for that one, and I don't know the towns over by that Indian quarry. Don't want to end up sleeping out in a cornfield in my car. No good can come of that. But you don't want to show up at a hotel where you're not known after dark. They pull back their curtains and see a black face staring at them out of the night, and the best thing you can hope for is that they just check the locks on their door. Sometimes it can be a lot worse.

So what to do with these boys? I couldn't just leave them on the side of the road. I'd spent a lot of time there myself, and it's a bad man who knows a pain and passes it on instead of doing what he can to stop it.

I was hoping I could hand them off to their own kind up at the Indian quarry. I knew the place a little. I'd been there once with my daddy when I was just a little sprout. I don't remember it much, except that I never saw so many Indians in one place before. All digging, singing, praying, doing Indian kind of things. Hear that "clunk, clunk" of steel on stone. No machines, no blasting, no nothing. Working man's music, my daddy called it.

I don't even remember why we'd gone there. I guess Daddy just wanted to see it for himself, a place where all these Indians came from everywhere to get this stone, not much different from the stone he cut out down at the quarry in Sioux Falls, but a lot harder to get.

I remember sitting by a fire with some of the Indians and my daddy bringing a bottle out and an Indian man telling him to put it away. No one ever told my daddy what to do with his bottle. But daddy put it back in his pocket. I never forgot that.

Seeing these little guys asleep behind me was bringing it all back: my daddy, those good days before he started drinking too heavy and he and Momma split ways. Before Miss Latrice and all those nights running and hiding and crying myself to sleep in doorways and fields.

It made me smile to see those little fellows all curled up against each other like puppies. Ragged little guys making little boy snores. Where that little one got that voice to sing, I'd never know. He was all walleyed, a little goofy looking. Hair sticking up in all directions like a dandelion. But that voice. Damn near the voice of an angel.

I could have made a lot of money bringing them along with me, just like Miss Latrice did with me when I was a kid. But that isn't my way. Miss Latrice was good to me, but a lot of that good was what I could do for her. I knew that even when I was a little boy, and it didn't sit so well. I was happy to be little Brother James, but I didn't want half my name to be cash money.

I'd never do that to these little fellows. We're walking different roads, these boys and me. They got some stone to get and I got some songs to sing. Best to help them as I can, then move on. If I can make their way a little easier, well, that's what the good Lord put us here for. Ain't much more to life than that.

MOTHERLESS CHILD

Brother James

All I remembered about that quarry from when I was a kid was them six big rocks, standing all by themselves like they had been dropped from outer space. Big as houses standing alone on the prairie. The Indians called them three maidens or three sisters or some such. Don't know why when there was six.

The Indians had some stories about them. Something about some maidens left over after a war and how you had to leave offerings there. There was handprints on them, some said. Right in the stone. And the stone wasn't like nothing else in the area. Big gray boulders right in the middle of the prairie.

I heard tell that science folk claim they had been carried down from somewhere up north by the glaciers, then left there when the ice melted. Didn't make much sense to me. Why just these? But I don't argue with science folk any more than I argue with religious folk. My job is to sing to make people happy. I leave science things to others.

I could see the night coming in the rearview mirror. Sky was getting ruddy, moving toward sunset. This was my favorite time to drive. The sun was all spent, ground cooling off a bit. Roll down the window, let my shirtsleeve flap in the breeze.

Sometimes I'd turn on the radio, listen to the preachers and the farm reports. Learn about the locals. Sometimes I swear I learned more about folks from the radio than I did from all the words and smiles in the dance halls and church basements.

I didn't know where I was going to drop the boys. Couldn't just leave them on the side of the road, what with dark coming on. One of these days that rain was going to come, and when it did it might just be a gully washer. And even if the rain didn't come, the mosquitoes was thick enough to lift you right off the ground. Didn't want neither of those sufferings to come to these young 'uns.

The night was getting heavy purple. Time to turn the car lights on. The little fellas was stirring in the back. Good thing, too. We was just about there. Ten, fifteen miles at most.

I figured to sing a little song, kind of soft, just to put a smile on their faces. When you come out of sleep and you don't know where you are, it can set you wrong, and these little fellas sure enough didn't know where they were. I hardly knew myself.

Sometimes I feel like a motherless child. Sometimes I feel like a motherless child.

I sang it soft as I could. Not much louder than breathing. It was the best "coming out of sleep" song I knew. Seemed about right for these fellas, too.

The little one popped up, looked around. Then his brother. Rubbed his eyes, scratched his hair.

I kept on singing. I wanted "soft" for them boys. Soft everything. Things were likely to turn hard soon enough.

It was full-on dark when we pulled around the corner and I could see them maiden rocks rising up all shadowy on the edge of the prairie.

"Here we are," I said. "This is the quarry place."

The two boys was sitting up in the back like a couple of terriers, all looking around, this way and that. There was something going on out by the rocks with campfires and tents and some kind of drumming.

A couple of Indians was standing in the road. They had set up two sawhorses to keep people from going in.

They come up to the car, put their heads in the window.

"Can't go in," they said.

They was nice enough about it, but I wouldn't have gone in anyway. Brought to mind something Miss Latrice said years ago when we was traveling through Oklahoma, seeing all these Indian reservations. "They ain't like us, Brother James," she said. "They didn't get dragged across no ocean and made to work in no fields. This was all theirs once, now we're squeezing them out of it. Pity shame, it is. It ain't that much to give when someone just wants to keep what's theirs and be left alone." I never forgot that, and it still fits inside my understanding just right.

Truth be told, I've crossed paths with most all kinds in my days, and I ain't never met an Indian that wants more than just a little respect. All that Custer and war paint stuff, well I never seen it. Just quiet as the land, like to blend in, that's how I knows them. And I'm happy to give them that as best I can.

So when them Indians said I couldn't go in and I heard all that drumming and dancing, I was good with that. Folks got to be able to keep some things for themselves if it ain't hurting no one else to let them have it.

Besides, it ain't my way to ask to be part of something where I ain't invited. Some of my folk, it puts them all in a lather that there's places they can't go and things they can't do. I figure the world's big enough and there's enough places to go without causing a stir. Maybe someday it'll be different, but I ain't living in someday. I'm living in the right now, and in the right now I've got me two little Indian boys that I'm about to set loose like a couple of tadpoles in a stream and I want to make sure I let them loose in good water. Once out, they're on their own. Nothing I can do to help them swim.

Still, it ain't too much to say I'd gotten real fond of the little fellas. I spend most of my days alone, and it doesn't take much to turn alone into lonely, and I was feeling lonely pretty strong.

I drove the car a good sight back from the sawhorses and pulled over to the side of the road. Them campfires flickered like the lights of home.

"Well, Mr. Levi, Mr. Reuben," I said. "Time for Brother James to say goodbye."

I looked over the seat at those two little fellas, sitting there all rumpled and ready to go, and I was like about to cry.

"Give me your hand," I said to little Reuben.

He reached out his hand and I took it and rubbed it against my hair. "Tatanka," I said.

"*Tȟatȟáŋka*," he said. He threw his arms around my neck and squeezed real tight. I let him hold it as long as he wanted. I ain't had an honest hug in as long as I can remember.

I looked in his little dark eyes, all gleaming. "What say?" I said. "One more time?" I started in on "Ol' Man River." Little Reuben picked it right up, sounding real funny with that high voice singing that low-voiced song.

We sang it together all the way to the end.

I shoved some dollar bills into Levi's hand.

"You take care of your little brother," I said.

He took them with a real serious face. I knew he'd do good with them.

There wasn't much more to be done. I knew we was all being pulled in two ways.

Levi put his hand on the door handle. He just held it there, not staying, not leaving.

"Best get going," I said.

Levi looked at me, pushed open the door, and pulled his little brother out. Reuben looked back at me, waved me his big wave.

I watched them as they run off toward them fires and them maiden rocks, dragging that pack behind them, headed toward their own kind.

I shoved in the clutch and set off toward the next town. The boys was gone, and there wasn't much cause left for me to stick around. I tried to pick up my spirits by singing "Ol' Man River." But my heart wasn't in it.

Drove on in the quiet, looking at my headlights cutting through the dark and listening to the tires on the road. Soon enough found myself humming.

Sometimes I feel like a motherless child.

My heart was in that one.

LISTEN TO *KHÉYA*

Levi

We were full running when I heard Brother James's car drive away. I did not want to look back. I did not want to see the lights of his car getting small in the dark.

Reuben was pulling hard in that way where he tries to just stop and not move. He kept turning back, looking for Brother James's car.

"Come on, Reuben," I said. "We've got to keep going."

"I like Old River Man," he said.

I kept on pulling. I couldn't make him come.

"I like Old River Man. He has *t̆hat̆háŋka* hair."

"I know he does. We have to keep going."

He was doing that snapping thing with his mouth, like trying to catch butterflies.

"Stop snapping," I said. "It's nighttime. There aren't any butterflies."

He kept snapping.

I was feeling afraid for him. Sometimes when he's scared he just does the things he knows. Sometimes if he can't get something right in his mind he falls on the ground and starts shaking. I was afraid for him to do that shaking now.

He kept pulling backward. "I like Old River Man. I want to go back to Old River Man."

I held on to his sleeve. It was the shirt from Missus Steinbach. It went way past his hand. I thought he might pull out of it and start running. I grabbed him by the shoulders.

"Reuben, look at me. That Brother James is gone. We have to keep going. Remember Grandpa's pipe. Grandpa's *čhaŋnúŋpa*."

I took out the red stone piece from Grandfather's *čhaŋnúŋpa*. I held it in front of his face. "Think of this, Reuben. Think of *čhaŋnúŋpa*. Remember Miss Ida. Remember what *khéya* said. Think of what *khéya* told you."

It helped to say about *khéya*. Reuben listened to *khéya*.

"Listen to *khéya*," I said. "*Khéya* told you to go the sunrise way. Brother James was driving the sunset way."

I could feel him calming down when I said about *khéya*. His arms got less stiff.

I wanted to move his mind away from Brother James. I wanted to move my mind away from him, too. Sometimes Reuben can see inside my mind and I didn't want him to see how much I was missing Brother James.

It was full dark now. We could hear the night sounds. The moon was small-sized way far in the sky. I could see the big stones like shadow houses and the Indian fires up ahead. There were tents near the stones. I heard drums. I did not know if we should show ourselves or hide. I had fear for Reuben. His mind was not working right. I had fear for him to say the wrong thing. I did not know these people. I decided to stay close but not to show ourselves.

Reuben was staring at the big rocks. I heard thunder. It was behind the sky. "*Wakíŋyaŋ,*" I said. "The thunder beings. We have to find a place to stay."

Reuben would not move. He was quiet now. He was staring at the rocks.

He made a shape in the air with his hand, like the shape of the rock. He made it over and over. He took *khéya* from his pocket. He held him up in front of him toward the rock.

"The rock is *khéya* shape," he said. He made the round shape in the air again.

"I like those rocks," he said. "We should stay by those rocks. They crawled here like *khéya*."

One of the rocks had a big part sticking out. We went under it. I could see prayer tie offerings. It made me feel good, like this was an

Indian place. Reuben found a hand shape in the rock. He put his hand in it. That made him quiet.

The thunder beings flew over but there was no rain. We slept close against each other. Reuben made sounds when he slept. We made a place for *khéya* with stones for walls so he could not get out. We filled it with water from the thermos jar. We ate the last sandwiches. It was a good night.

◊ ◊ ◊

When I woke up it was full day. Reuben was gone.

I could see across the field. There were Indians moving.

I could see a creek. There was stone all along it, like a wall, not smooth, but like piled chunks. The stone was red. It was the blood stone. *Čhaŋnúŋpa* stone. I felt strong joy.

I saw Reuben across the field. He was sitting with a woman. She was Indian. He was moving his hands big, talking loud. The woman had a small fire. She was cooking. She was making coffee. I could smell it. I heard hammer sounds. There was laughing. It was a happy place.

I thought to go to Reuben. The woman was half old, like an auntie, not like *Uŋčí*. She was laughing with Reuben.

I came close. Reuben saw me. "That's Levi," he said. His voice was big. He was talking proud.

The auntie woman waved at me with her hand. "Come, come," she said. She had a full smile.

Reuben was showing the woman *khéya*. "This is from Miss Ida," he said.

The woman was listening. She was kind. I can tell kind people when Reuben talks. He is half inside his mind when he talks. No one knows what he is saying. This woman was smiling. She was listening to Reuben talk. She was looking at *khéya*.

The woman called me close.

"He is your brother?" she asked.

"Yes. He is Reuben. He is other-minded."

The woman shook her finger at me. "Don't you say that. You be proud of your brother," she said. That gave me peace. Reuben was not making her angry.

"Here." She gave me fry bread. She was making it in a black kettle. "I'm Auntie Alberta. Where is your family?"

She was looking hard at me, in the learning way.

"We are alone, Reuben and me."

"Why are you here?"

She was asking inside of me. I don't like it when people ask inside of me. But she was an auntie. I had to answer her.

"We want to get a new stone for *Thuŋkášila*'s *čhaŋnúŋpa*."

"Where is *Thuŋkášila*?"

"He is at home."

"What is your name?"

"Levi Lone Dog."

"Lone Dog. A Lakota name."

"Yes."

"And you are here alone?"

"Yes. With my brother."

"How many winters do you have?"

"I have eleven winters."

"And you are alone?"

"Yes."

She looked thought-like at me. "You wait here. Eat your fry bread."

She went across the field. Reuben was dancing and waving his arms in the fire smoke.

I heard hammer noise from far away. Metal sound. Stone sound.

Auntie Alberta was gone a long time.

When she came back she had a man with her. He was big like Mister Steinbach, but full square. His shirt was all covered with sweat. He had dust on him.

Reuben ran over from the fire. "*Thezí tȟáŋka,*" he said. He was pointing at the man. He was calling him a "big belly."

I squeezed Reuben's arm hard. "Be quiet, Reuben," I said.

Reuben made that round shape in the air again, this time up and down, not like *khéya*'s back but like the man's belly. I squeezed him hard again.

The man looked at Reuben.

Reuben's sleeves were long, way past his hands. His hair was sticking up, all spiky. *"Thezí tȟáŋka,"* he said again.

The man looked long at him. I was scared for Reuben. Then the man laughed, really loud, almost like Brother James, but with a big wheeze in it. The woman laughed, too.

"Thezí tȟáŋka," the woman said. She had a big smile. She patted the man on the belly. "Too much fry bread."

Reuben made his big grin. He was happy. He had made people laugh.

"Thezí tȟáŋka. Thezí tȟáŋka," he kept saying. The man and woman were smiling. I felt safe.

We sat by the fire. We ate fry bread. The man and woman drank coffee. Reuben played with *khéya*.

"Alberta says you have a little *khéya* from a Miss Ida," the man said. His voice was deep and big. "Who is Miss Ida?"

I thought to answer before Reuben started talking. "She is old-like. She is from here," I said. "She can't walk. She said for us to come here for her. She said to bring her spirit home."

The man thought long. His hands were all scarred.

"She is from here," he said. "And you are Lakota. And you are alone. And you are doing this for Miss Ida."

He was doing that looking-inside thing. There were thoughts between his words.

He stood up and cracked his knuckles.

"You come with me," he said. "Both of you."

Reuben held up *khéya*.

"Yeah, the *khéya*, too," the man said.

We walked across the field. We were going toward the place of red stone. There was a creek running through. Not small, like the place where we stopped with Brother James, but rushing, with a bubbling sound.

The man walked fast, not looking at us. We were on a path. There were trees and bushes, with water going through strong like through a canyon with red stone sides. The rocks were piled on each other, like making a wall. In some places Indians were hitting on the rocks with hammers, breaking pieces from the wall, sometimes down in a hole, two or three of them, hitting hard and sticking metal bars in the rock to pull out pieces.

There were birds in the bushes, making singing sounds.

Reuben was holding *khéya* and looking around. Sometimes he would make singing sounds like the birds.

"I see a man," Reuben said. He was pointing to some rocks. They were like a face. It was like an old man face, sideways facing, with a nose sticking out. The *thezí tȟáŋka* man smiled. "Good," he said. He kept walking.

We got to a hole-like place where a man was working. He was breaking stone. There were piles of it all around him. He did not look up when we came.

He picked up a piece of stone and threw it down hard against another stone, making it break. It was hot, he was hard sweating.

"Ho, Lionel," the *thezí tȟáŋka* man said. "I got some boys for you. They need some help." The Lionel man turned to us. He was not young, not old. He had like maybe thirty winters. He was strong looking. He had a bandanna on his head. He was wet with sweat. He grinned big. He had a good spirit.

I thought to have the *thezí tȟáŋka* man talk to him, but he was already walking away. The Lionel man smiled at me. He had the Indian way; he was waiting for me to talk.

I took out the thermos jar. It had fresh water from this morning. I handed it to him.

He took the thermos jar. He drank deep. The water ran down his chin.

He made a big "aah" sound.

"*Philámayaye*," he said. He was Lakota.

He pointed to a big rock. "Sit, *hokšíla*." It was hot from the sun. "So you need some help. You're pretty little guys."

I told him about Grandfather and the pipe. I took out the stone piece from my bag. He took it in two hands, in the sacred way. I could see him moving his lips soft, with no sound, like praying. He handed it back to me.

Reuben was sitting on the ground. He was playing with *khéya*.

"Why does your brother have a *khéya*?" the Lionel man asked.

I told him about Miss Ida and her wanting us to bring her spirit home.

"Did Miss Ida have you bring the *khéya* here?"

"She talked to *khéya*. She said *khéya* would help. *Khéya* pointed us here."

Reuben held *khéya* up. "Miss Ida gave *khéya* her spirit," he said. He was talking proud-like.

The man looked far distant. He moved his eyes inside. He said some words real quiet.

"Put *khéya* on the ground," he said.

Reuben did not want to let *khéya* go. He pulled *khéya* close to him.

The Lionel man looked strong at Reuben. Not angry, just strong.

"Put *khéya* on the ground."

Reuben made a hard face, all tight and angry-like. He put *khéya* down.

Khéya stayed in his shell, with his legs and head in.

The Lionel man said something soft.

Khéya put his head out, slow-like. He waved his head around, like looking. Then his legs. He looked to the Lionel man, then to Reuben, then turned in a circle and went toward the wall, all fast. He climbed over a rock and went in a crack in the wall.

The Lionel man smiled. He picked up his metal bar. He stuck it in the crack where *khéya* went. He pushed hard. He hit the bar with his hammer. There was a crack sound. A piece of stone fell out. It was big like a *wašíču* book at the boarding school. The Lionel man spit on it and rubbed it with his hand. It went bright red, the same color as Grandpa's pipe.

"What is your grandfather's name?" he said.

"Amos Lone Dog."

The Lionel man handed me the stone. "This is for Amos Lone Dog," he said. "From a Lakota brother." I took it two-handed. It was heavy. The Lionel man smiled.

Reuben was standing at the crack where *khéya* went.

"*Khéya*," he was saying. "I want *khéya*."

"Let *khéya* be," the Lionel man said. "*Khéya* has gone home. *Khéya* showed us this stone."

He rubbed his hand on Reuben's sticking-up hair. "Maybe you should get yourself a porkypine instead of a *khéya*. Now you two get going. I got work to do."

I thought to Grandpa, to what he said about a Lakota, about how a Lakota always gives what is most important to him.

"Mister Lionel," I said.

I held out the thermos jar.

"Here. From my grandpa."

It was hard to give. I felt my hand not want to let go.

Mister Lionel poured some water from the jar on his head. He took a big drink. He made the "ahh" sound again.

"You're a good man," he said. "You thank your grandpa for me."

"I will do that," I said. I felt good in my heart. I would tell Grandpa that the Lionel man had called me a man.

LIKING CHOCOLATE

Levi

"*Khéya. Khéya.*"

Reuben was crying. He was sitting by the side of the road. He did not like the porkypine joke.

I felt sad for Reuben. Brother James was gone. *Khéya* was gone. We had gone back to see Auntie Alberta and she was gone. I could feel his aloneness. I was feeling aloneness, too.

He made his hands into fists and made his face tight. He had his eyes closed.

I thought to stop him from being sad. I wanted to make him happy, to make him proud for what we did.

I put my hand on his shoulder. "*Khéya* showed us the stone for Grandfather's *čhaŋnúŋpa*," I said. "*Khéya* helped Grandfather. *Khéya* carried Miss Ida's spirit home."

He would not listen. "I want *khéya*," he said. He pounded his fists in the air. He would not open his eyes.

I thought to tell him about giving away what is most important to you, like Grandpa taught me, but he was too young. He saw everything with little boy eyes. *Khéya* was his friend. He did not want to hear about *khéya* doing spirit teaching.

"Do you not think *khéya* went where he had to go?" I asked. I was trying to talk like Grandfather, making a question for learning that you answered in your mind. "*Khéya* is old. *Khéya* is wise, like Grandpa. You must trust *khéya*."

Reuben pulled his head down. He was trying to make his head disappear like *khéya*.

We needed to walk. It was late day. The sun was hot. The road was straight-line-like, and long. I was afraid. The stone for Grandfather's *čhaŋnúŋpa* was heavy in my bag.

I had thought to walk on the road Brother James had used, but I didn't remember it. This was a new road, tar, not dirt. I was feeling small, not brave. There were cars, but not too many. I was afraid to let them see us. I could not let Reuben see my fear.

"Come on, Reuben," I said. "We need to get to Grandpa."

"I want Old River Man," he said. "I want to ride in his car."

He was talking like a *wašíču* now, only talking about wanting things. He was making me mad by not moving.

"Reuben, you are thinking only about you. Think like Grandpa says, like a Lakota. Think other people first."

He made his fists tight.

"I'm not thinking about me. I'm thinking about *khéya*."

I thought to change his mind. "We have money. We'll get food," I said. Reuben likes to eat. "We will go to a store. We can get meat. We can get chocolate."

He opened his eyes.

"I like chocolate," he said.

I could feel his mind turning.

"You can have lots of chocolate."

"How much?"

"Three bars."

"I want three bars."

His mind had almost full turned.

I grabbed his sleeve. "Let's go then. We need to hurry. We need to find a store. We need to get chocolate."

We walked in the sunset direction. It was hard walking. The sun was hot. I had thought to find a train again, but I had told Reuben we would find chocolate. He was saying it now, over and over — "Chocolate, chocolate." I had made a promise. I had to keep it. I had to find a store.

I was close to crying. I could feel it in my eyes. Momma said a

Lakota boy does not cry. When they would hit us in boarding school we would not cry. I would not cry now. Being afraid makes me closer to crying than being hit. I was full afraid. I did not know where we were.

My back was sore. The stone was heavy. I had strong thirst.

I wished I had kept the thermos jar. I was proud to give it to the Lionel man. Grandpa said to give away the thing you want most. Right now I wanted that thermos jar most. Grandpa would be happy for what I did. It was hard for me to feel happy for it.

I was scared for a car to stop. Reuben was in a dark mind and he would say things. Not many cars came. When we saw them we would run into the field. There was corn. It was easy to hide.

Reuben pulled off an ear of corn and opened it. It was hard, but he ate at it. I tried it. I spit it out.

"Come on. We'll find a store."

We went back to the road and hid in the side grass. When there were no cars we ran. We could not see the end of the road. It was a straight line and the air over it was wavy.

Ahead of us a wagon came out of a field pulled by horses. It came right in front of us from a road in the corn. We could not hide before the man saw us. He had a flat-like hat and a big beard and straps to hold up his pants. He said something to us, but I couldn't understand him. He pointed to the wagon. It was long with square-like hay bales on it. He kept pointing, like to tell us to get on.

We got on. We sat on the bales.

The man didn't look back at us. He kept making the horses go. The horses went slow on the side of the road. We rode there, just sitting. Cars went past us. The road dropped down toward a river. There were trees all small by the side of the river around some buildings, like a little town. The man turned his horses onto a dirt road. He stopped. He did not say anything. He pointed to the town. He waited until we got off. Then he went down the dirt road.

"Chocolate," Reuben said. "Chocolate." He was smacking his lips. That was all he was thinking. I had moved his mind away from *khéya*.

We walked into the town. It was small, like only a few buildings. I felt safe. There was a dog, oldish, in the street. Reuben ran toward it. I saw a store. There were clothes in the window and some tools. I thought they maybe would have chocolate and food.

I told Reuben to stay with the dog. I told him I would get chocolate. "I want three bars," he said. He went to the side of the road and sat down with the dog.

The woman in the store was nice. She asked where my parents were. "Outside," I said. It was not a full lie.

I tried to buy things a *wašíču* might buy. I did not want her to ask me questions.

It was hard. I do not know money. I pointed to some cheese. Some bread.

There was a banana. I pointed to that, too. I wanted to show Reuben. We got a banana in boarding school and I didn't know what it was, so I bit it the way I got it and the matron hit me on the back of the head. She said I was trying to be funny. I didn't know you had to take the skin off to find the part to eat. I thought Reuben would like to see one.

There was a picture on the wall of a *wašíču* family on a swing next to some brown round cakes. It said "Hostess Cupcakes." I said to give me some of those, too.

Then I got the chocolate. I got three bars. I knew the kind Reuben liked from going to town with Momma. He would be happy.

I gave the woman the money that Brother James had given me. It was green paper money. The woman looked at me. I smiled at her. I thought to show clear eyes.

She took one and left me one and gave me some coins. "You keep these," she said. I think she knew I couldn't do it myself. She put the things I bought in my bag and handed it to me.

"*Philámayaye*," I said. I didn't mean to say it. It just slipped out.

She smiled at me. "You're welcome," she said. She had kind eyes.

SOME BOYS TO FIND

Danton

I was really beginning to think I had made a mistake.

These gravel roads were endless and the boys could have been on any of them. The stands of corn or alfalfa lining either side would have provided them with easy hiding places whenever a car went by.

This was not like the west side of the Missouri, where the long, winding ribbons of asphalt snaked through the hills and arroyos, allowing you to see for miles and perhaps get a glimpse of two tiny figures walking along the side of the road before they had a chance to see you and take cover. But I was where I was, and I had to make the best of it.

If I hadn't made a promise to Ree, the Steinbachs, and Ida, I would have turned around and gone home. But I had given my word that I would protect the boys, and my word is about the only thing I have that is worth anything. But I couldn't protect what I couldn't find, and driving through identical fields on identical gravel roads was not a promising way to find two little boys who probably didn't want to be found.

And the heat. My God. Every time I stepped out to get my bearings or to let Mister Bones empty his bladder, the sun was so hot on the back of my neck that my skin burned, and my shirt was drenched with sweat before I was even able to get back into the truck. Luckily, I had a mason jar full of water that the Steinbachs had given me. I had already drunk and refilled it three times at local stores and gas stations along the road since I had left their home this morning, and it wasn't even sundown.

I wouldn't say I was driving aimlessly, but it was close. I knew that the boys were heading to the quarry near Pipestone, just across the Minnesota line, and I figured that if they had arrived there, someone would have seen them. But I was a white man, and the quarry was one place that the Indians could call their own, so there was a good chance that even if anyone had seen the boys, they weren't going to share that information with me. Better, I thought, to stop in the few small towns along the way — white towns, all — and ask if anyone had noticed two young Indian boys passing through. Nothing goes unnoticed in small towns, and, once noticed, the word spreads like wildfire.

The only question was how long I could keep this up in this infernal heat.

Mister Bones, too, was suffering from the temperature. He was alternating between sticking his head out the window and turning in circles trying to get comfortable on the hot, sticky vinyl seat. I felt sorry for him, but there was nothing I could do.

Though he was not the world's best smelling dog, I had grown incredibly fond of having him riding shotgun next to me. Despite his age and his infirmity, he was exceedingly smart and was proving to be an excellent traveling companion. He was one of those rare dogs who gives every appearance of understanding you when you talk, and I had been in the mood to talk.

By the time we had been on the road for half a day, he had heard about my childhood in Michigan and how I had made everyone call me Danton because I was so ashamed of the French-sounding "Adrien," about most of my old girlfriends, about the guilt I felt for avoiding military service, about my feeling of dislocation living in the waterless West, about my fears that I might never have a home and a family, and about my realization that driving around in a truck through featureless farm fields was not my life waiting to happen, but was, in fact, my real life, and I'd better get used to it. Through it all he had just cocked his head and looked at me, half lovingly and half curious, through big brown eyes that were both soulful and deep.

I kept thinking that Sweet Girl would have approved of him and that the two of them would have been friends had they met, happily sniffing each other's sphincters and snuffling through the grass in fruitless geriatric pursuit of squirrels and prairie dogs.

In many ways he was so much like her — very thoughtful, more watchful than vocal, self-contained in his manner, and needing very little attention and stimulation to be happy. Aside from letting out a tiny yip when he had to get out to relieve himself, which he accompanied by placing his paw gently on my thigh, he had ridden the entire way without making a sound beyond the chewing and smacking that came as he finished off the crusts of my sandwiches, or the rhythmic slobbering from his incessant licking at his elbows where the fur had long since been worn off.

"You know, Bones," I said. "This isn't half bad. You're a good sidekick."

He looked up at me with big, doleful eyes.

"Yeah, I know, you're spoken for," I said. He wagged his tail and licked at my hand. "Best to keep to the task before us. We've got some boys to find."

Though my chances of finding the boys on these identical back roads was nearly nil, the one thing in my favor was that there were only a few towns — small settlements of several hundred souls with a few stores, a bar, and, if they were big enough, a bank where the local farmers placed their money in good years and begged for loans in bad.

These towns were usually no more than a dozen miles apart; you could count the number of them in a fifty-mile radius on two hands. By keeping the road map in front of me and crossing them off as I visited them, I could cover most of them in the course of a long day of driving.

There was, of course, the possibility that the boys hadn't gotten this far yet, or that they were cutting through fields, but I really had no other course of action unless I wanted to continue the fruitless task of driving randomly, hoping to get lucky.

The people in most of the towns were sympathetic. They didn't ask for much explanation. It was enough for them to know that these were two little kids wandering alone in this unrelenting heat. They were more worried about the welfare of the boys than they were about why I was looking for them. After all, most of them understood the dangers of this weather, just as they understood the dangers of winter snowstorms, and most of them had children or grandchildren of their own.

But in town after town I got the same answer: no, they hadn't seen any boys, but they would keep their eye out for them and take care of them if they saw them. Since the towns were too little to have police departments, there was really nowhere to contact and nowhere to send them. In a way that was good. It meant that I was outside the network of officialdom that might pass on my whereabouts to Two Finger if, indeed, he hadn't gotten rebuffed in Nebraska and turned his sights toward home. But it made it hard to establish any safe harbor where the boys might go if they did happen to show up in one of these towns.

Finally, the stops and conversations reached the point where it was too hot to keep Mister Bones cooped up in the cab, so I decided to move him to the back of the pickup where he could stick his head over the side of the truck when he needed a breeze and curl up against the back of the cab when he wanted shade.

I made him a little bed out of some of the boys' clothes that Lillie had sent along after having washed them, put a pan of water on the truck bed next to him, and left him to his own dog devices as I continued my stop-and-go visits to the small farm towns that straddled the Minnesota–South Dakota border.

I was having no success until one stop at a gas station for refueling. The man at the pump was a grizzled sort with a three-day stubble of beard and oily overalls that screamed "bachelor" at best and "sleeps in the back of the gas station" at worst. He was gregarious and affable and obviously proud of his little stucco station with its single garage bay and portico overhang. The front door was covered with license plates from various states and he had a sign in the window that read, "357 miles to Wall Drug."

"Old Bill Hustead himself gave that to me," he said, pointing to the sign with obvious pride, though I had no idea who Bill Hustead was. "Said if I sent them in his direction, he'd send them in mine."

"Well, it must have worked, because here I am," I said.

The man flashed me a crooked grin. "What can I do you for?"

"I'm looking for some gas for the truck, some water for the dog, and some information for me," I said.

"I can do the first two, but as to the third, it depends on what you want."

He had already unscrewed the gas cap and was pumping fuel full force into the tank. Mister Bones came across the pickup bed and nosed against him, curious about the presence of this newcomer. The man ruffled Bones's head and the old dog wagged his ratty tail in appreciation.

"So, what kind of dog is this?" the man asked.

"Don't really know," I said. "A little shepherd, a little Lab, a little of whatever lived in the neighbor's yard."

The man laughed. "Sounds like most of the dogs I know."

The sun was beating down with that afternoon heaviness that defeats the body and wilts the soul. I wanted to ask straightaway about the boys, but I had long since learned that small town folks are wary, even suspicious, of outsiders too quick to seek information, and you'd better meet them on their own terms if you want to meet them at all. This man wanted to talk about dogs and trucks and the state of the world, and I was not going to push him in any direction he didn't want to go.

"Ford, eh? I've always been a Chevy man myself. That straight six is damn near bulletproof. What's this got?"

"Flathead V-8."

"255? That new one?"

"Yep."

The man let out a long whistle. "I've heard about them. Mind if I take a look?"

I unlatched the hood and the man stuck his head inside. I was glad my dad had taught me about engines. I could always revert to vehicles if the conversation got too close to crops or livestock, neither of which I knew or cared anything about.

The man checked the air filter, tightened the plug wires, and checked my oil for good measure.

"You keep her pretty neat," he said.

"My daddy wouldn't want it any other way."

"Good daddy."

"The best one I had."

He grinned at my humor. "So," he said, "what's this information you want?" I had obviously passed the test of trustworthiness.

"I'm looking for a couple of kids. Little Indian fellows, maybe eleven and seven."

"Runaways?"

"Nah. Kids of friends."

The man cocked his head sideways. That wasn't much of an answer, but he knew that it would have to do. You ask a question, you get an answer, and that's as far as things go. Any more is prying.

"Nope," he said. "None came through here."

He scratched his stubble for a minute, then held his finger up like he was remembering something.

"There was a hay wagon went by earlier today with a couple of young kids on the back. One of them religious types that still use horses and wear them big hats. I didn't look close enough to know if the kids was Indian or not. I don't pay them kind much mind. I don't sell feed, and horses don't use gas." He chuckled at his joke, took my bills, and filled Mister Bones's water dish from a red rubber hose.

"Good luck. Hope you find them. Too damn hot for little fellows to be out on their own. Even Indians."

"Maybe we'll get rain," I said.

He looked at the cloudless sky. "That'd be good. That'd be damn good. But I don't count on nothing or nobody. Best way I've found to get by."

BANANA

Levi

The chocolate was melting. I had to let Reuben eat it. He'd said, "Three bars." I wanted to make him happy. He was eating them all. His hands were all covered with chocolate. His face, too.

He held up his hands to me.

"See?" he said. "Chocolate." He had a big smile.

"We need to find a place to rest," I told him. It was too hot. We had walked like a mile. The *čhaŋnúŋpa* stone was heavy. I didn't think I could go much further.

I didn't know what to do with all the food. I'd bought it to seem like a *wašíču* so the store woman wouldn't know. It was too heavy to carry. The cheese was melting.

"There's a pond over there," I said. It was small, like a place for cows to drink, right off the road. There were tall weeds around it. We could sit in the weeds and not be seen. We could eat the bread.

I could put the bag down. The stone for Grandpa's *čhaŋnúŋpa* was getting hard for me to carry.

We went to the pond. It was mostly dry. The dirt around the edges was shriveled up and cracked.

"*Khéya* would like this," Reuben said.

"*Khéya*'s happy," I said. "Stop worrying about *khéya*."

Reuben got sad-faced. He was thinking about *khéya* again. I thought to give him the banana. I thought to make him laugh.

"I have something for you. We need to wash your face and hands."

We went to the water. It was dirty. It smelled like cow.

I splashed it on Reuben's face.

He squirmed and fought. "I don't want to drink this."

"Your face is all chocolate. I have to clean it. Momma doesn't like us to have a dirty face."

"I'm not drinking it."

"You don't have to drink it."

I thought to the thermos jar. I wished we still had it. I was thirsty. I didn't want to drink the cow water, either.

"Here," I said.

"What's that?"

"It's a banana. *Wašíču* eat them. We had them in school."

He bit on the skin, just like I did. He pulled at it with his teeth.

"I don't like this," he said.

"Pull and twist," I said.

He twisted the end with his teeth and pulled like at jerky. The banana split partway and the peel part came open.

"Put your finger in there," I said.

He pulled out some of the eating part.

"Taste it."

He smiled big. "It's good," he said.

I showed him how to take the peel down. He ate it all.

"I like this banana," he said. "I want to go to that school."

"They hit you there," I said.

"How hard?"

"Pretty hard. On the back of the legs with a stick. Sometimes with a belt."

"Like a horse?"

"Kind of."

"I don't want to be hit like a horse."

"It hurts a lot."

"Do you have another banana?"

"No."

"What's in the bag?"

"I have cheese. I have bread. I have some cake things."

"I want the cake things."

I gave him the Hostess cake. He stuffed it all in his mouth. He made funny noises and opened his mouth wide so I could see all of the cake.

"They hit you at that school if you do that."

"What?"

"Open your mouth wide like that with food in it."

"Do they have these at that school?"

"No."

"I don't want to go to that school then."

He was talking in circles, but he was talking with a smile face.

I did not want to stay there. There were mosquitoes. Reuben was hitting at them. They were biting everywhere.

Reuben started to cry. The mosquitoes had him scared. "I want to see Grandpa," he said. When he got scared he asked for Grandpa. "I don't want Grandpa to be dead."

He had not talked like this since the train.

"Grandpa's not dead," I said. I didn't like that thought. I didn't know why he was having it. I took out the chunk of red stone and spit on it and rubbed it red. "See? This is for Grandpa. It is the same as his pipe."

Reuben put his head on me. "I want Grandpa to have a pipe. I'm happy now," he said.

His talk had made me feel fear. I had not thought of Grandpa dead. I took the bread. I tore off a piece. I gave part of the piece to Reuben.

"Throw it in the water," I said.

"Why?"

"For Grandpa's spirit," I said. "He will hear us and know we are coming."

We threw our bread in the water.

Reuben put his arms around my neck.

"I hear Grandpa now," he said.

I hid my face so Reuben wouldn't see. I knew my eyes were showing tear-like.

The sun was hot. The mosquitoes were biting.

I did not hear Grandpa. I did not hear anything.

PHONE CALL

Danton

I had not gone more than several hundred yards from the gas station when a woman came running out of a storefront and flagged me down.

"You're looking for some Indian boys?" she asked.

"Yes, that's right." I had no idea how she knew. I had only just mentioned them to the gas station proprietor a few minutes ago.

"Clint from the Sinclair called. He had Mrs. Johnson open the lines so we all could hear."

I realized then that this was one of those rural South Dakota towns that had somehow managed to get phone service. I had never thought much about it when people back in West River bragged about how Deadwood had gotten phone service only a year after they got it at the White House, and I'd heard stories about farmers here in East River getting together to put up poles and string wires so the little towns could be connected.

I wished it had been this way back on the reservation. Tracking the boys and keeping connected would have been a whole lot easier. But at least I was reaping the benefit in this town, especially if this woman had any information that might assist me. And it sounded like she did.

"Yes, ma'am, I'm trying to find two little Lakota fellows who are heading to the quarries to get some stone for a new pipe for their grandfather."

It seemed like honesty was the best way to go, even if it was limited in its scope.

"Well, I don't know about two of them, but a little Indian boy — I think he was Lakota — came into the store and bought an armload of food a few hours ago. Bread. Cheese. Salami. Even some Hostess cupcakes. He looked to be about ten.

"I can't say if he was the youngster you're looking for, though. He was alone. He said his family was waiting outside. I figured either they weren't comfortable with white folk or they were just letting the boy spread his wings a bit. All I know is he had cash and he didn't know what to do with it."

This dampened my spirits a bit. I couldn't imagine Levi going somewhere without Reuben and I knew he didn't have any family along. But I decided to persevere on the outside chance that it had been Levi.

"What can you tell me about him?" I asked.

"He was very polite and well mannered. He didn't really seem to know what he wanted or how to shop."

"How did he look?"

"Just a typical Indian boy. We don't see many of them around here. He had a bag that was like a pack sack. A white muslin shirt, dungarees. They both could have used a good scrubbing. And a belt with a cowboy on a bucking bronco. I got kind of a kick out of it, him being an Indian and all."

That was all I needed. Steinbach had told me about fitting the boys into clothes before they left, and how hard it had been on Lillie to see them wearing Joseph's pants and shirts.

He said Levi had gotten Joseph's favorite belt — one with a bucking bronco that Steinbach had bought him at a county fair for his birthday. "Joseph was so proud of that belt," he said. "He was looking forward to wearing it to school. He hardly had anything that wasn't homemade. It was hard giving that to Levi."

I had listened respectfully, never thinking that it would be important in finding the boys. But here it was — as close to proof as I was ever going to get that the boys had been here and that I was only a few miles or hours away from finding them if they hadn't taken a ride with some passerby. And, even so, it told me that I was at least on the right track and that finding the boys was now less a matter of "if" than "when." But I wondered what had happened to Reuben.

"Which way did he go when he left?" I asked.

"I didn't see. I hope it was somewhere with a bath. He was pretty much covered with red dust. Made the little red man even more red."

She chuckled at her joke. I didn't find it very funny, but as far as information went, it was pure gold. It told me the boys had already been to the quarry and were now on their way back home, or, at least, going in that general direction.

I thanked her for her help and hurried out to the truck with more enthusiasm than I had felt since leaving the Steinbachs. There was only one road out of town and it was heading straight west.

Bones was sitting up in the pickup bed waiting for me. When he saw me he stood up and wagged his tail excitedly.

I leaned over and gave him a hug.

"Save it," I said. "If we're as close as I think we are, you'll have plenty of reason to be wagging soon enough."

WINDMILL

Levi

Reuben was crying. I wanted to cry, too, but I had to show strong. The bugs were biting hard. We couldn't stay here.

"I hate these bugs," Reuben said. He was waving his arms all around his head. The sleeves on his shirt were flapping like bird wings.

"Come on, let's go," I said. I had bites all over me.

Reuben was slapping at his neck and making angry sounds. He was growling at the bugs.

I took my bag. We ran out to the road.

"Maybe the Old River Man will come," Reuben said.

"Maybe," I said. "Or maybe the farmer and the wagon." I was saying anything to make him not afraid.

Reuben started singing the old river song. It was loud singing, more like shouting than singing. It was like he was calling to Brother James.

We ran down the road. There were no cars. There were still bugs biting us, but not so many. My mouth was dry and sore. I was wishing we had the thermos jar.

Reuben would not stop singing. It made me scared. It was like he was not in his right mind.

There was a windmill in a field. It was old, with broken pieces. It was not moving. There were cows in the field.

"Let's go there," I said. "Maybe there's water." I knew windmills from by our home. They pumped water for cows.

We went into the field. There was a wire fence. We went between the wires. Reuben tore his shirt a little. He would not stop singing.

"Be quiet," I said. "This is *wašíču* country." I was scared for a farmer to hear him. *Wašíču* get mad if you go across a fence. I did not want us to get caught.

The field was hard to walk. It was all rocks and holes.

We got to the windmill. It was all rusted. There was a tub. I looked for water. It was dry and full of dirt.

My clothes were sweat soaking. I was thirsty. There were bugs like flies. They were landing in my hair. Reuben was singing. It was like screaming now, not like singing.

I laid down and pulled my knees up. I pulled my shirt over my head. I started to cry. I could not make myself stop.

I was feeling full shame. I had promised to protect Reuben. I had told Missus Steinbach that I would be careful for him. I had taken Mister Steinbach's thermos jar as a man gift, but I was not acting like a man. I was not showing *wóohitike*. I could not protect my little brother.

I put my hands over my ears. I tried to sleep. Sometimes the sleep place is the only place to go for getting away.

EVERYTHING CLOSING IN

Danton

I drove slowly. If the boys were nearby, I dared not miss them.

The fields were opening; there were occasional stretches of pastureland now.

The day had reached its hottest point. A breathless haze hung over the landscape, sucking the life out of everything. The bushes looked wilted. Cows stood immobile in the pastures, slowly swishing their tails. A lone hawk sat motionless in a long-dead tree.

It was as if everything was waiting for nightfall and the release that a cooling nighttime breeze would bring. If the boys were out here, I could not imagine how they were protecting themselves from this heat. For the first time, I felt real concern for their safety.

I didn't know where they would have gotten money. I had to hope they hadn't resorted to thievery. And Hostess cupcakes and a banana? None of it made any sense. I began to wonder if maybe I was mistaken; that maybe it had been a different Indian boy in the store. But the belt buckle could not be a coincidence. All I could do was keep on driving and looking.

I had already drunk half the water I had gotten at the gas station. It was lukewarm and tasted of rubber, but it was like ambrosia in this heat. I was worried for Mister Bones in the pickup bed, but he was probably better off being able to stick his head over the side of the truck than he would have been cooped up in the sweltering cab with me.

I opened both wing vents and aimed them directly at me to get the blessed rush of moving air as I drove down the road. Still, my shirt stuck to the vinyl seat.

Outside, the sun was an orange fireball moving toward the horizon. The whole earth was alive with a fiery glow. I shielded my eyes from the blinding sun, knowing that soon the sky would fade to violet, then purple, then descend into night. As much as I longed for it, I dreaded its coming. If I hadn't found the boys by then, I was not likely to find them at all. I would have to find a place to stay, and these towns were too small to have a hotel. Everything was closing in on me.

Suddenly Mister Bones started barking. He scrabbled frantically back and forth across the pickup bed, mewling and whining and barking out the driver's side of the truck. He was close to jumping out, and probably would have if we hadn't been moving.

I banged on the window to quiet him, but it had no effect. He had never done anything like this before.

Thinking that there was some animal on the side of the road, or that something had happened in the pickup bed, I pulled over to assess the situation. The second I stopped, he was over the side and off into the field. He was like a different dog, barking and whining and zigzagging across the pasture.

He was headed toward an old windmill.

CAPTURE

Levi

I heard a scream. It was Reuben. I thought a farmer had seen us. I sat up fast. I thought to be ready to run.

Reuben was running toward the road. He was waving his arms. His sleeves were flapping.

There was a truck. A man was getting out of it. A dog was running toward Reuben.

I knew that dog. It was Mister Bones. He was with the *wašíču* school man.

I did not know why they would be together. I thought I might still be in the dream place.

The school man was climbing through the fence. He was coming toward us. I yelled to Reuben to run away. He would not run. He ran to Mister Bones. He was hugging Mister Bones.

The school man was coming fast. I thought to grab Reuben, to hide in the cows. I ran to Reuben, tried to pull him away. He wouldn't let go. Mister Bones was making squeal sounds. He was licking Reuben. His tail was wagging hard.

The school man came up. I tried to hit him. I kicked and bit.

He did not hit back. He held my arms.

"Levi," he said. "Are you okay?"

He was talking soft-like, not mean.

I did not know how he knew my name. I yelled to Reuben to run. I thought to fight more with the man.

Reuben wouldn't listen. He did not have fear of the school man. He only cared about Mister Bones.

The school man whistled, sharp-like.

Mister Bones stopped licking and turned to him.

"Come here, Bones," he said.

Mister Bones pulled loose from Reuben. He ran to the school man. Reuben chased after him.

I kicked and tried to hit again. I did not want Reuben to get near to the school man. I thought this was a trick. School men use tricks to get kids for school. Sometimes they have candy. Mister Bones could be a trick. I could not let Reuben get taken to that school.

"Reuben, Levi, listen to me," the man said. He knew both our names. "I come from your mother and grandpa. I'm not trying to take you to the school. Mr. Steinbach. Mrs. Steinbach. They are my friends. Miss Ida, too. They sent me to find you. They sent Mister Bones with me."

He let go of me. I thought to kick him again, to get Reuben and run. But he knew our names.

"Are you thirsty?" he asked. "Are you hungry? It's hot in this field."

Mister Bones was licking my face. I was angry crying. Mister Bones was licking my tears.

"It's okay," the school man said. "I want to help you. I know you went to get stone for your grandpa. Miss Ida told me."

He reached in his pocket. He pulled out a *khéya*. It was made of the red stone.

I knew that *khéya*. It was from the shelf in Miss Ida's house.

"She gave it to me," he said. "Here. You can have it."

He held out the *khéya*.

I was afraid to take it. I did not know how he would have a *khéya* from Miss Ida's house.

"It's yours. It's a gift."

Grandpa had taught me never to turn down a gift. "It's an insult," he said. But I was thinking this could be a trick.

I did not know what to do. The man reached over and put his arm around me. I started hard crying, the choking kind. I couldn't stop.

The man didn't say anything. He kept his arm around me, soft-like. He put the *khéya* in my hand. It made me think of Miss Ida. It made me cry more.

He held his hand on my hand. The *khéya* was in between. I had no more fight. I leaned into the man. He felt strong. I put my head on his chest. His holding was all soft.

"You must be thirsty," he said. "I have water in the truck."

Mister Bones licked my face more. He was making little squeak sounds. I felt the *khéya*. I felt Grandpa's stone in my bag. I was still sob crying.

I looked up. The man was smiling.

"Where's Reuben?" I asked. "Where's my brother?"

The man pointed to the field.

Reuben was talking to cows.

Return

WHAT WILL BECOME OF US?

Lillie

I am so troubled by what I'm seeing in Karl-Martin. He has become a man of brooding silence. For a moment, when those boys were here, his spirit lifted. Now all I feel in him is darkness.

I see the light in his shed at night, the flickering lantern. I hear the sound of the file on wood. Sometimes it sounds angry, sometimes soft, almost weeping. Sometimes I wake when it's close to dawn, and he is still there.

What is he making? Why does he not come to sleep? I would go to comfort him, but that is his place. His and Joseph's.

I cannot escape those moments in my memory — summer days like this when Karl-Martin would rise early and go to Joseph's door.

"Good morning, son," he'd say.

He would speak so softly. It was a greeting, a welcoming him to the day. There was such love in his voice.

Soon I would hear Joseph rise and there would be the heavy boy footsteps on the stairs, then the clinking of plates and pans from the kitchen and the smell of coffee rising up, and the two of them talking, Karl-Martin's voice low and calm and Joseph all excited with his voice half boy and half man.

How often I wanted to go down to be with them. But that was their time. I would pull myself deeper beneath the covers and give thanks to Creator for the quiet happiness in our home.

Karl-Martin would make sandwiches, fill his thermos, and they would head to the barn. I would go to the window and see them walking, laughing, Karl-Martin with his hand on Joseph's shoulder, Joseph taking two steps to keep up with each of Karl-Martin's long strides.

I would watch Joseph's blond hair catch the light — his blond hair so different from my Lakota hair, so dark like a raven's wing, and I would wonder how he could even be a child of mine.

They would stay all day, just the two of them. I did not ask why. This is what it meant to be a *wašíču* wife and mother, with only the husband and children as family, only the husband and children held close.

I could see them from the window — Joseph working so hard, trying to be like Karl-Martin. He did not like the farmwork; I could tell. But he did whatever his father asked.

I would see him through the open barn door, in shadow, only thirteen, lifting bales, trying to keep up with his father.

Karl-Martin was so strong. He never needed rest; he could work from morning to night. Joseph was not strong like him, and his spirit wandered. It was his father he loved, not the farm.

I know Karl-Martin wanted to hand this farm to Joseph. But I did not believe this would happen. This was Karl-Martin's land, the land he had purchased in the white man way. Joseph's land was our people's land, far from here, where our ancestors had lived, where their blood and bones were in the earth, growing up through the plants and giving nourishment to the animals, feeding us and becoming part of us until we did not know where the land left off and we began.

I knew this knowledge ran deep in Joseph's blood. His hunger for home would be like mine, never giving him rest. He could never find ownership in a piece of paper and a promise from a bank.

I should have listened to Ida and the others, and stayed with my people. I would not have known Karl-Martin, and that would have hurt my spirit. But Joseph could have been born on the land where his blood spoke to him. When I tell white people this, they say, "Well, if you had not been with Karl-Martin, Joseph would not have been born at all."

I don't believe this. In our way, the spirit is waiting. It waits to be called forth. I could have called forth Joseph with another man. He still would have been Joseph. It makes me cry to think that he had to come to a body he did not love, only because I loved a man who was not of my blood.

Sometimes I talk to Creator. Why did I go to work in that school place? I ask. Why did I fall in love with a white man with strong hands and kind eyes? I should have listened to my mother, my father. I should have listened to Ida. But I never listened to anybody. I was a headstrong girl. I wanted to make my own way. I had Lakota fire in my blood.

And Karl-Martin had called to my spirit. He was not like other *wašíču*. That's why I fell in love with him. He had the peace of calm silence. The same silence I see in Lakota men. But after Joseph died his silences became dark. They lost their peace.

Now he is brooding, like the skies before rain.

I wonder what will become of him. I wonder what will become of us.

My life is filled with silences and ghosts.

THE TIP

Danton

Once I had calmed Levi down and cajoled Reuben with the promise of a warm meal, we had set about getting out of that sweltering pasture and into a more comfortable setting.

I had let the boys make their peace with the situation in their own way. They had drunk the entire mason jar of water, spilling as much down their shirts as they got in their mouths. Reuben had poured some in his hand to give to Mister Bones, who drank it almost as greedily as the boys themselves.

Levi was so full of fear and anxiety that he could not stop shaking. He did not know whether to be frightened of me or look to me as a savior. He kept talking about how he had made a promise to his mother and how he had to help get his grandpa a new *čhaŋnúŋpa*.

He spoke in a low, almost inaudible voice with his eyes cast down, so it was hard to know if he was speaking to me or to himself. All that was clear was that he had been overwhelmed by his efforts to take care of his little brother, and that he was now filled with a confusing mixture of anguish and relief as he sat huddled in the front seat of this strange white man's pickup.

Since getting in the truck, Reuben had been chattering and singing and talking to Mister Bones in some strange private language. Once Bones had seen the boys get in the cab, he had yipped and pawed until we let him ride up front with us.

He had been silent for almost the entire trip, but now he was whining and mewling and making all manner of sounds I had never heard from him or any other dog before.

Reuben would listen, say something in his special dog language, and Mister Bones would yelp, put his wet nose up by Reuben's face, and start licking his cheek until Reuben squirmed and laughed and pressed his head against the old dog's forehead.

We proceeded in this way until we came to the next small town. It was a simple farm town with a few residential streets that headed off at right angles from the single main street before petering out into an endless sea of corn and wheat and soybeans.

I drove slowly, looking for some place to get us a meal. Things did not look promising. It was the end of the day and the town barely had any going concerns to begin with. There was a feedstore, several boarded-up storefronts, a thrift shop with some ceramic tchotchkes in the window, and a brick bank building that had been converted into something like a VFW or Elks club.

As luck would have it, there was one restaurant in town — a café called Wilma's — that appeared to be open. I could see a woman inside wiping off the tables. She was obviously closing up for the evening. I hurried in and told her I had a couple of hungry boys in the truck and asked if she could give us a meal. She said she still had some meat loaf and mashed potatoes, if those would suit our needs. I said that sounded fine and hustled the boys in to an empty table.

It was clear that Reuben had never been in a restaurant before. He kept walking around and staring at the various tchotchkes with awe. A shelf of ceramic cows and chickens especially piqued his interest. The woman saw him looking at them and took them down and placed them in the center of our table.

"You can play with them if you wash up and roll up your sleeves," she said.

Reuben's eyes got wide and he ran over to her and hugged her legs. She cast a sideways glance of mild disapproval toward me for having let him reach such a state of dirt and dishevelment, and pointed toward the washroom door.

Levi, sensing that they might have done something wrong, took

Reuben by the hand and hurried off to clean up. He glanced over his shoulder to make sure the woman wasn't angry. All his interactions with white people were governed by fear.

The woman shooed them with her hand and they disappeared through the washroom door.

"Cute little fellows," the woman said. "Especially the little one."

"They're good boys," I said, not wishing to get involved in an explanation of why I might have a couple of dirty little Indian boys with me.

The woman got the message and went back to the kitchen to prepare our meals.

After a few minutes Reuben burst out of the washroom door looking fresh and scrubbed. He rushed back to the table and began setting the cows and chickens in alternating positions in a marching line.

"I like cows best," he said.

Levi came out moments later. His face was flushed from hard scrubbing and his hair was wetted and slicked into an approximation of a combed style. His eyes were wide and darting. I could see he was still frightened.

"Have a seat, Levi," I said. "You like meat loaf?" I was trying to use his name as much as possible to calm him down and establish a human connection. "It's one of my favorites."

He nodded seriously and sat silently while Reuben made sounds and moved the cows and chickens across the table. After a few moments he quietly put his hand in his pocket and pulled out the pipestone turtle I had given him.

"Here, Reuben," he said, handing the turtle to his brother. "*Khéya* wants to be in the parade, too."

Reuben squealed and grabbed the turtle and put it at the head of the line.

The woman emerged from the kitchen carrying three plates of mashed potatoes and meat loaf, one in each hand and one balanced expertly on her forearm.

"You boys look hungry," she said. "I put an extra portion on each plate. If you can't finish it, I'll bag it up for you."

She looked at Reuben's lineup of animals. "A turtle leading the parade," she said. "Won't go very fast." The humor eluded the boys. Levi nodded politely, but Reuben got excited at the mention of the turtle and held it up to her.

"Pipestone, eh?" she said. "That where you've been? That explains the dirt and dust."

Something in her comment got Reuben worked up.

"The pipestone place," he said. "The Old River Man took us there. He had *tȟatȟáŋka* hair."

The woman looked confused, as was I. Levi was obviously nervous about Reuben talking so much. "His name was Brother James," he said. "He was a Negro man. Reuben thought his hair looked like a buffalo."

The woman's face brightened. "Ah, Brother James. He comes through here a couple of times a year. Sometimes even eats in my restaurant. Gives a powerful show, he does. You boys know him?"

I had no idea what they were talking about, but whatever it was, it was filling in some of the blanks about how the boys had gotten here and what they had experienced.

"I sing with him," Reuben said. "I sing the Old River Man song." He stood up next to his chair and launched into a high-pitched version of "Ol' Man River." We all sat as he sang it through to the end, not stumbling once. It was more words than I had ever heard come out of his mouth since I had first met him.

At the end of the song the woman applauded. Seeing Reuben's smile, I did the same.

"That's amazing, Reuben," I said. "How did you learn that? Did this Brother James teach it to you?"

"Reuben remembers things," Levi said.

Reuben had climbed onto his chair. He was bouncing up and down. "We saw a farmer. He had a tractor. I sang the song to him. It made him smile. I made a *wašíču* man smile. I waved my arms like Miss Ida told me. *Wašíču* men like that."

He was bubbling over with words. Though they made little sense, they made the whole place feel warm and friendly. I was happy he was talking. Even Levi was smiling.

"Well, you eat your meat loaf," the woman said. "You've come a long way. And as far as I'm concerned, you've paid for your meal with that song."

"Little Tommy Tucker sings for his supper," I said.

The woman winked. We were of the same generation.

The boys ate ravenously — Levi with a certain politeness and Reuben hunched over his food like an animal. They both finished every bit of what had begun as a huge plate of meat loaf and gravy-covered mashed potatoes. Reuben picked up his plate and licked it. Levi kicked him under the table, but it had no effect.

"We should leave a tip," I said, giving Levi a good-hearted nudge.

He furrowed his brow. He obviously didn't know what a tip was.

"It's what you do in restaurants when someone gives you a good meal. You leave them money as a way to say thank you."

"Is that what *wašíču* men do?" Levi asked.

"The good ones," I said.

"I want to do that then."

"Here," I said. "Let me give you some money."

"No," he answered. "I have money. I want to leave a *wašíču* man tip."

I took the ceramic animals and repositioned them back on the shelf. When I turned around Levi was standing proudly by his chair. There was a stack of coins piled like a tower in a moat of gravy in the middle of his plate, with the quarter on the bottom, two nickels on top of them, then several pennies and a dime.

"Levi," I said. "Why did you do that?"

"You said to leave a tip. I wanted to make sure that the restaurant woman would see it."

BITTERSWEET

Danton

We left the restaurant just as the sun was sinking below the horizon. The relief I felt — I think we all felt — was almost palpable. As we headed off into the growing darkness, the old love of the open road overtook me and I just wanted to drive.

I know I should have looked for a hotel. But sometimes a moment just seems so full of magic that you don't want to let it go. This night, with the boys and Mister Bones asleep next to me, the engine of my truck humming beneath me, and the star-filled vault of the prairie sky arching above me, was one of those moments.

I kept the windows open so a cooling breeze could pass through. The scent of the earth and the fields wafted through the cab. A shooting star arced across the sky, and a night bird, involved in its nocturnal hunt, swooped low in front of the windshield before lifting off and disappearing again into the darkness. The parched desolation of the daytime landscape seemed a million miles away.

I looked at the two boys curled up on the seat next to me. They were like pups or kittens, so accustomed to sleeping together that they almost formed a single entity. Reuben had his head tucked against Levi's chest, and Levi had both arms wrapped around his brother like a mother embracing a baby. Reuben had the pipestone turtle clutched in his hand, and they were making little chirps and wheezes as they shifted position trying to get comfortable in the tight confines of the pickup's front seat.

Mister Bones had found a place on the floor and was stretched out and snoring in that snuffling way that dogs do when they fall into a deep sleep. It reminded me of nothing so much as Sweet Girl on our long-distance jaunts.

I reached down and touched Levi lightly on the cheek. He shifted slightly, but didn't wake. The night wind blew soft and an endless river of stars twinkled overhead in the prairie darkness. If I could have frozen this moment in time and driven through this night forever, I would gladly have done so.

I drove this way until the first hint of lavender creased the morning sky. I had made the decision that I would bring the boys to the Missouri River before we made our way back to their home. It was the river of their people; the river of their blood. In some way I could not articulate, it seemed like a necessary act of atonement or reparations for what I had put them and their family through when I had been working for Two Finger.

With drowsiness overtaking me, I pulled to the side of the road, made myself as comfortable as I could, and drifted off to the growing chorus of morning songbirds that filled the air around me.

It was Mister Bones's whining that finally woke me. His bladder was not as strong as the young boys', and he had crawled across the hump of the driveshaft and was pulling on my pants leg with his teeth.

"Okay," I said, and quietly opened the door and let him scramble out to relieve himself for what seemed like five minutes before he finally finished and came back to the truck.

Levi and Reuben had begun rustling and making little sounds. I was happy to see them starting to wake. The sky was blue and cloudless, and I wanted to get going before the heat descended. We had miles ahead of us, and I was anxious to drop off Mister Bones and let Lillie and Karl-Martin spend some time with the boys before I took them back to the Lone Dogs'.

I knew it would be a bittersweet meeting for all of us. Mister Bones had filled a void in my life, and I was guessing that the Steinbachs' brief time with the boys had filled a void in theirs. And in some way, we had all begun to form a fragile friendship — Ida included. Goodbyes would be hard, but we had all seen enough comings and goings to accept them as a sad but inevitable part of life.

The boys had pushed themselves upright in the seat, and were blinking and rubbing their eyes.

"Ready for breakfast, guys?" I asked.

We didn't have much, but I knew the boys would be hungry.

There was a leftover hunk of bread from the loaf Levi had purchased, as well as the remnants of the block of orange cheese with an odd chunk bitten out of it, complete with teeth marks.

"Did you do this, Reuben?" I asked, pointing to the missing chunk. Reuben showed his teeth and grinned.

"Well, we might as well finish it up. Mister Bones here will take care of anything that's left."

We sat together against the side of the pickup, shaded from the growing sun.

I had filled the mason jar at Wilma's, and Levi took charge of passing it around to each of us, making sure that Mister Bones got his turn. When we had eaten and drunk our fill, the boys climbed back in the truck. I could tell they were excited. They knew we were heading toward home.

Levi had decided to ride in back in the pickup bed with Mister Bones. Reuben had clambered into the cab and was sitting upright on the seat, facing forward, with an earnest vigilance. I had a momentary recollection of old Lone Dog looking in my pickup when he had walked me out to the truck. "I think the Creator chose well when he chose you," he'd said. "That will be a good seat for Reuben when you find him."

Reuben was holding the mason jar between his knees and marching the little stone *khéya* up and down its side. He looked up at me and grinned. "*Khéya* wants a drink, too."

"Give him as much as he wants," I said. "We've got plenty."

Reuben leaned his head against my shoulder.

Maybe, I thought, the old man had been right. Maybe the Creator had chosen me. And maybe, in ways I was just beginning to understand, he had, indeed, chosen well.

WAKȞÁŊ WATER

Levi

I liked riding in the back of the truck. I could smell the air and sit down against the window when it got too hot. I liked it better than sitting with Reuben. Reuben moves too much.

I was happy Mister Bones had wanted to ride in the back. It was like he liked being with me, too.

I could see the school man talking to Reuben. Reuben was laughing.

I did not know how to think of this school man. He had got us food. He laughed with Reuben. He had taught me about the *wašíču* tip.

He said his name was Mister Danton. He said Momma had sent him to get us. He knew about Grandpa and Mister and Missus Steinbach. He said he was not here to take us to the school.

I thought to trust him. He had Mister Bones with him. He had Miss Ida's *khéya*. But I was still afraid it might be a trick.

I thought to ask Reuben. Reuben knows this kind of thing.

When we stopped for the school man to go into the corn, I asked him.

"What do you think of this Mister Danton man, Reuben?" I asked.

"I see nice around him," he said. "And some sad. Mister Bones says to like him."

"I'm scared to like him," I said. "Momma said not to trust *wašíču*. This man was with the *iyéska* school man who broke Grandpa's *čhaŋnúŋpa*."

"Mister Bones says to like him," he said again.

Reuben did not think new things once he found a thought he liked.

The man was coming out of the field. Mister Bones had gone with him.

"See?" Reuben said. "Mister Bones likes him."

Reuben was holding Miss Ida's *khéya*. He would not let go.

"He gave us this *khéya*," he said.

The Mister Danton was smiling. He was talking to Mister Bones. I thought what Grandpa had taught me: Believe what your eyes see, not the words people say. This Mister Danton had given us the *khéya*. He had made Reuben happy. He was friends with Mister Bones. Maybe Momma was wrong about not trusting *wašíču*.

Mister Danton said he would take us to Mister and Missus Steinbach. He said they would be proud and happy. He said I could show them the stone I got for Grandpa.

I felt shame for being so dirty in the clothes we were wearing. Momma said Lakotas should never be dirty. She said we should wash every day. She said it is respect to Creator to keep yourself clean and respect to be clean when you go to someone's house.

Our other clothes were in the back of the truck. They were all folded. I saw them when I was sitting there. Mister Bones had been sleeping on them.

"Can we put on our old clothes?" I asked. I was afraid to say it. In the school we got hit whenever we asked for something. A Miniconjou boy got hit for asking to go to the toilet. He peed all down his pants. It went in a puddle on the floor. Some of the other boys laughed. I felt sad. I thought of Reuben.

"Good idea," the Mister Danton man said. "We're taking a little detour so we can stop at a river. You boys can wash up there and put on fresh clothes."

I was happy to hear those words. I thought to show respect to the Steinbachs.

We came to the river. It was not little, not creek-like, but wide, too much to swim across.

"That's the Missouri," the Mister Danton man said. "The one your people call *Mnišoše*."

I had never seen a river like that. It made the air breathe. There were small waves, chopping white-like all over it. It was moving slow, like a snake, so wide to hardly see across. Grandpa had talked about it. He said it gave life to all Lakota people. He said it was *wakȟáŋ*.

There was a place by the edge where it made a pool. "You can wash there," the Mister Danton man said.

Mister Bones jumped out of the truck. He ran to the river. He drank for a long time.

Reuben took off his clothes and went in the water. I don't like having my clothes off around other people. I did not want to be without clothes around a *wašíču*.

The Mister Danton man said he would go away and let us wash. He was a kind man to see my fear.

He went over by the truck and looked the other way. Reuben was grabbing at butterflies. Mister Bones splashed in the water. I took off my clothes.

The water was good feeling. I lay down. I could see clouds moving in the sky.

"I like this water," Reuben said. He was splashing with Mister Bones. He was throwing sticks out in the water. Mister Bones would swim out and bring them back.

I was happy to be in this water. I would tell Grandpa that I had been in the *wakȟáŋ* river, that I had been in the *Mnišoše*. He would be proud to know that.

We washed. The water around us turned red from the dust in our hair.

We laid there long. The Mister Danton man was sitting in the back of the truck. He was reading a book.

Mister Bones went out. He shook water on everything. We put on our clothes. I was happy to be in my own pants and shirt. I kept on the belt with the jumping horse buckle from Mister Steinbach.

Reuben did not want to change his clothes. He liked the flapping arms of the long-like sleeves. "I can be *šišóka*. I can be *waŋblí*," he said. I told him *šišóka* and *waŋblí* smelled clean-like. I told him he smelled more like a horse. He thought that was funny.

The Mister Danton man was sitting up. He called me to come to him. I was afraid.

He said to me to sit next to him on the back of the truck.

"You know that stone you have for your grandfather?" he said.

I had fear that he was going to take it.

"What do you think about washing it in the *Mníšoše*? Placing it in the *wakȟáŋ* water?"

I did not know that he knew these things. I did not know that he knew *wakȟáŋ*.

"Do you think that would be good?" I asked.

"I think it would be good," he answered. "I think your grandfather would like that."

I took the stone. I carried it down to the water. It was heavy. I placed it in the water. I watched it turn red, the same as the piece of pipe, the same as the stone *khéya*.

The Mister Danton man was smiling. I felt strong pride. The water made the stone alive. It would make a good pipe for Grandfather.

STRONG HANDS
FOR GRANDPA

Levi

I was glad we had stopped at the *Mníšoše*. The Mister Danton man had said it was my people's river. He said he wanted me to see it before we went back to the Steinbachs'.

I was feeling excitement to see Mister Steinbach again. He had shown trust in me. I wanted to show him the stone, to let him see what I had for Grandpa. I had liked helping him in his barn. I had liked his horse. I had liked lifting hay. He had smiled at me and put his hand on my shoulder.

I was feeling man-like pride. Now I had two *wašíču* men who gave me trust. I thought to tell Grandpa. He said *wašíču* men could have good hearts. Mister Steinbach and Mister Danton had good hearts. Brother James did, too. I thought to tell Grandpa that *hásapa* men could have good hearts, too. I had looked in their eyes, like he said. These men had kind eyes.

I would tell Momma about the good men, too. Her spirit is closed to *wašíču* men. I do not know what she feels to *hásapa* men like Brother James. Momma is strong, but her strength is of the anger kind.

I would be happy to see Missus Steinbach, too. She did not have anger in her like Momma. She was full of peace. Reuben said he saw sad in her eyes. He said he saw sad in all their house. When he said that, it made me feel good that I had helped Mister Steinbach. Maybe I had made him less sad.

I was feeling strong, like a full man. I had helped Brother James

with the tractor man. I had gotten a stone for Grandfather's *čhaŋnúŋpa*.
I had helped bring Miss Ida's spirit home. This was the man way, always helping. I was feeling strong when we drove to the Steinbachs'
house.

I was standing proud in the back of the truck when we drove in. I
waved in the *wašíču* man way.

Mister Steinbach was on the porch. Missus Steinbach came running out through the door. Mister Bones was barking to see them.

Reuben was bouncing up and down in the seat. He was making the
whole truck shake. He pushed open the door. Mister Bones pushed out
ahead of him.

Reuben ran to Missus Steinbach. He put his arms around her. She
bent down and put her arms around him. I could see crying in her eyes.

I got down from the back of the truck. Mister Steinbach came to
me. He put his hand out to me. We shook hands in the *wašíču* way, with
the strong grip. The Mister Danton man was standing by the truck.

"Well, well, well. Levi," Mister Steinbach said. "You're back. I'm
so glad to see you." He was smiling big. "Did you get your stone?"

I reached in the bag. I took out the stone. It was heavy to lift. He
took it two-handed and held it.

"Look," I said. I spit on the stone and rubbed it. It became full red.

"Good work, Levi," he said. He did that thing where he put his
hand on my shoulder and made me feel peace. He kept his big smile.

The Mister Danton man was standing far back. He had his hands
in his pockets. He was leaning on the truck.

Mister Steinbach was still holding the stone. "So, how are you
going to make a pipe out of it, Levi?"

I told him I thought to give it to Grandpa. Grandpa knew how to
make a pipe, I said. His grandpa had taught him.

Mister Steinbach looked at me. It was a thinking look.

"Just a minute," he said. "Let me talk to Mr. Danton."

They went over by the side of the house. They talked, serious-like,
for a long time. I petted Mister Bones, but I was trying to hear.

Mister Steinbach came back. He got down on one knee right in
front of me.

"Levi, you have done a man's job to get this stone," he said.

I put my eyes down. A man should never praise himself.

"That's all right. You can be proud. Now, you told me a man must have courage, is that right?"

"Yes, sir," I said. "*Wóohitike.*"

He was looking at me hard, right at my eyes. I don't like it when people look right at my eyes. I kept my eyes from looking at him.

"Mr. Danton says you have already shown courage," he said. "He said you fought to protect your brother. He said you walked lots of hard miles. He says you are a good man in the making."

"I want to be," I said. I was feeling blushing in my cheeks.

"Now, I want to ask you something hard, Levi."

He was asking about asking again. I did not like it when he did that.

"Yes, sir."

"For there to be courage there must be something to lose," he said.

"Yes, sir," I said, even though I did not understand the path he was walking.

"You want to give your grandfather a gift," he said. "You want to give him a new *čhaŋnúŋpa*. From this stone."

"Yes, sir."

"Mr. Danton and I were talking. Your grandpa is old. His hands are not strong. He does not see well. We think you should be his hands and his eyes."

He stopped long to draw me into listening.

"We think you should make the *čhaŋnúŋpa*. You are old enough and strong enough. We think you should make the *čhaŋnúŋpa* with your own hands."

I was afraid when I heard them say that. I had seen the Lionel man break the stone in the quarry.

"I don't know how to make a *čhaŋnúŋpa*," I said. "I am afraid the stone will break."

"That's why you need to have courage. For there to be courage there must be fear. Your fear will put courage into the *čhaŋnúŋpa*."

He was talking like an Indian now, about putting spirit power into something.

"I have tools," he said. "Mr. Danton knows how to make things. We can help you." Mister Danton nodded.

Missus Steinbach was standing quiet on the porch. She had been listening.

"What do you think, Levi?" she asked.

I thought to speak my heart to her. I spoke in Lakota. "*Wašíču* men do not know about *čhaŋnúŋpa*," I said.

She came over and sat next to me. She spoke soft to me, real quiet-like.

"Yes," she said. "But Miss Ida does."

LAMPLIGHT

Danton

From the moment we had driven up to the Steinbach home, the boys had changed. It was as if, in some way, this was their home, too.

Reuben had disappeared around the side of the house with Mister Bones, running as if he owned the place, and Levi had lost much of that stiff formality that seemed to characterize all of his dealings with white people. When he handed the piece of pipestone to Karl-Martin he had barely been able to suppress a grin.

I was fascinated by Levi's obsession with becoming a man. As boys growing up in Michigan, we had just bumbled into manhood through paper routes, girlie magazines, and occasionally being stuffed into a stiff, ill-fitting suit for weddings, funerals, and family affairs. Other than that, we were left to our semi-feral boyhood existence. Manhood was something that happened to us, not something we achieved.

Obviously it meant something quite different to Levi, and Karl-Martin seemed to understand. So I stood back and let Karl-Martin take the lead on the issue of the pipe.

Karl-Martin had immediately grasped the significance of Lillie's suggestion to consult with Ida, so it was determined that we would all go to visit her in the morning.

We spent the remainder of the evening sitting in the living room sharing relaxed conversation. Levi and Reuben, freed to be just boys again, sat on the floor playing games with Mister Bones, whose idea of fun was to lie on his side and snap at pieces of cloth that Reuben and

Levi waved in front of his face. The rest of us drank sassafras tea and shared stories of our pasts.

We talked long into the night. The summer breeze rustled the edges of the curtains, and the soft light of the flickering kerosene lamps Lillie had lit gave the night a treasured intimacy.

Eventually, the boys fell asleep and Karl-Martin carried them upstairs and tucked them into bed. Soon the lamps burned low and the conversation waned. With the boys occupying the upstairs bedroom, I was relegated to the couch in the living room. But this was less an inconvenience than a pleasure. After the last evening's few hours of fitful sleep in the front seat of my truck, it was a joy to curl up on a couch beneath a soft blanket.

I fell asleep easily, listening to the sounds of the cicadas and killdeer, thinking of what good people these Steinbachs were, and how easily we had come to some deep unspoken understanding. Sometimes, I thought, you don't even know your own hunger for friendship until you see it mirrored in someone else's eyes.

HOLDING HANDS

Danton

The morning brought a flurry of activity. It was clear that the visit to
Ida's was going to be something of a celebratory event. Lillie was
packing provisions to bring to Ida, and Karl-Martin had risen early to
dust off the old DeSoto and make sure that it was running smoothly. I
could sense Lillie's excitement. She was finally going back to visit her
dearest friend.

If Levi knew this was all being done on his behalf, he didn't let on.
He was following Karl-Martin around holding tightly to the chunk of
pipestone that was to be his grandfather's *čhaŋnúŋpa*.

Reuben was lying in a patch of grass behind the house, touching
noses with Mister Bones. He appeared more interested in talking to the
old dog than in *čhaŋnúŋpa*s or journeys or anything else. It seemed a
good time to engage him in casual conversation.

"You know we're going to visit Miss Ida," I said.

"Miss Ida is *khéya* woman," he responded.

He took the small stone *khéya* from his pocket and marched it
across Mister Bones's back, saying, "*Khéya, khéya, khéya,*" in time to
the turtle's marching.

Mister Bones lifted his head for a moment, then lay back and
closed his eyes. He pulled Reuben's hand close to him with his paw.

"You like Miss Ida," I said.

Reuben smacked his lips and pantomimed chewing. "*Wagmíza-
wasná,*" he said with a big grin.

I smacked my lips in response. "*Wagmíza-wasná*. I bet she'll have some for us."

"She's not there," he said, turning his attention back to Mister Bones.

It was a strange comment, and mildly disconcerting.

"What?"

"She's gone."

The comment, spoken so matter-of-factly, sent a shiver through me. Had Ida died and Reuben was aware of it through some strange psychic intuition?

"What do you mean?"

"She went with *khéya*. He went in a wall."

"I don't understand, Reuben. Can you explain it to me?"

"*Khéya* is old. *Khéya* went home."

I sat down on the ground next to him. He was making no sense.

"Tell me about this, Reuben," I said. "What do you mean about Miss Ida? And what's this about *khéya* going into a wall?"

Mister Bones kept pawing at Reuben's hand. Reuben moved away and sat up and looked at me with huge serious eyes.

"The Lionel man made *khéya* go into the wall. It made me mad. *Khéya* talked to me. *Khéya* was my friend."

I put my hand on his shoulder.

"Who's the Lionel man? What wall? Why did *khéya* go into the wall?"

"At the *iŋyaŋ* place. Where we got the stone. *Khéya* was carrying Miss Ida's spirit."

"How did *khéya* get Miss Ida's spirit?"

He screwed his face into a scowl, as if frustrated by my obtuseness.

"She gave it to him. She said to take it to the stone place. She wanted to go home." He made his snarling sound. It was clear that my questions were making him angry. I decided to change the subject.

"Are you excited to get the stone to your grandpa so he can have a new *čhaŋnúŋpa*?"

"Grandpa's like *khéya*. He's old."

He was obviously intent upon talking about *khéya*s, so I returned to the subject.

"How can you tell if a *khéya* is old?" I asked. "They all look about the same to me."

He exhaled theatrically. "Not years-like. Not like Mister Bones. Old-like. Like the old river."

Upon hearing his name, Bones pawed harder at Reuben's hand. Reuben yanked his hand away and growled something in his dog language.

"Can I see your *khéya*?" I asked.

Reuben marched the little stone turtle along Mister Bones's back, then handed it to me. I held it up in front of my face, as if I was going to engage it in conversation.

"Can I talk to this *khéya*?" I asked.

Reuben looked perplexed, as if he couldn't believe he had to explain everything to me. "That *khéya* can't talk. It's not *wamákhaškaŋ*. It's stone. It can't move. Things that don't move can't talk. They make feelings."

"Right, I'm sorry. I forgot. But you can feel them?"

He put his hands in the air like someone beseeching the heavens. "Yes!" He was making the growling sound again.

I had pushed him as far as I dared. It was clear he was reaching a point of profound irritation with my questioning. But I had gotten a glimpse inside his world — a place where everything had a voice or a presence, and everything either spoke to him or chose not to, where everything was alive and connected by sounds and feelings I couldn't even imagine.

I looked at him sitting there, a little boy of six with his fierce determined scowl and his crazy dandelion hair, and I just wanted to grab him and hug him. He was so earnest, so adamant, so protective of his understanding, and so unaware of how far it was from the way the rest of us saw the world.

I could see why he preferred spending his time with Mister Bones. Both of them looked out on the same world we did, but each of them understood it in a way that we could never understand. Perhaps the two of them really could talk to each other. Perhaps they understood each other better than any of us understood them.

"Come on," I said. "Let's go see what Levi and Mister Steinbach are doing. I'm thinking about Miss Ida's special *wasná*."

Obediently, he put his *khéya* in his pocket and stood up next to me. I started toward the shed where I could see Karl-Martin looking under the hood of the DeSoto. Reuben didn't move.

"Come on," I said.

He set his jaw and looked straight ahead.

"Come on, Reuben," I repeated. "We've got to get ready to go."

He stood there, unmoving, with his arms stiff at his side. He had taken on that dark look of adamance that I had seen in him before when he didn't want to do something.

I walked back to him and knelt down beside him. "Why aren't you moving?" I asked as softly as I could.

He refused to look at me.

"Mister Bones says you are my friend," he said. "He says friends should hold hands. You aren't holding my hand."

Then, without changing his gaze or looking at me, he reached out and took my right hand in his. With our hands firmly clasped together, he took the lead and marched us off toward Karl-Martin's shed.

Mister Bones, wagging his tail, followed close behind.

The Visit

FAR SIGHT

Lillie

Oh, how good it is to be in the car with these boys. Ida will be so happy to see them, and I will be so happy to see her, too. She is my oldest and closest friend. She is like my big sister.

I should have visited her more often. She lives so close. But my grief has stopped me. My grief and my shame. She has far sight; she saw where my love for Karl-Martin would lead me. I believe she knew of Joseph's fate even before he was born. I am ashamed that I didn't listen. But I need to listen to her now.

I want her to talk to me about the boys. I want to know why she thinks they have come to us, and what she thinks they should do with the stone. I want to know what her far sight tells her.

Ida knows these things. She always has. What she says will not be the thoughts of her own mind.

Little Levi sits behind me holding that stone. He is so serious, so solemn. I believe he will grow up to be a leader. He is such a watcher. He holds his counsel so well.

And little Reuben, he feels like one of the special ones. He is so dark and fierce, like he is protecting a great prize inside himself.

I wonder if he understands his gift. I wonder if he even knows he has a gift.

I want us to do right by these boys. But I don't know what right is. But Ida will know.

I remember being with her grandfather when I was just a girl. We were out in the field, just the three of us — her grandfather, Ida, and me. We heard a horse screaming. We ran to see it. It was tangled in barbed wire, tearing and ripping. There was blood everywhere. It had terror in its eyes.

"Stay here," her grandfather said. He walked up to the horse. It was kicking and thrashing. He spoke soft to it, said something in Dakota. The horse stopped kicking. It stopped screaming. It lay still, not moving. He touched it on the flank and took the barbed wire off, piece by piece. He had to pull it from its flesh. All the time he kept talking, speaking softly. The horse closed its eyes. It never moved. When he was done he walked away. He took the barbed wire and put it in a pile. "Don't ever touch this, girls," he said. "Ever. I will bury it and we must never think of it again." Then he said something to the horse and the horse got up and ran away. We never talked about it after that.

Then there was the time after Ida got hit by that post and was in her bed. I went to see her. She was just lying there, hardly breathing. She looked like she was dead. I couldn't stop crying. Her grandfather came and put his arms around me.

"I am so sad for Ida," I said. "If I had been there I could have stopped her. I could have pushed her down when that post came."

He pulled me close and stroked my hair.

"My girl, you couldn't have stopped that post from hitting her. Nobody could have stopped it."

"But why, Grandpa? How can a wind pull up a fence post and throw it at someone?"

He took my head in his hands and looked right in my face.

"You are young, my girl," he said. "You have much to learn. That was not an ordinary wind."

BURDENS

Karl-Martin

It is good to be driving this DeSoto again. Good but hard. There are such strong memories here.

I remember going to that old fellow's house when I saw the card on the wall in the butcher shop. "'42 DeSoto. Stopped driving. Make offer." I was so excited as I drove out to his place. The car was sitting in his garage, jammed in amid piles of boxes and old furniture. He said he'd tarped it over before the war, thinking he was going to drive it again. But that never happened. Now he and his wife were moving into a home, and he just wanted it gone.

It was like a gift from the heavens for me. Here was something Joseph and I could do together. I had dreams of us tearing that engine down, learning together, fixing it together, working long into the night until it was too dark to see, then going in for a late supper, talking about what we had done, and planning what we were going to do the next day.

But that had never happened either, so I just tarped it over, just like the old man had, and left it. I didn't much care what happened to it. It was just too hard, too damned hard.

So much about these times is hard for me. The first thing I see in my mind when I wake up each morning is the image of Joseph after I heard that shot. Even if he had not been my son, what I saw would have scarred me forever. But he was my son, and there is no darkness so great as the darkness that overtook me at that moment. Had it not been for Lillie, I swear I would have walked out that door and kept walking until

I came to the end of the earth. I was dead, and would have remained dead had it not been for these two little boys behind me.

But these boys showed up and something came alive in me again. Suddenly my heart was filled with thoughts I hadn't entertained since the seminary.

Providence. Grace. Redemption. Redemption most of all, because that's what I need most of all — redemption and healing — a way to rise above the wound of Joseph's death. And that's what these boys offer me.

If I can help these little fellows in their lives, perhaps my Joseph will not have died in vain. That is my fondest hope — that somewhere in helping Reuben and Levi there is some redemption and healing to be had. But I need to find a way to help them that fits inside their traditional ways. That's why I took the chance and sent them off. There must be no more Josephs, caught between worlds.

Can little Levi make a pipe? I don't know.

He is so serious, so determined, so intent on becoming a man. To me, he is too young to have such a hunger for manhood, but who am I to question his Lakota ways? And, somehow, he did manage to get that stone.

How did he do it? Hundreds of miles, and with his little brother in tow.

If he could make that journey and come back with a stone, why can he not make it into a pipe?

Ida will know. She knows such things.

I am so thankful for Ida. Her knowledge runs so deep. And her heart is so full of good cheer. I think if my back had been broken in the bloom of life, leaving me in a wheelchair forever, I would have sunk into a darkness not so different from the one I live in now.

But she has no darkness, at least none that I can see. Her life's meaning runs so far beyond her birth and death. Perhaps when you are held in the hands of the ancestors, peace is easier to find.

I have none of that. I sit alone in my shed, trying to shape my anguish into forms, to give it flight in the small birds I create. I sometimes feel like one of those medieval painters, placing in the images of birds all their yearnings to fly free from the torments of the earth. But I can fly free from nothing. My grief is earthbound. I sit there night after night, trying to find peace in the rhythm of a file.

I see Danton in his truck ahead of me, a man with a lonely freedom, trapped only by his own demons. How I wish my life were so simple. I have the ever-present vision of Joseph, I have the unreachable sadness of Lillie, I have the burden of a farm that won't produce, and the weight of a faith I can neither embrace nor deny.

But now I have these boys — two innocents, arriving like a gift of grace, bringing joy where there was sadness, replacing despair with hope.

How did two Indian boys — the very kinds of boys whose spirits I wounded with my teachings in the boarding school — find their way to my country road? How did they find their way into Joseph's room, Joseph's clothes, Joseph's place in my heart? If this is not grace, I don't know what is.

I can feel the weight of Lillie's silence next to me. Grace is not part of her life. She has no urge to rise above her past, only to honor it.

I love Lillie so much. I gave up the life I had planned in order to be with her, and I would do it again. But would she?

We came together from two different worlds. Joseph was the bridge. Now he is gone and I feel only the distance between us.

Those boys in the back seat of this old DeSoto are the closest thing we have to a bridge now. They will soon be gone, too.

What, then, will we have to reach across from our separate worlds? What, then, will we have to keep us each from disappearing into our own private loneliness?

CRYING

Levi

R euben won't stop kicking the seat.
He has his tight face, all dark and mad.

"Stop kicking," I tell him.

"I'm not kicking."

"Yes, you are. Look at your legs."

I'm trying to talk soft so Mister and Missus Steinbach in the front seat don't hear. Reuben is breathing in and out real loud and being all squint-eyed and banging his heels against the seat.

"Why are you doing this?" I ask.

He points his lips at the Mister Danton's truck on the road ahead of us.

"I want to be with Mister Bones. I want to be with Mister Bones and the Mister Danton man in his truck. He likes *khéya*."

"Stop talking so loud," I say. "Missus Steinbach wants us in this car. They don't want Mister Bones in this car."

"Why?"

"It's a special car. They never drive it."

"Then why are they driving it now?"

"We're going to Miss Ida's. She's going to help us make a *čhaŋnúŋpa* for Grandpa."

That makes him calm down a little.

"Miss Ida is *khéya* woman," he says. "She has *wagmíza-wasná*."

I can feel his mind turning around.

"Here, look at Grandfather's stone," I say.

I hold out the stone from my lap. All night I have been rubbing my hands over it so it will get to know me. Grandpa says that stones know things. He says they are wise because they are the oldest and do not need anything else. He says they see us and can help us. I want this stone to tell me about how to make it into a *čhaŋnúŋpa*. I want Reuben to help me. Sometimes he can hear and feel things that I can't.

"Reuben, feel this stone," I say. "Can you feel what's inside of it?"

Reuben stops kicking. He puts his hands on the stone. I put it in his lap so he can feel it.

He closes his eyes and sits quiet-like, listening. "I feel *khéya*," he says.

It makes me mad to hear him say this. "All you think about is *khéya* now."

He makes his hard face. "No. I feel *khéya*."

I take Grandfather's stone back from him. I don't want to hear him talk about *khéya*.

He takes Miss Ida's stone *khéya* out of his pocket and marches it up my arm. He is singing the Old River Man song really soft. He has turned happy.

Missus Steinbach is looking over at us from the front seat. She is soft-smiling. I like it when people soft-smile. It means their spirit is happy.

She keeps smiling that soft way at Reuben and me. That's why I don't want him kicking. I always want to show respect. But Reuben doesn't know respect. He just does what he does.

"I'm sorry for Reuben's kicking, Missus Steinbach," I say.

She reaches back and takes my hand. "It's okay," she says. She is sending feeling through her hands. There is kindness. She does not let go.

"Levi?" she says. She is still soft-smiling. "It would make me happy if you called me Miss Lillie. Would you do that?"

She is giving me her name. It is a great honor. I can feel my face get hot.

"Yes, ma'am," I say. "I'll try."

"Good," she says. She touches my cheek, just soft, with her fingers. I can feel full kindness.

"We're going to stop for a minute now. Then we'll go to Ida's. You and Reuben stay in the car."

Her soft-smiling has turned to smile-crying, like when it rains in the summer but the sun is still out.

Mister Steinbach turns the car off the road. He goes up a track path with grass in the middle. I am small in the seat but I can still see out. I have to hold tight to Grandpa's *čhaŋnúŋpa* stone because we are bouncing so much.

We drive to a clearing place with a little fence. It is a burial place. There are graves, but not too many.

Miss Lillie gets out. Mister Steinbach does, too. They go to a place and stand over it. They are holding hands. Then they come back. They are different quiet, sad-quiet.

"You're such good boys," Miss Lillie says. Her eyes have full tears.

We drive back down to the road and go toward Miss Ida's house.

This is the most happy-sad ride I have ever taken.

DOG THOUGHTS

Danton

Ah, Bones, it does my heart good to look in the rearview mirror and see that old DeSoto rumbling down the road behind us, with Karl-Martin in his old fedora and Lillie next to him in that cotton farmwife dress. They look for all the world like a happy farm couple out on a Sunday drive.

And I can just imagine Levi and little Reuben sitting in the back seat — Reuben squirming and worming around while Levi is sitting there stock-straight with that serious set of the jaw that he always has when he's trying to look grown-up.

I know that Reuben had wanted to ride with us. It made me feel good, though I'm sure it mostly had to do with you. And I'm sure you wanted to ride with them. But you got exiled to my truck so the upholstery of the DeSoto wouldn't get covered with fur. An occupational hazard of being a dog.

We could easily have fit the boys in with us. We've done it before. But Lillie wanted them to ride with her and Karl-Martin. I think she liked the idea of making this drive with her stitched-together family. It reminded her of better days, or at least of imagined better days.

I can't blame her. And I'm happy to drive alone with you as my sidekick. It brings back memories of all those miles on all those lonely back roads with Sweet Girl asleep beside me in that very place where you're sitting.

You know, Bones, I never thought another dog would ride in that seat. But here you are, and it feels good.

I think you would have liked Sweet Girl, Bones, and I think she would have liked you. You're really different, but you're both such good dogs. Sweet Girl was always right up-front with her feelings. She wore her heart on her dog sleeve.

But you seem to be watching from way back inside — always thinking, processing. You've got a kind of wisdom, just like little Reuben has a wisdom. It's as if you know something the rest of us don't know, even if you can't articulate it. It makes me feel protected, even understood.

I tell you, buddy, you can't imagine what a joy it is to see you sitting there, all raggedy and smiling, with your head out the window and your ears flapping in the wind like airplane wings. You never ask for anything. You're just happy to be along for the ride.

People who don't know dogs will never understand. We humans struggle so damn hard in this life, hardly getting it right even half the time. But you dogs don't care. You only see the good part of us. You fill up all those "should have" and "could have" and "ought to" places with your unqualified dog love.

You just look at us and say, "You're good enough."

And, God knows, we need it. At least, I do.

I look at those good people behind us in that rattly old DeSoto — a couple of wandering Indian boys, a not-quite-priest, and a woman lost between two worlds — a makeshift family with a ghost at its center, and it almost breaks my heart.

How can Karl-Martin and Lillie live with the ghost of their son? How can they live in the house where it happened?

Who found him? Was Karl-Martin out in his shed? Was Lillie in the yard hanging up clothes? Did they hear the shot and come running?

And how about you, Bones? Where were you? Were you with him? Or had he sent you off so you wouldn't have to be witness?

And what has this done to you inside your dog soul? Did you sleep at the foot of his bed every night? Were you his best friend? Do you feel it all and just keep it hidden, knowing that your job is to help Lillie and Karl-Martin heal? Do you go out to that shed thinking you're supposed to be with that boy, wondering where he is?

These are hard times for all of us. Everywhere I look I see people struggling. So many of them are hurting so bad they can hardly even help each other. But they keep on trying. That's the way poor folks are. The ones who have the least are always willing to give the most.

Maybe it just comes down to doing whatever you can. Helping a little Indian boy make a pipe for his grandpa. Or letting two little fellows sleep in your son's room and wear his clothes, though it breaks your heart.

That's what makes you dogs such a comfort. You don't try to weigh things out. You just see what needs to be done and do it the best you can — protecting those around you, having an open heart for people's pains and joys, bringing a ball back to someone with a smile on your face. Why should it be any harder than that?

I look at you sitting there with your ears half chewed off, skin all raw on your elbows, fur coming out in chunks. Yet all I see is that smile. Love, pure and simple. When there's that much love coming out of something, nothing else matters.

I wish it was that simple for us humans, but we're a compromised species. Nothing is simple for us.

I think about those two little fellows sitting in the car back there and I'm afraid for them. What if Levi can't make a pipe? What if he breaks that stone? What happens then? Will he break, too? Will his dreams of achieving a worthy manhood and honoring his grandfather break? Will his Lakota spirit, so strong and innocent and hopeful, be killed?

If that happens, that will be on us — Karl-Martin and me. We're the ones who set him on this path. Two more white men, thinking they know what's best for the Indian, thinking they're acting out of love when maybe they're really just setting up a young boy's spirit to be crushed.

I don't want that to happen. God, I don't want that to happen. But in the end it's all the same. A spirit killed by love is just as dead as a spirit killed by cruelty. Not a whole lot different than a young boy putting a gun in his mouth and blowing off the back of his head.

PROMISE

Levi

I am excited to be going to Miss Ida's to show her the stone. We will tell her about the *khéya* going into the wall. I will let Reuben do that. The *khéya* was his friend.

At first when we started driving I did not know where Mister Bones and Mister Danton were. When we stopped at the burial place Mister Steinbach had opened his window and waved them to keep going. I did not know where they had gone.

When we got to Miss Ida's, then I knew. Mister Danton's truck was already there.

Mister Bones ran to us, wagging hard and making squeal sounds. Reuben made squeal sounds, too. He tried to get out of the car even before we stopped.

I tried to hold him back. He wasn't listening to anybody. He ran to Mister Bones. Then he saw Miss Ida. "*Khéya* woman! *Khéya* woman!" he said. He ran to her.

She was sitting on the porch. Mister Danton was next to her. Mister Bones pulled on Reuben's pant leg, playful-like, while he ran toward her.

She had her arms out for Reuben.

"Oh, you good boy," she said. That was the same thing Miss Lillie had just said. I was feeling proud. They thought we were good boys. I would tell Grandfather. He would be proud, too.

She held Reuben close. He put his head on her chest. She rubbed his hair. "We'll have *wagmíza-wasná*," she said. Reuben licked his lips. "*Wagmíza-wasná*," he said. They were both full smiling.

There was a ramp to get down the steps. It was on the side of the porch. I hadn't seen it before.

Mister Danton pushed Miss Ida's wheelchair down the ramp. She was looking across the yard at Miss Lillie. They were both crying. I felt to cry, too. When people are joy-crying it spreads all over. Miss Lillie came to her. They held each other for a long time. I could see their sobs.

Miss Lillie and Miss Ida talked for a long time. They mostly spoke in Indian. I was too far away to hear. They kept looking over at me.

I was holding my *čhaŋnúŋpa* stone. I was excited to show it to Miss Ida.

Then Miss Ida said we should all go in the house. She was talking a strong way, like we all had to listen. It was like when Grandpa spoke.

We all went in the house. She said we should sit at the table, even Reuben. I could feel power in her. I hadn't felt power in her before. I had only felt kind.

She looked at my stone.

"You put that stone in the middle," she said to me, strong-like.

I put it on the table.

Mister Danton was standing in back.

"You sit, too," she said.

He sat down. Then we were all at the table.

She lit some sage in a shell. The smoke gave me peace. It made me think of Grandpa.

Miss Ida made us all put our hands on the stone. Reuben liked that. I think it made him feel big. It made me feel big, too.

Miss Ida said a prayer soft in Indian. It was a singing prayer. She sang it three times. Then she said a talking prayer. She said it in *wašíču*.

"*Tȟuŋkášila. Wakȟáŋ Tȟáŋka*," she said. "You have brought us together around the *čhaŋnúŋpa-iŋyaŋ*."

She closed her eyes. I closed my eyes, too. I do not know what the others did.

I could feel our hands on the stone. I could feel the stone get warm. It was like there was sun in it.

She spoke more. She was talking to the stone.

"*Íŋyaŋ*, of all creation you are perfect in yourself. You have no need of food. You have no need of water. The seasons do not change you. You have come out from the earth for us. You have called us. Creator has sent you out of the earth to us. We place our good hearts before you. We offer our good hearts to you. *Mitákuye oyás'iŋ.*"

"*Háu*," Miss Lillie said. Then we all said, "*Háu.*"

We opened our eyes.

Miss Ida turned her eyes to me. "Levi, you talk now. Say how this *čhaŋnúŋpa-íŋyaŋ* came to you."

I was scared to talk. She had made this place *wakȟáŋ*. I thought to talk in the sacred way, like Grandpa does. I thought of Grandpa in my mind. Then I talked.

"I ask Reuben to help me. I ask Reuben to say if I speak the truth." Grandpa had said that you should always have someone be witness when you want to speak the truth.

Reuben kept his hand on the stone. He had his big smile. He nodded up and down. He was feeling big.

"We went to the *Inyan Sa K'api* place," I said. "We slept under some big rocks. Reuben met a man and a woman. The man took us to a place where another man was digging the *čhaŋnúŋpa-íŋyaŋ*. He was Lakota."

Miss Ida smiled strong at me. I was feeling brave to continue.

"Reuben had the *khéya*. The man made us put *khéya* on the ground. *Khéya* crawled into a crack. The man hit that place with his hammer. This stone fell out. He gave it to us. He said it was a gift to Grandfather to be his *čhaŋnúŋpa*."

Miss Ida's eyes were black like small stones, but full of light. The *čhaŋnúŋpa* stone was feeling more warm.

"Does your brother speak the truth, Reuben?" she asked.

Reuben's eyes got big. Miss Ida was calling to his spirit.

"Yes," he said. "Levi says the truth."

Miss Ida smiled, warm-like. "That's good, Reuben," she said. "Now, Levi. Tell me about the place where you found the stone."

"There was a man's face in the rock," I said. "It was by a fast stream. The digging man was in a pit-like hole. We had to look down on him."

"Reuben, is this right?"

Reuben nodded.

"I know this place," she said. She was full smiling. "Now I want you to tell me about *khéya*, Reuben."

Reuben was full excited to talk. He could hardly keep his hand on the stone. "The Lionel man made me put *khéya* on the ground. *Khéya* went fast over the ground, right to a crack where the Lionel man was digging. He said *khéya* was taking your spirit home. He put a metal rod-like into the stone where *khéya* went. He hit it hard with a hammer. He hit it a lot of times. The stone cracked. A piece came out."

"And this is that stone, Levi?"

"Yes."

Miss Ida was smiling strong. Her face was full of lines like smiles. She put her hands on top of all of ours. We were all still touching the stone. She spoke quiet-like, but strong, making words toward all of us, not just one of us. "*Čhaŋnúŋpa-iŋyaŋ* has brought us together here. Now you must tell me why you have all come to show me *čhaŋnúŋpa-íŋyaŋ*."

I looked to Mister Danton and Mister Steinbach. I thought for them to talk.

They were looking at me.

I looked to Miss Lillie. She told me with her eyes to talk.

I did not have words to talk. I only had fear in my mouth.

I thought back to Mister Steinbach when he said that to have courage there must be fear. I was filled with fear.

I thought of Grandfather. I thought to put Grandfather in my heart. Grandfather would give me courage.

Then I said it.

"I want to make this *čhaŋnúŋpa-íŋyaŋ* into the *čhaŋnúŋpa* for Grandfather."

The words came out hard. When you say a word it is in the world. You cannot take it back. My words were in the world now.

"You are brave to ask," Miss Ida said. "Do you have courage to make this?"

Everyone was looking at me.

"I have courage," I said. I said the words. But my courage was only in my mouth. For Grandpa I would try to put the courage in my heart.

"And how will you make this *čhaŋnúŋpa*?"

"Mister Danton and Mister Steinbach say they will help me."

Miss Ida looked strong at all of us.

"They are not part of this," she said. "If you choose to do this, you must do it alone. They can help you, but only with words. They must not shape the stone. They must not place their hands on the stone while you are shaping it. Only Reuben can help you."

I was scared to hear that. "But Reuben can't do work. He doesn't understand."

"Reuben can hear the stone. The stone will tell him what to do."

Reuben had his wide-open eyes. "I hear the stone," he said. He was nodding his head up and down.

She turned to Mister Danton and Mister Steinbach. "If he will do this, you can help him with words, but you cannot touch the stone. Do you understand?" She was talking strong now.

They nodded.

"I ask you again, Levi. Do you have courage to do this?"

My spirit was filled with fear. My hands do not know how to shape a stone.

"I have courage for Grandpa," I said.

"You have said it twice. We have heard it. Now you must take your courage from your mouth and put it in your hands. You will make the *čhaŋnúŋpa*."

She took her hand from the stone. The stone was hot-like now.

"Now, I want you to go upstairs. There is a bag up there." She held up her hands to show the size. "You bring it downstairs. We will wait."

I went upstairs. There was all dust on everything. I saw the bag. It was in a corner. I picked it up. It had a bead design on it.

It was the shape of a *khéya*.

THEY HAVE BEEN WAITING

Danton

I swear to God the stone got warm when we put our hands on it. And it kept getting warmer, like it was pulsating.

When Lillie had suggested we go see Ida about Levi making a pipe, I had figured it was just to get her approval or blessing. It had never occurred to me that Ida had some kind of special power, or — God help me — that she could actually draw some spiritual presence out of the stone. But I swear that stone pulsated when we touched it. And I know it went from cold to warm.

Listening to her talk to little Levi reminded me of nothing so much as listening to old man Lone Dog talk to me about my responsibility to Reuben. It was as if they tapped into some other dimension of being, taking on a tone of formality that came from somewhere way beyond themselves. One minute Ida was this happy, rollicking Indian grandma clapping her hands and laughing and talking about *wagmíza-wasná*; the next, she was like a hollow reed letting some ancient wind blow through her.

I could see that Lillie and Karl-Martin were accustomed to this. The minute we sat at that table they had become deferential. They knew they were in the presence of true spiritual authority. I was like an outsider brought into something he did not understand.

What struck me most was that Ida was not playing at this or trying to fulfill some role. She was truly assessing little Levi's spiritual readiness and somehow connecting that readiness with the spiritual presence in the stone. I almost blush to say it, but it was as if in some way she was performing a spiritual marriage between a boy and a stone. If ever I had been out of my depth, this was it.

We sat there in silence listening to the creaking floorboards above us as Levi searched for the bag Ida had sent him to retrieve. Even Reuben sat quietly. I think being in Ida's presence reminded him of being with his great-grandfather.

Soon enough Levi came clumping down the stairs with a leather bag in his hands. His hair was covered with cobwebs. He was probably the only person to have been in that upstairs for years.

Ida tapped the table with her finger. Levi put the bag down next to the stone. Little Reuben's eyes got wide. "*Khéya!*" he said, pointing to the beaded figure on its side.

Ida smiled. "*Khéya,*" she affirmed.

I had no idea what this connection with turtles was, but *khéya*s seemed to be everywhere in this entire enterprise.

"Levi, open it," Ida said.

Carefully, almost fearfully, Levi undid the laces that held the bag shut.

Inside were tools — old files, some saw blades, some kind of wax or grease in a little canister, some beaded sticks and prayer ties, a small buckskin medicine bundle.

"They have been waiting," Ida said.

Levi's hands were shaking. I don't know whether it was from fear or joy or a little of both.

She put her hands on his. "They have been waiting for you. They were my grandfather's."

"I will make the *čhaŋnúŋpa,*" he said. His voice had a solemnity I had never heard from him before.

"Yes. You will make the *čhaŋnúŋpa,*" Ida said.

The rest of us sat in silence.

"No one else must touch these," she said, looking straight at Levi and gesturing to the tools. "If they fall on the ground Reuben can pick them up. But only Reuben. From this moment forward no one else can touch this stone or these tools except you or Reuben until the pipe is in your grandfather's hands."

"You take them now," she said. "Reuben, you can carry the bag."

Again, Reuben nodded adamantly.

We all sat watching, distant observers of something that felt sacred and ancient, as Reuben and Levi carried the bag and the stone out the door.

After the boys had left, Ida relaxed into her more informal, grandmotherly self.

"Those are good boys," she said.

"Yes," Karl-Martin responded, almost inaudibly.

Lillie was watching through the door as the boys walked toward the car with the stone and the tools. "I just love them," she said softly, with no little tinge of wistfulness in her voice.

Ida touched her gently on the arm. "Oh, Lillie, my friend," she said. "Have patience. Creator sees things. Creator knows." The undercurrents of the conversation ran so deep that I almost didn't want to hear. "Come, help me in the kitchen. We will have a feast before you leave for home."

As she wheeled past me, she reached up and took my hand and held me in her gaze. "And you, Mr. Danton. What do you think?"

I did not know quite how to answer. "I'm honored to be here," I said. "But I don't understand."

She squeezed my hand tightly. "That's all right," she said. "Understanding comes in its own time. Sometimes you must wait until things are revealed."

NIGHT THOUGHTS

Danton

The ride back to the Steinbachs' was uneventful.

There had been a palpable feeling of release after the heavy solemnity of the encounter with the stone. The ceremony — and it had felt like a ceremony — had been like an investiture, and the meal of ham and corn that followed had felt like a quiet communion. By the time we left, an air of resolved peace and calm had settled over us all.

Once on the road, the short six-mile drive seemed like a procession. Karl-Martin drove slowly, almost triumphantly, and I followed close behind.

I could not believe how sacramental the whole day had felt. Mister Bones slept the whole way back, stretched out across the entire seat next to me, wheezing and flubbering in that way I had grown to love. By the time we had reached the Steinbachs', the day had cooled, dusk had settled in, and the air was alive with the whisper of crickets and the distant calls of night birds.

The boys had both fallen asleep. Karl-Martin and I carried them to the upstairs bedroom and tucked them in next to each other. Neither of them had even stirred. Levi had kept the stone clutched so tightly to him as we carried him up the stairs that I don't think we could have pried it from his hands even if we had wanted to. Reuben, even in sleep, kept that furrowed brow expression that always made him seem slightly perplexed about the world around him.

As we were leaving the bedroom, Lillie came in. She gestured for us to go and closed the door behind her. She stayed up there for over an hour while Karl-Martin and I sat in the living room sharing stories about our upbringings and the strange circumstances that had brought us together in this forgotten corner of the country.

The intensity of the day had created a feeling of intimacy between us, and once again Karl-Martin opened his heart to me, much as he had done on that first evening out in his shed. I soon discovered that he had led an incredibly complex and interesting life. There had been an Indian massacre in his little Ohio hometown of Gnadenhutten in the 1780s, and though it had never really been explained to him — it was just a blip in the story of the pioneer settlement of the area — he and his friends had played around the monument that stood in the park in town, and he thought it might have worked its way into his subconscious and been a driving force in his interest in Indians and the Native world.

During his seminary years he had actually studied in Europe at the University of Tübingen before getting sent back to America for involving himself in protests against anti-Semitism, and had found himself branded by the Church as a radical and assigned to the Indian boarding schools out west, where it was assumed his views could cause little harm.

Once in the West, he had fallen in love with the clarity and simplicity of the Native way of life, and had soon found that love taking human form in his affection for a quiet, deeply thoughtful young Lakota woman who worked in the school library.

A short courtship, carried on outside the view of both his church and her family, had resulted in his leaving the church and her leaving her cultural roots, and the two of them setting out to make a life as a prairie farm couple on this abandoned piece of property in this drought-ridden, dust-choked part of the state.

He didn't say much beyond that, choosing not to broach the subject of his son or his death, and I did not see fit to push him. But his willingness to speak about his own personal journey and the common bond we had formed around our concern for Reuben and Levi, soon had me opening up about my estrangement from my parents for my refusal to join the military, and the wound that I had carried inside ever since.

I almost started crying when I recounted the moment when I had walked away from my parents' home and refused to turn and look at my father because I couldn't face the look of shame in his eyes. And then never getting back to see him before he died because I was afraid to set foot in a town where every face in every window was etched with the sorrow of a son or brother who had been lost in the war, and each knew what I had done in order to be able to be walking down the streets where their sons would never walk again.

Karl-Martin had been sympathetic — more than I might have expected. "Perhaps you were not meant to kill other men," he said.

"I wish it was that elevated," I responded. "But I think I was just afraid."

He had smiled gently. "You're pretty hard on yourself, Adrien Danton."

He stood up and walked to the window. The night outside was filling with stars.

Above us we could hear the door to the boys' room opening. Soon Lillie appeared at the top of the stairs. We could see that she had been crying.

A look of absolute shock came across Karl-Martin's face.

"Are you okay, Karl-Martin?" I asked.

Lillie covered her face and moved quickly from the landing into their bedroom.

He turned toward me, looking stunned and confused.

"The last time I saw Lillie cry was on the day we buried Joseph. She told me then that nothing could ever make her cry again."

SOMETHING MOVING INSIDE

Lillie

Last night sleep would not come to me. I spent all night listening to my heart, to the boys, to voices that have been silent too long.

I know Mr. Danton and Karl-Martin and even Ida think Creator has brought these boys into our lives to help them make the *čhaŋnúŋpa*. I had thought so, too. But last night, as I was sitting next to their bed, hearing their breathing and watching Levi with his arm around little Reuben, something happened to me — something I did not think possible. There, in the darkness, my son, Joseph, came to me. For the first time since his death, I felt his presence, not his absence.

Since Joseph's death I have tried to keep my heart a sacred burial ground for his memory. I swore that it would be his place, and no one else would be allowed to enter. But last night, in my sadness and loneliness, he spoke to me.

He said that my heart should not be a burial ground for his memory. He said that I should be at peace. He said I had wrapped myself too tightly in the Christian way, where the dead leave never to return.

"I am not gone," he said. "I have just walked on. Now I am reaching back to you through these boys."

"You have been blinded by your Christian thoughts of guilt and failure," he told me. "You must let these go."

He said he had not been trapped in that half-Lakota, half-*wašíču* body, but that Creator had called him into the world through that body to do a task.

"I did not take my life, Momma," he said. "I gave my life. I came into the world through you so that when I left there would be an empty space in your heart big enough to accept these boys. I want you to help those boys, Momma, like you would help me."

When I heard those words, my spirit turned around. It began to face outward toward the world again.

This has been a hard year, a year of death, both in the land and in my heart. But now that Joseph has spoken to me, I feel that something is being born. Something is growing.

I felt Karl-Martin next to me. I heard the boys in the next room.

I lay there until the sun came up. I watched the light stream in through the window. I heard the birds begin their morning song. For the first time I felt something move inside me. It moved like Joseph had before he was born.

It was something I had forgotten. It was something I did not think I would ever feel again. It was a feeling of hope.

Making
Čhaŋnúŋpa

EVERYTHING WE CAN

Danton

Today the boys will begin carving the *čhaŋnúŋpa*. I'm nervous and worried. We all are. So much is at stake.

Lillie has fed them a good breakfast. She lit sweetgrass for them and gave Levi a blanket her grandmother had made, telling him that her grandmother's spirit would help give him strength and courage. Karl-Martin even read the prayer he has tacked above his workbench.

Karl-Martin and I have shown Levi how to use tools, shown him how they work. We have done everything we can except the one thing that would truly help — held his hands in ours as he tries to cut and shape the stone.

But this is the one thing Ida says we cannot do.

It seems so wrong and unnecessary. There is a way to move a boy toward manhood without making everything into a test.

I could see the fear in Levi's eyes as Ida told him that no one else could touch that stone. I saw his lip quiver and his hand shake when she told him that the task must be his, and his alone. Yes, she said Reuben could help. But how much help can Levi get from a little six-year-old brother? He looked as alone and frightened as an eleven-year-old boy can be.

It breaks my heart to see this. I love this little guy. I would take him in a heartbeat to be my little brother or my son.

I could help him make this pipe. I could guide his hand in a way that made it his, not mine.

But Ida has stopped me.

This seems so wrong, even cruel.

What will little Reuben think if the stone breaks? He idolizes his brother. If Levi fails, it will break two hearts, not just one.

But Ida stands in our way. She says we can explain, but we cannot touch. Prayers and incantations and verbal instructions are fine, but none is a substitute for the gentle guidance of a knowledgeable hand.

I know these Lakota ways are designed to produce a strong man. And I'm sure that Levi's manhood, when he reaches it, will be a worthy one.

But for now he's just a boy.

And I can't help but think that sometimes the first step in helping a boy succeed is doing what you can to make sure that he doesn't fail.

PRAYER SONG

Levi

Today I will begin.
I am happy Mister Steinbach said I can use his workshop. He gave me a hay bale to stand on so I would be tall enough to reach the workbench. He said it was one that I brought in, so it should be mine to use.

My hands are afraid to start. I try to fill my heart with Grandfather. I am trying to remember everything about when that school man broke his *čhaŋnúŋpa*, everything he said, everything he did.

I have the broken piece of his *čhaŋnúŋpa* in my hand. I am touching it to the stone Mister Lionel gave me. I am hoping they can feel each other. I am trying to be strong.

Reuben is standing next to me holding the bag of tools.

"Make the *čhaŋnúŋpa*, Levi," he says. "Make Grandfather's *čhaŋnúŋpa*."

I want him to be quiet. I am trying to hear the stone. Grandfather says that stones can talk. I'm thinking that if I touch the piece of Grandfather's pipe to the stone they will talk to each other. I am hoping that maybe they will talk to me.

I wish Mister Danton or Mister Steinbach could help me. They know how to make things. But Miss Ida said that only Reuben can touch the stone. Only Reuben and me. Miss Ida knows the old ways. I must do what she says.

I have a blanket from Miss Lillie. It is from her grandmother. She told me to put it under the stone when I work. She says it has her grandmother's spirit. She says her grandmother's spirit will help me.

This is why I need Reuben. Reuben hears the spirit world more than I do. I am counting on Reuben to help me now.

Mister Steinbach let me file on a little bird he was making. He said that would help me. It felt good to use his tools. But that was wood. It was not stone like the *čhaŋnúŋpa-íŋyaŋ*.

Mister Danton showed me how to make a drill from two pieces of wood and some string. He said he learned that from his uncle. He said it would help me when I had to drill the hole in the pipe.

I think I can do this. I have used tools to fix shoes in the boarding school. The priests said I had talent in my hands. But this is not like fixing shoes. Shoes don't care if I nail them wrong. They have no life. But the *čhaŋnúŋpa* stone is alive. Mister Lionel said it spoke to him when *khéya* went in the wall. He said the stone wanted to give itself to Grandpa. I am afraid it will break if I hit it wrong. I am afraid it will be hurt, that it will cry out in the *íŋyaŋša* way. I am afraid it will be angry.

Reuben is pulling on my sleeve. He keeps telling me to start. But I don't want to start. I am not ready. I am trying to do this in the sacred way, the way Grandpa would want.

This morning Miss Lillie lit sweetgrass for us. She gave it to me in the shell to bring out here to the shed. The smoke went up high. I hope it reaches Creator. I want Creator to hear me.

I wish Grandpa was here. But I only have Reuben. I must trust him and the things he knows.

Miss Lillie made us wash before coming out here. She said our bodies should be clean and pure when we work for Creator. She combed my hair and made it lay flat. She tried to comb Reuben's but it would only stick up. She made us rub our bodies with sage. She had washed our clothes.

I tell Reuben I am ready.

Reuben makes his wide-face grin.

"I know a song," he says. "It's a prayer song."

"You should sing it," I say. "Maybe the stone will hear."

He sings the prayer song. It is the same song Miss Ida sang over the stone at her house. He sings it just like she did.

I climb up on the hay bale. I make the first cut with the saw. The saw cuts smooth. It feels good in my hands. Reuben keeps singing.

The blade moves with Reuben's song. Reuben is singing the *čhaŋnúŋpa* out of the stone.

I am no longer afraid.

SINGING OUT *KHÉYA*

Levi

I have been working on this *čhaŋnúŋpa* for three days now. I have a good heart for what I am doing.

Each day Mister Steinbach and Mister Danton walk with us to the shed. They do not come in. Miss Lillie says that if *čhaŋnúŋpa* sees them it will hide its spirit from us.

Miss Lillie lights sweetgrass for us every morning. She has clean clothes for us and she makes us wash. She says we must be clean when we meet Creator.

Reuben sings Miss Ida's prayer song every day before I begin, and I read Mister Steinbach's Christian-like prayer on the paper over the workbench. I don't know what the words mean, but it has *Tȟuŋkášila* in it, so I think that maybe *Tȟuŋkášila* will hear his name and help guide my hand.

Reuben sings all day when we work. He will not stop. He sings with each pull of the saw. The saw moves soft in the stone. It wants to move with his song. The file, too, when I am filing.

I am happy. *Čhaŋnúŋpa* is trying to come out. *Čhaŋnúŋpa* is listening to Reuben.

It is past the high sun time now. We came out here at early sun. I should be tired, but my hands are happy. I see the *čhaŋnúŋpa* coming out of the stone. I see it like in a dream. Reuben is singing it out. It is asking to be born.

I would like to work all day and all night. I do not want to sleep. I hear *čhaŋnúŋpa* calling. *Čhaŋnúŋpa* is giving me strength.

Reuben is pulling on my arm. He has stopped singing.

"Stop!" he is saying. He is talking loud. "You have to stop!"

I don't want to stop. *Čhaŋnúŋpa* is calling to me.

Reuben will not be quiet. He is pulling hard on my arm. He has not done this before. "You have to stop," he says. There is fear in his voice.

"Why?" I ask. "The saw and the stone are happy."

"You will hurt *khéya*," he says. He is almost crying.

I am angry to hear him talking about *khéya* again. Now I have to stop because I don't want to put anger into Grandfather's *čhaŋnúŋpa*.

I put the stone down.

"Why are you talking about *khéya*?" I ask.

"*Khéya* is in the stone," he says.

He points to the place on the stone where I am cutting. "*Khéya* is there," he says.

He takes Miss Ida's stone *khéya* from his pocket. He sits it on top of Grandfather's *čhaŋnúŋpa* stone. It fits the same as where I am cutting.

"Bring *khéya* out of there!" he says. "*Čhaŋnúŋpa* says you have to bring *khéya* out!"

I do not understand what he is saying. All he talks about now is *khéya*. I am trying to think about Grandfather and the *čhaŋnúŋpa*.

He is almost screaming now. "Let *khéya* out! Let *khéya* out! Don't hurt *khéya*!"

I am starting to feel afraid. Reuben is talking from his other mind.

"How should I do that?" I ask. I have to listen to his spirit power. Miss Ida said he could hear what is in the stone.

"Make the *khéya* shape!" he says. He makes the round-like shape with his hand, like the rock shape and the *khéya* shell shape and the *thezí tȟáŋka* shape. "*Khéya* will come out, just like he went in the rock place. Make it!"

I think to make a round shape on the top of the pipe. I do not want the spirits to be angry.

I think to how Mister Steinbach showed me how he made the round shape on his wooden birds, how he pushed the file from the middle going both ways so the sides would be the same.

Reuben is singing again now. "Make my song!" he says. I do not know what he means. His song is a new song. I do not know it. It goes high in the middle and low on each side. It sounds like the way *khéya* looks.

I take the file. I make it go like the song.

The stone is starting to look like *khéya*. *Khéya* is coming out of the stone.

HOLDING HANDS TOGETHER IN MY HEART

Levi

It has been four days now. We are coming to the end. *Čhaŋnúŋpa* is almost done. I can feel it.

I have let Reuben make the *khéya* on the back of *čhaŋnúŋpa*. I was afraid to let him do it. He has little boy hands. They are good for grabbing and climbing but not for making.

I showed him how to use the tools the way Mister Steinbach showed me. But he got mad and said he didn't need that. He said he could hear *khéya* in the stone and would not hurt him. He said he would let him out. I thought to how Miss Ida said that Reuben could hear the stone. So then I was not so afraid.

Reuben is singing loud when he works. There is joy in his voice.

Yesterday I made the big hole on the top of the stone. It is where the *čhaŋšáša* goes.

Tomorrow we will make the small hole to reach the big hole. It makes me proud to think of Grandpa putting the *čhaŋšáša* in a *čhaŋnúŋpa* we have made.

Reuben is excited. He says he wants to see the two holes touch. He says that will make the stone into a pipe. He likes things that turn into something else. That's why he likes butterflies, he says. He says they were worms and then they got wings. He says he wants to see the stone turn into a pipe.

Miss Lillie is happy now. She sings in the morning. Reuben likes to hold on to her when she gives us our clothes. Sometimes they sing together.

Mister Danton and Mister Steinbach go out with us every morning. I do not let them see the pipe. I keep it covered with the blanket Miss Lillie gave me. Sometimes Mister Steinbach will say his prayer. He knows it in his mind. Then they go off into the barn or the field. They are making a strong friendship.

Mister Bones likes to be with Mister Danton, but sometimes he comes in the shed to be with Reuben and me. Mister Danton talks to Mister Bones all the time. Mister Bones has strong love for him. Reuben says they are spirit friends now.

I am happy in this place. I am putting happy in the stone along with courage.

Tomorrow when the holes touch the stone will become a *čhaŋnúŋpa*. We will take the grease in the small tin that was in Miss Ida's grandfather's bag. I will let Reuben rub it in. It will make the *čhaŋnúŋpa* the color of the piece of Grandfather's pipe I have in my pocket. They will be the same, like brothers, like Reuben and me.

Mister Danton says when we are done we will go back to see Grandpa. My heart is like two horses running different ways when I hear this. I will be happy seeing Momma and Grandfather and bringing him the *čhaŋnúŋpa*. But I will be sad with the leaving behind of Mister Steinbach and Miss Lillie and Mister Bones. I will be sad to not see Miss Ida, too. She is like *Uŋčí*. I feel strong love from Reuben for her. He will want to hold on to her. He will not want to let her go.

Reuben is singing strong now. We are near the end. Maybe this is another thing for being a full man, to hold happiness and sadness together at one time.

I hope so, because right now they are holding hands together in my heart.

A BOY NEEDS A MOTHER

Danton

The house has gotten very tense, like the sky before a storm. Even Mister Bones has noticed it. He is pacing, making little sounds. He can't find a place to lie down.

Karl-Martin is silent. He is standing at the window with his hands behind his back, staring. It's like he is waiting. We all are waiting.

It has been five days since the boys started. They have not let us see what they are doing. Levi says that Reuben is singing out the pipe. I'm not even sure what he means.

Levi said this is the day they will drill the holes. This is the moment I fear the most. This is when the stone could break. I wish Levi would have done the drilling when the stone was just a block. It would have been stronger, less fragile. But he said Reuben told him to do it this way.

Lillie is sitting alone in the kitchen. She is lighting herbs in the abalone shell, fanning them, and pulling the smoke around her.

We are all looking at the shed, watching, wondering.

◊◊◊

Lillie heard it first. A wail, a screech, a high-pitched scream.

It was hard to know what it was. It didn't even sound human. It was coming from the direction of the shed.

Karl-Martin turned toward the sound. "My God, is that the boys?"

We ran around the side of the house. Lillie was already running toward the barn. The screaming was coming from the shed.

Thoughts raced through my mind. Something had happened to one of the boys. Levi had cut himself with one of the tools. The stone had broken.

I felt a tightening in my chest. Everything I had feared was coming to pass.

The shed door flew open. Reuben came running out, wailing. He had his hands on his head.

"*Khéya*! We hurt *khéya*!"

We ran past Lillie. She had taken Reuben in her arms. He was sobbing and choking. He was burrowing his head in her chest.

I made it to the shed first. Karl-Martin was right behind me. My heart was pounding.

As we got there Levi stepped through the door into the sunlight. He was holding the blanket in front of him like a baby or an offering. He stood, straight and solemn, staring past us. His eyes were empty.

"Levi, are you all right?" I said.

He did not answer.

He walked past us into the yard where Lillie was holding Reuben.

He walked up to Reuben and held the blanket out.

"Open it," he said.

Reuben looked up with terrified eyes. His lip was quivering.

"Go ahead. Open it."

Slowly, Reuben unfolded the blanket, layer by layer. I could see a form emerging as the layers were peeled back.

Reuben began crying again. "*Khéya, khéya*," he said softly, like a child staring at a dead pet.

Lillie looked up at Karl-Martin and me. There was anguish in her expression.

She pulled little Reuben closer to her.

Levi's eyes remained blank. There was no way to know what he was thinking. He stood with the blanket in front of him, letting Reuben open it at his own pace.

Reuben's hands shook and he turned back and buried his head in Lillie's chest. He could not stop sobbing.

"Go ahead, Reuben," she said. "I'm right here." Slowly, he turned back and lifted the last layer of the blanket.

Inside was a stone pipe, round and whole, with a small turtle figure crawling up from the stem to the bowl. Nothing was broken.

This was the first time any of us had seen it. It was a thing of beauty.

Reuben let out a wail of joy.

"*Khéya*'s not hurt!" he said.

Lillie held him tightly as he sobbed uncontrollably into her shoulder.

"What happened, Levi?" I asked.

"We were making the hole with the string drill. Reuben was holding the pipe and he dropped it. It slipped out of his hand."

"But it's not broken?"

"No. He ran out when it happened. He didn't want to see."

Reuben was alternating between gasping sobs and kissing the little stone turtle on the stem of the pipe.

He looked up at Lillie with undisguised joy. "*Khéya*'s not hurt, Miss Lillie," he said. "*Khéya*'s not hurt." His face was beaming.

"Come on, Reuben," she said softly. "Leave Levi and the men to take care of the *čhaŋnúŋpa*."

The two of them stood up. She took his little hand in hers and they headed back toward the house. Reuben stopped for a minute to wipe his nose on her apron. She turned and looked back at us while she waited. There was coldness in her eyes.

"Trying to be a man is fine," she said. "But sometimes a boy just needs a mother."

Storm

DECISION

Lillie

Tomorrow morning Mr. Danton and the boys are leaving. I dare not wait any longer. I have to tell Karl-Martin. I have to tell him about Joseph and my decision.

I waited until we were in our room and the moon was high. Karl-Martin's heart is softer at night.

"Karl-Martin," I said. "You know how I have been quiet."

"Yes," he said. "I've noticed. And I have left you alone. I know it has been hard for you to have the boys here."

"But it has been good, too."

He looked at me with kind eyes.

"Yes, they have filled an empty place in our hearts."

He could see my nervousness.

"What is it, Lillie?" he asked. "Something is troubling you."

"Oh, Karl-Martin," I said. "I've tried to be a good wife in the *wašíču* way. I have done your wishes and tried to have none of my own."

He ran his hand through my hair. "I know that. And I have asked more of you than I should."

"But something happened to me that night when I was sitting with the boys."

He put his hands on my shoulders. "I know," he said. "I saw your tears. You can tell me." His eyes were kind. They took away my fear.

"When I was watching them sleep Joseph came into my heart. I felt his spirit move inside me like his body moved inside me before

311

he was born. He spoke to me with his spirit. He told me I should be at peace. He said it was wrong for me to think that he had been trapped in his body. He said that Creator had called him from the spirit world and put him in that body to do a task, and that my task was to respect Creator's will."

Karl-Martin smiled and kissed me on the forehead.

"That's very Christian," he said. "Taking on a human body and coming to earth to do the Creator's will."

"It is not Christian," I said. He was not understanding me. "It is Lakota. Our way was here long before your people brought your Christian ways to this land."

Those were hard words for me to say. I do not like to contend with Karl-Martin. He is a kind and gentle man. I was taught never to argue about the Creator. But I did not want him to make my thinking fit inside the shape of his Christian mind.

I tried to turn away, but he would not let me go. He held my face softly in his hands. They are so large; they have such power.

"Say more," he said. "Tell me what Joseph told you."

I looked in his eyes. They were showing a good heart.

"He said I am called to be a mother to those boys. That I should not let them out of my sight until they are safely back in their home."

Karl-Martin said nothing. He was waiting for me to speak.

"So I have made a hard decision, Karl-Martin. When Mr. Danton takes them, I will go with him."

Karl-Martin stood up and walked around the room. His silence was heavy, full of thought. The moon sat full over his shoulder in the midnight sky. When he spoke, his words were slow.

"You're a good woman, Lillie," he said. "Better than I deserve. Our life together hasn't been easy. I've asked things of you that have been hard. You have never asked anything of me. Now you are asking something of me. If I am the man I want to be, I must listen."

I could feel the tears coming to my eyes again. I stood up and put my head against Karl-Martin's chest. He held me soft and strong.

"If you feel you must go, we will go together," he said.

Then my tears came, like they hadn't come since the day of Joseph's death. And I held him close, almost bursting with joy.

HEARING *HIŊHÁŊ*

Levi

This morning we are leaving.

I am sad to leave but happy to go. Last night I heard *hiŋháŋ*. It was making night "hooing" sounds. Grandpa said people are afraid when they hear *hiŋháŋ* at night. They think it is a death sound. Grandpa said *hiŋháŋ* is a good thing to hear. He said *hiŋháŋ* flies at night, like dreams. He said that when you hear *hiŋháŋ* and then have a dream, *hiŋháŋ* is bringing that dream.

Last night I dreamed of Grandpa. I think he sent that dream for me. I think he sent *hiŋháŋ* to tell me he was waiting.

Reuben does not want to get up. He wants to stay here. He is only seeing close. He is only seeing Miss Lillie and Mister Steinbach and Mister Bones. I want him to start seeing Grandpa and Momma. Then he will want to go.

"Reuben, it's time to get up," I tell him. "It's time to go home."

He pulls the quilt up over his head.

"Come on, Reuben," I say.

He makes a growl sound. He is in his stubborn mind.

"Reuben, Mister Danton is taking us home today. You have to get up."

He makes more growl sound and goes more under the covers.

"I am *khéya*," he says. "I am in my shell. This is my home."

DEPARTURE

Danton

I'm not happy about leaving this morning. This doesn't feel like a good day to travel. There is something disquieting in the atmosphere. Maybe I'm just projecting my ambivalence about leaving onto the weather. But there is something I don't like in this sky. It's dark and brooding, like some great malevolent force is looming overhead. The wind is hot — too hot — and in my experience a hot wind always bodes ill.

I would rather we waited a few days. But Karl-Martin and Lillie feel it would be unfair to the boys' mother and grandfather to keep them apart any longer.

I can hear the boys moving around upstairs and talking back and forth. As always, Levi is the little man, all serious in his tone and manner. Reuben is making squeals and snarls. He sounds more like an animal than a boy.

I'm concerned about the *čhaŋnúŋpa*. I hope that Levi is wrapping it well. We've come too far on this journey to have anything happen to it now. The truck rides smoothly, but the reservation roads are rough. A wrong bounce, an unexpected jostle, and what happened to his grandfather's old *čhaŋnúŋpa* could happen again.

Lillie has laid out two piles of clothes for the boys — Joseph's all, I'm sure. This cannot have been easy for her.

I heard Karl-Martin drive off early this morning. I think he, too, senses something unsettled in this air and wants to finish the morning chores as soon as possible.

I wish he would have asked me to come along. This is the end of our time together and it would have been good to do something to show my appreciation for his friendship and hospitality. But I'm guessing he just didn't want to bother me. That's the kind of man he is, always thinking of others first. I'll wait until he returns before we get on the road. He deserves a chance to say a proper goodbye to the boys.

Lillie is preparing breakfast — a full farm feast with ham and eggs and pancakes and potatoes. She was up and dressed and had coffee waiting for me. She has a placid smile on her face, but I can imagine what lies behind that calm demeanor. She has taken these boys to her in a way that only a mother can understand. This parting must be breaking her heart.

It breaks my heart, too, to think of taking the boys away from this good couple. But what can I do? These are not their boys any more than they are mine. Circumstances threw us together and we each met those circumstances as best we could. Letting go is part of life. But what they are letting go of is far greater and more painful than what I will be losing when I let the boys off at their home.

It will be a hard change, returning to my life of a propane camp stove and blankets and an old mattress on a metal-frame bed. This whole experience has shaken something loose in me. Maybe that Romanian girl was right. Maybe all my talk about the joys of adventure and movement are really just my way of trying to make a virtue out of my fears. Maybe I'm really not cut out to be a wanderer. This time with the Steinbachs and Ida and the little guys has certainly given me pause. And the thought of parting ways with Mister Bones hits a taproot of emptiness in me that I didn't even know existed.

I need to spend some time thinking about this. But there will be time enough for that when I get back home. Right now I need to focus on the boys and Lillie and that unsettled sky.

I hear Reuben coming down the stairs. His footsteps have a distinctive clomp, as if he is stamping on a bug with every step.

"You got everything packed?" I ask.

"Levi's doing it."

His fists are clenched and he's wearing a dark glower.

"Something bothering you, buddy?"

He scrunches up his face.

"*Hiŋháŋ* kept me awake last night."

"*Hiŋháŋ*?"

"The owl," Lillie says, placing a plate of eggs and ham in front of Reuben.

The thought just increases my unease. I don't know what the owl means to the Lakota, but in my world the owl is the harbinger of death. You don't want to hear it if you are inclined to premonitions.

"*Hiŋháŋ* stopped me from sleeping," Reuben says. "Levi made me get up. I wanted to sleep more." His face is screwed up into a full scowl and his hair is sticking out like porcupine quills.

Lillie pours him a glass of milk. "Just eat some breakfast," she says, "It will make you feel better."

It pleases me that Reuben, with his strange connection to unseen forces, has not drawn any dark conclusions from the sound of an owl. But my consternation must be apparent.

Lillie sits down across from me and places her hand on mine.

"It's okay, Mr. Danton. There are lots of barn owls around here. It's a common occurrence." Then, turning back to Reuben, "Do you want some bread, my child?" The phrase tears at my heart.

Reuben slams his hand on the table. "I'm mad about going home," he says, staring hard at Lillie.

"You just eat your breakfast," Lillie says. "Your grandpa's waiting for his *čhaŋnúŋpa*." Her voice is soft and soothing, and her face wears a benign, motherly smile.

She brushes her hand against his cheek and his whole manner relaxes. It hurts me all the more to see how wonderfully she manages to calm Reuben and pull him gently out of his dark moods.

I'm about to add my support when I hear Karl-Martin's old pickup clatter into the yard. There's commotion and clanging and the sound of the tailgate dropping, followed by thumping and jostling on the front porch.

The door opens and two figures emerge in the doorway. Karl-Martin is pushing Ida in her wheelchair.

"You packed yet, Lil?" he asks.

Ida is beaming. She has a beaded traveling bag clutched on her lap.

UNDERSTANDING

Danton

"Why do you think I've been working on that old DeSoto?" Karl-Martin said. He was grinning from ear to ear. "Can't fit all of us into that pickup of yours."

A thousand thoughts were going through my mind, but they all came down to this: Ree and old Lone Dog had sent me off to find two boys, and now it looked like I would be returning with two boys and a carful of strangers whose reasons for coming I did not fully understand or trust.

My concern centered mostly around Lillie. Though my time with Ree had been brief, I could tell she was a tough one, and there was something in the potential dynamic between her and Lillie that was worrisome.

Levi and Reuben had been protective of their mother when I had been at their house, and they obviously loved her. But there had been none of the warmth that I had felt between the two of them — especially Reuben — and Lillie. She had claimed a kind of motherhood with them, and I did not know any families that had room for two mothers.

Nonetheless, I was sure that it was Lillie who was behind this decision for them to accompany me. There had been a self-satisfied manner about her this morning that had seemed quite out of place in a woman who was about to lose two young boys who had become the center of her life.

"So what's this about?" I asked. "This decision to come along."

Her back was to me. She was clearing dishes off the table and straightening the kitchen.

"We are part of this," she said. Her voice had a tone that closed down any further possibility of discussion.

I turned to Ida.

She was sitting in her wheelchair in the corner, smiling. "Oh, I just thought it would be fun to go for a little drive," she said, following it up with a wink and a happy chuckle. She obviously had been in on this and was taking great pleasure in watching it play out.

Karl-Martin stood quietly in the background, saying nothing.

Reuben and Levi were standing on the stairs, watching. Reuben was bouncing up and down and making faces. He was clearly excited about having all his friends together. Levi was standing stock-still and stern, holding the blanket with the *čhaŋnúŋpa* tight to his chest.

Karl-Martin went to the refrigerator and took out two large brown paper bags full of food. "I arranged for the Petersons to look after the place for a few days," he said to Lillie. "I'll take these out to the car. We should get on the road before the weather picks up. Feels like something going on in the air." The wind banged the screen door open and shut as he spoke.

Lillie straightened a few things and shooed the boys toward the door. "Time to hurry," she said.

"What about Bones?" I asked. I couldn't imagine they were leaving him, and the thought of saying my final goodbye to him here tore at my heart.

"Mister Bones comes," Lillie said. "You've got room in the truck."

When Reuben heard that, he ran to Mister Bones and threw his arms around the old dog's neck. "I want to ride with the Mister Danton man and Mister Bones," he blurted. Bones thumped his tail and licked Reuben on the face.

"No, you ride with us," Lillie said.

"Let him go with Mr. Danton," Ida said. There was authority in her voice.

Immediately Lillie backed down.

I stood back, not really understanding what was going on, but filled with relief that my time with the old dog was not yet coming to an end.

Ida was staring at me strangely, almost as if she was looking past me at something else.

"You let Reuben sit right next to you," she said. "Right next to you. You understand? Right next to you."

"I understand," I said.

A rush of wind blew a thin wisp of dust across the floor.

I remembered old Lone Dog's comment about how my passenger seat would be a good place for Reuben. The wind had been blowing strong on that day, too, and I wondered if I really did understand. In fact, I wondered if I really understood anything at all.

SOMETHING ISN'T RIGHT

Karl-Martin

Something isn't right. I don't want to let on, but something isn't right. There's a weight in the air, like something is pushing down on us. I'd like to think it's the coming of rain, but it doesn't feel like rain. It doesn't feel like anything I recognize. The whole sky is unsettled and angry.

At least the DeSoto is running well. Thank God Danton is a good mechanic.

We had to put Ida's wheelchair in the back of the pickup. Danton strapped it down with a piece of rope. He kept looking up. I can tell he's worried about this weather, too.

I've never seen a year like this. Dust storms, heat waves, insect swarms. Everything but rain. The old-timers talk about the Dust Bowl and the Depression. Sometimes I think they revel in it, kind of like old soldiers revel in their wartime experiences. But even those who went through the Dust Bowl say that this year reminds them of those times. And when they say it, there is fear in their eyes.

What's painful is that they approached this drought year as if they were fighting the last war, and that has only made things worse. At the first sign of locusts, they were out spraying their crops with kerosene and digging trenches and lighting fires in hopes that the smoke would keep the insects away. And when the infestation never happened, they were left with poisoned ground and poisoned crops and rain that never came to set things right.

Now the soil is sick and the crops are diseased.

I haven't really been paying attention to how widespread this is. I don't read the papers, and our radio reception is spotty. I've mostly kept to myself and tried to hold things together. So aside from an occasional conversation with neighbors or the mailman, I haven't had much news about what's going on in other parts of the state.

But now that we're on the road I see how bad this really is. We're only a couple hours out and already it feels like a war zone. Farms are abandoned. Crops are withered and stunted. Just up ahead a half dozen emaciated cattle are gathered around a dry water tank. They're just ribs and spines; they look like they're just waiting to die. Everything everywhere is covered with dust.

We just crossed into plains country. Danton is leading us. He says he knows the fastest way. I have no choice but to trust him.

The world here seems even more desolate. The arroyos are dry. The few trees look like burnt skeletons. It's a landscape of suffering and death.

Lillie has disappeared inside herself. She's sitting quietly with her hands in her lap. She seems not even to be noticing the dying land around us.

Ida is in the back seat talking quietly in Dakota to little Levi. He's listening intently, but I can see him glancing around at the landscape. I think he knows he is nearing his home country.

Danton is several hundred yards ahead. He's driving cautiously. I'm sure it's because he's worried about the DeSoto. I wish he would hurry. This sky is churning, and whatever it's bringing does not feel good.

I don't know how far we have to go before we get to the boys' home — I should have asked — and I don't know what we are going to find when we get there. I want to arrive while it's still daylight, if you can even call this daylight. It's more like some kind of illuminated darkness, and it's getting darker by the mile.

I've never seen anything like this before. The sky is nearly black, but the trees along the arroyos are a shimmering silver. Where there should be shadows there is light, and where there should be light there are shadows. I've turned my headlights on just to keep track of the road. It shouldn't be this way, not so early in the afternoon.

I should have listened to Danton when he proposed putting this off for a few days. But we're here now, and there is nothing to be done.

I only wish I was more of a practical man, confining my thoughts to seed catalogs and the *Farmer's Almanac*, like the old-timers around here. But I've read too much and seen too much, and my thoughts keep running to some lines I remember from Milton's *Paradise Lost*: "Where all life dies, death lives, and nature breeds, perverse, all monstrous, all prodigious things...."

I'm not sure this hard country was ever paradise, but whatever nature is breeding here is prodigious and monstrous, and if I were inclined to fantasy it would not be hard to see this weather as Satan scouring the sky on swift and solitary wings.

LOTS MORE ON FIRE

Danton

We shouldn't have left this morning. I knew it. But no one would listen to me. When Karl-Martin came in with Ida, I knew there was no resisting. So I just finished my breakfast, packed up my things, and made ready for a journey I didn't want to take.

"An ill wind blows no good." I think that's the phrase. And that was an ill wind this morning if ever I've felt one. It was hot, too hot for the day. It kept gusting and banging the door while we were loading, like some kind of animal trying to get in, or something trying to give us a message. The pieces just didn't fit.

Now we're on the road and we're driving right into the teeth of whatever this is, and I don't like it. It's big — that's the thought that keeps coming to mind — it's big and indifferent and dark and roiling.

Reuben is banging his heels against the seat and making little sounds with his lips. He seems unconcerned, even unaware. But Mister Bones is acting strange, and that concerns me. Dogs have a sense that picks up everything — thunderstorms, earthquakes, full moons, bad people. And he's picking up something. He's normally quiet and relaxed, but right now he's on high alert.

Karl-Martin and the rest of them are about a half a mile behind me in the DeSoto. I'd be pushing harder if I didn't have to keep in touch with them. But they don't know where they're going except by following me, and other than a couple of test drives along the dirt roads near their house, that DeSoto hasn't had any real shakedown.

I wish I would have checked it out more closely, but it never occurred to me that it was going to be taken on a several-hundred-mile journey. I assumed it was just going to be puttering back and forth to town.

I hope Karl-Martin is paying attention to it. He has basic farmer skills with machines — the kinds of skills that keep things running — but he doesn't have a mechanic's head. He can't see systems and think out in front of things. The implications of rusted brake lines, fan belts cracked from age and disuse, things like that — he doesn't see them coming. And that DeSoto had been doing a lot of sitting before we fired her up.

I'm trying to keep these worries out of my mind and think about the moment when those boys will pile out of the car and run to their mom and grandpa. It will be a celebration, and I should be proud of the part that I played in it. And I will be. But right now there's the weather, the DeSoto, my concerns about Lillie and Ree, and the tension I'm feeling in everything around me. Add the twitchiness I feel from Mister Bones and the lonely emptiness of this back country route I've chosen, and there's not much room inside me for feeling too good about anything.

Sometimes I wish I would have stayed in Michigan, married one of the local girls, had a couple of kids, and never looked much further than the corner bar and the local tackle shop. It would have made life a lot easier. But I'm here, somewhere on these accursed Dakota plains, with darkness closing in at one in the afternoon and a whole lot of people depending on me for something I don't really quite understand. All I can do is make the best of it.

Mister Bones has started making an odd, almost ultrasonic high-pitched squeal. He's jerking his head around, like he's looking for something. The sky is dropping low, turning the whole landscape dark. But there's a glow behind it, shining through the darkness with an unearthly light. It's like midnight at midday. It feels completely wrong.

Both Karl-Martin and I have turned our lights on. I can't make out if this is dust or fog, but it is obscuring everything on all sides. The DeSoto is only several hundred yards behind me, but it has been reduced to just two pinpricks of light in my rearview mirror.

I need Reuben to help me out. I need eyes in all directions to help me get through this.

"Reuben," I say, "I want you to help me."

Reuben is still making motorboat sounds with his lips to the tune of "Ol' Man River." Where he learned that song, I have no idea.

"I want you to get up on the seat and watch out the back window. I want you to let me know if we lose sight of Mr. Steinbach's car."

He nods and stands up on the seat.

"I see them," he says.

"Good. You keep your eyes on them. I have to concentrate on driving."

The road is almost completely obscured. It's like driving in a snowstorm of blackness.

I crack the window slightly, but the air is thick and noxious, like fire or soot, so I quickly close it again.

"Do you still see them, Reuben?"

"I see them."

The visibility is almost zero. I don't know whether to speed up and try to outrun this or to pull over to wait it out.

"Can you still see them?"

"I see orange."

It's a strange comment, and not what I need.

"That's fine. But can you still see Mr. Steinbach's car?"

"I don't see a car. I see orange. Like the sky is on fire."

The comment catches my attention.

"On fire?"

"Like the orange is moving in the clouds."

I need to check this out. I pull to the side of the road and step out. The dust is acrid. It blinds my eyes and fills my nostrils. Mister Bones scrambles out behind me and runs frantically along the ground, mewling and whining and sniffing the earth.

Reuben has stuck his head out of the window and is looking back down the road. He's right, the sky is orange, as if seen through clouded glass.

"I can't see them," he says.

I cover my face and wait for Karl-Martin to catch up, but his car doesn't appear. Something has gone wrong.

"We've got to go find them," I say. "Get back in the truck, Mister Bones."

Bones limps back to the truck. I lift his rear end and push him onto the seat. "Sit down, Reuben," I say. "We've got to go back and get your brother."

I head back in the way we came. The sky is turbulent. The roiling darkness has a strange coppery edge. It's so bright that I have to shield my eyes.

I drive for a mile, heading into the orange glow.

An object rises up in the darkness. It's the DeSoto, sitting motionless in the center of the road. Karl-Martin is standing in front of it with the hood open and a handkerchief over his mouth. The wind is blowing strong. The dust makes him look like a ghost.

I roll down my window. "What's wrong?" I shout.

"Car's overheating," Karl-Martin says. His voice is almost lost in the wind. Steam or smoke is rising from the engine.

"Let me check," I say. I jump out and put my head under the hood. The sweet smell of antifreeze fills my nostrils.

I put my hand near the radiator cap. It's too hot to touch.

"I'll get a flashlight," Karl-Martin says.

He hurries around to the passenger side and returns with a silver metal cylinder. The wind and dust are pelting us. Its light is weak against the swirling darkness.

I shine the light down the front of the radiator. The entire surface is covered with bugs and straw and what appear to be remnants of a mouse nest.

"Damn," I say. "Radiator's plugged. We should have checked. We'll have to let her cool down then clean it out. Nothing else we can do."

Karl-Martin heads back to the car. I stick my head further in the engine. I need to make sure no hoses have split and there aren't any leaks from the engine block.

Reuben is standing next to me pulling on my sleeve.

"Not now," I say.

I try to shake free from his grasp. He pulls on my sleeve again. "Mister Danton man. Mister Danton man," he says. He is adamant.

"What?" I ask. "Make it quick."

He points off to the north. "See? Over there, behind those hills. The sky is lots more on fire."

DO WHAT *UŊČÍ* SAYS

Levi

We are stopped.

There was a sound, loud-like, and Mister Steinbach stopped. He got out of the car. He opened the engine part. There's dark sky everywhere, like a storm, but with smoke. It burned my eyes when he opened the door.

He is looking at the engine place. Mister Danton is there, too. I can hardly see them. They look like shadows.

I want to stay in the car. Miss Ida is looking at the *čhaŋnúŋpa*. She is smiling at the *khéya*. She says that *khéya* means "long life." "That will make your grandfather happy," she says. She is not showing fear.

The wind is blowing hard against the car. There are sticks and weeds flying across the road. The dust is hitting hard-like on the windows. It sounds like rain. I feel to be more scared, but Miss Ida is talking calm. She is holding my hand. She has told me to call her *Uŋčí*.

I hear hard banging on the door. It is Reuben. I can see him through the window. He's pounding on the door with his fists.

"Levi, Levi. Let me in." His voice is frightened-like.

I don't want to let him in. I want him to go back to the truck.

Reuben keeps hitting on the door. "Let me in, Levi. There's a fire sky."

"You let him in, Levi," *Uŋčí* Ida says. "He is your *nisúŋkala*, your younger brother."

I feel shame for not wanting him in the car. Momma and Grandpa say I always have to think of Reuben first. He is blood, they say. He is your little brother. But I want *Uŋčí* Ida just for me.

"Yes, *Uŋčí* Ida," I say. I have to do what an *uŋčí* says.

I try to push open the door. The wind pushes it back. Reuben is pulling hard from the outside. He is shouting about a fire sky.

We get the door open and he climbs in fast-like. The wind grabs it and pulls it full open. I can't get it shut.

The car is filling with dust. It's burning my eyes. The wind is making a roaring sound.

Mister Bones is at the door. He is making squeal sounds. He can't climb in. "We have to get Mister Bones in," I say. "Help him, Reuben."

Reuben can't help him. He is too small.

I get down and lift Mister Bones in. He licks my face. He is all covered with dust and soot.

"We have to shut the door," I say.

Reuben has crawled up close to *Uŋčí* Ida.

"You have to help me," I say.

"I can't," he says.

"Stop being little," I say. "Be man-like." I am getting angry with him. This wind is hot. There is burning in my eyes.

"I'm going to push hard on the door," I say. "You pull from the inside." Reuben makes a face. He pulls hard on the door. We get it closed. I get in just before it shuts.

Reuben is back up against *Uŋčí* Ida. He has his arms around her. It makes me mad to see him making her his *uŋčí*.

He pushes close against her. "I don't like this day," he says. He is being little boy–like.

Uŋčí Ida strokes his cheek.

"It will be okay," she says. She is smiling. She is not showing fear.

That makes me feel better. I do not want to show fear. I want to be man-like. I want to show *wóohitike*. *Uŋčí* Ida makes me feel less fear.

The wind is loud, like when we were on the train. Mister Bones is licking at Reuben's feet. Reuben is pulling at me.

"There's a thunder sound," he says.

I tell him there is no thunder.

"Shh," *Uŋčí* Ida says. She puts her arm around Reuben's shoulder. "What are you hearing, Reuben?"

"It's an everywhere sound. Like the whole earth is making noise," he says.

He stands up on the seat. He points out the back window. "Over there. The sky is more fire-like. See?"

I look behind. It is like the dark is filled with orange.

I see Miss Lillie outside the car. She has a scared look. She pulls the door open. The air is full of noise and dust.

"Ida, you have to get out," she says. "We'll all have to go in the truck. Levi, go get Ida's chair."

I go to climb out to get the chair.

Uŋčí Ida grabs my arm. "No," she says. "Go to the trunk. Get my bag."

Miss Lillie is full scared-like. "Forget your bag, Ida," she says. She is full shouting. "This is coming fast. We have to get out of here."

Mister Steinbach has gotten back in the car. He is turning the key. The car makes noises. It doesn't start.

Miss Lillie is pulling on Uŋčí Ida. "Come on, Ida. We'll get your chair."

Uŋčí Ida pulls away. She turns to me. "Get my bag, Levi," she says. "Do what your uŋčí says." Her voice is strong-like.

I don't know what to do.

Grandpa told me I must always do what an uŋčí asks. Miss Ida is my new uŋčí. I think to do what she says.

There is a loud sound. It is like a thunder sound. It is the ground sound Reuben heard. It is everywhere. It is big like the whole sky.

Miss Lillie is coming back. She is almost running. She is pushing the wheelchair. Mister Danton is helping her.

"I'll get Ida in the chair," he says. "Levi, Reuben. Get Mister Bones. Get in the back of the truck. Cover your faces."

The smoke smell is strong. My eyes are burning.

I see Mister Steinbach. He is on the ground. He is on his knees, praying-like. His hands are folded like church hands. He is shaking.

"What's wrong with Mister Steinbach?" I ask. I'm scared for him. I have never seen him in this shaking way before.

"We'll get him," Mister Danton says. "Help me get Ida in her chair, then take Reuben and get in the back."

The sky is now full orange everywhere. Birds are flying fast. They are making screaming sounds.

Uŋčí Ida does not move. "Where is your *čhaŋnúŋpa?*" she asks. She is talking to me. Her voice is calm-like.

I show it to her. It is on the seat rolled up in Miss Lillie's blanket.

"You bring that with," she says. "Now get me in my chair and push me."

"We haven't got time for this," Mister Danton says. He is doing shouting talk. He is angry scared. "You boys get in the truck. I'll push Ida."

"No," Miss Ida says. "He will do what I say." She is talking to Mister Danton. She looks at him with strong eyes.

"This is not your time," she says.

Mister Danton steps back. She is talking *wakȟáŋ*.

She slides herself across the seat. I help her into her wheelchair.

"Put my bag in my lap. You push me, Levi. You come, too, Reuben." She points backward, up the road.

Mister Danton is angry. Miss Lillie is sitting on the ground by Mister Steinbach. He is still prayer-like. She is holding him close to her.

"Ida," Mister Danton says. It's a shouting voice. "This fire is going to kill us."

Uŋčí Ida does not answer. She points back behind the car. "Push me there," she says. It is a small hill.

I do not know what to do. I am afraid of the fire. I'm afraid for Mister Steinbach. I'm afraid to make Mister Danton angry.

"Do what your *uŋčí* says," *Uŋčí* Ida tells me.

Reuben is with Mister Bones. The smoke is strong. I call him to come help me. We push *Uŋčí* Ida up the road. She is singing a prayer song. It is the same song as when we touched the stone in her house. It is in Lakota. Reuben sings it, too.

Mister Danton is yelling at us. The thunder-like sound makes it hard to hear. *Uŋčí* Ida says not to listen.

We get to the top of the hill. The sky is brown with orange. The burning feel is everywhere.

Uŋčí Ida opens her bag. She has four sticks. They are green on the bottom, then blue, then yellow, like the earth color, then the sky, then the sun.

"You take them, Levi," Miss Ida says. "You put them on either side of the road. You push them in."

I am full scared. I do what she says. Reuben helps me. The sky is more orange and hot. It is burning. My eyes are full stinging. I can't see anything.

"Now lift me up," she says. "Get under my arms."

She is hard to lift. Reuben isn't strong. She pushes with her hands. She half stands.

"Now hold me up."

We hold her.

"I'm going to sing," she says. "Reuben, you sing with me."

She starts a song. It is loud-like and strong. I am afraid for it. It is low like a different voice. It does not sound like her.

She puts her arms out. I'm afraid for her falling. She makes her hands sky-ways. Her song has loud sounds in it, like thunder sounds, not words. Reuben is singing it, too. I don't know how he knows it.

"Levi, hold up your pipe," she says. "Toward the sky. Toward Creator."

I unwrap the *čhaŋnúŋpa*. I hold it sky-ways.

The orange light is strong. The whole sky is wind and hot and dust.

I feel a hit, like someone slapping me. It hits again. I do not understand it.

Reuben makes a loud cry-like sound. He is looking up.

I see something hit his face.

It is wet.

It is rain.

Aftermath

THE AXLE BUSTER

Danton

I don't know what that was and I hope I never see anything like it again. All I know is that it moved in on us with a fury that was almost human and that we all would have died if the rain hadn't come.

As long as I live I'll never forget the image of Ida silhouetted against that roiling wall of darkness with her arms lifted skyward while Levi and Reuben held her up. I can still hear the echo of that strange dirge or prayer or whatever it was that she and Reuben were singing.

I can't believe I let her lead those boys right into the teeth of it. I should have stopped her, but I didn't know how. It was like everything around her was terror and chaos and heat and horror. But she exuded an aura of peace, of control, of something that I couldn't challenge. When she looked at me and said, "This is not your time," it was like she had a knowledge that was too deep to challenge.

And that rain. I've never experienced a torrential downpour like that since coming west. Most storms out here pass over and empty themselves in a brutal burst that lasts for a few minutes, then move on. Not this one. From that first gunshot report that hit the roof of the car, it must have lasted three-quarters of an hour.

Did Ida's chanting really have something to do with it? The sky had been so strange all day — unsettled, dark, half fog and half dust, illuminated by that unearthly half-light. Did she recognize it and know what was coming and want to offer some Lakota prayer for our safety? Or did she really have something to do with calling forth the rain? I'll never know and I can't even guess. This is simply way beyond my understanding.

Right now my job is to keep us moving forward. Miraculously, Karl-Martin's car started. Perhaps it only needed to cool down. We were able to get enough of the muck off the radiator so that I think it will drive without a problem. But I don't trust it any more than I trust that the fire is out. There are fingers of burnt patches still smoldering on the hillsides. I can't tell if the mists rising from them are steam or smoke, and there's no saying that they won't catch fire and start moving again. I remember what Karl-Martin said about the prairie fire that attacked him.

We'll drive cautiously, but we have to drive. I can't count on Ida's magic or the rain or anything else. I've got to get us out of range.

Now that the sky has cleared I can get a feel for where we are. Red Shirt Mesa is off to our right. That puts us about five miles from the Lone Dog place as the crow flies. But this road is one I've never taken. I've seen it from a distance and know where it cuts off from the main road, but I've always avoided it. The locals call it "the axle buster," and most folks will drive an hour out of their way rather than drive on it. The only ones who ever use it are drunks or people running from the law or kids in stolen cars. Had I known we were going to end up on it, I would have gone a different way. I just routed out a shortcut on the map to make things easy on the DeSoto. I didn't realize that the route I'd chosen would end us up on a road that was legendary as a car killer.

But now we're stuck with it and I've got no choice but to get us through, even if we have to do it at five miles per hour.

I'm worried about Karl-Martin. He completely fell apart during that conflagration. Once we got him off his knees and into the car he just sat there holding tightly to the steering wheel and mumbling some sort of incantation that sounded like it was in Latin.

I was concerned that I would need his assistance to get his car back on the road, but he seemed almost catatonic. He was shaking and breathing hard the whole time. It was like he was in shock.

The truth is, I think we were all in shock, and still are. None of us, with the possible exception of Ida, really understands what has happened.

What amazed me most was how everything changed when the rain finally stopped and the dust cloud lifted. What had been some kind of hell storm of fire and smoke miraculously transformed into a blue sky, rolling with banks of fast-moving pillowy cumulus clouds. If it wasn't for the charred hillsides and the smell of the burnt earth, you would never know that this was land that only hours ago had been parched almost to the point of death.

But now that has passed, and it is the road, not the sky, that's challenging us.

It's laced with diagonal fissures a foot wide and a foot deep. Over the years the rains have dug them into trenches that can snap a car's tie-rod like a matchstick. In several places there are actually small boulders sticking up through the dirt. Either they had been too difficult to remove when the road was built or the construction crew had never even made the attempt.

I'm inching my way slowly over the protruding rocks, trying to take care not to allow them to scrape the undercarriage and punch holes in the oil pan. Karl-Martin is about a hundred yards behind me. I hadn't wanted him to drive, but there had been no other choice. Neither Lillie nor Ida knows how to drive and the boys were obviously out of the question.

Karl-Martin assured me that he was okay, but his voice had been hollow and distant. I don't know if I can count on him to be attentive to the realities of this road.

I'm worried, too, about the *čhaŋnúŋpa*. I have to hope that Levi has a tight grip on it. Some of these dips and fissures are truly bone-jarring.

Almost worse than the fissures and gullies are the stretches where the rain has reduced the road to a slippery viscous gumbo. In these places even the slightest grade can set the car wagging and fishtailing. If you don't navigate these patches judiciously, the car can spin itself into the muck up to its wheel wells. You'll never get moving again until someone comes along to pull you out. And that isn't going to happen on the axle buster.

Reuben is standing on the seat next to me, jumping up and down. I'm trying to make him sit, but he refuses. I think he senses that we're getting close to his home. The jostling keeps tossing him against me.

"Reuben, damn it, you've got to sit down," I tell him. "You're going to get hurt."

"No, I'm not." He glowers at me and sticks out his jaw.

"Yes, you are. Now sit down."

I hit a deep fissure and the truck jolts violently. Mister Bones lets out a yelp from his place on the floor. I manage to grab Reuben just before he catapults into the dash.

"Reuben, this is a bad road. You've got to sit down. I need to concentrate. This isn't a joke."

He makes a snarling sound and turns away. Reasoning isn't working with him.

"Listen, this road is slow going. Why don't you tell me a story?"

"I don't know any stories."

"Then why don't you sing me a song? You know lots of songs."

"No, I don't. I don't know any songs."

He folds his arms fiercely across his chest and drops down on the seat.

"Sure you do. How about that song you and Miss Ida were singing in the storm?"

Something in him suddenly changes.

"Don't talk about that," he says.

"Why not? It sounded like a beautiful song. Sing me just a little bit of it."

He puts his hands over his ears and kicks the front of the seat hard with his heels. "No! No! I won't sing that song."

His lip is quivering. His eyes have gotten wide.

"What's wrong, Reuben?"

He looks up at me. His face is that of a scared little boy.

"I don't want to sing that song."

"Why?"

His face is pleading.

"I don't want to make it rain again."

SIDE-EYES

Brother James

Sometimes you do the wrong thing for the right reasons.

When I dropped off them little fellows, I figured I was leaving them with their own kind and they'd find their way home in their own way. Tried to put them out of my mind. But every time I got up onstage and started singing "Ol' Man River," it was like I was singing with a ghost. I only heard half the song. The other half was out there somewhere in the cornfields or the quarries or I don't know where. I wasn't going to have no peace until I found out.

I figured the best way to find them boys was to retrace my steps. Figured I'd start with the Indians. Indians don't have no truck with a Black man. Since the Civil War we been living with them anyway. Run away from the white slave owners, ended up with the Indians, and they took us in like we were some of their own. Now and then you see a kid, look at them one way and see an Indian. Look at them another, and you see a little Black boy, little Black girl. People live together, things happen. When you're on the outside, you got to huddle together. Don't matter what color you are.

So I went back to that place where I dropped them off. Parked the Studebaker a ways away. Got to be respectful. Folks would rather talk to someone on foot than through a car window.

The place looked different during the day. Lots quieter. All that drumming and fires must have been for something special. Now, it was just the wind in the trees and the clink of the hammers off in the distance. Working man's time.

I walked along the path, keeping my eyes down, listening to the creek flowing by. Folks was working hard in their quarries. Nodded when they saw me.

I wasn't sure how I was going to find the boys. Poor folks don't offer much when they don't know you. Indians don't offer nothing at all. Just their way.

So I just kept walking and nodding and hoping. At least no one stepped up to say, "What are you doing here?" That's the white man way. Indians, they just kept hammering and nodding and keeping about their business. I figured if the good Lord wanted me to get an answer, he'd find a way to get it to me. No need to be asking any questions on my own.

First edge of fall was coming on. Still hot as the devil, sweat pouring down. But you could tell something was out there. The light changes in August, colors lose their edge. The air starts smelling of distance.

I was walking the path, listening to the water rushing and the wind moving in the leaves, thinking about my daddy and how hard he'd had to work to survive hammering in those quarries down by Sioux Falls. For a minute I nearly forgot about the boys, caught up as I was thinking about my old man. But them little fellows kept coming into my mind, tapping me on the shoulder, telling me I wasn't there for memories. I was there to right a wrong.

So I was watching close, even if I didn't look it. Just force of habit. Growing up on the streets, you learn to pay attention. Otherwise you might miss something that ain't going to miss you.

I wasn't looking for anything in particular. Just looking and hoping. My daddy used to say you can't make luck, but you can sure enough leave the door open. I was keeping that door open by keeping my eyes open. Maybe I'd see something that meant something. Maybe I'd see the boys themselves.

Now, some of them quarry pits, if you want to see what's going on you got to go right up to the edge, stick your head over, and put yourself right in the middle of someone else's business. Never a good idea. But you can always give something the side-eye, maybe catch a glimpse of what you need.

That's what I was doing, nodding if someone saw me, otherwise keeping my business to myself.

Soon enough I come near one pit, about as deep as two men standing. I heard some hard hammering down there, heavy thud on the rocks, a deep sound, the strokes of a strong man working hard.

I give it the side-eye and there's the backside of a man, broad as a bull, swinging a big hammer, sweat pouring down in a big V in the back of his shirt. He was about square as a house, looked like someone who had never missed a meal and never lost a fight. Next to him, sitting on a rock, was a thermos. The same thermos them little Indian boys shared with me back on the road in my car.

You can't waste no time when you're talking to a working man. So I figured I might as well get right to it.

"Good morning, my friend," I said.

I knew I was taking a risk. It ain't always a good idea to claim a friend for someone who ain't offered you their friendship first. But it was about the best "hello" I could think of.

He put down his hammer and looked up at me. Took off his bandanna and wiped his forehead. Nodded. That was good enough. There wasn't no "why you here?" or "what you want?" in his look. Just an honest nod.

I can tell a good man pretty easy. There ain't no face that don't show something when they look up and see a colored man standing before them. Sometimes it's a full shutdown, sometimes it's just a quick flash before they settle in to where they want to be. Sometimes it's something you don't want to see. But it's hardly ever straight across with nothing in between. When you see that straight-across look, that's a man you can trust. And this man was about as straight across as a man can be.

I wished I had a gift to give to him. That's the Indian way and it's a damn sight better than any other way as far as I'm concerned. But all I had was a good hand and an honest heart. Best thing I had to offer was my name, so I give that up right away.

"Name's Brother James," I said. No need to give him my last name because it don't connect to nothing, not like an Indian last name.

He give me another nod. He wasn't offering nothing, but at least he was letting me come further.

I could see he was in the middle of working and didn't want to do some dance, so I come straight to the point.

"That thermos you got there. I shared a drink from that with a couple of young Indian boys about a week ago. They was on the run. I let them off here, thinking they might be better off with their own kind. Now I'm thinking I might have let them go too soon. Just trying to fix my wrong. Make sure they're okay."

As I was speaking it came to me that maybe this man had come by that thermos in a bad way, so I didn't want to say their names.

The man wiped his hands on his bandanna and come to the side of the pit.

"Why they with you?" he said.

"I found them in a cornfield. Trying to get here to the quarry. Something about making a pipe for their grandpa. Figured I'd save them some shoe leather. So I put them in my back seat of my Studebaker and drove them down here. I left them off down by them sister rocks. Figured they'd make their way to where they ought to be."

The man thought for a while. I never begrudge a man who takes his time. Give a man time to speak, you know that what he says is what he wants to say.

"I seen them," he said when he'd done enough thinking. "They had a turtle."

I could see he was testing me.

"Yeah. The little fella. It was kind of like his pet. Called it his *khéya*."

The man smiled. "Indian word."

"He kept rubbing his hand on my hair. Called me *ťhaťháŋka* head."

The man burst out laughing. It was a good belly laugh, the kind a man makes when he ain't hiding nothing.

"So what you doing now?" he asked.

"I don't know where they were going. I didn't ask. But I want to make sure they get there. It can be a cold world."

The man went quiet again. The wind moved the leaves in the trees.

You can't outwait an Indian, but I was damn sure going to try. He moved slow, reached over and took a swig out of the thermos bottle, spit it on the ground.

"Lone Dog," he said. "That's their name. I give them a stone for their grandpa. Sent them on their way. Pine Ridge, I think. Maybe Rosebud."

It wasn't quite a road map, but it was damn close.

"You're mighty helpful," I said. "Much appreciated."

He nodded again and reached the thermos up to me. "Have a drink before you go. Getting to be another hot one."

I took a swig from the thermos and handed it back to him.

"Hope you find them," he said. "I done some running myself."

"Yeah," I said. "I been there, too."

NO PLACE TO BREAK DOWN
Danton

It took me close to an hour to get through the worst of the axle buster. But, gradually, the road was becoming more passable. There were still craters and boulders, but they were becoming smaller and farther apart.

I kept a close watch on Karl-Martin behind me, never letting him out of my sight. This was my country, not his, and I was still worried about his mental state and the shape of the DeSoto.

The sky had opened into a towering blue vault. Cotton-white clouds raced in from the west. The rain was gone, as were the dust and the grit. It was almost as if a fever had broken.

Ahead of me the land spread out in an awe-inspiring panorama, with hills and swales stretching for miles toward the horizon.

I rolled down my window and cracked open my wing vent. The air was bracing, almost celebratory. It was nearly impossible to remember the smoke and haze and darkness of only a few hours ago.

Off to the north Red Shirt Mesa rose silent and solitary into the cobalt-blue sky. I was glad to see it. It was one of the landmarks of the reservation, long held sacred by the local tribe. I was told that young boys still went there on their vision quests. Red-tailed hawks and peregrine falcons floated lazily above it, small dots in an azure and limitless sky.

The road had taken on a familiar rhythm, rising and falling in its march toward the western horizon. A few bison wandered on the dun-brown hillsides, but there was no sign of human habitation anywhere.

"No place to break down," I said to Mister Bones.

Mister Bones made no response. He had climbed up next to

Reuben and the two of them were curled up together like newborn kittens, breathing and snoring in unison.

I descended to the bottom of a deep dry wash and began the long climb to the top of the next rise. The tires spit rocks as the truck labored its way up the grade.

The road, though less rocky and rutted, was still difficult and treacherous. It had turned from a ragged gash in the land to a narrow shoulderless hogback barely wide enough for a single vehicle. I had no idea what I would do if I met another car coming from the opposite direction. But that was the least of my worries; we hadn't seen another vehicle since we had first turned onto the axle buster miles ago.

My biggest concern was how much further we would have to go on before we intersected with Lone Dog Road. My hope was that I would get a better view from the next summit.

As we topped the rise the view almost took my breath away. Spread out before me was an endless series of low rolling hills stretching for what seemed to be a hundred miles to the horizon. In the far distance a few bald knobs and cones of extinct volcanoes punctuated the landscape. Red Shirt Mesa stood like a lone sentinel off to the north; the rays of the afternoon sun glanced off its surface and sent shadows racing down through the hills and draws.

I wanted to wake Reuben so he could see his land from this amazing vantage point. But I decided to let him sleep. The day had been hard on him and there was excitement enough coming to him in just a few miles.

"God's country," I said under my breath. It was about as close to a prayer as I was likely to get.

Ahead of us, the thin gravel roadway snaked its way downward and disappeared into the rolling hills, only to reappear a few hills farther on, ever smaller and more distant, barely even visible against the shooting rays of the afternoon sun.

I sat there transfixed by the stark majesty of it all, when a small movement far down in the next valley caught my eye. At first I thought it might be an animal grazing by the side of the road. But upon closer examination it appeared to be a vehicle with a man crouched beside it. How he would've ended up out here and what he was doing was anybody's guess.

A REGULAR PARADE

Brother James

Folks out here, they're a different breed. Less farmer, more cowboy. Their "what can I do for you?" ain't got much help inside of it.

Not that I expected much — Black man looking for a couple of Indian boys can't expect a whole lot of welcome. But I had to ask.

I probably could have picked someone better than that big fella sitting on that bench to ask for directions. But his was the first town I come to and he was the first person I saw. And he cut it pretty much down the middle — part Indian, part white. Figured he might not shut down like a full-blood or ask too many questions like a white man.

I give him the name — Lone Dog. Seemed to register with him. He thought for a while — he was a slow-moving sort — then told me to go straight out on this road, ten, fifteen miles, and take a right at an old dead tree just past a tire on a fence post.

Either he give me bad directions or he was a bad man making sport of a stranger, because just after I took that right turn the road turned into something you don't want to drive on. All rocks and ruts, hardly no road at all. Tore up the Studebaker pretty bad. Blew a tire like popping a party balloon. Lucky I always carry a spare.

Now, I ain't much for car work. I mostly confine my efforts to keeping things clean and polished. But a man's got to know how to change a tire if he's going to be spending any time on the road. I had that old Studebaker jacked up and the lug nuts loose when this Ford pickup come rumbling down from the top of the rise. I can tell you I was awful glad to see it. Hadn't been another car on the road since I set out. Soon enough, an old DeSoto come following up behind. A regular parade in this country.

I waved down the pickup as much for directions as for help. If this road was going to keep on this way, I didn't want to take it. If I was going wrong, I wanted to know it.

Driver pulled over and stuck his head out. Middle-aged white guy. Hair combed back. Clean shaven. Looked more like a schoolteacher than a rancher.

"You doing okay?" he asked. Decent-seeming fellow. Neighborly tone in his voice.

"Fine. Nothing a little elbow grease and a little time won't fix."

There was some ruckus inside the truck and a little head popped up. Heard a scream that just about froze my blood. Door swung open and, as I live and breathe, out come the little fella, Reuben, running toward me and shouting "Old River Man!" at the top of his lungs.

Home

A BOY SHOULD HAVE A DOG

Levi

I see Red Shirt Mesa. We are close to our house.

I'm feeling good to give the *čhaŋnúŋpa* to Grandpa. I'm feeling good to see Momma. I want to show them my new friends.

But there's strong sadness in my heart. I'm trying to hide it behind my face.

Mister Steinbach is humming. He is tapping on the steering wheel.

"Happy to be getting near home?" he asks.

"Yes, sir," I say.

He looks at me in the mirror. I do not look at him. I am not good at hiding sadness.

"Something bothering you, Levi?"

"No, sir."

Miss Lillie turns to me. She is mother-like. She can see my heart. She does not like to see me lie.

"What is it, Levi?" she asks.

I don't want to tell her. I am thinking about Mato, when we used to play in the hills. He liked to chase prairie dogs. Right here is where he got shot. I see where we found him. I am thinking about when he got shot.

"I'm thinking about my dog," I say. It is a truth lie. I feel strong shame to say it.

"You have a dog?" Mister Steinbach says. "I'll bet you're excited to see him."

"He's dead," I say. There are full tears in my eyes.

Uŋčí Ida takes my hand. She pats it soft-like.

Mister Steinbach looks at me in the mirror. "Sorry to hear that," he says. "What was his name?"

"Mato."

"That's a good name," Miss Lillie says. "Bear. Was he like a bear?" She is showing kindness.

"Kind of," I say. I am choke-talking now.

"I bet you miss him, don't you?" she says.

"Yes, ma'am," I say. I try to hide my face.

Mister Steinbach stops his humming. He stops his tapping. He looks at Miss Lillie. They do not say anything. They are doing eye talk.

"A boy should have a dog," Mister Steinbach says.

"Yes, sir," I say. My voice has more choke sound.

They sit more silent. They are doing more eye talk.

Mister Steinbach smiles at Miss Lillie. It is a big smile.

"What do you think, Lillie? Can you think of a dog that's available?"

"There's one that comes to mind," she says. She is smiling strong, too. "He's pretty old, though."

"Let me ask you, Levi," Mister Steinbach says. "Do you ever have pork chops for dinner at home?"

"Yes, sir," I say. I do not know if they are making jokes.

"Well, that settles it," Miss Lillie says. "I think we have just the dog for you. How would you like to have Mister Bones for your dog?"

GREETING

Ida

It is a good thing I have come.

I had been thinking a lot about Lillie, but I had not thought to come along. Then when Karl-Martin came to my house and told me that Lillie was going with Mr. Danton to bring the boys back to their mother, I said, "My little *maškè* needs some watching over." I had a feeling for what she was doing, and it worried me. She's a soft-hearted one, my Lillie, all full of book learning and love for everybody. But she has the heart of a library girl. Sometimes she thinks too much inside of books and gets herself in trouble.

This has been a bad road. I don't know why Mr. Danton took it. Sometimes I think he is like Lillie. He has a good heart but lacks good sense.

For a while I thought maybe he had gotten us lost. But when little Levi started watching close, I knew we were close to his home.

The Lone Dogs' house was way back in the hills. It was mostly tar paper and boards and some old windows. A woman and an old man were standing out in front.

"That's Grandpa and Momma," Levi said.

They must have heard the cars.

The old man was smiling. He had a *wóksape* look, like he'd seen some things and wasn't letting on. The momma had hatchet eyes. Ice blue and cold. They made me worried for Lillie if what I was thinking was right.

We drove in together, all in a line, Mr. Danton first, then Karl-Martin, then the *hásapa* man we had found on the side of the road. Little Reuben was bouncing up and down in Mr. Danton's truck even before it was stopped. I could hear him squealing and screaming from all the way back here.

As soon as the truck had slowed enough, he pushed open the door and ran to his momma and grandpa with his arms out. Mister Bones jumped out and limped behind him.

I kept my eyes on the momma and the grandpa. I wanted to see how much love was in their greeting. Sometimes there are good reasons for sending boys off, sometimes there's not.

The grandpa smiled and held back. He was leaving Reuben to the momma and keeping his eye on the rest of us. The momma squeezed Reuben tight. She had full love in her eyes but her face was hard. I could see her looking past Reuben. I knew she was looking for Levi.

Levi was sitting next to me in the back seat. He was all straight-backed, but his hands were shaking.

"Levi, you're home," I said. I could tell he was gathering himself, wanting to be all proper when he stepped out. It made me smile. He was full Indian; he wanted to own himself before showing out to anyone else.

He was holding tight to the blanket with the pipe. "You leave that with me," I said. "You can give that to your grandpa later. I'll help you. Right now you hurry out and see your momma and grandpa before your little brother takes all their loving."

"Yes, *Uŋčí*," he said. My little joke made him smile.

"I should tell Reuben about Mister Bones," he said. "I should tell him Mister Steinbach and Miss Lillie gave him to us."

I put my arm around him. "You're a good brother, Levi. But they gave him to you because your heart is sad for Mato. Reuben can love him, but Mister Bones is your dog. Remember that."

He put the *čhaŋnúŋpa* blanket on my lap and stepped out slow and proper. Then the little boy in him come out and he ran to his grandpa and momma and threw his arms around them with all the scaredness and loneliness he'd been hiding since the day he and his little brother had first run off. It made my heart warm to see this. There was love in this place.

Lillie was watching close from the front seat ahead of me. I knew what she was seeing. I put my hand on her shoulder. That was all the words we needed.

Karl-Martin was just still, watching and waiting like the rest of us.

Mr. Danton was staying in his truck and the *hásapa* fellow was holding way back in his car.

"You go get my chair out of the pickup," I said to Karl-Martin.

I did not know what was going to happen, but I wanted to be in front. I knew that Creator hadn't brought me here for nothing.

◊ ◊ ◊

We got out one by one. The mother looked at us flat-eyed. She had a smile on her face but it didn't run deep.

The old man kept that *wóksape* look. He give us a big "hello" smile and shuffled out to us. A small one he was, not much taller than Levi. But he had big-hearted eyes. I kept the pipe blanket held tight on my lap. He looked at it and smiled. I think he knew.

Levi was trying to show strong, but little Reuben was all full of excitement. He was running and holding and pulling, dragging his momma out toward us and going on about Mister Steinbach and Miss Lillie and the beautiful *wašíču* house with lights and pictures of the Jesus man, and *tȟatȟáŋka* heads and *khéya*s and most anything that passed through his mind. When he saw the *hásapa* man he started up singing real loud something about rivers. It put a smile on all of us, even the momma with the cold eyes.

The grandpa come out to where we were. He had his arms wide in full greeting. "*Taŋyáŋ yahípi*," he said. It made me happy that he was speaking Indian.

He went around to each of us, shaking our hands in the two-handed way.

"I am glad you are here," he said. "Welcome to our home."

He turned to Levi. "And who are your friends?"

He was a smart one, this *wičháȟčala*. He was making Levi take the man part.

But Reuben started in before Levi could speak, talking faster than his thinking. The *wičháȟčala* stopped him. "Let your brother talk, Reuben. You listen. Make sure he speaks the truth."

Reuben nodded strong. He wanted to make his grandfather happy.

Levi stepped up, all formal and stiff.

"This is *Uŋčí* Ida," he said.

He was a good boy. He was placing the elders first.

I was ready to tell of my family so they would know who I was, but Levi was saying only names. I think he knew the *wašíču* would not know the traditional way.

He went around to each of us, saying our names. The old man shook our hands again, one by one. We would tell more of ourselves later.

Only when he spoke of the *hásapa* man did this change. When he said, "This is Brother James," Reuben ran over and threw his arms around the man and started singing that song about a river. That Brother James bent down so Reuben could rub his hair. "*Tȟatȟáŋka* head, *tȟatȟáŋka* head," Reuben said. The Brother James laughed. I could see he had a good heart.

The *wičháȟčala* was full of kindness. He had a giving spirit. "I am Amos Lone Dog," he said. "This is my granddaughter, Ree Lone Dog. We are honored to have you in our home."

The granddaughter did not send kindness toward us.

It was good to be around an Indian man. He did not ask why we were here. I have been so much around *wašíču* who want to know everything right away.

"We have brought food," I said.

"Good. Good," the *wičháȟčala* said. "You will all stay. I have special *tȟatȟáŋka* meat from the *Pahá Sápa*. It fed on the sacred grasses. We will have a feast." He spoke Lakota. I spoke Dakota. We could understand each other.

"Levi. You will push *Uŋčí* Ida," he said.

Levi looked at me. He was scared for the *čhaŋnúŋpa*. I whispered to Lillie to take it back to the car and place it under the seat.

Levi smiled strong. He was full of relief.

He pushed me toward the house. It was hard pushing.

"You are strong as a man," I said. The *wičháhčala* heard me.

"I would help you, Grandson," he said. "But I am old." He winked in my direction.

Oh, he was a crafty one, this old man Amos Lone Dog. He reminded me of my grandpa. He saw everything and said little.

It was so good to be back in Indian country.

TALKING CHRISTIAN

Lillie

The boys went off with the men. It was only Ida, the Ree woman, and me.

This Ree was showing respect, but she was showing no kindness. I was glad that Ida was along.

"You come in," the Ree woman said.

She pulled Ida up the small step to the house. She was as strong as a man.

I came in behind with a box of food.

She pointed to the table. "Put it there." She offered no words of greeting or thanks.

I was raised in the Lakota way, even though we lived in *wašíču* farm country. My mother taught me that when you open your house you must open your heart. This Ree was not showing an open heart.

I looked to Ida. We are like sisters. She knew what I was feeling.

"I am happy to be here," she said. "I am honored to share your kitchen." She was trying to show kindness.

The Ree woman said nothing. Her quiet was full of distance.

I felt ashamed of my *wašíču* farm dress. This Ree wore blue jeans and a man's shirt tied at the waist — clothes for outdoor work, not clothes for farm cooking or caring for a house. Her skin was like mine, but we had different hearts.

Her grandfather had said we should prepare a feast together. I did not know how we should do this. This was not my kitchen.

I looked to Ida. She had her caring smile. She would know what to do.

I did not like this kitchen. It was cold. It had no heart.

Ida was singing and wheeling around by the table. She was making the kitchen her own. She was an *uŋči*. She could do that.

We had brought turnips and eggs and chokecherries and bread I had made. Ida took them out of the box and gave them each to this Ree, one at a time. I knew what she was doing. She was touching hands through the passing of food.

She gave Ree the chokecherries. I had picked them earlier that summer.

"Oh, these are good," Ida said, holding them up. "Our Lillie picked them in her special place. They are the best." She smiled at me. I smiled back. Ree took them but did not smile.

"That Reuben," she said. "He likes the *wagmíza-wasná*. I had some for him when he came to my house. He said it was good, but that yours was better. We should have *wagmíza-wasná*. Will you make it, my *maškė*? I will watch and learn your way."

I love to watch Ida. She is like *Iktómi*. She knows how to weave a web. She was calling Ree *maškė* — her sister friend — just like she called me.

"Lillie, you will prepare the *thíŋpsiŋla*. We will make *wóhaŋpi*. Old men like soup. No bones. I will pound the meat so it is easy to chew."

Ree was watching closely. I had never seen eyes like hers. They were like looking at fire through ice.

Ida took Ree's hands in hers.

"I am so happy to be in your kitchen," she said. "I live alone. I don't get to make meals for others. Thank you for this gift." She squeezed Ree's hands tight. Ree did not pull away.

Ida has a happy smile. It is full of sunshine. No one can keep a dark spirit when Ida is around. Seeing her with Ree gave me courage to speak.

"I was so honored to have your boys at our home," I said. "I tried to treat them as my own. They are such good boys."

Ree looked at me. "Yes. They are good boys." Her answer was flat. It had no thanks in it.

She picked up the chokecherries and held them in front of her.

"You are married to the *wašíču*," she said.

"Yes. Karl-Martin."

"Reuben says you have a picture of Jesus in your house."

"Yes. It was from my husband's grandmother. It is all he has of her from his homeland back east."

She looked at me and then at the chokecherries. She set them back on the table and wiped her hands on a towel in the corner.

"I hope you did not talk Christian to them," she said. She did not even ask how the boys happened to come to our home.

A BAD DAY

Levi

I had thought Reuben would be glad to be home. But he was full angry. He was walking in his clenched-fist way.

"Reuben, don't say anything about the *čhaŋnúŋpa*," I said. "We want it to be a surprise for Grandpa."

Reuben was mad. He had his bear face.

"I want to tell him," he said.

"No. *Uŋčí* Ida said to wait. She said we should give it to him in the honor way."

"I don't like *Uŋčí* Ida."

"Yes, you do. You're just mad."

"I want to show Grandpa the *khéya* on the *čhaŋnúŋpa*."

"So do I. But *Uŋčí* Ida said to wait."

I was talking low. I did not want Grandpa to hear. He was walking ahead with Mister Steinbach, Mister Danton, and the Brother James. They were going around back. Mister Steinbach was holding Grandpa's elbow so he didn't fall.

Reuben was growling and doing bear-stomp walking. He was making me mad again. He was only thinking inside himself. I thought to move his mind to something else.

"Why don't you talk to Mister Bones?" I said. Mister Bones was walking right with us. He was limping. He had a sad face.

"I don't like Mister Bones."

"Yes, you do. Mister Bones is your friend."

Reuben made more pinch face and pulled his head down. He would not answer.

"Well, then, why don't you sing the Old River Man song?" I thought to turn his mind to singing. Reuben always gets happy when he sings.

"I forgot it."

"No, you haven't. You never forget anything. You sang it with Brother James."

"I don't like Brother James. He's mean."

"Brother James is the nicest man I ever met."

"He's mean."

I was full angry now with Reuben. He was using his mind for fighting.

The men were up behind the house. They were all standing close. Mister Danton looked sad. Mister Steinbach was helping Grandpa by holding his arm.

"We should go up and help Grandpa," I said.

"No," Reuben said. "I want to stay here."

He sat down on the ground and crossed his arms. Mister Bones licked his face. Reuben swatted at him.

"Reuben, why are you being like this? Aren't you happy to see Grandpa and Momma?"

"This is a bad day. I don't like this day."

I always want to be a good big brother. I want to show Reuben the good way. But he was being full stubborn. I sat down next to him. He made a snarl sound and turned away.

"Remember how happy you were when you saw Old River Man where his car was stuck? Remember all the hugs you got from Momma and Grandpa when we got back? This is a good day."

He took out his stone *khéya* and walked it along the ground. He made motor sounds with his lips.

I put my arm around him. Grandpa says that you should show calm when there is fighting. I closed my ears to his sounds and pulled him close to me.

"That's a good *khéya*," I said.

"I like this *khéya*," he said.

It was the first "like" thing he had said.

"Does the *khéya* like to walk on Mister Bones?"

He walked the *khéya* along Mister Bones's back. Mister Bones wagged his tail.

"We should go in the house if we don't go up with Grandpa," I said.

Reuben leaned against me. I could feel crying in him.

"Why are you crying, Reuben?" I asked.

"I don't want them to go," he said.

"Who?"

"All of them."

"But they can't stay here. They have to go home."

He put his head on my chest. He was doing full sobbing now.

"That's why it's a bad day."

SHE WASN'T ANYTHING

Ida

I could see from the first that she was a hard one, this Ree. There was no thanks in her for all that Lillie and Karl-Martin had done for the boys. I was afraid for my Lillie.

I looked around the kitchen. The cups and dishes were set upside down so they wouldn't collect dust. The dishcloths were all folded square and put in a pile. The plates were school-type plates, all white and washed and leaned against each other like trees blown over in the wind. There were no pictures or strings of herbs. There was no vase for flowers.

A kitchen should be a place full of love. This was like a kitchen in a hospital or a boarding school. It was a place without life.

"You keep your kitchen so nice," I said. I wanted to make the room warm with my words.

"I keep things clean," she said.

She was chopping carrots with a big knife. Her chopping was harsh. It had no care or attention.

I knew she could not be a bad woman. I had met her boys. They had been brought up well. It came to me that she had just been raised too much by men.

"Let Lillie do the chopping," I said. "She likes to cut vegetables. You make Reuben's special *wagmíza-wasná*. I know he is waiting for it."

Lillie was across the table. She had pushed herself back against the wall when she heard my words. She did not want to be in this woman's house.

"Come, Lillie," I said. "It will be good to work together."

Lillie always brings love to the kitchen. When we were young she would come to my grandparents' house and wash and cook and help my grandmother bake. She made the kitchen happy when she was around. She would sing while she worked. She was not singing now. She was only watching. We were all just watching.

I did not like this. Where there is only watching, there is no trust. I thought to move us to sharing. I thought to bring happiness to the room.

"Tell me about your *wagmíza-wasná*, my Ree. Did your grandma teach you?" All Indian people like to talk about their grandmas.

Ree's cold got even colder.

"She could not teach me," she said. "The *wašíču* stole her spirit."

Her words came out black and angry. A dark spirit filled the room.

"Oh, my girl," I said. "What happened?"

She nodded toward Lillie.

"I don't want to talk with her here."

I took her hand. "You should not be like that. Lillie is like blood to me. She was as a mother to your boys when they were lost. You should trust her."

"I do not trust someone with a picture of Jesus in their house."

I could feel anger rising in Lillie. "That picture is my husband's," she said. "When he sees that, he remembers his grandma. Would you have me take his grandmother's memory away from him?"

I had never heard Lillie speak like this. She was speaking without fear.

I thought to put softness in the room.

"What Lillie says is true," I said. "Karl-Martin is a *wašíču*. But he is a good man. He puts everyone else first. He helps me and tells no one. He asks nothing for himself."

Ree pulled her hand away from me.

I could feel dark anger in Lillie. I had never felt it before.

"I do not tell my husband how to live," she said. "And he does not tell me. I practice the ways I was taught by my mother and grandmother. He may practice what he will. I married a man, not a picture on a wall."

She laid the knife down on the table and stood up. Her anger filled the room.

"I came here to honor you. I came to bring your boys back. I have washed their clothes. I have fed them at my table. I have treated them as my own and kept you always in my heart as I cared for them. Now I give them back to you whole and healthy as a gift from my hand to yours. Tell your grandfather it has been an honor to be in his house. I will leave now."

I could not let this happen. I knew this was not why Lillie had come.

I wheeled my chair in front of the door.

"My girls. My sisters," I said. I took hold of each of their hands. "I wish you to listen. You have each given everything you have to those boys in the way that was asked of you. You must not become small. Keep your arms open to each other. Creator did not bring you together to fight over a picture on a wall."

Lillie pulled her hand away. "This woman has insulted me," she said. "She has insulted my husband. She has not respected us as guests."

"Lillie, Lillie," I said. "She is protecting her boys. She does not know you."

Lillie did not care. "I was not raised to be insulted," she said. She moved toward the door.

I would not let her pass.

"You must not let your anger harden your heart," I said. "Sit. For your dearest friend, Ida. Sit. Stay." I understood her insult. It was not right the way Ree was acting, but I would not say it. I hoped that Lillie would let the insult pass.

Lillie thought long. Outside the boys were laughing and squealing.

When she spoke, she spoke to me, not to Ree. Her voice was quiet but strong. "I love those boys. I do not see an insult as love. But you are my dearest friend, Ida. For you I will stay."

I could see Ree was listening. I could not tell her thinking. She sat for a long time. She was measuring her words. They would not come without thought.

When she spoke, her words came slow. But her words, too, were strong.

"I do not mean to insult you. You are married to a *wašíču*. I do not know your heart. But I, too, will do what *Uŋčí* asks. You may stay if you want to. You can hear what I have to say. But you will not understand."

I grabbed both their hands. "*Philámayaye*, my girls. Thank you. You make me happy."

Ree took a photograph from beneath a bowl on the shelf. It was the one bowl that was different. It had been carved from wood.

The photograph was yellow and worn. It showed a *winúhčala* with dark skin and sad eyes. She had a blanket wrapped around her shoulders.

Ree placed the picture on the table in front of Lillie.

"You speak of your mother and grandmother. You cut carrots. You pick chokecherries. You smile when you work. This is my *uŋčí*. She would not cut carrots. She would not pick chokecherries. She would not speak. She would not even say her name. She would only sit. What would you know of this?"

She pushed the photo closer.

"Look at her. What do you see?"

"She looks kind," Lillie said. She was trying hard for me.

"She was not kind," Ree said. "She was not anything."

She put the picture in her pocket, as if to remove her *uŋčí* from Lillie's presence. I did not like this. There was too much darkness filling the room.

"It would be good to burn some sage," I said. "Lillie, get the shell. It is in my bag."

Lillie took the abalone shell from my bag and prepared the sage. We had done this together before.

"Will you light it, my Ree?" I said. I wanted her hands working with ours.

Ree lit the sage. The smoke rose and filled the room. It was chasing the darkness.

"Now, some sweetgrass."

Lillie placed some sweetgrass in the shell.

"I have saved this for a long time," I said. "It was from my grandfather. It will call the good spirits."

Ree lit the sweetgrass. Her hands were moving more gentle now. She respected the old ways.

"Now, Lillie, give sister Ree the feather."

Lillie took the eagle feather from my bag and handed it to Ree. Their hands touched. It was as I had hoped.

Ree fanned the smoke. I said a small prayer.

"There is more peace now," I said. "Now, my *maške*. Talk to us. Why do you say this about your *uŋči*?"

Ree placed the picture back on the table. She fanned the sweetgrass with the eagle feather. "I do not like to tell this story. I do not like to make bad things come alive by speaking them. But because you have brought me my boys, I will tell you."

This was a great gift. She was opening her heart.

"We are honored to hear it," I said.

Lillie said nothing.

Ree turned her spirit inward to find her memories. When she spoke, she spoke soft, from inside herself.

"I loved my *uŋči*," she said. "My whole life I wanted to make her happy. But she was so sad. From the time I was a small girl she was always sad.

"I asked Grandpa why *Uŋči* was always sad. He said that when she was little a priest in the boarding school had come into her room and thrown water on her. She had tried to hide under the bed, but he had found her and threw the water on her head and said, 'Now you are a Christian.'

"She didn't tell anyone, but it made her so afraid. She kept trying to act Indian, but in her heart she thought she had been made Christian.

"The priest told her that Indian language was the devil's language. He said if she spoke it she would go to the hell place. He said it was full of devils and fire and it burned you up without ever killing you. You could never get out.

"Grandma told the priest her parents spoke Indian. She asked him if they were going to this hell place.

"He told her she should pray and not ever speak Indian and maybe her prayers would keep her mother and father out of the hell place. So all day she prayed. All day and all night. She prayed in English. She hardly knew any words.

"When her parents died she cried and cried. She put her hands in fire. She said her parents were going to the hell place and she wanted to feel what it was like. The doctor had to wrap them in bandages. She said she didn't care. She said her parents were in the hell place because she had not been able to make them go Christian.

"When she married Grandpa, he told her to stop thinking about the hell place. He told her that Creator had made a special place for Indians so they did not have to go to the hell place, but she didn't believe him. She said that Grandpa hadn't had water thrown on him, so he didn't know."

Ree looked at Lillie. Lillie had her eyes closed. She was fanning the sweetgrass. She would not look at Ree.

Ree talked more. Her voice got more soft. Her heart was coming open.

"Momma died while I was being born. *Uŋčí* said it was her fault because she had not been Christian enough. She said she had made Jesus mad. She cut off all her hair and cried all day and wouldn't talk.

"She sent me to boarding school to make me more Christian. But I kept running away. When they caught me the priest said I had the devil in me. That made *Uŋčí* even more afraid.

"She stopped doing anything Indian. She would not let me play with Indian dolls. She would not cook Indian food. She would only chop wood and carry water and pray. Grandpa and I had to do everything.

"Grandpa moved us out here to help her spirit. But still she would not talk. She sat all day holding beads and trying to pray in English. It was like something had stolen her spirit.

"She tried to make me pray with her. I threw the beads on the ground. She cried and hit me with a stick.

"I wanted to leave, but I could not leave Grandpa. I tried to cook, but I only knew peeling potatoes in the boarding school way.

"I was so lonely. I had no friends.

"There was this neighbor boy come by sometimes to help Grandpa. I thought it would be good to feel a man, so one day I lay with him. That day gave me Levi.

"I wanted Levi to have an Indian name, but *Uŋčí* cried and cried and said he would go to hell unless I named him Christian. So I named him Levi from the Bible book. I had heard the name in boarding school. I liked its sound. That made Grandma happy. She would hold him and rock him and say this name, 'Levi, Levi,' because it was a Bible name. That was the only happiness I ever saw in her.

"The neighbor boy went away and never came back, except one time years later. I wanted a husband so I lay with him again. But he did not want to be a husband. This time I had Reuben. I gave Reuben a Christian name, too, so Grandma would be happy. But Grandma was afraid of Reuben. She said she saw an Indian spirit in him. She was afraid it was a devil spirit. She would not let him be in the same room with her.

"One day Grandma was acting funny. She was crying out and would not talk to us. She said she was going to Jesus and she went up into the hills.

"We found her the next morning. There were birds flying over her. She was curled up holding a little cross covered with beads. Her spirit had left her.

"Now I have Levi and Reuben and that's all I have except for Grandpa. I would do anything for my boys. But I cannot forget what happened to my *uŋčí*. I cannot forget that the *wašíču* stole her spirit and left her afraid of everything and holding beads and saying white man prayers to keep people out of hell. I cannot forget that they made her afraid of her own grandson.

"I will always be angry for that. I will always be angry for my *uŋčí* and all my people who had their spirits stolen by the *wašíču* with their beads and their Bible books and their pictures of Jesus.

"Grandpa says we must accept this world. I am not like that. I will never accept what was done to our people. Grandpa says I should take joy in my boys and leave such things to the Creator.

"I love my boys and I will protect them until the day that I die. But I will not forget my *uŋčí* and my people. I must fight for them with every breath. It is not enough just to be a mother."

Lillie had been quiet. She had been listening with full respect. She fanned the sweetgrass. The smoke came up between them.

"It is for me," she said.

WITH HIS OWN HAND

Lillie

I do not like this woman. I do not like her coldness. I do not like her anger.

Yes, she has known great hurt, but she is not alone in that. Creator has given her what he has taken from me. Her anger should not be greater than her love.

"Tell her about the boys," Ida says. "How they came to you."

How good Ida is. She is trying to reach across.

I do not want to reach across. But for Ida and the boys I will try.

Outside we hear the boys talking. They have their serious voices — little men solving problems and making plans. It makes my heart full.

I look across the table at Ree. There should be love in her eyes, too. But there is none. Her eyes are like fire beneath ice on a winter day. I have never seen eyes like that before.

"I'm sorry for what happened to your *uŋčí*," I say. "Your life has known great sadness."

Ida smiles at me. She knows that I am trying.

"Let me tell you about your boys and how they came to our house," I say. I think that by opening my heart to her she will open her heart to me. But Ree says nothing.

"My husband found them walking along the road. They were hungry and dirty. They said they had been running. They were good boys, both of them, full of respect. Levi was brave and strong — a good protector for his little brother. Reuben was just a boy full of joy."

Still, this Ree does not speak.

"Levi told us that the school men were after them. He said that you had told them to run and hide. We did not know what to do. We knew we couldn't keep them; they were not ours. We couldn't send them back; you had sent them away to protect them. But they were so young to be out alone. So we fed them and clothed them and sent them to Ida. We treated them as our own."

Still, this Ree is silent.

I am filling with anger. I am opening my heart to this woman, but she is showing no interest in what I am saying, no gratitude for what Karl-Martin and I have done. Her heart is a closed fist.

I feel disrespect in her. I have given her boys the love I have kept inside since Joseph passed. When she disrespects that love, she is disrespecting my Joseph.

I reach in my pocket. I will do something that I never thought I would do.

"You have shown us a picture," I say. "Now I will show you a picture."

I take out the small photograph that I keep in my pocket. It is my secret. No one knows I have it, not even Karl-Martin or Ida. I keep it with me always, close to my breast, close to my heart.

I place it in front of her.

It is a picture of Joseph. He is wearing cowboy boots and a bandanna, standing with his feet wide apart and his thumbs looped in his belt. It was taken at the county fair when Karl-Martin bought him the belt. He is smiling his happiest smile, looking right at me. The photo is smudged where I have kissed it so many times at night.

"Here," I say.

Ree picks it up. Her face has no expression.

"Who is this?" she asks.

"It is my son, Joseph."

I can see Ida growing tense. She has never heard me talk of Joseph since his death.

Ree looks at the picture for a long time.

"Why is he not with you and my boys?"

"He has walked on," I say. The words come hard to my mouth.

Ida squeezes tight on my wrist.

Outside I hear Levi and Reuben arguing. Their voices make Joseph even more alive. I feel the tears rising in me.

Ree looks at me. Her eyes are changing.

"I'm sorry to hear that," she says. "When did he pass?"

"A year ago. April twenty-third."

"How old was he?"

"He had thirteen years."

She puts down the photo and stares at me.

Everywhere is filled with Joseph's spirit.

◊ ◊ ◊

Outside Reuben and Levi are shouting. Mister Bones is barking and whining. I want to stop my ears — Mister Bones had been Joseph's dog; I'm hearing Joseph in the voices.

"Come, I will make some tea," Ida says. I can tell she's worried to hear me talking like this.

Ree waves her off. She is staring at me.

There is stomping outside the door. Reuben pushes in and runs to his mother. He is covered with dust and dirt. Mister Bones is barking and scratching at the door.

Reuben pulls on his mother's sleeve. "Can Mister Bones come in?" he asks. He is all out of breath.

Ree wipes the dirt from his cheek. "Who's Mister Bones?" she asks. She keeps her eyes on me.

"Mister Bones is our dog friend."

Levi pushes in through the door. He is covered with dust and dirt, too.

"I told you not to ask Momma," he says. I can see he is angry.

"But Mister Bones goes in Miss Lillie's house."

Ree gets down on one knee to be at Reuben's height. She takes his face in her hands. "We do not let big dogs in our house. They have their own place and their own life."

Reuben does his bear stomp.

"But he's my friend."

"I told you," Levi says. He is being the big brother.

Ree moves the boys in front of her and straightens their shirts and pants. Clouds of dust fill the air.

I am embarrassed. I had washed their clothes and made them bathe before we left. I wanted to bring them home clean. I wanted to show respect.

Ree straightens Levi's shirt. She reaches to tuck it in his pants.

"What is that?" she asks. She is looking at Joseph's belt. "You didn't have that when I sent you off."

Levi stands up tall. "Mister Steinbach gave it to me," he says. He turns the buckle toward his mother. "See? It has a cowboy and a horse. Like in a rodeo." His face is full of pride.

Ree picks up the picture on the table. She stares at the photo, then at the belt.

"Yes," I say. "It is the same. It was Joseph's. My husband wanted Levi to have it."

She holds out her hand to Levi. "Let me see it."

Levi unbuckles the belt and pulls it off. "See, Momma? The cowboy is waving his hat in the air. The horse is trying to throw him off. Just like in the movies."

Ree runs her hand over the buckle, then turns the belt over. On the back is Joseph's name, scratched into the leather with a knife.

"Who made this name?" she asks.

"Joseph," I say.

"With his own hand?"

"Yes."

She runs her fingers over the letters. She traces each letter slowly. I want her to stop. It is like she is touching my Joseph.

"And yet you gave this to my son?"

"My husband did. He wanted Levi to have it."

"Did you agree?"

"Of course. I would do anything for these boys."

She sits for a long time.

"Wait here."

She goes to a back closet. I pull the belt close and hold it to my chest. I do not want to let it go.

She returns with a small buckskin cross covered with beadwork and lays it on the table. She runs her fingers over the beads, like she ran them over the letters on the belt.

"This is from my grandmother's hand," she says. "It was what she was holding when we found her."

She pushes it across the table to me.

"I want your husband to have it."

I feel tears coming.

She folds my hand around the cross. She holds my hand tight.

"You are a good mother," she says. "And your husband is a good father."

The fire is gone from her eyes. And the ice.

INTRUDER

Danton

I could feel fear rising in my chest when I heard the car door slam. I knew that sound.

Then the heavy footsteps and the labored breathing, and Two Finger appeared in the doorway. The light from outside silhouetted him in the doorframe like a monster.

He didn't look at me or Karl-Martin. He walked straight across the room to where little Reuben was talking to his grandfather. Reuben saw him coming and crawled under the table.

"I'm taking him," Two Finger said.

The old man clapped his hands in apparent glee. "Ah, good," he said. "Good. I have been hoping to see you."

It was a strange response, completely out of context and completely inexplicable.

Two Finger brushed him aside. "You shut up, old man. This's got nothing to do with you."

"Oh, sure it does," Lone Dog said.

He gestured to a wooden kindling box by the stove.

"Sit down. Sit down."

The rest of us watched in stunned silence. Two Finger's violent intrusion had frozen us all in place. Old Lone Dog's behavior was making no sense.

Old Lone Dog hoisted himself out of his chair and reached out his hand in a welcoming handshake. "Creator told me you were coming," he said.

Two Finger ignored him. "I ain't here for your tom-tom bullshit. I'm here for the kid."

Lone Dog hobbled past him over to the bookcase. He pulled out a baseball and his old, worn baseball glove. "I think you are here for something else," he said.

Two Finger glared at him. "I know what I'm here for."

The old man bent over like a fielder getting ready for a ground ball. He pounded his fist into the glove. "Come on, batter, batter," he said, mimicking an infielder awaiting a pitcher's delivery. It was a practiced movement, surprisingly agile for someone his age.

He grinned at Two Finger. "I was a pretty good shortstop in my day. Nothing much ever got past me." He had a mischievous twinkle in his eye.

"I said to shut up," Two Finger said. I could feel his irritation growing. I was getting afraid for the old man.

Lone Dog continued undeterred. He kept tossing the ball into the glove as he talked. "Yeah, I was pretty good. We had this barnstorming team. Back in the twenties. All Skins. Mostly played on reservations. A few small towns. We weren't much. Just a bunch of bucks who loved the game. But we had this one guy. Big Lakota fella. Must of gone six four, 250. Had a curveball like no one had ever seen. Looked like it was coming straight at your head, then dropped down across the outside corner of the plate right at the knees. Strike every time."

Lone Dog took the baseball and gripped it between his thumb and his pointer and index fingers. He pantomimed throwing it with a snap of his wrist. "Violent thing, that curveball. Never met a man who could hit it."

I was watching Two Finger carefully. His face muscles were twitching and his hands were tensing.

"I told you to shut up," he said.

"He could've been something," Lone Dog went on. "Another Chief Bender. Hell, we even called him 'the chief.' There were even some scouts for the bigs sniffing around him. But he was a hard drinker. Couldn't count on him. Would disappear for days at a time. Come back looking like forty miles of bad road. Couldn't hardly even stand up."

Two Finger was on the edge of violence. "Stop wasting my time with this, old man," he said. "If you think you can stall while them boys get away…"

Lone Dog raised his hand for Two Finger to be quiet.

"Oh, that Chief, he liked the white women. They liked him, too. Met this one outside of Eagle Butte. Pretty young thing. They really hit it off. We didn't see him for three days. When he come back, he was married."

He got an impish grin on his face.

"Must have been a hell of a three days."

Two Finger's eyes had been reduced to slits.

"They had a kid. Cute little fella. Kind of our mascot. But Chief couldn't keep his pants on. Kept on snagging. One day his wife decided she couldn't take it no more. Took him to court. White man judge, white man justice. Gave the boy to the mother. Told Chief he had to stay away or he'd put him in jail and throw away the key. Broke Chief's heart. Oh, he loved that kid. Used to say, 'The only good things I ever had in my life were that kid and my curveball.'"

The old man pantomimed throwing the ball again.

"Even named the kid after that pitch. Called him 'my little Two Finger.'"

The room fell deathly quiet.

I had been around Two Finger for almost three months, and I had never seen a look like the one that came across his face.

All eyes were watching him to see what he'd do next. I glanced over at Karl-Martin, thinking that the two of us might have to try to stop him if he went for the old man. But he did nothing of the sort.

He took a step forward, drew a couple of deep breaths, then sat down heavily on the kindling box and stared at the floor. It was like all the angry tension had drained out of him.

Lillie and Ree and Ida were watching from the kitchen door. Ree was holding a large butcher's knife. I had no doubt that she intended to use it if Two Finger went for her boys.

Levi was standing behind her. Reuben was peering out from under the table.

We sat in silence for what seemed like two minutes, listening to Two Finger's labored breathing and the loose tar paper flapping against the side of the house in the wind.

Finally, Two Finger lifted his eyes to the old man and spoke.

"My dad," he whispered in a voice as plaintive as a child's.

Lone Dog nodded.

Two Finger's face filled with anguish. It was as if he was suddenly stripped bare of all the anger and rage and cruelty of forty years, leaving only a hurt and wounded and frightened little boy.

"What was he like?" he asked.

Lone Dog shuffled over and set himself down on the edge of the kindling box and put his hand on Two Finger's shoulder. I had never seen anyone touch Two Finger before.

"He was a good man," Lone Dog said, his voice almost as soft as Two Finger's. "Big sensitive guy, he was. He didn't want no one to see it. Always put on that gruff face. We used to bunk together sometimes on the road. Talk late into the night.

"He said that kid of his was going to be something. Wasn't going to be a drunk like he was. He wanted him to learn the old ways. But the Skins on the rez wouldn't have nothing to do with him. Said he had too much *wašíču* in him."

Two Finger was staring at the floor. His breathing was coming in gasps.

"When his mother took him to visit her white friends — she was a churchgoing type — they'd put down a blanket and make her put the little tyke on it. They said they didn't want a bastard half-breed touching their floor. The poor little fellow had to sit by himself while the other kids played together. They wouldn't let him go anywhere near them."

Two Finger said nothing. His breathing was heavy. He opened and closed his hands and stared at the floor.

Slowly he lifted his head and looked at the old man. His words came out slowly, as if he was afraid to say them.

"Did he like me?" His voice was barely audible.

The old man smiled and patted him on the knee. "More than anything."

"Do you know where he is now?"

"Dead, I guess. Someone said he froze to death over in Whiteclay."

Two Finger stood up and lumbered to the door. He pushed it open and walked out. The door banged several times and fell silent. We all looked at each other. None of us dared move.

Lillie was still standing in the kitchen doorway. She walked quietly across the room to where Karl-Martin was sitting and bent down and whispered something to him. He whispered something in return and squeezed her hand.

They stood there silently for a moment, holding each other's hands. Then she kissed him on the cheek, pulled herself up straight, and walked out the door after Two Finger.

TAKING A LIFE

Lillie

When that Mr. Two Finger had looked up at grandfather Lone Dog, I had seen a little boy — a little boy all full of sadness and hurt.

Still, I was afraid to approach him. I had seen him at our house; I had seen him push into the Lone Dog house to come after the boys. He was an angry man, and there is a place where anger turns to danger. I understood why Ree had carried that knife with her to the living room.

His back was to me. He was sitting on a log all slumped over. His face was buried in his hands.

"Mr. Two Finger," I said.

I spoke softly. I did not want to bring out his anger.

He did not answer.

I knelt beside him and touched him on the shoulder.

"Mr. Two Finger," I said.

He did not look at me.

"Mr. Two Finger."

I did not know what to say, but Joseph's memory gave me strength. "I once had a son. He was like you. He had both the blood of *wašíču* and the blood of Lakota flowing through him. But he was not strong, like you. He took his own life."

Mr. Two Finger turned to me. His eyes were empty. He understood what I was saying. But he was not there. His life had been taken from him long ago.

BAD TALK

Levi

I was glad when the bad school man had gone out the door. Momma told Reuben and me to run. She was holding her big cutting knife. "I will kill him if he touches you," she said.

We ran to our secret hiding place. It was down in the gully. We always came here when Momma got mad at us.

I had the *čhaŋnúŋpa* wrapped in the blanket. I had got it when we ran out. I did not want the school man to get it.

"Reuben, we have to hide the *čhaŋnúŋpa*," I said. "That school man will break it."

"I hate that school man. He tried to grab me."

"He didn't get you. What shall we do with the *čhaŋnúŋpa*?"

"Why was Grandpa nice to him?" Reuben asked. He was really upset. "He showed him his baseball."

"Grandpa is nice to everybody."

"But he showed him his baseball."

"I don't know, Reuben. Grandpa is nice to people. Even mean people."

"I heard Momma say she would kill him. She was holding her big knife."

"Momma's not going to kill him."

"I want her to. I want her to kill him."

"Stop talking that way, Reuben. That's bad talk."

"Momma talks that way."

"She shouldn't. Grandpa says the words you say might move into your hands. You can't talk about killing."

"But he's going to break the *čhaŋnúŋpa*."

"You can't talk about killing."

"I'll tell Mister Bones to bite him."

"Mister Bones won't bite anybody. He doesn't even have any teeth. Stop talking this way."

"He will if I tell him."

I pulled Reuben close to me. He was doing fast breathing and his eyes were blinking. I was afraid he might fall on the ground in that shaking way. I had to stop him. I had full fear, too. But I am his brother. I have to show strong. I have to show *wóohitike*.

"Let's go up the hill," I said. "We can go to the butterfly rock."

"The butterfly rock. The butterfly rock," Reuben said. He stopped his fear breathing and made a snapping with his mouth.

I was glad I knew how to move his mind around.

NO PART OF THIS

Brother James

I'm pleased to be here, but I ain't part of this. I just wanted to see that the boys got where they was going without something bad happening to them. I would have been good going on my way once they got me out of that ditch, but the old woman told me I had to come along. The way I was raised up, when a grandma tells you to do something, you'd better do it.

I could see from the get-go that there was things going on here that weren't none of my business. So I kept to the outside, wearing my good smile and keeping my peace.

It was pretty easy, what with the women doing all the talking and cooking in the kitchen and the menfolk sitting around in that little front room. Hardly enough space for all of them. No need for me to fill it up all the more with my being there. So I just said my "hellos" and went outside to be on my own.

I'm pretty much used to being alone, so I got no problem passing time. As Momma used to say, just turn your waiting into contemplating. And there's lots to contemplate out here, what with the big sky and the wind singing songs and the land going on halfway to tomorrow. So I found a little gully a ways up from the house and lay back to stare at the sky. Figured I'd go in the house when someone come out to get me. I don't go no place where I ain't been asked.

I kept thinking about all that darkness off to the east a couple of hours ago. Lots of cracking and rumbling. Lightning bolts cutting through the clouds, sky dark as night. Now all of a sudden it's all blue and sun streaming down. Different world out here.

I was lying there thinking about how the wind was almost more like remembering than hearing when I seen little Levi and Reuben go running past me out the back of the house. Levi was carrying something all wrapped up in a blanket like a baby. They was running full-on, like trying to get away from something.

"Hey, Levi," I shouted. "Reuben. It's old Brother James. No need to be in such a hurry. Stop and talk awhile."

Boys kept right on running, paid me no mind.

"Reuben," I shouted. "It's Old River Man, *t̃hathánka* head."

Little fella stopped for a second, turned around. His face was as frightened as any face I had ever seen.

"That bad school man is here," he said. "The one that broke grandpa's *čhaŋnúŋpa*. We have to hide."

Then it all fell together in my mind. That wasn't just some blanket Levi was carrying. There was a *čhaŋnúŋpa* in there, all wrapped up like a baby. They must have got one made from the stone that they got from that quarry place. They was afraid that the school man was going to break this one just like he did the old one.

"Ain't no one going to harm what you got as long as Brother James is here," I said. "Why don't you leave it with me? I'll take care of it."

"No," Levi said. "No one can touch this."

I didn't know the whole piece of what was going on, but it sounded like some kind of Indian thing that wasn't none of my business.

"Fair enough," I said. "Then stay here with Brother James. We'll watch over it together."

Little fellows didn't have to be asked twice. They run over and huddled down tight against me, shaking real hard.

I put my arm around them. It felt good to be holding them; good to be feeling like I was doing some good.

Levi put the rolled-up blanket between us, like to hide it. I could feel a lump in it.

"That your grandpa's new *čhaŋnúŋpa*?" I asked.

He looked up all wide-eyed, and nodded.

"Can I take a look at it?"

He unwrapped the blanket real slow and careful-like. Showed me a red stone pipe, all polished and bright with a little turtle crawling up its side. It was a real beauty.

"That's a heck of a pipe," I said. "Your grandpa's going to be really proud. Who made it for you?"

"Me and Reuben made it."

That was close to impossible from what I knew about making things.

"You made it? You two little guys?"

Little Reuben pulled hard on my arm. He was itching to talk.

"Mister Danton and Mister Steinbach told us how. But *Uŋčí* Ida said they couldn't touch it. You can't touch it either. We had tools from *Uŋčí* Ida's grandpa. I made the *khéya*. I sang it out."

He was talking a mile a minute and not making a lot of sense. But I had heard enough to put some real steel in my spine. I don't care if it's a Indian pipe or a painting or a little boat made out of wood scraps — when a kid works that hard at something, Brother James'll stand in the way of anyone trying to do it damage. Kids work from love, and when you hurt a kid's love you're sending a hurt all the way through the rest of their life.

"Ain't no one going to hurt that pipe," I said. "Not while Brother James is around. And I sure enough ain't going to try to touch it."

Little fellow looked up at me all full of trust and thanks.

Down the hill I seen a man come walking out of the house. He was slow moving, a big sort. I recognized him right off. He was the same man I talked to in town who give me directions.

Levi grabbed hard on my arm. "That's the bad school man," he said.

It made me feel bad. He must have followed me up here, or at least been put on the scent by my asking.

It got me angry thinking of that big man putting the hurt on a couple of boys. Fair is fair, and there wasn't no fair in that.

"I'm going to go down and talk to him," I said. "I come out here to see that you boys is okay, and I guess I ain't seen it all the way through, yet. Not till that pipe's in your grandpa's hands."

"No," Levi shouted. "Stay away from him. He's a bad man." He grabbed hard on my arm.

I gave him my best calm-down smile. "Listen, Levi. Brother James seen a lot of bad men in his life. This one ain't no badder than the rest."

Little fellow wouldn't let go.

"What are you going to do?"

"Not sure. But you got no need to worry. Most country folks ain't real comfortable with a Black man. Give them a little hoodoo talk and they think they're looking at some kind of deviltry. Turn tail and run."

I give him a little wink to take some weight off what I was saying. "Course some of them want to hang you from a tree."

I shouldn't have been joshing with him. "I don't want you hanging from a tree," he said. He was half on to crying. He was full-on terrified.

"Ain't going to happen. Nobody going to hang nobody out here, what with the folks we got. I just need to put myself in between until things get straightened out. Nothing he can break on me that ain't already been broken. But just in case, you might want to skedaddle up further when he ain't looking. Nobody ever got hurt by being too careful."

I tried to make it all matter-of-fact, like there wasn't nothing to be afraid of. But anyone who ain't got any fear in him is either a fool or a crazy man, and Brother James don't claim to be neither. So the face I was showing on the outside wasn't the face I was feeling on the inside. I had seen that school man close up, and his eyes didn't have no light. Inside I was thinking there was probably more hanging tree in him than I had let on.

Still, you make your stand where you make your stand, and I was making my stand between that dead-eyed school man and the boys. We all got our time and none of us knows when it is. Best leave that to the man upstairs and get on with what you got to do.

So I stepped from the gully, keeping a close eye on the school man as I did. He was walking around, kind of agitated looking. Made me even more cautious. Dead-eyed men when they get angry don't know no limits.

I held back, waiting for the right moment. Soon enough he sat down on a log and put his head in his hands. Made me come up short. One thing dead-eyed men don't do is show sad. And I was looking at sad.

Minute later that Lillie woman come out, the one married to that tall farmer fellow who was driving the DeSoto. She looked kind of cautious and frightened-like. She walked up behind the school man and put her hand on his shoulder. Made no sense by anything I knew. And if there's one thing Brother James has learned in life, it's that when something makes no sense, you better stand back and watch until it does.

I turned around and went back up the hill to find the boys. If you're going to try to stand between someone and trouble, you best be sure where that trouble is coming from.

BLUEBIRD

Karl-Martin

The room was stifling and dark. Why old Lone Dog had a blanket over the window, I don't know. He was settled back in his chair with his eyes half closed and a tiny smile on his lips. The room was silent except for the creaking of his rocker.

I could hear muffled words from Lillie talking to Two Finger outside the front door. She has a lot of courage, and this was a side of her I'd never seen before. But I was worried. There's a cruelty about Two Finger that frightens me. Just because old Lone Dog shocked him with the revelations about his father, doesn't mean that the cruelty is gone. It might even have made him more dangerous.

I wanted to go to Lillie, but I knew from my time working in the boarding school that it's an insult to walk out on an elder unless you're excused. And I didn't want to insult this man. We were his guests and he had a strange authority about him that I did not want to challenge.

I was hoping Danton would help me. But he was staring at the floor with his elbows on his knees and his hands folded like a man in prayer.

We were all feeling the silence between us. With every passing moment I was getting more anxious.

Old Lone Dog was saying nothing, but I could tell he was catching everything.

He pulled a cigarette from his shirt pocket and lit it with a wooden match that he struck on the thigh of his jeans.

"Don't worry," he said with a wry grin. "Your wife's going to be all right." It was like he was reading my mind.

He took a couple of deep drags from his cigarette. "You need to trust things more. Creator's taking care of a lot of things."

He pecked the cigarette toward me like a man making a point.

"I've known lots of guys like you," he said. "You think too much. Try to control everything. A man can make himself miserable that way. Get himself all tied up in knots. *Wašíču* mind."

He nodded toward Danton. "Still, it's better than your friend here. He don't try to control enough. Every time he comes to a hard place he just turns and runs in a different direction. Tries to get away from the hard stuff. Everything. People, questions. Don't matter. Just gets up and runs."

He drew hard on his cigarette to punctuate his point. "That's why I sent him after the boys."

I had no idea why he was talking like this or what it meant. I just wanted to go to Lillie.

Danton shifted in his seat. He kept staring at the floor. The old man reached over and patted him on the knee.

"Yep," he said. "The minute I saw you, I knew that you could help me. I could tell you weren't no kid catcher. You didn't have the eyes for it. Just a wanderer like all *wašíču*. Moving all over trying to figure out how to stop being lost on the earth.

"But you were one of the good ones. I could see that. The good ones, they turn their wandering into seeking. With just a little nudge they can turn that seeking into hunting. Just got to give them something to hunt."

He drew a long, theatrical drag on his cigarette.

"I gave you the boys."

He leaned back in his chair and let out a flat laugh.

"And sure enough, you found them."

He leaned in close until his face was only a few inches from Danton's.

"What I don't know is why you come back with a parade."

Danton kept his eyes down and said nothing.

The wind flapped the tar paper against the side of the house.

Lillie's muffled voice came drifting in from the doorway. The old man just rocked and waited and smiled.

His question sat out there like a hard stone. Someone was going to have to pick it up. The question had been to Danton, but I had been part of the parade. It felt like an act of disrespect not to give the old man an answer.

"Mr. Danton didn't ask us to come," I said. "We came on our own. We came because we loved the boys. They'd stayed at our house a bit. We wanted to be sure they got home safely."

Lone Dog creaked back and forth in the chair. "Um-hmm. Um-hmm. Loved the boys. Loved the boys." He chewed on the phrase as if to extract all meaning from it.

He pulled a shard of tobacco from his teeth and spit a thin reed of brown saliva into a coffee can he kept by the side of the chair.

"So the boys stayed at your house?"

"Yes, sir."

"Tell me about it. What did they do there?"

"Levi helped me with chores. Reuben mostly stayed with my wife. He liked our old dog."

"The one that come with you? The one he wants to come in the house?"

"Yes, sir. Mister Bones."

Lone Dog laughed at the name.

"Talked to it, I bet."

I nodded.

"And the dog talked back?"

"Far as I could tell."

Lone Dog let out a belly laugh. He spit again into the coffee can and slapped me on the knee.

"How about Levi? How'd he do?"

"He was a good worker. Pushed himself hard. Threw hay bales as good as a man."

"Tried to make him a *wašíču* farmer, eh?"

"No, sir. He was just being a respectful Lakota boy. Wanted to do his part."

Lone Dog considered the answer.

"How about with Reuben? Was he a good brother?"

"I've never seen a better one. Watched over him. Guided him. Slept with his arm around him. Never heard a cross word between them."

Lone Dog smiled. "A good little protector, eh?"

"The best. Firm but gentle."

Lone Dog fell silent again. He sucked on his teeth and closed his eyes.

"So who's the *winúȟčala*?"

I knew the word for "old woman." Ida had used it jokingly when talking about herself.

"Ida. She's my wife's best friend. Since childhood. She helped the boys, too."

I didn't want to mention the pipe. I knew that Levi wanted it to be a surprise for his grandpa. Old Lone Dog seemed satisfied with the answer.

"And that *hásapa* man. The Black fellow. Who's he?"

I looked to Danton. I had never seen this Brother James before. I had no idea who he was or what he was doing here. Danton realized he would have to answer.

"He helped them on the road, too, I guess," he said. "We found him with a flat a ways up the axle buster. Reuben ran to him and hugged him like they were old friends. They sang some old spiritual together like they both knew it. He said he was coming to make sure the boys got home, too."

Lone Dog chuckled. "You come in on the axle buster? Maybe you ain't so good at tracking after all."

He fiddled a bit more with his cigarette and scratched the side of his cheek with his knuckle. He was still chuckling to himself. "The axle buster. The axle buster." He shook his head in mock disgust.

"So you all come to my home because of the boys. All of you. Even that Two Finger out there. Ended up here together." He sucked in his cheeks and chewed on his lip. "Um-hmm. Um-hmm." He was putting together information.

He remained quiet for a few more seconds, then hoisted himself upright in his seat. "Well, I'm damn glad you all came," he said with a surprising finality. "Damn glad."

He reached out and shook both of our hands again. "Damn glad."

His manner, though inscrutable, was comforting. He might be a man who kept a lot hidden, but what he showed was warm and genuine.

Almost without thinking I reached in my pocket and took out the little bird I had been working on. It was my favorite one I had ever made. I'd painted it blue, giving it a bright color like Danton had suggested. I'd made a little beak for it out of a snuff cover and wings for it out of some blue feathers I had found. I'm not quite sure why I'd brought it along — some kind of good luck charm or talisman, perhaps — but giving it to Lone Dog seemed like the right thing to do. I'd never given one of my birds to anyone before.

"Here. I'd like you to have this," I said.

I held the carving out to Lone Dog. He took it gently in his hands and cradled it like it was an actual baby bird. His concern almost seemed to make it come alive.

He looked down at it, then up at me, then down at the bird again, then back up at me. His smile widened.

"*Ziŋtkátȟo*, the bluebird. Sign of a new beginning. *Philámayaye. Philámayaye.*"

He continued to smile at it as if at a newborn.

Danton came over and stood behind me. I think he was as amazed as I was at what I had just done.

Lone Dog grinned at him. "You're a better hunter than I thought. You brought me a good one here."

Behind us we heard the front door open. A shaft of light cut across the floor. The sudden illumination broke the spell of the moment.

I turned to see what was happening.

Lillie was standing there, motionless, with the sun surrounding her like a halo. Two Finger was standing next to her like a great hulking shadow.

The two of them were holding hands.

BUTTERFLY ROCK

Brother James

"Let's go up the hill a bit, boys," I said.

I tried to say it all calm and relaxed, but now I was full-on concerned. Something wasn't right here. That old man had some Indian juju and the weather was changing again, too, with the wind picking up and the clouds rolling in out of nowhere, dark as nightmares.

I had to show strong for the boys, but I wasn't feeling much strong inside. I was in a place I didn't know with people I didn't know in country I didn't know. All I knew was these two boys, and they was more scared in their own home than they'd been when they was lost in a field. And when someone is scared in their own home something ain't right.

I was pretty much out of breath trying to keep up with the little fellows going up the hill. I got plenty of breath for singing, but not much for climbing. But the boys seemed to know where they was going, and they was doing it fast, so I just followed, keeping one eye on the sky and one eye on the ground. The wind was making a crazy sound and the grass was hissing like a basket of snakes.

"Let's go to the butterfly rock," Levi said. "That school man won't find us there."

Reuben did some snapping with his mouth and took off running faster. "The butterfly rock, the butterfly rock," he said. Levi was right behind him, holding that pipe in the blanket like a baby.

He stopped and looked back at me all scared-like. "You won't let that school man get us, will you?" he said.

I was panting like a dog, bent over with my hands on my knees.

"If I can't hardly make it up this hill, that school man ain't making it up here. I'm puffing like a steam engine and he's about the size of two of me."

Levi give me a happy grin. He thought that was funny. It made me feel good to make him smile, even though I wasn't that sure about what I was saying. Crazy people and angry people can do stuff you can't imagine and I didn't know if that school man was crazy or angry, but I figured it was one or the other if he was trying to catch a little guy like Reuben and was knocking pipes out of an old man's hand.

Levi grabbed my arm. He pointed up the hill to where Reuben had made it to a big craggy rock that stuck up like a jagged tooth.

"Come on, Brother James. This is our secret place."

Reuben was waving his arms and dancing in a circle. There were butterflies everywhere, yellow and white, landing on his shoulders and in his hair, dancing and darting and filling the sky like snowflakes. He was singing some kind of song, just a tune with no words, making it go up and down with the butterfly flights.

"Reuben says he gets a lot of his songs here," Levi said.

"I can see that," I answered.

Reuben was twirling and waving his arms.

I couldn't hear much because the wind was blowing hard and Reuben was singing in his little boy voice. But if I know anything — and Brother James has been doing this for a lot of years — the tune the little fella was singing had exactly the same pitch as the sound of that wind.

◊◊◊

I knew right away that the top of this hill wasn't no kind of place I wanted to spend time. The wind was moaning and the sky was moving fast. Made me feel naked. But I could see why the boys liked it. It was a full-circle kind of place, higher than everything around, rolling off in all directions with just this one big rock at the top, half sticking out of the ground, all jagged and pointed like the end of a spear — the kind of meeting place boys like, good for adventures and making up stories and running away when your momma is coming at you with a switch. Probably the kind of place folks come to in the old days to do rituals and such, too, but that ain't no world I know nothing about.

Little Reuben was jumping and waving and snapping his mouth like some kind of lizard. The butterflies was flying all in circles and landing on him and sitting in clumps on the rock.

"What you doing there, Reuben?" I asked.

I was breathing so hard I could hardly get the words out. This might have been a hill to them boys, but it was half a mountain to Brother James.

"Grandpa said if you catch a butterfly in your mouth it will give you a song. I'm trying to get a butterfly song." He pretty much seemed to have forgotten about that school man.

Levi, though, he hadn't forgotten. He was looking down the hill toward the house. There was no sign of the school man and the farmer woman. "You don't think he's coming up here?" he asked. He was holding the pipe blanket close to his chest.

"No chance of that," I said. Took me two breaths just to get the sentence out.

He come over and stood close to me. The clouds was darkening up and pushing off toward the west like galloping horses. When one passed in front of the sun, a shadow raced across the whole land about as fast as a man can see. Enough to take a man's breath away if he had any breath left to take.

"Special place up here," I said.

"Grandpa says it's *wakȟáŋ*."

"That ain't no word I know."

"Sacred-like."

The sun caught the edge of that pointed rock and sent a shadow shooting out like an arrow across the hills.

"I can sure enough see that," I said.

Levi sat himself down and wrapped his arms around his knees. I could tell this place was making him feel safe.

I set myself down next to him. I was damn happy to stop. There wasn't much climb left in me.

He lay back and put his hands behind his head. He pulled the pipe blanket in close to his chest. "Do you ever look at the clouds and see things in the shapes, Brother James?" he asked.

I was glad to hear him use my name. Made me feel close to him.

"Every kid that ever lived done that," I said.

"Can I tell you something?"

"Anything you want."

"When we were in the field by the road where you found us, I saw a *čhaŋnúŋpa* in the clouds, like the one that I made. It was kind of like a dream."

"Clouds and dreams, they ain't that far apart."

"Reuben says he gets songs from clouds up here, too. That's why I like to bring him up here. He's most happy when he has a song."

Couldn't help but smile to hear those words. "True that for Brother James, too."

He moved over close to me.

"Do you like Reuben?" he asked. His voice was real quiet, secret-like.

"'Bout as much as anyone I ever met," I said.

"Grandpa says I'll have him for my whole life."

"Better to have someone than no one."

He slid himself even closer to me. "Sometimes I get sick of him, though."

"Everybody gets sick of everybody sometimes. No shame in that."

We stayed there quiet, looking at the clouds. Reuben was behind us, up at the rock, jumping and snapping, waving his arms at the butterflies. He was wearing about the biggest smile I ever seen.

Levi kept twitching around. I could tell he had something more going on inside.

"You still worried about that school man?" I asked.

He shook his head.

"Come on. Something's on your mind."

He kept moving and twitching, keeping his eyes down.

"Do you ever sing other kinds of songs, other than the river and the chariot kind?" he asked.

Gave me a laugh. It was a funny thing to ask.

"Oh, Brother James'll sing most anything, so long as folks want to listen. Why do you ask?"

He stayed quiet for a while, like a boy deciding what to say. Then he pushed himself straight up and took the pipe blanket and unrolled it, real careful and formal-like.

Right there in the middle, like a little baby, that pipe lay there soft and protected and gleaming in the afternoon sun, with that little turtle crawling up its back all shiny and red and polished to within an inch of its life.

"I made a song for it," he said. His voice was so soft I could hardly hear.

"Making songs is about the best thing a man can do," I said.

He got real quiet again. I let him carry it out as long as he wanted.

"I could sing it if you want."

That brought up some tears. Hadn't expected it. All the years of me singing songs for other folks, ain't no one ever offered to sing one for me.

"I'd like that a lot," I said.

"I'm not very good at singing. Not like Reuben."

"Ain't many of us are. No shame in that."

He took a deep breath. Made his voice soft, just about like a whisper.

For Grandfather's pipe we got this stone.
A long way we went to get this stone.
Many people helped us get this stone.
For Grandfather's life we got this stone.
For Grandfather's pipe we got this stone.

He said it like reciting, more talking than singing. Just words. No tune. More like a poem than a song.

He kept his head down. I could see him blushing.

"Them's good words," I said. "But where's the song?"

He got quiet still. Stayed that way for what must have been near onto a minute. Then looked up at me. Big eyes full of hope.

"I thought maybe you could make it."

Just about tore my heart out to hear those words.

I put my arm around his shoulder. It was the nearest to being a father Brother James ever felt. "I'd be glad to help. But Brother James don't do no making, I just do the singing. Maybe we should ask your brother. He might be getting a song from them clouds."

Boy got quiet again.

"I already asked him. He said he would only do it with Brother James."

That had my heart near exploding. Lots of folks want what Brother James got. Not too many won't go forward without it.

"Then we better have a talk with him," I said. "Figure out how to make this happen."

I kept my arm over his shoulder. Never felt so close to a boy in my life.

Reuben had stopped his jumping. He was standing with his arms down, fists all tight, staring out over the hills. The butterflies was mostly settled in on the rock or gone off to find some place to spend the night.

We come up quiet, not wanting to bother him if he was all inside himself.

He had on his pout face, all puckered and serious.

"Reuben," I said, real soft. "Your brother said you want us to make a song together for your grandpa for when he's giving him the pipe."

He looked up at me. Didn't say nothing. Just kept staring with that pucker look. Then he opened his mouth. Out come a little white butterfly, fluttered off up into the sky.

"I already got one," he said.

Thought he might burst for the grin that come over his face.

LIKE THE TICKING
OF A CLOCK

Danton

When Karl-Martin pulled that little blue bird out of his pocket and handed it to the old man I almost fell over. I thought I'd understood this half priest, half farmer, but every time I thought I knew him another layer would come off and there'd be someone else inside.

Lillie, too. Who would follow Two Finger out into the yard? Who would follow him anywhere? He was a man you tried to get away from, not a man you went to.

Nothing was making sense.

The day was waning. The light creeping in around the edge of the blanket over the window was strange and orange. I was afraid that the weather was taking another turn.

I wanted to get us all on the road. My drive home from here was easy. But Lillie and Karl-Martin and Ida had several hard hours of road time ahead of them. Even if they stayed off the axle buster — and I would make sure they did — they would be on reservation roads in a car that had already failed them once. Night can swallow you up out here.

But the old man had us trapped. And he wasn't letting anyone go.

Two Finger had set himself down on the kindling box and was staring at the floor. He was like a ghost of the man I had known. Lillie was sitting next to him, still holding his hand like a mother holding the hand of a frightened child.

Ida had rolled herself in from the kitchen and was sitting in the corner. She had the same kind of enigmatic smile on her face as old Lone Dog. They seemed like brother and sister.

I didn't know where the boys were, or Brother James, either. Ree was almost invisible in the shadows. All I knew was that the old man was using his authority as an elder to hold us in place, and he showed no signs of letting us go. The creaking of his rocking chair was like the ticking of a clock.

He gestured Ida to come over to him. The two of them talked softly in their language. She nodded and smiled, once squeezing his arm and letting out a small laugh.

We all sat there, held in place by the authority of the old man, until Reuben burst through the door and ran past us, all hunched over, as if by making himself small no one would notice him. He scuttled into the bedroom and emerged with a buckskin roll held tightly to his chest.

He tried to make it back out the door without being stopped, but Ida grabbed him by the arm. She pulled him close and talked to him in a low whisper. She made shapes with her hands like squares. She talked to him like this for what must have been five minutes. Reuben nodded and scowled. Old Lone Dog steepled his hands and smiled approvingly.

The light around the edge of the blanket was fading. The room was almost in complete darkness. No one made any attempt to light a candle or a lamp.

Lone Dog lit another cigarette and drew heavily on it. In the flare of the match I could see that his eyes were half closed.

Ida lifted the corner of the blanket. A shaft of orange light shot across the floor.

"Is it time?" the old man asked.

"Yes," Ida said.

"Good."

He lifted himself out of his chair, hobbled toward the door, and gestured us to follow. He touched me lightly on the shoulder and pointed to Ida as he passed.

I got behind Ida and pushed her toward the door.

It was a struggle to get her down the steps. Her wheelchair was old and the boards were uneven.

The old man stood aside, waiting for us to pass. The strange orange light from outside was neither daylight nor night.

He nodded his approval as I wrestled Ida's chair down the step.

He smiled down at Ida and she smiled back at him. Though I couldn't be sure, I thought I saw him give her a wink.

SPIRIT VOICES

Ida

O h, that look. That *wóksape* look.

I should have known. I should have known back when we first got here and he give me that same wink about little Levi pushing my chair. I should have known when I saw him pull the poison from the spirit of the school man.

He might not be a *wičháša wakȟáŋ*, but I can see he knows the old ways. He's like my grandfather. Always keeping things hidden. Always making you hunt. Always talking just around the corner from what he wants you to see.

Oh, he's a crafty one, that Lone Dog. I'd been thinking I was coming along just to help Lillie. I thought it was just something I wanted to do. But now I know. It was that old man that was calling me to come. He's been behind all of this.

It makes me think back to when I was a girl and got hit by that fence post. I was all crying about why it had to happen to me, and the doctor was saying it was just an accident. After he left, Grandpa come into my room and touched my cheek and brushed my hair back and said, "There are no accidents, my girl."

Now I'm seeing that me coming along on this trip was no accident. None of this is an accident. That fire was no accident. Me bringing Grandpa's sacred bundle was no accident. No, nothing going on here is an accident. I just haven't been paying attention.

I'm paying attention now.

Blood
Moon

HELPING

Levi

The wind is getting strong up here. The butterflies are all gone now. I keep looking down at the house. Grandpa has all the windows covered.

Day is almost gone away. *Aŋpétu-Wí* is taking away his light. *Haŋhépi-Wí* is starting to show her face in the sky.

Reuben is back. I'd sent him to get the pipestem. He knew where Grandpa kept it under his bed. *Uŋčí* Ida had grabbed him when he ran by. She'd told him they all will be coming when *Haŋhépi-Wí* shows her light. She told him what we have to do.

"We have to hurry," I tell him. "*Aŋpétu-Wí* is going away."

Reuben isn't listening. He's talking to Mister Bones.

I'm feeling to get mad at him. This is not going to be easy. I need his help.

"*Uŋčí* Ida told you we have to make the earth square," I tell him. "Altar-like."

He shows his teeth and does his pinch face.

I don't know why we have to do this. But *Uŋčí* Ida says it is important. She says we have to put sage on it. I want to do what she says.

"Reuben, help me," I say.

I am pulling on the ground with my fingers. The grass is too strong. I can't get down to the earth.

Reuben is making a growl sound. "I am helping," he says.

"No, you're not. You're talking to Mister Bones."

He makes more growl sounds.

Brother James is standing next to me. "I can help," he says.

"No," I tell him. "*Uŋčí* Ida says only Reuben and me."

I am full angry and scared. *Haŋhépi-Wí* will be giving light soon.

But *Aŋpétu-Wí* is staying bright. He is keeping the sky orange so *Haŋhépi-Wí* does not have to show her light. I say a *wóphila* prayer to Creator.

I am on my knees. I am digging more with my hands. The grass will not come out. I'm feeling strong fear now. I cannot do this.

Reuben will not stop talking to Mister Bones. He is making more dog talk.

"Reuben, you have to help me. They will be coming soon."

He will not look at me.

I put my head down. I close my eyes and say more prayer. I will do this. I will turn my hands to blood if I have to. I will do what Miss Ida says. I will make the earth square and altar-like. I will do this for Grandfather.

I hear a sound behind me, a strong digging sound. I look up. Reuben is there. He is standing next to Mister Bones. Mister Bones is pulling up dirt with his paws, fast-like.

Reuben makes his pinch face and sticks his jaw out.

"I told you I would help," he says.

NIGHT SUN

Danton

It has to be the dust. The dust and what's left from that prairie fire. There's nothing else it can be. I've lived here for almost a year and I've never seen anything like this. The whole sky is orange, not like a normal sky at all. It's more like the photos of Mars we used to see in our schoolbooks. The moon looks like a drop of blood coming up over the horizon. The wind is high in the air and blowing strong.

Old Lone Dog seems completely unconcerned. When we left the house he pointed up at the moon and said, "*Haŋhépi-Wí*. The night sun." Then he grinned and kept on walking.

I can't believe how sure-footed he is. Even with his limp and his tremor, he moves over this rough ground with confidence, more confidence than any of the rest of us have.

The moon is rising fast. It's brighter than it should be, brighter than makes any sense. It's a world in reverse — strange and unearthly — like a memory or a dream.

We are all staying behind the old man. Ree is close, just close enough to catch him if he falls. Karl-Martin and Lillie are behind her, holding hands.

I'm in the rear, pushing Ida in her chair.

Further up the rise, I can see the boys and Brother James gathered around a mound of dirt. Levi is on his knees, digging feverishly with his hands. Reuben is standing next to him talking to Mister Bones. Brother James is bent over the mound, watching intently. Something important is going on.

Night birds pass overhead like apparitions. The wind moves and the distant hills are full of sounds. But it's this sky that haunts me — this unearthly sky and that red moon rising like a bloody lifeless eye.

I don't know where the old man is leading us. I don't know what we are doing. All I know is that one moment we were sitting in that darkened room, marking time to the creak of his rocking chair, the next he was leading us out into this impossible twilight with a purpose that feels almost urgent.

Pushing Ida is hard. The ground is rocky and uneven.

I have to watch every step. I can't let Ida fall.

The others are getting far ahead of me. The old man keeps turning back. He sees me struggling but he just smiles and keeps going. I don't know why he is so unconcerned.

I look toward Karl-Martin, hoping he can help me. But he's looking the other direction. Lillie has broken away from the group and is hurrying down the hill. She is headed toward the shadows at the corner of the house. There's a small light glowing like a firefly in the darkness.

JUST A WOMAN

Lillie

I wouldn't have noticed him if it hadn't been for the glow from his cigarette ash.

"Karl-Martin," I whispered. "What's he doing?"

"Who?"

I pointed to the dot of light in the shadow by the house.

"Mr. Two Finger."

The form in the shadows shifted slightly. A match flared. Mr. Two Finger's face lit up for a second.

"He's probably just having a smoke," Karl-Martin said.

"He should be with us. Grandfather Lone Dog told us all to come."

Karl-Martin shook his head. "Just leave him alone."

"No," I said. "It feels wrong to leave him." I struggled to get free of Karl-Martin's grip. "I'm going to go get him."

Karl-Martin would not let me go. "Just leave him," he said. "He's not your concern."

I could not do that. I had seen the boy in the man. I had seen his hurt.

"I reached him before," I said. "I can do it again."

I pulled free and ran down the hill.

Mr. Two Finger was leaning against the wall of the house, out of the moonlight, hidden in the shadows. I approached respectfully. I knew the violence inside him.

"Mr. Two Finger," I said.

I could not see his face. It was hidden in the darkness.

"Mr. Two Finger."

I reached for his hand. He pulled it away.

"You should come and join us."

He drew on his cigarette and spit hard on the ground.

"I ain't staying," he said.

I tried again to take his hand. Again, he pulled away.

"No. Please. Mr. Lone Dog wants us here. He's an elder. We should respect his wishes."

"Respect what you want. I ain't staying."

I could feel his cruelty returning. I could not let that happen.

"He knows about your father. Don't you want to know more about your father?"

"My father's dead."

His disrespect for Mr. Lone Dog was making me angry.

"So is my son," I said. "You are not the only one who carries wounds."

I could not believe those words came out of my mouth. It was the same thing I'd said to Ree. Joseph must have been speaking through me.

He looked hard at me. He wanted me to be afraid, but I would not be afraid.

His eyes got narrow. He spit again into the dirt.

"You don't know nothing about my life."

My heart was turning dark with anger. "I don't know why you are being like this. When I sat with you, your spirit was soft. Mr. Lone Dog is giving you a gift. This is how you repay an elder?"

He snuffed out his cigarette between his thumb and forefinger.

"You don't know nothing about these Indians. I grew up around them. I know how they are."

I could hear sadness below his cruelty.

"I think you are just afraid," I said.

He made a harsh sound and spit again.

"Afraid? Why would I be afraid? I just don't trust them."

"But you trust me. I'm an Indian. I'm Lakota, just like you."

"Just like me? Pretty little Indian schoolgirl? You ain't just like me. You ain't nothing like me. You don't know nothing about me."

His words were making my blood hot.

"And you know nothing about me."

The anger was growing strong between us. I had to make it stop.

I reached for his hand. "Then tell me," I said. "Tell me why you don't trust them. I want to know." I spoke with a soft heart. "Please."

He thought for a long time. He did not pull away.

"Okay," he said. "You been straight with me. I'll tell you.

"I was just a little kid. All I wanted to do was get along. I'd go sit with the elders like the other kids, try to learn stuff. The other kids wouldn't even talk to me. They'd just laugh and move away.

"I wanted to be a medicine man. Hah. A *wičháša wakȟáŋ*. Hell, they wouldn't even let me be an Indian."

"But your dad?" I said. "He was an Indian. Wasn't he a good person? Mr. Lone Dog said he loved you."

"First I ever heard of it. We'd go out in the yard, try to play 'catch.' But I couldn't see. Bad eyes. Missed the ball a couple of times. He cuffed me on the head, swore at me. After that he had nothing to do with me. Far as I could tell, the only thing he ever loved was the bottle and baseball and snagging with women he didn't even know.

"I'll tell you what. I was glad when he left. Beating up my momma all the time. Going off, taking any money we had. Leaving us hungry, leaving Momma crying."

His words were harsh, but the pain was strong in his voice.

I took his hand. This time he let me hold it.

"Tell me about your mother," I said. "I am a mother. I care about these things."

"My mother." He let out a bitter laugh. "She tried. Christ, she tried. Me and my sisters...."

"You had sisters?"

"Three of them. Took them away. Sent them off to white families. I don't know where they are. Left me with Momma. Just the two of us. I wasn't even good enough to take."

He lit another cigarette.

"We didn't have nothing. Lived in this old railroad shack on the edge of the rez. Momma had to turn tricks just so we could eat. All these white guys, get off the train, they'd come in, go in the bedroom with her. I'd hear them grunting, making noises like animals. They'd come out wiping their crotches, not even look at me.

"I'm all huddled up in a corner, scared to death, eight, nine years old, not knowing what's going on. Pull on their pants. Slap some dollar bills on the table. Leave. Then Momma would come out, tell me to take the dollars and go to the store to get us some food. I'd see her looking like she was crying, feel those sticky fucking dollars, and I'd want to kill those sons of bitches. Kill every fucking white man who ever lived.

"Then I'd think of my dad and how if he was there this wouldn't be happening. But he was off drinking and snagging and playing baseball with his Indian buddies, and I'd look at my crying momma and then I'd want to kill every fucking buck on the reservation. Don't talk to me about trust."

"You've had a sad life," I said.

He shrugged and drew on his cigarette. "Same as any other."

"And your mother was a good woman."

He flicked the cigarette into the darkness.

"Just a woman," he said. "Doing what she had to do to get by."

PUSHING IDA

Danton

I don't think I can make this. Pushing Ida is too hard. The hill's too steep; the ground is too rutted.

I'm worried about this wheelchair. It's an old metal thing with hard rubber wheels. They keep getting lodged in cracks and crevices. I'm afraid one might come off and Ida will fall out. I need some help. I need Karl-Martin. But he and Lillie are somewhere back down the hill.

I'd yell to him, but I don't dare violate the silence.

I'm tempted to wedge some rocks behind the wheels and go get him. But Ida's not strong enough to stop the chair if it starts rolling, and I can't trust these little hand brakes to hold.

"I don't know what we're going to do, Ida," I say. "I don't think I can push you."

She just sits there with her hands folded over the bag on her lap.

"Oh, you'll figure something out," she says.

I'm getting frantic. I don't know what to do. Old Lone Dog is almost at the top of the hill. I don't know how he can be so steady on his feet on this ground in the dark.

I dig in my feet and give the chair another push. One of the wheels slips and drops into a crack.

Ida almost falls out of the chair.

"Are you okay, Ida?" I ask.

"I'm fine," she says, and reaches up and pats my hand.

I try to lift the wheel out of the hole, but it doesn't budge.

I don't know why the old man isn't paying attention. He knew how hard this was going to be.

I pull on the wheel again. Nothing happens. I get behind and lean into it with all my weight. Nothing moves; the chair is stuck. I'm not going to be able to get it out.

I feel someone behind me. I turn to look. It's Two Finger.

"I can help," he says. Lillie is standing beside him.

He gets next to me and grabs the wheel.

We pull together. The wheel lifts out.

He gets behind and takes one of the handles.

We push together. The chair moves forward. Our shoulders are touching.

Old Lone Dog has stopped. He's looking back at us.

He nods once and gives us that strange *wóksape* smile. Ida smiles back at him.

Then he turns and continues up the hill.

A GIFT FOR GRANDFATHER

Danton

I don't like being this close to Two Finger. I feel his shoulder against mine. We've never made physical contact before.

The moon is high in the sky, hanging like a blood-red dot in this strange darkness.

The old man has reached the mound. He's standing still and silent, facing Brother James and the boys.

Levi is standing stern and erect, like a little soldier, facing his grandfather. Brother James and Reuben are behind. Reuben is holding on to Brother James's leg and staring up at his brother.

Ida gestures us to push her up close. She grabs at my sleeve.

"Here, give them these." She reaches in her bag and pulls out the four sticks she had placed in the ground when we were facing the fire.

Reuben grabs them from me and pushes them into the four corners of the mound. It's as if he knows what to do. He looks wide-eyed at Ida, who smiles broadly at him.

Ida grabs again at my sleeve. "Here," she says. "These, too."

She takes four long cloth ribbons from her bag — one red, one yellow, one white, and one black. Reuben takes them and ties one to the top of each pole. They move soundlessly in the hot night wind.

He looks over at Ida. She is smiling even more. He clenches his fists and makes a little squeak. His face is shining like the sun.

The moon is nearly at the top of the sky. I can't guess what hour it is. In this strange half-light, time seems to stand still.

Old Lone Dog steps forward and holds out his arms. *"Hiyú po,"* he says. He beckons us to come in close to him.

We all gather around the mound, as if around some kind of ceremonial altar. Even Two Finger joins the circle.

Lone Dog nods to Ida. She reaches in her bag and takes out a round piece of pipestone, flat and polished like a plate. It is the same color as the moon — like a drop of blood come down from the sky. Levi takes it and places it in the center of the mound.

He takes the blanket with the pipe from Brother James.

He steps forward, squares his shoulders, and holds it out in front of him.

"Grandfather, we have a gift for you," he says. His voice, though still a boy's, is strong and formal. It cuts through the night silence like a knife.

Lone Dog stands before him, more like a man receiving a military commendation than a grandfather accepting a gift from a grandchild. His eyes are moist and liquid.

He unwraps the pipe and lifts it toward the sky. It glows blood red in the moonlight. *"Wóphila, Tȟuŋkášila,"* he says, and whispers something in Lakota. Ida and Lillie respond, *"Hahó."*

Levi gestures to Reuben, who steps forward with the buckskin roll that he had taken from the bedroom. The old man opens the buckskin and lifts out a long wooden pipestem. He takes the pipestone bowl in one hand and the wooden stem in the other and holds them both at eye level, as if presenting them to the sky.

Levi nods to Brother James, who is standing behind with his head bowed.

Brother James takes Reuben by the hand and they move directly in front of old Lone Dog.

Reuben opens and closes his mouth several times, as if waiting for words to come out, then begins to sing in a sweet, otherworldly, childlike voice:

For Grandfather's pipe we got this stone.
A long way we went to get this stone.

It is somewhere between a chant and a song, like nothing I have ever heard in my life.

Brother James takes a deep breath, lifts his head, and begins to sing along with Reuben, at first softly, then with growing power, until the whole night is alive with their voices.

For Grandfather's pipe we got this stone.
A long way we went to get this stone.
Many people helped us get this stone.
For Grandfather's life we got this stone.
For Grandfather's pipe we got this stone.

I'm not a religious man. Never have been. But standing on that hillside in that haunted moonlight, hearing those two voices, one as dark and rich as the earth itself, the other floating childlike across the heavens while the old man held the pipe and stem upward into the night sky, touched me in a way I had never experienced in my life. It may be as close to religion as I am ever likely to get.

EVERYTHING IS SPEAKING

Karl-Martin

Lillie's hand is warm in mine. The faint scent of smoke remains on the wind. The light from the moon touches the red of the stone. A coyote howls. The night birds cry, the grasses rustle. Everything is alive; everything is speaking. In a way that I have never known before, I feel that I am standing on sacred land.

Little Reuben is holding on to his grandfather. He is beside himself with joy. This is the world he knows, where every creature has a name, every creature has a voice.

Ida's eyes are closed. The old man is smiling. There is a peace here beyond my understanding.

I'm afraid I have lived too much with a God of judgment. The prayers I learned were prayers of supplication and fear, not prayers of thankfulness. "Give us this day our daily bread. Forgive us our trespasses. Deliver us from evil."

The old man, holding his pipe to the sky, had no apology in his prayer. It was an offering, a consecration.

Mitákuye oyás'iŋ. "All my relations." Not "Deliver us from evil."

Lillie reaches up to me. She whispers quietly. "What are you thinking, Karl-Martin?"

I hardly dare break the silence with my words. "How everything is alive. How everything is speaking."

She grabs my arm and pulls me close to her.

"Yes, I know," she says. "Even Joseph."

PHILÁMAYAYE

Danton

We stood there together, Karl-Martin on one side of me, Ida on the other.

The old man had taken full control of us with his presence.

He handed the parts of the pipe back to the boys — the bowl to Levi and the stem to Reuben. He touched each boy on the forehead, then turned to the rest of us. His eyes had an earnestness I had never seen from him before. The irony, the cleverness, the sense of mirthfulness were gone. In their place was a deep and abiding kindness.

"*Háu, mitákuyepi,*" he said. "*Lé-aŋpétu kiŋ čhaŋtéwašteya napéčhiyuzape ló.*"

I leaned over to Ida.

"What's he saying? Is he going to talk in Lakota?"

"Quiet," she said. "He's doing this in his own way. He's greeting us. He's saying he shakes our hands with a happy heart."

He looked around at the group, holding us with his eyes. His pace was measured and slow.

One by one, he moved his gaze across each of us. I wanted to look away, but didn't dare. I couldn't imagine what the others were feeling.

When he was finished, he put his hands on the shoulders of the boys.

"Come," he said, and gently moved them forward as if presenting them to us.

Levi stood erect, his face stern and his back straight, a boy trying to have the bearing of a man. Reuben was beaming and twitching. He could hardly contain himself.

The old man reached out his hands, palms up.

"Greetings, my relatives," he said in English. "I thank you for coming. I have a good feeling in my heart for all of you. This day my boys have come back to me. They have come back from a long journey. You have all helped them on this journey. I have a warm feeling in my heart for all of you."

It was both a welcoming and an incantation, spoken slowly and deliberately, with genuine warmth and affection.

"I am old," he continued. "A leaf ready to fall from the tree. Creator has named my day. It is not long from now. When you are leaving this earth, you have many cares for what you are leaving behind. By watching over my boys, you have taken many of those cares from my heart. For this I thank you."

It was strange to hear such formal language coming from a bent-over little man in blue jeans and a cowboy shirt. But old Lone Dog's powerful presence made it all seem right.

"I have waited for this day to have us all together," he continued. "Now we are here."

I looked around at the others. What, I wondered, did we have to do with each other, beyond the accidental circumstance of having crossed paths with these boys in the course of their journey?

"I am going to speak now," he said. "I have many things to say. May *Thuŋkášila* guide my tongue."

He closed his eyes and began to pray in Lakota.

The moon hovered high above us — a tiny bead, still red as blood, and distant.

Off to the north, Red Shirt Mesa loomed dark and solitary. The wind rustled the ribbons on the stakes. Lone Dog's prayer wove seamlessly through it all.

When he finished, he opened his eyes and extended his hands in front of him again.

"Hear me now, my friends," he said. "I wish to show you my heart. Come. Come closer."

We all stepped nearer, forming a half circle around the mound.

He took a deep breath that seemed to go to the very core of his being, and began to speak.

"My brothers and sisters. It is not by accident that you are here. In this life there are no accidents. Creator causes each leaf to fall.

"We are living in difficult times. These times have troubled me. There is anger in the people and anger in the earth. It makes me fear for the children. In my own life it makes me fear for Reuben and Levi. How will these boys find their way in times such as these?

"I have prayed to Creator about this. I have asked for guidance. I have asked for a sign so that when my time comes I might walk on in peace.

"In *Čaŋpȟásapa-Wí* I received such a sign. The *čhaŋnúŋpa* made by my grandfather's hand was struck to the ground and broke into many pieces.

"*Čhaŋnúŋpa* is strong. *Čhaŋnúŋpa* does not break. *Čhaŋnúŋpa* is made from the blood of the people. If *čhaŋnúŋpa* broke, it was because she let herself be broken. If she broke, it was because Creator was speaking to me.

"I knew then that this was the sign I had been seeking.

"I did not know what this sign meant. I gathered the pieces together and buried them here so that they would not be scattered. The spirit of *čhaŋnúŋpa* lives in every piece.

"I knew that in his own time Creator would make *čhaŋnúŋpa* whole again. What I did not know was how this would happen."

He knelt down and scraped away a bit of the earth and picked up the shards and fragments of the broken pipe. He cupped them gently in both hands and held them out to us.

"Now I know."

He smiled lovingly at his two great-grandsons.

"Come, Levi and Reuben. Show me again the *čhaŋnúŋpa* you have brought me."

Levi took the pipe from the blanket and handed it to Reuben. Reuben held the pipe before him, his face as bright as the sun.

Lone Dog took one of the fragments and held it next to the bowl of the new *čhaŋnúŋpa*. They seemed to be made of the same stone.

He pulled his boys to him and spoke quietly to them.

"I do not know the journey you have made to bring me this *čhaŋnúŋpa*. But I know that none of us makes our journey alone."

He turned toward us.

"My brothers and sisters," he said. He held the handful of fragments toward us.

"Look again on these pieces of my grandfather's *čhaŋnúŋpa*. You are like these pieces. You were scattered on the earth. But like these pieces you have come together. *Čhaŋnúŋpa* called you together to help my boys. By helping them you have helped make *čhaŋnúŋpa* whole. By caring for them on their journey you have brought *čhaŋnúŋpa* back to life."

He moved his gaze around to each of us and smiled.

We all remained silent. I think we were all humbled by the tone of his words and the way he had knitted us together in a common, preordained journey.

He moved slowly to a place behind the center of the mound.

"There is a reason why *čhaŋnúŋpa* chooses," he said. "I have watched. And I have listened. I think I know these reasons."

The moonlight glistened on the stone fragments in his hand. The cloth strips on the four poles at the corners of the mound rustled softly in the nighttime breeze.

Lone Dog closed his eyes. I could feel him almost physically disappearing to some private place. He remained this way while the rest of us stood facing him, unsure of what to think, unsure of what to do.

Slowly he lifted his head and opened his eyes. He placed all the fragments in his left hand and held up his right, as if in benediction.

He began to speak in a voice so soft we had to lean forward to hear him.

"When I was a child, the black robes taught me about the *wičháša wakȟáŋ* — the man they call Jesus. There was much about him that I thought was good. He shared his food in the way of an Indian. He healed those who were sick and did not ask for money. He used his power to serve and he loved the children.

"When the black robes told us these stories, my heart was open. But there was one story I could not understand. There was a man who loved this Jesus but who the black robes hated. This man was named Judas. This Judas became angry when Jesus allowed himself to be honored with sacred herbs. He said those herbs could have been traded for money that could have been used to help the poor."

I looked at Karl-Martin. He gestured me to be silent. He was watching Lone Dog closely.

"It did not seem to me that the anger of this Judas was wrong," Lone Dog said. "But the black robes told us this Judas was a bad man and that he had done a bad thing. They said that because of him the *wičháša wakȟáŋ* was nailed to a tree and died.

"I thought that if this was true, then this Judas was perhaps a bad man."

He looked at us and smiled, as if he expected us to understand.

"But the black robes said that Creator had wanted Jesus to be nailed to that tree and die so that the great spirit father would pay attention and keep us all from going to the hell place where we would burn forever."

"That made me open my heart to this Judas. If the *wičháša wakȟáŋ* had to die to keep everyone from the burning place, and this Judas helped the *wičháša wakȟáŋ* on this path, he did not do a bad thing, he did a good thing. He was doing Creator's will."

Karl-Martin smiled slightly and shook his head.

Lone Dog paused for a moment to let his words sink in, then walked up to Two Finger. Two Finger towered over him. He was fully a foot taller than the old man.

"Mr. Two Finger," Lone Dog said. "You are like that Judas. By breaking my grandfather's *čhaŋnúŋpa* you set us on this journey. Without you we would not all be here. Without you, my great-grandson Levi would not have set his foot on the path to manhood. Without you, my great-grandson Reuben would not have found his spirit voice. You are like that Judas. You think you did a bad thing, but you did a good thing. Because of you, I can pass on in peace."

He took Two Finger's hand and placed a fragment of pipe in it. He gently closed Two Finger's hand around the fragment and held it firmly. "*Philámayaye, kȟolá,*" he said.

Two Finger looked down.

"*Philámayaye, Tȟuŋkášila,*" he answered.

I had never heard him utter a word in Lakota before.

"What's going on?" I whispered to Karl-Martin. Karl-Martin put his finger to his lips.

Lone Dog moved over to Lillie and Karl-Martin. Lillie was holding tight to Karl-Martin's hand.

"My sister, my brother," Lone Dog began. "I wish to speak to you as one, because you have come here as one. I have heard your story. It is a sad story. *Wačhíwiŋ* has told it to me." He was using Ida's Indian name.

"You began your journey in different worlds. You came together through love. But your love experienced a great sadness, and now you are bound together in grief. Grief comes to us all. It is a journey that makes us all one."

He placed his hand on theirs.

"When Creator took your child from you, he left a great empty place in your hearts. Grief rushed in to fill that place. But it was a place meant for love.

"When my boys came to you, they were lost and afraid. They needed love. You put aside your grief and opened that place in your hearts to them. You fed them and clothed them. You gave them hope and courage and peace. You did not try to own them or change them or make them take *wašíču* ways. You took them into that place in your heart and surrounded them with love."

He looked at Karl-Martin. "I listened closely when we spoke. When I said that Levi was being a good *wašíču* farmer, you stood against this. You said, 'No, he was just being a respectful Lakota boy.' You were protecting him with your words. You were standing strong for his Lakota heart. This told me that you were a good man, that you were not like so many *wašíču* who wish to make everyone like them."

He placed a fragment of the pipe in Karl-Martin's hand. "*Philámayaye*, my brother," he said.

"*Philámayaye*, Grandfather," Karl-Martin said.

Lone Dog turned to Lillie. "I see your eyes. The hunger in your heart for a child is great. The memory of the child you lost is strong. Yet you cut the clothing you made for your son with your own hands so that Levi and Reuben would be warm on their journey."

He pressed a pipe fragment into Lillie's hand.

"*Philámayaye, Iná*," he said. "You have the heart of a true mother."

Lillie's eyes filled with tears. She held his hand tightly, as if reluctant to let it go.

"*Philámayaye, Thuŋkášila,*" she said, and lowered her eyes.

I was nervous that he was about to come to me, but he turned instead to Brother James.

"I do not know you, my *hásapa* friend, but Levi and Reuben know you. I see the love they have in their hearts when they are with you.

"I do not know what you did to call forth this love. I only know that trust is at the heart of love, that Levi stands tall in trust next to you, and that you have called forth such trust from Reuben that he sings in the spirit voice that I feared would be hidden forever.

"I do not know how they met you or what you did for their bodies on this journey, but I know what you did for their hearts. And for this I honor you."

He squeezed the pipe fragment into Brother James's hand.

"*Philámayaye,* my friend."

From behind him, Reuben let out a tiny squeal.

Brother James broke into a grin. "And to you, my brother," he responded.

There remained only Ree, Ida, and me.

I was afraid for what he would say when he got to me, but he turned instead to Ida. He spoke to her in Lakota, paying no attention to the rest of us. I tried to understand but I recognized only a few words.

Lillie saw me listening. She moved close to me.

"I can understand him, Mr. Danton," she whispered. "He's telling her that Creator called her to this moment to protect the spirit that is alive in Reuben, so that his gift can be shared with all the people. He is telling her that Creator gave her *ič'ič'upi*, the true power of sacrifice, so that she would have the strength to give up her legs and live in one place for all her life to protect the sacred stone. He says she is like the sacred water of the *Mnišoše*, that she has been kept inside her banks for all these years to bring life to the people, that she is the current on the river that has kept the boys to the sacred ways and has carried them safely on their journey home."

Lone Dog nodded to Ida in a gesture of deference and placed a piece of stone in her hands. She held his hand tightly, clasping it in both of hers.

Unlike the others, she chose to speak back to Lone Dog. She spoke in her own language.

"Can they understand each other?" I asked Lillie.

"Lakota and Dakota are very close."

"What's she saying?"

"She's thanking him. She's saying that through their hands the ancestors are touching. She's saying that her spirit leapt when Reuben came into her house and that she heard her grandfather's voice in her heart."

The old man and Ida held their hands fast. They looked at each other with an understanding that was more than personal. I felt a shiver move across me. Truly, it felt like through them the ancestors were touching.

The strange light had almost disappeared. Shadows were filling the hills and valleys. Above it all the moon hung red and small in the darkening sky. One by one, like tiny pricks of light, stars were beginning to emerge.

Lone Dog turned to me as I had known he would. He stood before me, no taller than my shoulders. I was afraid of what he was going to say.

"You, my friend, my little brother, my hunter. When I first met you I had strong doubts. I could see that you were strong in your *wašíču* ways, that you knew the ways of the mind but had little understanding of the ways of the spirit. But when Ree sent the boys off, I knew that the time might come when I would have need of a man who knew the *wašíču* world; someone who could get through doors a Native man could not enter. But it had to be a *wašíču* I could trust.

"When you stood against the cruelty of Two Finger and told Ree that Reuben should not go to that school, I knew I had found that *wašíču*. You had courage to stand against what was wrong even though you did not always know what was right.

"I could see that your heart was good even if your mind was confused. You heard me when I spoke. You heard my Ree when she spoke. You did not argue. You listened with an open spirit.

"So we gave you our trust. We trusted you to find our boys. We trusted you to be their hunter. It was good that we did so.

"What we did not know was that you could also be their protector. But once you found them you led them with a gentle hand and kept them safe from harm.

"For this I will always honor you. For this you will always be my friend."

He pressed a fragment of the broken *čhaŋnúŋpa* in my palm.

"*Philámayaye, kȟolá*," he said.

I was shocked and humbled. I had feared he would berate me as he had done in the house. But there was nothing but warmth and gratitude in his voice. When he placed the fragment into my hand I felt like I had been given one of the greatest gifts I had ever received.

"*Philámayaye*, Grandfather," I mumbled.

He smiled at me and turned toward his granddaughter.

Ree stood before him as firm and erect as little Levi. The history of their whole relationship was written in their faces — the love, the defiance, the mutual respect. It was the belief in the old ways meeting the challenges of the new.

Lone Dog took her hand in his. "My Ree," he said. "My granddaughter. The mother of my great-grandsons. I have often spoken harshly to you because you carry such bitterness in your heart. I have done so out of love, because I have not wanted to see you raise up that bitterness and make it sacred. One should never make bitterness sacred. It will take you on the black road where anger seems like goodness. Anger can never be goodness. It is like poison water, good to drink in the moment, but it leads to death.

"I understand that your road has been difficult. You have had to be both mother and father to your boys. I have tried to take the father part, but I am old. I am like the stars to them. I can give them guidance but I am too distant to be felt.

"But the old, too, can learn. I now see that your anger has given them a gift. When softened with love, anger can become strength. By your anger you have placed courage in Levi's heart. By your love you have softened it to strength. This strength is now bearing fruit.

"Reuben has a knowledge that is not of this world. He will live his life needing a protector so that he can share this knowledge with our people. Levi's strength has shown that he can be that protector. He has led his little brother through a harsh world and returned him to us, and he yet has only eleven years.

"If he can do this for his brother, he can do this for his people. You have created a strong man in the making, and it is a man with the heart of a leader. Though his journey has just begun, you have set his foot on the good road. Because of you, I have been allowed to see the man who he is and the man he yet can be."

He took the largest remaining piece of the *čhaŋnúŋpa* and pressed it in her hand.

"*Philámayaye*, my granddaughter. You have taken the fear from my heart and replaced it with hope."

They stood there facing each other in silence. I thought for a moment that they might embrace, but it was not in their character. Instead, Ree stepped back and let her grandfather bring the boys forward to the rest of us. Levi stepped up, straight and serious, looking every inch his mother's son. Reuben squeaked and squealed and jumped forward to be even with his brother.

"My friends," the old man said, facing the rest of us. "*Wóphila* for hearing me. My heart is lighter now."

From a distant ridge a coyote called. From somewhere behind us another answered in the darkness.

He turned to the boys. "Hand me the *čhaŋnúŋpa*," he said. "It is time that we smoke together and touch the spirits of the ancestors."

GRANDPA SMILES

Levi

I am full scared now. Grandfather is putting the *čhaŋnúŋpa* together, the man part and the woman part. Reuben says they will fit. He says he has always watched when Grandpa took out his pipe. He says he knew the stem part was finger size. When we made the *čhaŋnúŋpa* he had me make the hole part finger size, too.

The red moon eye is watching us. *Haŋhépi-Wí* is showing strong, right above us. The circle stone Miss Ida placed on the *owáŋka* is looking back at it.

The sky has turned full dark. Only *Haŋhépi-Wí* has light, except for *Wičháȟpi-Oyáte*, the star people. They are out now, everywhere. They are watching, too.

Reuben is jumping up and down. I want him to stand still. I want him to show respect.

Grandpa stops me with his eyes. He has full love for Reuben.

Grandpa takes the *čhaŋnúŋpa*. He puts the man part and the woman part together. "*Hahó*," he says. They fit. Momma is crying. I have never seen her cry. It is quiet crying. Joy crying. Miss Lillie is crying, too. They are like sister crying.

Grandpa hands the *čhaŋnúŋpa* to *Uŋčí* Ida. She touches the bowl part to the circle stone. They are the same, like *Haŋhépi-Wí*.

"*Hahó*," he says.

Grandpa closes his eyes. He is doing in-looking. He talks low in Lakota. He is talking to the ancestors.

Reuben is making sounds. It is like he is understanding. Grandpa puts his hand on Reuben. He puts his other hand on me.

431

"*Wakȟáŋ Tȟáŋka*," he says. "*Tȟuŋkášila*. You have brought my boys back to me. You have brought *čhaŋnúŋpa* alive again through their hands. You have kept the blood of our ancestors alive through their hands."

He puts both hands on Reuben. "*Wakȟáŋ Tȟáŋka*, see this boy. His spirit sees backward. He sees the old ways. The knowledge of the ancestors is in him."

He puts his hands on my shoulders. "*Wakȟáŋ Tȟáŋka*, see this boy. This boy looks forward. He sees the world that is coming. The hope of the people is in him."

He takes the pipe from Ida. She reaches in her bag. She has *čhaŋšáša*.

Grandfather gives it to me. "You," he says. "It is time."

I am afraid proud. *Uŋčí* Ida is smiling.

I hold the *čhaŋšáša* to the four directions, like I have seen Grandfather do. Then to the sky and to the earth.

I am looking at Grandfather. He is smiling, too.

I put the *čhaŋšáša* in the pipe. I use only my right hand, like he taught me. He has never let me do this before.

I pack it slow, sacred-like. I say a prayer when I do it.

Grandpa takes the *čhaŋnúŋpa* back.

He looks at the bad school man.

"You," he says.

The bad school man looks scared.

"You," Grandfather says again. He points to the pipe.

The bad school man reaches in his pocket. He has wood matches.

He strikes one on a stone. It makes a strong light in the dark.

He puts it to the *čhaŋšáša*.

Grandpa draws in the smoke. The *čhaŋšáša* glows orange.

Grandpa passes the *čhaŋnúŋpa* to me.

He has never let me smoke before.

I draw in the smoke. I cup it around me, like washing myself in it, like I have seen the men do. I turn the pipe sunwise and hold the stem toward the sky.

The smoke goes up toward *Haŋhépi-Wí*.

Haŋhépi-Wí is small. She is watching down.

Grandpa smiles. I pass the pipe on.

WE ARE NOT FINISHED

Karl-Martin

I used to think that rituals have power because people believe in them. Now I think it's the other way around. People believe in rituals because they have power.

In the seminary I would watch the old monks on Good Friday reciting the Stations of the Cross. But they weren't just saying them, they were in them. When three o'clock came — the time when it is said that Jesus died — something inside them died, too. They would weep and tremble. They were one with the crucifixion.

I'd sit there like the man in the Gospel of Mark, crying out, "I believe, I believe. Help my unbelief," but I couldn't enter in.

Tonight on this hillside, taking in that smoke from the pipe the boys had made, then watching it rise up into the night sky toward that blood-red moon, I entered in. I was taken to a place I did not know that I could go.

It was a kind of a communion. All of us together, beneath that haunted sky, passing the pipe from one to the next and turning it so it would honor the four directions. I don't know exactly what it meant, but I know what it did. In that passing, everything became one. All of us, that moon, the birds, the night sounds, the wind.

We could all feel it. I know we could. I could see it in Lillie's eyes. There was a peace to her that I had not seen before. She had returned to a home she had never known, but somehow had never forgotten. And Ida, and Danton, that Brother James, and even Two Finger — there was that same look in their eyes.

Even Mister Bones lay quiet as if he understood.

And who am I to say that he didn't?

Who am I to say anything about what this means?

I was the last to receive the pipe. I could feel the old man watching me as I cupped the smoke around my head, bathing myself in it, as I had seen the others do. He had a calm, almost beatific look on his face. He had given Reuben the responsibility of holding the pipestem as we passed it among us. Reuben's eyes were luminous.

Levi stood at his place in the circle, motionless and impassive. He had been included with the adults. It's as if all his seriousness of intent had come to fruition. Finally, he was being allowed to be the man he had always wanted himself to be.

There was a finality about this — a wholeness, a completion. We had done it. We had protected the boys, helped them with their mission, brought them safely home. We had all played our parts.

As I finished, the old man took the pipe from my hands. He nodded to me, in deference, in thanks.

"*Wóphila,*" he said. "I thank you all. You have given me a great gift. The boys and I will stay up here until the star that divides the night from the day arrives. The rest of you may go."

We turned to walk down the hill. Lone Dog raised his hand to stop us.

"You may leave this place," he said. "But you must not leave my home. This night is not yet finished."

I DIDN'T GET TO CHOOSE

Brother James

Miss Latrice always said, "If you get yourself in a situation and you don't know what to do, make yourself useful."

When the old man told us to go down the hill but not to leave, that pretty much felt like a situation to me. So I figured to build a little fire. Not a big one — this is dry country. But these high plains nights can get pretty cold, even in the summer. Making a little fire seemed like a useful thing to do.

I was still thinking about what had happened up there with that pipe. Reminded me of some of the times when you're singing, and just for a moment something happens and there ain't no time or space. You're just there, inside that song.

That's what it was like when that pipe went around the circle. It took us all inside.

I don't know what was up with that mound that Levi built. I seen a lot of altars in my day, and I guess that was one. But the stones and the pipe touching, I didn't know what that was about. But it's like everything else — when people believe something, you don't get in their way unless they're putting the hurt on someone. And the old man wasn't putting the hurt on any of us. He was calling each of us out, but it was all to lift people up.

That old man was someone you take serious. He was one of those folk you meet every once in a while — the kind that can see right through you. One look in your eyes and he knows stuff about you that you don't even know yourself. So, if he said we should stick around, well, then, we stick around.

The women, they went in the house to do some cooking. I don't know how they were going to stay awake — I figured they'd been up since morning — but I was happy they was trying. I know that my tank was pretty much empty, but my hungry was bigger than my tired. I think it was for all of us. Miss Lillie brought out some apples and bread to keep us going, and that took the worst edge off. Beyond that, we just had to sit and watch that sky and wait.

I got the fire going pretty easy. Found a little pile of wood right outside the back door. Flamed right up.

Soon enough that Two Finger fellow come over. He didn't say nothing, just stood there.

He didn't make much more sense here than I did, so I figured I'd be neighborly and talk him up a bit.

"Sit down, take a load off," I said. And it was a good-size load. He was a hefty one, maybe 250, 300. He had meanness ground into him — ugly mouth with darting eyes. Even his clothes showed mean — dirty shirt with tears in the elbows, jeans with pockets ripped halfway off, hanging down below his belly. Had a smell about him, too.

But old Lone Dog had put a change in him when he had him light the pipe. Now he seemed more lost than mean.

He give me a nod and set himself down on a log by the fire. I didn't feel much friend in him, but like recognizes like, and there ain't too much more alike than two folks who spent their lives on the outside looking in. So I figured I could find some place where the two of us could meet.

"Hell of a thing up there," I said. "What with that pipe and all."

He give me a nod, but nothing more.

"Old man said you set all this in motion, coming after them boys, breaking that pipe."

He give a shrug but that was all. He was a hard one, that was for sure. Answered questions like slamming a door.

I stirred the fire. Sparks was dancing upward.

Thought I'd try again.

"Never been to nothing like this before. You?"

"Once or twice."

"Pretty much an honor to have the old man ask you to light the pipe, I'd guess."

"Wasn't expecting it."

Talking to him was like tending a fire. Have to poke it every once in a while to keep it going. I wasn't getting anywhere with soft poking, so I thought I'd push a little deeper, see if I could get him talking.

"You Lakota?" I could see some Indian in him, mixed up with something else.

A dark look come across him. I wondered if that was too much of a poke.

"Part."

His face was flat-eyed, but he was squeezing his hands together. Hands tell you a lot. His squeezing was more nervous than angry.

I was starting to feel sorry for the man. If there's one thing I know when I see it, it's "lonely." I been wrestling that angel for my whole life. All that shut-door stuff he was giving me, that was just for keeping people away. I was looking at a lonely man.

Now, lonely can be real sad or it can be real hard, like a dog biting to keep from being touched. I was thinking this Two Finger's lonely was probably the biting kind. So I wanted to move careful. But I'd seen him sitting with Miss Lillie and I'd seen the old man call him to light the pipe, so I knew there was some good in there, even if he was a school man and he'd put the fear of God into the boys.

"You know what the old man was talking about?" I asked. "The star that divides day from night?"

He lit a cigarette. Coughed several times. Sounded bad. Come from down deep. Something to worry about.

"*Áŋpó-Wičháȟpi*. Morning star. Indians think it means new beginnings."

"You know this stuff?"

"Not much. Just heard my old man talking. He was mostly full of bullshit."

He coughed again. All rattly and wet.

"Them cigarettes can't be helping that cough."

He looked hard at me. Squint eyed. That was too much of a poke.

"Sorry. Don't mean to be prying. I just think about them things. What with me making my living singing and all, I got to pay attention to coughs and such."

"I don't sing."

Took a big chance. "And I don't cough."

He paused for a second. Thought I might get the biting dog. But he give me something close to a smile. There was someone inside there.

"You ain't bad for a colored man," he said.

"Didn't get to choose."

He took another big drag on his cigarette, stared off like he was thinking. Then flicked it head over tails into the fire.

"Yeah. I know. Neither did I."

CHILDREN

Ida

I am happy to be in the kitchen, but my heart aches for the boys. This will be a long night on the hill for them.

Levi will do fine. He wants to be a man; he will show strong. But Reuben is young. It will be hard for him to go through the night without sleeping.

I wonder what *Tȟuŋkášila* Lone Dog is telling them. *Aŋpó-Wičháȟpi* is the dawn star, when the old gives way to the new. If he is having them wait for that, there is something he wants to say.

I'm glad to be preparing this feast with Ree and Lillie. The men will be hungry when the sun comes up. It is good to be making food for men.

I have sent Mr. Danton back to his truck. I could see his eyes were heavy. He has had a hard day. He needs to rest. He does not have the strength of a Lakota.

It made me smile to see the old Bones following right behind him. They have become friends, Mr. Danton and that old dog. I'm happy for that. Mr. Danton is a good man, but he has a lonely heart. A *šúŋka* will take away that loneliness.

It is good, too, to have met *Tȟuŋkášila* Lone Dog. He reminds me of my grandfather. He says he is only an ordinary man, but I do not believe this. I believe he is a *načá*. I believe he has been called to give counsel. Tonight he gave counsel to all of us.

The words he said to me gave me a strong peace. I have lived a quiet life with only my grandfather's stones for family. I have often wished for a husband, for children. It has often seemed to me that my life has been wasted. But *Tȟuŋkášila* Lone Dog did not see my life in this way. He honored me for how I have lived. He said the stones have been my children.

Tonight when we touched my grandfather's stone with the pieces of the broken *čhaŋnúŋpa*, and the *čhaŋšáša* from my grandfather rose up from the *čhaŋnúŋpa* that the boys had made, all my children came together. In that moment, I forgot I had no legs. In that moment, my spirit danced. I was one with my children, the *íŋyaŋ*. They have no legs, either.

A WEIGHT TO LAY DOWN

Lillie

I'm so tired that I can hardly stand. But my heart is smiling. It is so good to be working in the kitchen with Ida again like when we were young. She makes her wheelchair dance, the way she moves from the table to the stove.

Ree is making her special *wagmíza-wasná*. Ida told her that Reuben kept talking about it when he was at her house. That made Ree smile. She had not smiled before.

There is a big pot boiling on the stove. Ida is making the soup for the feast. We have cut the vegetables — the carrots, the potatoes, the *thíŋpsiŋla*. Ida is preparing the *t̃hatȟáŋka* meat that Grandfather Lone Dog said was fed on the sacred grasses of the *Pahá Sápa*. I'm kneading the dough for the fry bread. It feels good on my hands. It has been so long since I have made bread in the Indian way.

The night is quiet, but my heart is singing. When Grandpa Lone Dog placed the piece of pipe in my hand and called me "*iná*," he made my spirit leap. He was calling me "mother." He knew. He understood. He was seeing into my heart. He was seeing Joseph.

I feel like I have come home. To see these boys with their grandfather, to hear their song, to smoke with my people, has filled me with such peace.

I believe that I have done some good here. I have drawn kindness from Mr. Two Finger. I have touched the sister place in Ree's heart. The spirit of Joseph has been strong inside me. I am filled with joy toward everybody.

I have wanted to feel closer to Ree. We are both mothers.

I went near to her. I took her hand in mine.

"Your boys are such good boys," I said.

I feared that she might pull away. But, instead, she smiled. I could feel her opening to me.

"Yes, they are good boys," she said. "But they have not been easy. Levi came into the world in a hurry to be a man. Reuben came trailing spirits."

"You have raised them well."

"I have tried."

She stopped stirring the chokecherries and looked at me. I could feel something heavy on her mind.

"There is something I want to say to you," she said.

"My heart is open to you, my sister," I said. "Say it."

"I did not honor what you did for my boys."

"You are a mother. You feared for them. You did not know me."

"Yes, but I met you with a closed spirit."

Ida was watching from across the room. She was smiling.

"It has been hard to raise boys alone," Ree said. "There is no father. We have no *thiyóšpaye*. There are no uncles to guide them. There is only Grandfather, and his voice is distant. I have no fears for Levi. His spirit will not be broken — not by the boarding school, not by the *wašíču*, not by anything in this life. But Reuben, he does not come from this world. He will be crushed by the *wašíču* ways."

Ida wheeled herself over to Ree. She did not want Ree's spirit to go dark.

"My girl," she said. "You look too much outward at what the *wašíču* have done. There are spirits watching over Reuben. You must look with your heart as well as your eyes."

"You are very kind, *Uŋčí* Ida. But you are not a mother. These are a mother's fears."

I felt what was in Ree's heart. "I understand what she is saying," I said.

"My girls, my girls," Ida said. "I am not a mother, but I have lived a long time. Did you see that *khéya* on the pipe that the boys made?"

Ree's eyes warmed with pride. "Yes. My Levi is gifted with his hands."

Ida shook her head. "Levi did not make that *khéya*. Reuben did. He sang it out. Levi only made the shape that Reuben sang. The boys told me.

"Do you know why Reuben called out a *khéya*? Why he did not make *tȟatȟáŋka*, or *waŋblí*?"

"No, *Uŋčí*. I don't know."

Ida was holding tight to Ree's hand. She would not let her go. "Tell me, Ree, what is Reuben's greatest fear?"

"He fears for his grandfather. His fears for his grandfather's death. His grandfather is his whole world."

"And what do the elders teach you about *khéya*?"

"*Khéya* is wisdom. *Khéya* is courage to keep going. *Khéya* is a long life."

Ida took Ree's hand in her two-handed way.

"*Khéya* came to Reuben in my house. He told the boys which way to go. He showed them where to find the stone. When Reuben sang *khéya* into the *čhaŋnúŋpa* he was calling *khéya*'s power for your grandfather. He was bringing your grandfather a prayer for a long life. He did not know he was doing this. These are not things he has learned. These are things the spirits showed him."

She looked up at Ree with an *uŋčí*'s eyes.

"You do not have to worry for Reuben. The spirits have been guiding him. The spirits will always protect him."

MORNING

Danton

I tried to stay awake but I just couldn't. I don't know how the rest of them managed it, or even if they had. I'd been drifting in and out of consciousness for the last several hours.

All I could think was that these people were made of tougher steel than I was, or that the stress of dealing with the firestorm and the axle buster and getting everyone here safely had taken all the stuffing out of me. Or maybe I'm just getting old.

Ida had seen my exhaustion and pulled me aside. "You go sleep for a while," she said. She didn't have to say it twice.

I made my way back to the pickup and climbed into the back. Mister Bones had followed faithfully behind me. I was going to let him sleep on the ground, but he had mewled and whined so loudly that I'd been forced to lift him into the bed and let him share the pile of rags that served as my blanket and a pillow.

I might have slept all the way through to daylight if he hadn't begun pushing against me and snoring and kicking his feet in some kind of dog dream.

"Jesus, Bones," I said, pulling an old jacket over me. "You're a hell of a bed partner."

He opened his eyes and breathed a blast of rancid dog breath on me, then fell back asleep.

I sat up and looked out into the darkness. It took me a moment to remember where I was. The edge of the eastern sky was beginning to crease with pink, and the distant hills stood like shadow cutouts against the night.

I could hear low voices coming from the Lone Dog house. Several figures were huddled around a small fire in the side of the yard.

Slowly, everything was coming back to me — pushing Ida up the hill, old Lone Dog asking Two Finger to light the *čhaŋnúŋpa*, Reuben and Brother James singing that haunting, otherworldly song.

With a start, I realized that we were supposed to be waiting for Lone Dog to come down the hill with the boys. The morning star that the Lakota said divided day from night was glowing just above the horizon.

"Come on, Bones," I said. "I hope we're not late." I lifted him out of the pickup and hurried toward the fire.

Karl-Martin, Brother James, and Two Finger were sitting across from each other on some old stumps. The fire had burned down to where it was little more than a pile of glowing embers. An occasional flame surged up as a random twig or branch flared, burned quickly, then settled into ash. The men were conversing quietly amongst themselves.

"Welcome back," Karl-Martin said. "Get a little beauty sleep?"

The hill was still shrouded in darkness.

"Are they still up there?" I asked.

Karl-Martin pointed to the morning star. "Began to show just now."

There was movement on the hill. The three figures were beginning to make their way down. They were walking close together.

As they got closer we could see that Levi was supporting his grandfather by his right arm. Reuben was holding his grandfather's other hand. Old Lone Dog looked unsteady on his feet.

When Mister Bones saw the boys, he took off limping and whining toward them, his tail whirling like a propeller.

"Should we go help them?" I asked.

"No," Karl-Martin said. "We should wait."

The three figures moved slowly, tentatively, over the uneven ground.

"I'll build up the fire so they can see better," Two Finger said. He poked the coals to stir up a flame.

As the three came nearer, I could tell that something wasn't right.

Levi was stiffer than usual. His jaw was set and he was staring straight ahead. Reuben was sniffling and clinging tightly to his grandfather's hand. He looked to be crying.

Brother James stood up to offer Lone Dog a seat.

The old man waved him off and remained standing.

"Go get the womenfolk," he said.

There was something in his voice that I had never heard before.

TOUCHING ON THE
HEART SIDE

Ida

The kettle on the stove was boiling strong. This *wóhaŋpi* was going to be so good. The *thatháŋka* meat *Tȟuŋkášila* Lone Dog had given us tasted sweet like prairie grass and flowers. I had added good spices. We were going to have a good feast.

Ree was just finishing the *wasná* when Karl-Martin come through the door. There was worry on his face.

"Grandpa Lone Dog wants us all out in the yard. I think something is wrong."

Ree dropped her spoon. Her face was full of fear.

"Is Grandfather okay?"

"I don't know. I think so."

"The boys?"

"I can't tell. Reuben is crying."

She pushed past us and ran out.

"Oh dear," Lillie said. "We'd better get out there. I hope nothing bad has happened."

"I think it's okay," I said. I had a strong feeling. "I think I know what's going on."

Lillie was feeling fear for the boys. "What do you think it is, Ida?"

"I think he told them something. I think that's why he wanted them on the hill."

"What? What would he tell them?"

"He will tell us if he wants us to know. Come, we'll go see."

Lillie ran ahead. She wanted to catch up with Ree.

Karl-Martin pushed my chair down the step into the yard. His pushing was strong, stronger than Mr. Danton's.

"I'm worried, Ida," he said.

I put my hand on his.

"We have to wait," I said.

The dawn was showing first light. *Aŋpétu-Wí* was coming up over the hills, not yet showing his face. *Áŋpó-Wičháȟpi* was still shining, but not strong. Night was turning to day.

Tȟuŋkášila Lone Dog was standing with the boys by the fire. When I saw him, I understood Karl-Martin's fear. Levi was standing strong, but he was shaking, like when boys try not to cry. Reuben's eyes had the look of a scared animal.

Tȟuŋkášila Lone Dog stood between them. He was still, as if without life. I could tell his spirit had gone somewhere and had not yet returned.

Mister Bones was making sounds and pawing at Reuben. He felt the fear, too.

"Give my boys some water," *Tȟuŋkášila* Lone Dog said. His words were soft, like he was hardly there. "They have earned their thirst." He did not ask for any for himself.

His eyes were far off. He was seeing a distant place.

"I have told the boys something," he said. "Now I wish to tell you all."

He waited until we were all still.

"I have been to the *wašíču* doctor. He says my time is short. He says I will not be here to see the first snow."

Reuben made a wail sound.

Tȟuŋkášila touched him soft on the shoulder. "No, Grandson. You should not cry. Creator gives us all our season. Mine is now done."

Reuben pulled his face tight and made hard fists and crying sounds. Levi had a look that sees nothing.

Ree showed tears, but no surprise. I think she had known.

"I want you all to sit," *Tȟuŋkášila* said. "This is important."

We all sat down.

"Levi, I want you to get Grandmother's bowl. It is on the shelf. Fill it with water from the jug on the floor. The one I have told you never to drink. I want you to bring it here."

Levi ran to the house. I heard water pouring. He came back with the wooden bowl from the shelf. He was walking fast, trying not to spill, holding it in front of him.

"Good, *t̆akóža*. Now place it on the ground."

Grandfather Lone Dog looked at all of us. "I want you all to take some earth in your hand. I want you to put it in the bowl."

The earth here was loose, easy to pick up. Mr. Danton put some in my hand. I placed it in the water in the bowl. We all did.

"Reuben, stir it," *T̆uŋkášila* said. "This is water from the *Mníšoše*. Stir it until the water and the earth become one."

Reuben was breathing fast. His hands were shaking.

T̆uŋkášila Lone Dog took a leather pouch from his pocket. He handed it to Levi.

"Pour it into the water."

The pouch was filled with red dust. Levi poured it into the water.

"This is from my *čaŋnúŋpa*. Stir it until the earth and the water and the dust are the same."

Reuben was stirring strong with his hands. He was breathing hard. He was talking animal talk. He had tears in his eyes. He stirred until the water became like mud.

"Stop now," *T̆uŋkášila* said. "Let me see your hands."

Reuben held up his hands. They were red with mud.

"Good. Now I want you to put your hand in this and touch each of our friends on the cheek. Make a hand mark." He pointed to the left side of his chest. "On the heart side. Can you do that?"

Reuben nodded. He was still crying and shaking.

T̆uŋkášila turned to us. He looked at us all.

"Will you let Reuben mark you with his hand?"

We all nodded.

Reuben put his hand in the dust mud. He went to each of us. He placed his hand on our cheek, making a hand mark. Levi came behind. He carried the bowl.

I reached up and touched my left cheek. The hand mark was warm on my skin.

The others touched their faces, too.

"He has marked you with this earth," *Tȟuŋkášila* Lone Dog said. "He has done it on your heart side. You may wash the earth off your face, but you cannot wash it from your heart.

"Come now, my friends. Let us build up this fire and I will tell you why you are really here."

MORE BROTHERS AND SISTERS THAN BLOOD

Danton

I have to say I was frightened by what was happening. The place where Reuben had touched my cheek was burning like fire.

The moon had lost its color and was disappearing like a ghost. A pale light was growing slowly beyond the eastern horizon, and the stars were fading. Only the morning star, the one Lone Dog called *Áŋpó-Wičháȟpi*, was still bright in the sky. The buttes and mesas stood like brooding, looming giants. They seemed almost to be advancing toward us as they emerged from the night.

I was afraid for what the old man was going to say. There were things going on here that I didn't understand.

We all kept our eyes cast down. We were all just waiting, but we did not know for what. The silence loomed ever larger as we stood there in the darkness waiting for Lone Dog to speak. I was suddenly aware of the night rustlings, the movements of unseen animals, the crackling of the fire, and the soft whispering of the winds. The only human sounds were Reuben's tiny whimperings and the heavy, rhythmic rasping of Two Finger's labored breathing.

Lone Dog stood for a long while in silence, regarding these unseen forces, then gathered himself, spoke softly under his breath, and turned his attention in our direction.

"My friends, my relatives," he said, taking on the formal manner he used when speaking of something important. "I have told you that *čhaŋnúŋpa* has called you. *Čhaŋnúŋpa* does not ask something of someone without offering something in return."

He gestured us to come closer.

"I want you to look upon these boys, my great-grandsons, Levi and Reuben Lone Dog. They are the ones who have brought us together."

He placed his hands gently on their backs and moved them toward us.

"Reuben's roots run deep. He hears the voices of the ancestors. Levi's branches grow and spread. He sees the way of the future. Together they are the strength and hope of our people, the tree of our Lakota life. Creator has given them to me to protect.

"Now that I'm about to pass, it will be up to others to protect these boys and help them grow. You are the ones Creator has chosen. You are the ones called by *čhaŋnúŋpa* to help them on their journey to manhood."

He paused again. He wanted us to feel the significance of his words.

"We have among our people a sacred way that binds one person to another. It is called the way of the *huŋká*. You cannot be made *huŋkáyapi*. You are not all Lakota and I do not have the power. But you have let Reuben touch you with the mark of the sacred earth. This has made you one in the task the Creator has placed before you. It is a sacred bond. You cannot betray it. You are now more brothers and sisters than blood."

The words sent a chill through me. More brothers and sisters than blood.

I touched the mark on my cheek. We all did. It felt like a claim, a binding, a promise. And though the words do not come easily to me, there in the great Dakota darkness it felt for all the world like we were all part of something sacred.

Reuben and Levi stared across the fire at us. Their faces flickered in the fire's orange glow.

Reuben's cheeks were shiny with tears. With his spiky hair and his quivering lip, he seemed small and frightened, not at all the bearer of some deep wisdom or the strength and hope of the Lakota people.

Levi had withdrawn to some far place. He was as distant as the disappearing moon. He had claimed something in himself and taken it deep inside where no one else could touch it.

Lone Dog smiled at us all — that kind and complicated smile that held both love and a challenge. The boys stood motionless. They knew they were being presented to us.

One by one Lone Dog called us forward.

"You," he said, pointing to Two Finger. "Mister Bazile. The son of my lost friend, the Chief. The one he called his 'little Two Finger.' Come closer."

Two Finger stepped forward.

"I have watched you now for years. I have seen how you fill the people in town with fear. You think this gives you great power. But it is a small power that faces outward, and you do not use it for good. If you would have true power you must learn to turn that power inward. Then it will become self-control, and you will be able to use it to protect others, not cause them fear.

"I have an important task to place before you. My boys are living in a harsh world. They need protection. I want you to become their protector. I want you to make sure no harm comes to them from the outside world on their journey to manhood."

Two Finger's eyes were turned toward the ground.

"In return I have a gift for you. You have said you wished to learn the old ways. I was raised in those ways and I have held them close. In honor of your father, my friend, the Chief, if you will use your power to protect these boys, I will teach you what I know while I am still alive."

Two Finger looked up. His eyes widened. I had never seen such a look of surprise on him before.

Lone Dog wagged a finger toward him.

"But you must know that this learning will not take you on the journey you had hoped. You are not called to be a *wičháša wakȟáŋ* as you once dreamed. You are called to follow the *akíčhita* way, the warrior way. But it will not be an easy journey. A warrior serves, he does not harm. He uses his strength to protect those who are weaker. You will have to learn to take the anger from your heart and get control of your spirit. This will not be easy and my time is short. But I will teach you what I can in the time I have left if you have the courage to learn."

He looked hard at Two Finger. His eyes were full of challenge.

"Do you have this courage, Mr. Two Finger? Do you have the courage to be the man your father dreamed for you to be?"

Two Finger looked at him with an almost childlike innocence. No one had ever asked such a thing of him before.

"Yes, *Tȟuŋkášila*," he said.

Old Lone Dog smiled and touched him gently on the sleeve. "*Hahó*," he said.

Then he turned his attention to me.

"Mr. Danton — you, the other school man, the *wašíču* wanderer. When you and Mr. Two Finger first came to my house, I knew that Creator had brought you two together, but I did not know why. Now I know.

"You were two men who belonged nowhere — Mr. Two Finger because he was born between worlds, and you because you believed in the *wašíču* way that tells you that you can be anything you choose. But you did not have the courage to choose. You ran from place to place. Because you did not have this courage, Creator chose for you."

He nodded at Levi and Reuben. "He chose these boys."

"I have watched you closely. It has been important that I understand you because of what I am about to ask of you. I believe now that I do. You live inside the small house of your mind. It is a *wašíču* house, but it is a good house. You know how to help others. You have a generous heart. You understand honor. You do not always seek to put yourself first. Though you do not always know what is right, you know what is wrong. That is a start.

"The spirits are knocking on the door of that small house of your mind. Soon they will come in. And when they do, you will know what is right, because the spirits will speak, and you will have no choice but to listen.

"Hear me closely now. I have thought for a long time about what I am about to say.

"In our way, all boys need a *lekší*, what you call an uncle. He is the one who watches and teaches and sets their feet on a good path in the world. Our boys have no *lekší*. They have no one to guide them.

"Though you are a *wašíču*, I believe that you could be the *lekší* to

Levi and Reuben. You are close enough to them in years that they hear you when you speak. You put no fear in their hearts. You have earned their trust.

"I believe *čhaŋnúŋpa* has brought you here. I believe *čhaŋnúŋpa* has called you to this place so you could help these boys and so you would find a home on this earth."

He looked directly into my eyes.

"Will you be their *lekší*, Mr. Danton?"

I nodded my head. There was no way I could say no. Lone Dog had a power I could not deny.

"Good. I want you to come to them every day. I want you to take them into the world. I want you to show them how to be good in the *wašíču* way. Show them how to live among the *wašíču* without becoming one of them.

"Your brother, Mr. Two Finger, will help you. He will help you by protecting the boys from the outside while you guide them from the inside."

Hearing Lone Dog call Two Finger "my brother" made me cringe.

Something must have shown on my face. He pointed his finger at me. "More brothers and sisters than blood," he said. "Do you understand? More brothers and sisters than blood."

I nodded my affirmation. I had no choice. "More brothers and sisters than blood."

He turned again to Two Finger.

"Mr. Two Finger? More brothers and sisters than blood?"

Two Finger looked at me. It was the first time ever that our eyes had really met.

"More brothers and sisters than blood."

"Good."

Lone Dog then moved close to Ida. His eyes softened. His voice became warm and caring. It lost its edge of challenge.

"My friend, *Wačhíwiŋ*, the keeper of the stones, you who the boys call *Uŋčí* Ida. I knew you were coming. I did not know you, but I knew you were coming. I thank you for hearing Creator's voice."

Ida smiled. There was a connection between them that was deeper than I could understand.

They spoke together quietly in Dakota and Lakota. Then Lone Dog turned to the rest of us.

"I will speak now in English so our friends can understand. There should be nothing hidden between brothers and sisters."

He took Ida's hand and stood facing her.

"*Wačhíwiŋ*, you have lived long in the *wašíču* world. You have learned the *wašíču* ways. But the old ways have always lived inside you. They were like memories, stuck away in the corners of your life like the stones your grandfather entrusted to you. You knew them in your spirit.

"When the boys came into your life, your spirit spoke. The voices in the stones called to you. You put away your *wašíču* mind and listened to Creator's voice. What you had been waiting for had come.

"Now you are here and we hold the boys between us."

He squeezed Ida's hand. Ida squeezed back.

"You said you felt the touch of our ancestors when we met. I felt it, too. I believe they were passing Reuben from my hands to yours. It gave me peace to feel this.

"Now I am asking you to pass on to our Reuben what our grand-fathers passed to us. Those things only we older ones know. I have a warm feeling and a great peace knowing this. *Philámayaye*, my dear friend. Creator has been good to us."

Ida looked at him with gratitude. She nodded quietly. In the flickering firelight her lined face seemed as aged as the stones.

I knew that Lone Dog was not done. He had not gathered us in this circle by accident.

He placed his hands gently on Levi's shoulders and looked at him with a grandfather's love.

"Levi, my great-grandson. The same blood runs through us. You wish to become a man. Very well. I will speak to you as a man. I will speak to you as my own blood.

"Though I have feared for your brother, I have known that Creator will protect him. But you are meant for the world, and the world is a hard place.

"You are being called to be a leader. I have seen it from your young-est days. I have seen it in the way that you have served your mother and the elders, never asking what needs to be done. I have seen it in the way that you guide your brother and care for him at all times, always putting him before yourself. When he is with you, we have no fear. We know that you will protect him and bring him safely home."

He smiled warmly at Levi.

"As you have done now."

Levi straightened with pride.

"Hear me now, my great-grandson. To be a leader, you must learn to spread your arms over both the weak and the powerful. You must learn to guide with both strength and kindness. You must have *wóohitike*. You must be prepared to guide the people through cruel and difficult times.

"Your mother has raised you well. She is a powerful woman. She has taught you strength and courage. She has made you an oak, able to stand alone on a hill in the fiercest of storms. But how, I have wondered, would you learn kindness? How would you learn not only to lead the strong, but to care for the weak and to leave no one behind?

"Kindness and gentleness have not been part of our life. We have had no family, and it is in a family where love is learned."

He turned toward Karl-Martin and Lillie, who were standing close to the fire holding hands.

"But now I see that Creator has sent you a family."

Lillie's eyes widened. She let out a small gasp.

Lone Dog opened his arms toward them — a welcoming, a beckoning.

"Creator gave us a great gift when he sent the boys to you. But it was not an easy gift. Before Creator sent you, he tested you. He tested you with a great loss. For many, such a loss drives them apart. They forget the family and turn in on themselves and seek only their own protection.

"But your loss has brought you closer. You have held hands through your grief, just as you are holding hands now."

He made a little inward chuckle.

"I did not think that Creator would send a *wašíču* man and a Lakota woman to teach my boys about strength through kindness and love."

He shook his head, as if reliving a private joke.

"But I long ago learned not to question Creator's ways."

He reached across and took both of their hands.

"I am sad that your great loss has opened a space in your heart. But a space that was once filled with love wants to be filled with love again. That is Creator's way."

He stared for a long time into the fire. He was thinking carefully about his words.

Slowly he lifted his eyes and pulled their hands toward him.

"I believe Creator is asking that the space in your heart be filled with love of the boys. I believe he is asking that you take them into your family."

On the other side of the fire, Ree's eyes hardened. Old Lone Dog shook his head slightly and smiled at her. It was a smile full of grand-fatherly warmth.

"Have patience with me, my Ree," he said. "I am not taking your boys from you. You are their mother. Creator has sent them into the world through you. That is a bond that will never be broken.

"I know your love for our boys is great, as is their love for you. But the wound of your *uŋčí*'s pain has filled you with anger, and that anger has taken all softness from your love. You are like *waŋblí*, the eagle, who would raise its young in the highest branches, to make them strong against the wind. But Lillie is like *ištáničatȟaŋka*, who raises its children protected from the cold and winds. Yours is the way of love as strength. Hers is the way of love as softness. To survive in this world our boys will need both.

"*Čhaŋnúŋpa* has brought you two together. You must lean against each other to bring these boys to manhood in the mother's way. *Wačhíwiŋ* will help. She will bring a grandmother's wisdom.

"The three of you will give these boys a mother's love that will make them strong against the harshest winds and the hardest times.

"Will you do this? Will the three of you do this?"

Lillie's eyes were bright with joy. She was being called to be the mother she had been longing to be. This was why she had wanted to come. Old Lone Dog was filling the empty space in her heart.

"I will, *Tȟuŋkášila*," she said, almost breathlessly.

Ree nodded her assent. There was something in her expression that was almost like relief.

Ida just smiled.

Old Lone Dog inhaled deeply and reached in his pocket and took out the carved bluebird Steinbach had given him.

"Mr. Steinbach," he said, holding the carving out toward Karl-Martin. "With this gift you have shown me your heart. If Mr. Two Finger will be the protector of these boys and Mr. Danton will guide them into the *wašíču* world, you must keep their hearts open to the power of the Great Mystery. You will show them that the spirit lives inside of everything, even in the *wašíču* world where everything is given a price and is bought and sold.

"I know you can do this. You are not Lakota, but your heart is open to the ways of the spirit. I have seen that. You can hear Creator's voice. You will make sure that the boys each find their path to the Great Mystery."

Karl-Martin straightened himself like someone receiving an honor. This was man to man, father to father.

"I give you my word," he said.

Old Lone Dog nodded in response. "I believe that word. And I accept it." He held out the carved bluebird. "As I accepted this gift."

This left only Brother James. What, I wondered, would Lone Dog say to this man none of us knew?

But Lone Dog said nothing to him. Instead, he bent down and whispered something to Reuben.

Reuben let out a squeal and ran to Brother James and threw his arms around him. Brother James picked him up and held him in front of him, like a father playing with a toddler. Reuben let out another squeal and hugged Brother James around the neck.

The sun was beginning to rise behind them. The sky was filling with color — first soft lavenders, then pinks, then oranges. Then, in an instant, the sun pushed over the horizon, an orange ball rising, and shafts of light shot to the heavens, setting fire to the clouds.

"Sing it," Reuben squealed. "Sing the waking up song."

Brother James looked toward Lone Dog. Lone Dog nodded.

He set Reuben down and drew in a deep breath. Taking Reuben's hand in his, he began to sing, at first so softly that I could hardly hear him as the two of them walked slowly toward the morning light. With each step his voice grew stronger, until the song filled the hills and the valleys and moved across the landscape like the very sunrise itself.

Sometimes I feel like a motherless child.

I felt a lump rising in my chest. This is the song my grandmother had sung to me as a child growing up in Michigan.

Brother James kept singing. His voice was smooth and rich. The words came from his mouth like a lullaby.

Reuben squealed and jumped up and down. "Sing it more!"

Brother James smiled and sang louder, cradling each word gently.

"Sometimes I feel like a motherless child."

Reuben buried his face against Brother James's leg and held tightly around his waist.

Brother James sang ever more loudly. This was more than a song, it was a lament.

"Sometimes I feel like a motherless child, a long way from home."

The old man had folded his hands in front of him. His eyes were closed and his lips were pursed in a tiny smile. The rest of us stood quietly as the words of the song filled the air and moved across the valleys.

Without warning, my eyes started to fill with tears. Though Brother James was singing this song for Reuben, standing there in that growing high plains morning with the sun coming up over this land as wide as the sky, it felt for all the world like he was singing it for me.

CHOOSING JUST RIGHT

Brother James

I suppose I ought not to have done that singing, what with the quiet over everything and morning just coming on.

But sometimes you get that feeling and a song just has to come out. Besides, little Reuben asked me. Come up and threw his arms around me and whispered to me in that squeaky little boy voice, like he was telling me a secret, "Sing that waking up song you did for me and Levi."

I had to think for a moment, but then I remembered. I had been looking for something quiet back there in the car, trying to wake them up gentle. And there ain't nothing Brother James knows that's more gentle than "Motherless Child." So I'd sung it soft, halfway to a lullaby. I didn't think the little fellow even remembered it. But now here he was, wanting it again.

I got to say, the little fellow chose just right. I should have known he would. He doesn't understand music; it just kind of comes through him. He must have felt something in this morning that called that song out of him.

I hummed it soft so only he could hear. "I like that song," he said.

"I do, too. Lot of love and sadness all wrapped up in there."

He looked up in my face. There was still tears on his cheeks.

"I have sadness, too," he said.

He put his head on my chest. "I have sadness for my grandpa. I don't want my grandpa to die."

I hugged him close. "Best not to think about that right now. Put away the sadness and think of all the good in this morning."

"But the *wašíču* doctor said Grandpa would be dead before the snow. What if it's going to snow tomorrow?"

I might have had to laugh if I hadn't been so touched.

"Not much worry about that. Summer's barely done. And doctors ain't always right. Just be glad you're home and feeling the love of all these folks that been waiting to love you."

He reached up and put his finger on the little handprint on my cheek.

"I like you, *tȟatȟáŋka* head," he said.

I squeezed him all the tighter. "Liking ain't even the half of it," I said, and started to sing, real soft, letting the song find its way in the quiet.

Pretty soon it fit right into the hills and valleys so I laid it out there with everything I had. I could hardly have stopped if I had wanted to; the day was calling it out from me, and singing it seemed as right as the morning sun. So I just kept singing it until I was all sung out. By the time I made it to the end I was pretty much empty.

The old man must have liked what he heard. He come up behind me and put his hand on my shoulder. I could feel that touch going right through me.

He said something soft in his own language, then took both my hands in his. He was smiling wide with something near to love in his eyes.

"More than for any other I have been waiting for you," he said. Made me blush, but made me feel proud.

He come in close. He was just a little guy, but he took up big space.

"We are a people who listen close for Creator's voice," he said. "We do not find it in churches or in human words. We hear it in the things Creator has given us. The trees, the animals, the grasses, the waters.

"Those voices do not speak so strong anymore. I don't know if they are leaving us or if we have forgotten how to listen. But they speak so soft now that we can hardly hear them. This gives me a great sadness."

He nodded at Reuben.

"But my little great-grandson still hears them. He hears them strong. He has heard them since he came into this world. He does not even know what he is hearing. But Creator's voice speaks through him."

He held tight to my hands, like he wanted to make sure I was listening.

"Our people need to hear that voice. They need to hear it so they do not forget who we are. I have been afraid that Reuben's spirit would be crushed by the *wašíču* world. I have worried that his voice would be lost.

"But then I heard him sing with you. I knew that you could keep his spirit from being crushed."

He kept holding strong to my hands. He would not let go.

"Reuben must never lose his voice. Creator has called you to protect that voice. You must come and you must teach him. You must sing with him. You must help him find his voice and bring it to the people. Will you do that?"

I was feeling close to crying. No one had never asked nothing like this from me before.

"I've been singing songs to the Creator my whole life, Mr. Lone Dog," I said. "If I can help this boy sing out the spirit inside of him, you can damn sure bet that I'll do everything I can to make that happen."

Maybe that wasn't the way I should have been talking to a man like this. But I was feeling something deep inside that had been trying to get out for years. It was the "thank-you" I'd been wanting to say to Miss Latrice for what she done to help a lost little boy find his voice back when he was alone on the streets and no one was listening to him.

If this was the way that I could do that, by helping another little boy find a voice of his own, well, there had to be a God in heaven to give me a chance like this. And you better believe that Brother James was sure enough going to take it.

THE THING HE LOVES MOST
Danton

The blood-red moon had faded into memory. The meadowlarks and shrikes were trilling in the grasses. Sunlight was moving across the landscape and filling in the gullies and the draws. The whole day was coming to life.

The yard was coming alive, too. Karl-Martin and I were putting the finishing touches on a table we had constructed out of some old planks we had found leaning against the house. Ida was giving instructions to Ree and Lillie, who were hurrying back and forth from the kitchen carrying bowls and utensils.

We were all happy to be doing something practical. After what we had just experienced, it was a relief to be involved in something over which we felt we had some control.

The smell of the buffalo stew and fresh fry bread drifted out from the house.

I was famished. I'm sure we all were. None of us, with the possible exception of Two Finger and Brother James, had eaten a full meal for almost a day.

Ree brought us each a chunk of bread lathered with *wóžapi* to hold us until the meal was ready. I glanced at Reuben. He was sitting next to Brother James on the hillside watching Levi throw sticks for Mister Bones. When he saw the *wóžapi* he made a little squeal and tensed his fists like he was about to explode from joy.

The old man was slowly making his way toward the house. His hands were shaking badly. I was worried that he had overtaxed himself. It made me think that the *wašíču* doctors were probably not far wrong.

Ida wheeled herself to the center of the yard. "Sit," she said, flapping her hands at us like she was shooing us all to the table. She had a smile as bright as the morning.

We all pulled up anything we could to serve as a chair and took a place at the table.

The old man came unsteadily out of the house. He was carrying something wrapped in a piece of red cloth. Levi jumped up and ran over to assist him. Mister Bones followed closely behind.

Lillie whispered something to Two Finger, and Two Finger hurried into the house and returned quickly carrying the old man's rocking chair.

He put the chair at the head of the table and helped the old man settle into it.

Lone Dog waved the boys toward him. "Levi. Reuben. Come here," he said.

The boys ran up and stood beside him, one on each side, like attendants.

He waited until we all gave him our full attention.

"Good," he said. "Now, Levi. I want to ask you a question. What makes a good Lakota man?"

It was a question that came out of nowhere. I didn't know if this was part of a premeal ritual or just something that had come into the old man's mind.

Levi straightened himself. It was as if he had been expecting this question and was prepared to answer it.

"A good man serves others and asks nothing for himself, Grandfather."

"Good. What else?"

"He honors the elders. He speaks softly. He raises everyone else up and puts himself last."

"Good, Levi. These are good things. You are learning well."

He turned away from Levi, as if the lesson was somehow complete, and focused his attention on the rest of us. "Now, before we eat I would like to tell you a story."

None of us knew exactly what was going on, and I'm sure we were all much more interested in food than a story, but we were his guests and we needed to honor his wishes.

Lone Dog leaned back in his chair. "Sit down, my grandsons," he said, gesturing Reuben and Levi to relax. "Let me tell you about when I was playing baseball, back in the thirties. I was one of the old ones, but I could still catch a fly ball and hit a little. So they let me play right field when the game didn't matter much.

"One night we had a game up in Bismarck, up in North Dakota. They had a team up there called the Churchills. It had a bunch of Negro fellows on it, like this here Brother James. I don't know why. There weren't no Negro folks living anywhere nearby. Most of us had never even seen one.

"They brought us up there, long bus ride, to play the Churchills. It was going to be the Indians against the Negroes. The whole town was excited. This was hard times and baseball was about all the *wašíču* farmers had to take their minds off their troubles. Families come from miles around."

I looked over at Karl-Martin. He looked back and shrugged.

"So we get off the bus and we see this pitcher warming up — tall lanky guy, doing this high-kick windup, higher than we had ever seen. Sounded like a rifle shot when the ball hit the catcher's mitt. Someone said his name was Satchel Paige.

"Come game time, we go up to the plate, one by one, stand there with our bat ready, watching this guy with that head-high leg kick. Then he'd rear back and let loose with that pitch and it would be in the catcher's mitt before we had time to see it. Heck, before we even had time to think it. Never seen anything like it.

"No one laid a bat on it all game, not even once, except for Chief. Either he was swinging blind or he was too hungover to know any better, but somehow he got that bat on the ball, sent it looping into center field, right past the second baseman. Don't know who was more surprised, that Satchel Paige fellow or the Chief.

"All I remember is that the crowd of farmers was going crazy, and Chief went wobbling down toward first base so slow they could have thrown the ball back to the catcher and he could have tagged him while he was going past.

"But he got to first, stood there huffing and puffing. Everyone cheering and jumping up and down.

"End of the game, that Paige fellow come up with a big smile, clapped Chief on the shoulder, and give him the ball he hit. Signed it and everything.

"Oh, Chief was proud of that ball. Carried it with him everywhere. Showed it off to everyone everywhere we went. Ended up with me when Chief disappeared. It's been sitting on my shelf ever since, just waiting for the right person and the right time."

He unwrapped the red cloth, took out the old baseball, and held it out to Two Finger.

"I'm thinking now is that time and you are that person."

Two Finger looked at him wide-eyed like a little kid, then took the ball and held it out in front of him, like it was the most precious thing in the whole world.

Lone Dog pointed at it with his gnarled finger. "See? That's the Paige fellow's signing right there."

The boys scrambled around to look at the signature. They didn't know who Satchel Paige was, but they knew that they'd been told that the ball on the shelf was never to be touched. Now their grandfather had given it to the bad school man who had broken the pipe and had wanted to kidnap Reuben.

Lone Dog sat patiently while the boys examined the ball. He waited until they were done before speaking.

"My great-grandsons, do you know why I have done this?"

Reuben furrowed his brow. Levi looked at him but said nothing.

Lone Dog pointed at Levi's belt. "Levi. That belt. The one you're wearing. That was the last thing Mr. and Mrs. Steinbach had of their boy and they gave it to you.

"Reuben. Those pants you're wearing and that shirt. Mrs. Steinbach made them for her boy with her own hands. She cut them up and sewed them so they would fit you. They had touched her own son's body. She had washed them and sewn them and got them ready for him every day. And she cut them up and sewed them and gave them to you."

Lillie was sniffling and crying softly.

"Do you boys understand what I am saying?"

Levi had a strange look on his face. He seemed to have withdrawn even further inside himself.

Lone Dog let the silence hang heavy.

I glanced at Ida. She had a knowing look on her face.

"All right," he said, as if he had made his point. "Now we will eat. Ree, would you give our friends the *wóhaŋpi*?"

Ree began ladling stew into bowls and passing them around.

Lillie drew some water from the pump and filled a mug for each of us.

"*Wačhíwiŋ?*" Lone Dog said. He nodded toward Ida's bag.

Ida took out her abalone shell and lit some cedar and sweetgrass and fanned the smoke over the entire table.

"This is a good day," Lone Dog said, lifting his mug.

We all lifted our mugs in response, as if in a toast.

The sun was rising higher in the sky and a soft wind was blowing warm from the west. The birds called to one another and the grasses whispered in the breeze. Up the hill the butterflies were gathering in splashes of yellow and white by the butterfly rock. The day was taking on the feeling of a celebration.

We all ate happily and hungrily. There were flavors of herbs and berries in the buffalo stew that I had never tasted before.

We sat there under the growing sun at this makeshift table, passing the food from one person to the next, talking together as a group for the first time. The air was warm with good feeling and camaraderie.

Two Finger and Brother James were involved in an animated conversation. It amazed me to see Two Finger interacting with anybody, but they seemed to have developed some kind of friendship. Two Finger would say something and Brother James would let out a booming laugh that shook the whole end of the table.

Ida was talking to everybody, touching everyone within her reach — even Ree, who had seemed so distant and averse to human contact. Karl-Martin was keeping mostly quiet, adding comments when they seemed appropriate, but otherwise appearing content to remain in the background. Lillie kept running back and forth to the kitchen, bringing coffee and fry bread and asking everyone if there was anything else they needed. She was beside herself with happiness. This was the family she had always wanted.

Reuben was wolfing down piece after piece of fry bread slathered with *wóžapi*.

Only Levi wasn't eating. He sat quietly, pushed slightly back from the table. He had his arms wrapped tightly around Mister Bones.

I was going to try to bring him into the conversation, but Ida saw me and shook her head.

When the meal was finished, Ree went into the house and returned with a pan of *wasná*.

Reuben let out a shriek and grabbed for it.

She shook her finger at him. "Pass it around," she said. "The elders first."

Reuben pinched up his face, went from person to person, offering each of us *wasná* in an overly formal and theatrical way.

When Reuben got to his brother, Levi shook his head and looked away.

"It's *wasná*," Reuben said. "Momma's."

Levi shook his head again. He quietly left the table and walked up the hill to the mound of earth where we had shared the pipe. Mister Bones followed closely behind him.

He stood there, motionless, facing away from us, staring out toward the east.

Ree and Lone Dog and Ida were watching closely. The rest of us kept up the conversation, but we could tell that something was happening.

Levi's stillness was disconcerting. He reminded me of one of those old posed Edward Curtis photos of chiefs in the Southwest — noble, distant, untouchable. I tried to stay engaged in the goings-on at the table, but I could not keep my mind off Levi's distant presence.

Lone Dog, too, had turned his full attention to Levi. He sat quietly with his hands steepled against his chin, watching intently as Levi and Mister Bones faced out toward the east.

Then, almost as if he could feel his grandfather's gaze, Levi turned and looked down the hill at him. It was not the look of a boy.

The two of them stared long at each other, neither one moving, their eyes locked in some kind of common understanding.

Then Levi straightened himself and walked down the hill and stood directly in front of his grandfather.

"Grandfather," he said. "You asked what a Lakota must do to become a man."

Lone Dog nodded. "I did."

"I told you he serves others and asks nothing for himself. That he honors the elders and cares for the weak and places himself last."

"And so he does," Lone Dog said.

We were all watching now. Lone Dog kept nodding, allowing Levi to express himself at his own pace.

"There is more," Levi said. "He must be prepared to sacrifice everything."

Lone Dog stared straight at him.

"He must be willing to give away the thing that he loves most. Like Mister Steinbach and the belt. Like Miss Lillie and the clothes."

Lone Dog nodded slightly and smiled.

Levi pulled himself up to his full height. He seemed taller, older, as if showing something to his grandfather that he had never shown before.

He walked over and stood directly in front of me. Mister Bones was close by his side.

"Here," he said.

I wasn't sure what he was saying.

He put his hand on Mister Bones's back and nudged him forward. "Here."

I looked at Lone Dog. Lone Dog nodded his assent. His face was stern, but his eyes were shining.

"No," I said. "No," slowly realizing what was going on.

"You don't turn down a gift, Mr. Danton," Lone Dog said softly.

Levi was looking directly in my eyes. He had never done that before.

Mister Bones seemed to know what was happening. He leaned his head against me and licked my hand.

Levi took a step back. He turned his eyes away. The passage was complete.

I had no idea what to say or what to do. "Are you sure?" I asked. "This is…"

Ida shook her head to stop me. This was about something much larger than personal feelings.

I was at a loss for words. This was outside of my way of understanding.

Reuben broke the spell by running up to Brother James. He was waving the little stone *khéya* Ida had given him. "This is the most good thing to me," he said. "I'm going to give it to Brother James. I'm going to do a man thing, too."

Brother James, bless his heart, knew just the tone to take. He put his arm around Reuben and bent his head down so Reuben could rub his hair. "Soon enough," he said. "But it ain't man time yet for you. Part of you is as old as the hills. The rest of you has a long way to go. Best to hold on to that little *khéya* until the two parts catch up with each other."

Brother James winked at Lone Dog. The old man gave him a toothy grin and a small salute. Reuben put a pout on his face and quickly put the *khéya* back in his pocket. In truth, I think he was glad to keep it.

Levi had not moved. He was standing directly in front of me, staring at the ground. Mister Bones was still licking my hand.

I was filled with something between gratitude and shame. Bones looked up at me with his gray muzzle and rheumy eyes. A feeling rushed through me that I hadn't known since that last day with Sweet Girl. I needed to say something, do something, to honor what Levi had just done.

"Thank you" seemed too inadequate and insipid. Hugging him seemed inappropriate.

Eventually I stammered out a response. "*Philámayaye*, Levi. Thank you. This is a great gift you have given me." The words sounded clumsy coming out of my mouth.

Levi nodded. He looked at me from a place I could never understand or reach. In the moment he seemed more the man and I the boy.

He moved over close to his great-grandfather. Lone Dog smiled and put his arm around his great-grandson. There was a pride in what passed between them that required no words.

"Come, we will smoke together one more time," Lone Dog said.

We gathered in a circle. Mister Bones stayed right next to me, staring up at me with soulful eyes. It was as if he understood.

Lone Dog unwrapped the pipe again and held it out in front of him. His pride at what the boys had accomplished was evident.

"Reuben, you may put the parts together."

Reuben made a little squeak of joy, then hurried to fit the stem into the bowl. He petted the *khéya* on the pipe and wrinkled his nose as he put the two parts together.

Ida dug into her bag and pulled out the pouch of her grandfather's *čhaŋšáša*. She handed it to Levi, who packed it in the bowl and tamped it down with his right hand. He acted with confidence and authority.

"Mr. Two Finger?" Lone Dog said.

For a moment, Two Finger looked surprised. Then he took out his matches and, with great formality and ceremony, lit the *čhaŋšáša* as Lone Dog drew in the smoke and let it out into the blue morning air. We all watched as it rose up sinuously and disappeared into the day.

One by one we smoked and passed the pipe, rotating it sunwise as we had been taught, before handing it on.

There was no fear in us this time, no uncertainty. The pipe moved around the circle from each of us to the next until it arrived back at Lone Dog. He pinched out the ashes and emptied them into his hand.

He stood quietly, looking at each of us as the clouds moved above us like spirits and the butterflies flew like ribbons of white and yellow among the prairie flowers and grasses.

When he was satisfied that we had understood the significance of the moment, he cocked his head slightly and said, simply, "I think we are done here."

Then he turned and limped toward the house. As he reached the steps he turned again and flashed us that impish smile.

"More brothers and sisters than blood," he said, and walked through the door.

Epilogue

I LIKE YOU, TOO

Karl-Martin

It had been an entire winter since we had seen the boys, and the winter had been hard. Hard and long. The snow had started early and had not let up until April — six months of howling winds strafing barren fields, snowdrifts piled as high as the eaves of the house. Hard weather for a man, but good weather for the earth. You could almost feel the land drinking in the moisture and replenishing itself under the blanket of winter snow.

Lillie and I had mostly spent the winter inside. We'd made an occasional foray into town to pick up supplies, but otherwise it had just been quiet times, reading and talking and readying ourselves for what we hoped would be a better year.

And waiting. Above all, waiting.

We had stayed in touch with Danton through weekly letters. He had kept us up-to-date on the goings-on with the Lone Dogs and the boys. And by and large, the news was good.

Despite the doctors' predictions, old Amos Lone Dog had survived the winter. Two Finger had conveniently lost any governmental communications regarding Reuben and boarding school, so Reuben had spent the year at home with his great-grandpa and mother. Levi had gone back to the school, insisting that he wanted to do it to "learn the *wašíču* ways."

Danton himself had taken a job working with an eighty-five-year-old German carpenter who still climbed on roofs and believed that taking a day off was a sin against God. But Danton had made it a condition when he signed on that he could take time off whenever he wanted. God and the old carpenter, he said, would just have to deal with it.

In his most recent letter he'd told us he was planning to bring the boys for a visit as soon as the roads were passable. The boys were looking forward to it, he said. Reuben kept talking about *Uŋčí* Ida's *wagmíza-wasná* and Levi said he was going to help me with the chores. Ree was more than ready to have them gone for a while, and the old man had given them his word that he wouldn't die before they got back. Now that the days were getting longer and most of the standing water was off the roads, it looked like the time was just about right for them to make the journey.

Lillie had been watching every day. She had sewn new clothes for the boys and fixed up Joseph's old room with new curtains and a braided rug she'd made from old rags we'd been saving. Each time a car went by on the road, she would rush to the window in anticipation, returning to her chair with a slightly sad look in her eyes. But behind the sadness was hope. She knew the boys would be coming soon.

I was full of hope, too. It seemed like the whole world had changed with the arrival of the boys in our lives. The sky seemed clearer, the fields seemed richer. The hell of the previous summer felt like a distant memory.

I was turning over the soil in the garden when I heard the throb of an engine approaching and the familiar sound of old Mister Bones's bark.

Lillie was already at the window.

"Karl-Martin," she shouted. "I think they're here."

I dropped my shovel and ran to the edge of the driveway. Danton's red Ford was churning down the road toward us. Bones was barking frantically and I could see two little heads bobbing up and down in the front seat.

The truck wheeled into the yard and pulled to a stop right in front of me. Danton rolled down his window and grinned. His hair was neatly combed and he was freshly shaven, a far cry from the slightly disheveled man I had become accustomed to.

"Danton," I said. "You look like you're going on a date."

He smiled broadly and stuck his hand out in greeting. "How you doing, Karl-Martin?"

We clasped hands and held them like long-lost brothers.

"Good to see you, my friend," I said.

"And you, Karl-Martin."

"Good trip?"

Bones and Reuben were tussling in the front seat. Bones was yipping and barking.

"It was better before this started," he said. "He's been like this for about the last five miles."

"Smart dog. Recognized the road."

"Or smelled pork chops."

Reuben had no interest in waiting out this conversation. He crawled across Danton and stuck his head out the window.

"*Wagmíza-wasná*," he said, smacking his lips.

"Patience, my boy," I said, ruffling his hair. "You just got here. There will be *wagmíza-wasná* aplenty soon enough."

As was his way, Levi was holding back. He sat straight and upright with his hands folded in his lap. He had the bandanna we had given him tied around his head.

"Hello, Mister Steinbach," he said with his usual air of stiff formality.

He had grown since I had last seen him. His voice had taken on the dusky edge of adolescence. "I'm ready to help with the chores if you like."

"Good of you to ask, Levi, but no more work today. You take your brother and go in and say hello to Miss Lillie. She's been waiting. Mr. Danton and I have some catching up to do."

Reuben pushed his way out the passenger door, followed closely by Mister Bones. It did my heart good to see the old dog again. He shot off to the edge of the yard and began relieving himself copiously on every tree and bush.

Levi stepped out more cautiously. His hair was slicked back beneath the bandanna and he had his white T-shirt tucked in his pants so we could see Joseph's belt. The buckle was polished and shiny. Joseph's old work gloves were stuffed in his back pocket.

"Should I bring in some water?" he asked.

"You're a good man to ask. But, no, we've got plenty. Just go say 'hi' to that woman in the window."

Lillie had been watching from the kitchen, staying back so Danton and I could have our moment. But when the boys emerged from the truck she hurried onto the porch, her arms held wide and her smile as bright as the sun.

When Reuben saw her he squealed, ran across the yard, and threw his arms around her. Levi stayed close to the truck, watching from a distance.

"Oh, Levi, Levi, Levi," she said, gesturing him to her. "Come and give Miss Lillie a hug."

With that, Levi dropped his reserve and ran to her. The three of them stood holding each other like their world depended on it.

Danton nudged me with his elbow.

"Worth the wait, huh?"

"You have no idea."

Lillie's eyes were brimming with tears. I hadn't seen her cry from happiness since Joseph was born.

"How long can we keep them?" I asked.

"Ree says that the way they're squabbling with each other, you can keep them forever. Just don't make them into shoemakers."

I put my arm around Danton's shoulder. "Ah, my friend, you haven't changed," I said. "Come on. Help me put away the tools. We can talk while we walk."

Bones had excavated a corner of the yard and was proudly limping over to us with a filthy bone in his mouth.

"How are you and old Bones getting on?" I asked.

"It's going well. He sleeps in my bed. Loves riding in the truck. But my yard is pretty much a wasteland." He swept his arm across the yard. "No treasure trove like this."

"Rome wasn't built in a day," I said. "He's been stocking this up for years."

We got the rake and shovel hung up in the shed. There were still some filings and chunks of pipestone piled on the edge of the bench. Danton picked one up and cupped it in his hand.

"I still can't believe those boys made that pipe," he said.

"More things on heaven and earth…"

"I think that pipe's what keeps the old man alive. He smokes it every day. Reuben brings him the *čhaŋšáša*. Stays right by his side."

"How's he doing?" I asked. "I thought the doc said he was supposed to be dead by now."

"He's not going easy. And he's pretty ornery about it. Says the ancestors are waiting for him and he'd just as soon get on with it. And don't get him started on *wašíču* doctors."

"How about Ree? How's she handling things?"

"The old man's fading has softened her. She's not real good at being a mother but she's damn good at being a daughter."

"And she's okay with us having the boys?"

"She's wiser than you think. She knows family when she sees it."

Through the door we could see Mister Bones digging up a storm in a corner of the yard. Dirt was flying in all directions. On the porch Reuben, Levi, and Lillie were pointing at him and laughing.

"I can't tell you…" I started.

"No need," he said. He put his hand on mine. "'More brothers and sisters than blood.'"

I wanted to ask about Two Finger, but I knew it was a touchy subject with Danton. He didn't like to be reminded that he had ever worked with the man. But I needed to know. Two Finger had been deeply affected by the events at Lone Dog's that night, almost more than any of the rest of us. And Lillie had been a big part of it.

I approached the subject cautiously.

"And Two Finger? How's he doing? Is he still grabbing kids for the schools?"

Danton seemed almost to relish the subject.

"Ah, Two Finger. He's still getting his paycheck, at least for now. Funny, though. Every time he goes out to do a grab, the kids somehow manage to get away. I would imagine he'll be seeking other employment soon."

"Hey, it's a government job," I said. "It could go on this way for a long time."

"But I'll tell you, Karl-Martin," Danton said, turning suddenly serious, "something has changed in him."

"How so?"

"Every evening he goes up to Lone Dog's and sits with the old man. Doesn't matter — snow, wind, he's there like clockwork. He's like a little kid. Lone Dog says he's hungry to learn. It's really kind of touching. What amazes me most is how he's taken to the boys. He's really taken that protector responsibility to heart. No one in town messes with those boys about anything. They've got to go through Two Finger, and that's nothing anyone wants to do."

He leaned back against the truck fender and chuckled. "The best part, though, is watching him try to play catch with Reuben. Seeing the two of them out there in front of the house, tossing that Satchel Paige ball back and forth. I don't think I've ever seen either of them actually catch it. Two Finger certainly doesn't have his old man's genes."

I was incredulous. "They really use that ball that Satchel Paige signed?"

Danton shrugged. "A ball's a ball, I guess."

"How about that Brother James? Does he show up like he said he would?"

That got a hearty laugh out of Danton.

"Brother James. Ah, yes. Brother James. He's become something of a fixture on the rez. Rolls in about once a month in that old Studebaker. Stays around for a couple of days, working with Reuben. If the weather's good, the two of them go up by that butterfly rock for two, three hours. Work on some private songs that Lone Dog taught them.

"He usually gives an impromptu concert down in town right before he leaves — he and Reuben sing those Negro spirituals together and the Skins love it. You've never heard anything until you've heard Reuben squeaking out 'Ol' Man River' at the top of his lungs."

"But he's accepted okay?"

"You mean because he's Black? Heck, Indians don't have any problem with Black folks. In fact, they kind of favor them. Just one more group under the heel of the white man's boot. Lucie feeds him for free and Two Finger even cleaned up that old jail cell so he can stay there."

He paused for dramatic effect.

"Course, I don't think he stays there much."

He had a mischievous twinkle in his eye.

"How so?"

"Well, he and Ree seem to have taken a shine to each other."

"What?"

"I'm just telling you what I see."

"But Ree and Brother James?"

He cuffed me on the shoulder. "No stranger than an Indian girl and a halfway priest. Come on. Let's get back to the boys."

We made our way past the pump toward the house. Bones came limping up with an even filthier pork chop bone held proudly in his mouth.

Levi and Reuben and Lillie were still on the back step. Reuben was sitting on Lillie's lap with his head leaning on her shoulder. Lillie was gently stroking his hair.

"How's she doing, Karl-Martin?" Danton asked. "How are you both doing?"

"It's still a pretty lonely life," I said. "But we're doing better. Lillie's spirit is lighter. She sings almost all the time. But she still keeps most everything inside her. Leaves me no one much to talk to other than the mailman, and if you've got half a brain you don't share too much with the mailman in farm country."

"But she's okay?"

"She and Ida have reconnected. That counts for everything. And these boys — she lives for moments like this."

Reuben was talking animatedly and showing Lillie something from his pocket. "Looks like they live for them, too," Danton said.

"How about you?" I asked. "You enjoying the carpentry work?"

"I get to use my hands, and I can do some good for some folks. And I can see the boys every day. What's not to like?"

"Any women? Now that Ree's spoken for?"

He flashed a toothy grin and shrugged.

"Maybe you're the one who should have been a priest," I said.

I hadn't realized how much I'd missed our conversations. I wanted to open up to him about that trip to the Lone Dogs. I was still embarrassed about how I had fallen apart in the face of that prairie fire, and I wanted to explain.

I was about to broach the subject when Lillie called out from the porch. "Ten minutes," she said.

"We can talk more after dinner," I said.

"I'd like that," he answered. There was genuine affection in his voice.

Lillie had set the table with a linen tablecloth and her best dishes. She had poured big glasses of milk for Reuben and Levi and piled their plates high with mashed potatoes and pork chops and buttermilk biscuits. I wished we could have had Ida with us, but she had told me that whenever the boys came it was important that Lillie have them to herself for a while.

"There'll be time enough for me," she'd said. "Keep them to yourself for a day or so, then bring them over. I'll have the *wagmíza-wasná* ready."

We ate together happily, just like old times. Levi was all full of "Yes ma'ams" and "No ma'ams" and Reuben ate hunched over his food like an animal. But his enthusiasm and obvious relish for Lillie's cooking made up for his lack of table manners.

When they were finished, Levi asked permission for them to be excused, and they ran out the door together. Reuben had the remainder of a pork chop secreted in his pocket.

Lillie poured us coffee and we sat together listening to the boys' laughter. The sun was coming in soft on an angle through the dining room window, casting long shadows across the floor. The afternoon had reached that quiet, contemplative time, just on the edge of twilight.

"It's good to see you, Mr. Danton," Lillie said, touching him lightly on the sleeve.

"It's good to see you, too," Danton replied.

He put down his coffee. "Just a minute. I have something for you. I'll be right back."

He hurried out to the truck while Lillie and I stared at each other quizzically. Danton was not the type to bring gifts.

Soon he returned with a book-size package wrapped in brown paper and handed it to Lillie.

"Open it."

She untied the string and carefully unfolded the wrapping.

Inside was a frame with a wire strung loosely across the back. She turned it over and her eyes softened with tears.

"Oh, Karl-Martin," she said, and held it up so I could see it.

It was a photo of Levi and Reuben dressed in white shirts and ties, with Levi's hair slicked back and Reuben's unruly spikes unsuccessfully brushed to one side. Levi was wearing his most serious face and Reuben had on some sort of goofy scrunched-up look like he was imitating a ferret or had just smelled something bad.

"It was the best the photographer could do," Danton said apologetically. "He was on a schedule. You should have seen the shots that Ree rejected."

Lillie looked up in surprise. "Ree did this for me?"

Danton nodded. "She wanted you to have it. She said there's another photo that you can put with it. She said you'll know what she means."

Lillie's lip was quivering. She placed the portrait on the top of the piano and reached into her pocket and took out a yellowed photo about the size of a postcard. She carefully fit it into the corner of the frame so that it didn't block either of the boys' faces.

I moved in close so I could get a better look at it. It was a photo of Joseph from the county fair when I had bought him the belt. His face was all smudged, but the rest of the photo was clear. He was standing with his thumbs in his belt like a rodeo cowboy, showing off the belt buckle. I had never seen this photo before.

Danton saw my surprise. "I'll wait outside," he said.

Lillie leaned her head against my shoulder. She was crying softly.

We stood there in silence looking at the two photos. I reached over and wiped the tears from her cheek.

Truth be told, hers weren't the only tears being shed in that room.

◊ ◊ ◊

Lillie did her best to get Danton to stay.

"I can make up the couch for you," she said. "In the morning we'll have a good breakfast, then we'll all go to Ida's. She's waiting to see you, too."

But Danton was having none of it. "Tell Ida I'll see her when I come back to get the boys," he said.

Lillie looked shocked.

"You're leaving? Why? Aren't you going to stay here with the boys?"

Danton shook his head and smiled.

"I've got to take a little trip back to Michigan."

"Michigan?" I asked. "What's left back there?"

"Oh, there's always loose ends. Sometimes you just need to touch the earth where you were born."

Mister Bones was pressing his nose against the screen door and whimpering.

"Or where your old dog is buried," I said.

"That, too."

Then he paused a bit, as if deciding whether to say more.

"Left something else back there, too."

He had a strange look on his face.

"What's that?"

"Yours aren't the only letters I've written."

He paused theatrically. His mouth was drawn into a tiny smirk.

"Romanian girl. Says she's always wanted to see the West."

I burst out laughing. "Oh, Danton. You are a sly fox."

"Yes, but not a quick one. A little slow on the draw."

"Well, you know how it is. 'If we knew then what we know now.'"

"Well, I know it now," he said. "Time to pick up the pieces."

He ran his hand through his freshly combed hair and smoothed his eyebrows.

"How do I look?"

"Who could resist?" Lillie said.

Bones was still mewling outside the door.

"And how about Bones?" I asked. "You're leaving him with us, aren't you?"

"Not a chance. It's our first road trip together."

"Taking the bride back to the old homestead."

"Something like that."

He stood up to leave. "Well, I'd best get going. The light's starting to fade. 'Miles to go before I sleep.'"

"You're a tough nut to crack, Adrien Danton," I said. "At least let me walk you out to the truck."

Lillie had put half a pie between two plates and wrapped it in the brown paper bag the picture had come in.

"That's for you, not for Mister Bones," she said.

"You'll never know," Danton grinned.

She stood on her tiptoes and gave him a little kiss on the cheek. I had never seen her do that to anyone other than the boys and me.

The light over the fields had turned from gold to lavender, and the cicadas were beginning to sing as we headed out to the Ford.

"There's something I've been wanting to ask you," I said. I knew this was my only chance. "All those things that happened. The rain, the fire, all of that with the turtles and the sticks, do you think old Lone Dog really had anything to do with it? I'm serious."

Danton shook his head. "Those things are above my pay grade, Karl-Martin," he said. "No sense trying to make sense out of things that don't make sense."

"I suppose. I guess I'm just not wired that way."

"Makes things easier."

"Still, there's coincidences and there's coincidences. Sometimes things just seem like messages."

Danton shrugged. "To each his own. I just keep my eyes aimed straight ahead and try to keep from going into the ditch."

He gave Mister Bones a ruffle behind the ear. "Isn't that right, Bones?"

Bones wagged his scraggly tail. He had found another pork chop bone and was holding it tightly in his teeth. It looked suspiciously like the one that Reuben had been carrying in his pocket.

"Well, it's time for us to put some miles behind us. Michigan's a long ways away."

"You want to say goodbye to the boys?"

"Let them be. They're off having fun. I'll see them when I get back."

He lifted up Bones's back end and helped him into the truck. The old dog climbed onto the passenger seat and positioned himself like a copilot, bone held high and proud.

"Well, Karl-Martin. Take care," Danton said, giving me one final handshake.

He slid into the driver's seat, shifted the truck into gear, and backed out toward the road. As he turned onto the gravel he reached his arm out the window and waved his hand in the air like a cowboy on a bucking bronco. Soon enough he was nothing more than two taillights disappearing down the road into the dusk.

Lillie had come over and taken a place beside me. She was holding tight to my arm.

"He's a strange man, that Mr. Danton," she said.

"Yes," I answered, "but a good one. That's what Lone Dog saw. Takes a while to figure things out but usually gets them right."

"It sounds like he got them right this time."

"We can only hope."

She squeezed me tighter.

"I can't believe Ree had that picture made for us."

"She's a good woman," I said. "Rough on the outside, but a good heart."

"And a good mom in her own way." Lillie smiled.

She took my hand and headed toward the barn. "Come on. Let's go find the boys. It's getting near dark."

We walked around to the back of the house. Levi and Reuben were standing out beyond the barn at the edge of the field.

We started to approach, but Levi held up his hand, motioning us to remain quiet.

We moved up slowly, step by step. Reuben was standing as still as a statue. His arm was extended and something was resting on his wrist.

I started to say something. Levi shook his head.

We got to within a few feet and I realized it was a bluebird. In all my years of living here I had never seen a bluebird on our land.

Reuben lifted his wrist and the bird flew off.

He turned and smiled at us. His eyes were wide and his spiky hair caught the last golden glint of the sunset.

He moved over and leaned against Lillie and took her hand.

"I like you," he said softly.

"I like you, too," Lillie answered.

Levi moved quietly next to me and took my hand in his.

We stood there silently, the four of us, watching the bluebird disappear into the fading twilight, out beyond the fields, out beyond the hills, out beyond the edge of anything any of us had ever dared to dream.

ABOUT THE AUTHOR

Kent Nerburn is widely recognized as one of the few American writers who can respectfully bridge the gap between Native and non-Native cultures. Novelist Louise Erdrich has called his work "storytelling with a greatness of heart." Nerburn is the author or editor of fifteen books on spirituality and Native themes, including *Chief Joseph and the Flight of the Nez Perce*, *Simple Truths*, *Small Graces*, and *Letters to My Son*. The volumes in his groundbreaking trilogy, *Neither Wolf nor Dog: On Forgotten Roads with an Indian Elder*, *The Wolf at Twilight: An Indian Elder's Journey Through a Land of Ghosts and Shadows*, and *The Girl Who Sang to the Buffalo: A Child, an Elder, and the Light from an Ancient Sky*, are considered core works in the multicultural curriculum of schools and colleges around the world. He and his wife, Louise Mengelkoch, live in Minnesota. His website can be found at KentNerburn.com.